Bad For Me

By Codi Gary

Bad For Me
Return of the Bad Girl
Bad Girls Don't Marry Marines
Good Girls Don't Date Rock Stars
Things Good Girls Don't Do
The Trouble with Sexy (a novella)

Bad For Me

CODI GARY

AVONIMPULSE
An Imprint of HarperCollinsPublishers

*For my stepfather, Charles Domecq, who taught
me you don't have to be blood to be a family.
I love you, Dad.*

Excerpt from *Rules to Be Broken* copyright © 2015 by Codi Gary.
Excerpt from *Changing Everything* copyright © 2015 by Molly McAdams.
Excerpt from *Chase Me* copyright © 2015 by Tessa Bailey.
Excerpt from *Yours to Hold* copyright © 2015 by Darcy Burke.
Excerpt from *The Elusive Lord Everhart* copyright © 2015 by Vivienne Lorret.

EPub Edition APRIL 2015 ISBN: 9780062372246

Print Edition ISBN: 9780062372260

AM 10 9 8 7 6 5 4 3 2

Chapter One

"AND THAT WAS John Michael Montgomery, with 'I Swear,'" Callie Jacobsen said into the microphone. "For all you Little Big Town lovers, this one's for you."

Turning on the next track, Callie stretched her arms above her head and yawned, groaning silently that it was only Monday. As the morning DJ for Kat Country 106.1, she was at work from four in the morning until noon, even eating breakfast while on the air. The small radio station had three on-air DJs during the week, and two part-time on the weekends. Although it might have been nice to sleep in and take the afternoon shift, Callie enjoyed the early morning callers.

Well, one caller in particular. He went by Rhett, which probably wasn't his real name, but who cared? He'd been calling in for over a year now, the same time every day, but what had started out as simple song requests wound up striking a chord with her every time—mostly because every one of the songs he chose was a favorite of hers.

Plus, he had an amazing voice. A rough, deep rumble that made her toes curl every time she heard him on the line. It reminded her of Deacon Claybourne's voice from *Nashville*, her favorite show, and maybe that was what had her so infatuated with Rhett. She loved her some Deacon.

It was crazy, really, but each time she heard his voice over the line, the butterflies he woke in her stomach fluttered like crazy. And it had been a long time since she'd had butterflies. Not since high school.

Not since Tristan, her high school and college sweetheart. They'd met sophomore year and seemed perfect for each other. When he'd asked her to marry him after their last year of college, she had imagined a future filled with happiness and babies.

Absently, Callie rubbed her chest and felt the bumps and ridges of the scars under her plain T-shirt, a constant reminder of how good love could go bad. Really bad.

Which was why she usually steered clear of romantic entanglements. It was hard enough to trust anyone, let alone someone looking to get into her pants. She'd had a few stress-relief partners over the years, but no one she'd felt even a zing of interest for, besides the initial getting-her-rocks-off impulse.

Kicking off her shoes, she rubbed her feet over Ratchet's belly. The 130-pound Anatolian Shepherd went everywhere with her but usually found that sleeping under her DJ table was the best way to get belly-rubs.

She'd jokingly called him "Killer" to a few folks when she'd first moved to town five years ago, and word had spread pretty quickly that there was a crazy new girl in Rock Canyon with a vicious beast of a dog.

In actuality, Ratchet was a trained therapy dog, but no one knew about that except for Gemma and Caroline. She didn't like talking about her past or her two years of insomnia that could only be cured with a bottle of Jack. Even now, nightmares left her filled with terror, soaked in sweat, and trembling like her muscles would explode.

But when she'd seen the ad in the *Sacramento Bee* for a litter of Turkish guardian dogs, she'd felt compelled to go see them. After what happened to her old dog, Baby, Callie hadn't thought she'd ever have another dog, but the minute she'd looked into Ratchet's soft brown eyes, she'd felt calmer. It was as if he'd understood that she needed him, and when she'd taken him home, she'd immediately started researching therapy-dog certification programs. She wasn't going to spend thousands of dollars just for a shrink to tell her she'd suffered a trauma but was "lucky to be alive." She didn't need to talk, not with Ratchet, who would crawl up onto the bed with her and snuggle close and who could sense her fear and loneliness. He made her feel safe.

No one else needed to know her problems. As far as the rest of the world was concerned, she just kept the huge sheep dog as a deterrent for criminals. And Callie liked it that way.

Little Big Town's latest hit came to an end, and Callie leaned forward to speak into the mic. "Coming up after the event calendar, we'll be taking requests for our 'Crack of Dawn' hour, so all you early birds can listen to your favorite hits as you start your daily grind," Callie said. She smiled, then, as their station intern, Dalton, held up a coffee cup in the control-room window with the Local Bean Coffee Shop's logo on the side. "And speaking of grind, try waking up at three-thirty and still being as entertaining as me. Let me tell you, it takes work and a lot of coffee, so we're going to take a commercial break. Callie Jay will get herself a little java pick-me-up, and you stick around for more of today's hottest country on the Kat."

Turning off the mic, she waved Dalton in. The kid was a big improvement over the little bastard the University of Southern Idaho had sent her last semester. Despite having known what kind of station he'd signed up for, the intern had been into punk rock and had sported an attitude about everything from the music to the people who came in. And instead of putting his whole heart into the job, he'd blanched at every task. Callie had sent him packing shortly after he'd given the concert tickets Justin Silverton had won to another winner who was supposed to get a singles' weekend package. The intern hadn't even bothered to apologize. Callie had put in a call to his professor about the kid needing a work ethic before being placed in another internship.

Of course, that mix-up had started the chain of events leading to Justin's and Valerie Willis's wedding next month—and to Callie deejaying the whole event—but still, you had to own your mistakes.

No matter how hard and painful it might be.

Dalton was a complete 180 from the little jerk: a good ole boy, just turned eighteen, and eager to learn. He had only been there a month, but he'd jump into the next job without her even having to ask. She couldn't have hoped for better.

Plus, he was pretty to look at, with a tall, rangy frame and sweet smile. Sure, he was just this side of jailbait, but Callie would have to be dead not to notice that he was a cutie.

As he came in through the studio door, Ratchet stood up to say hi. Most of the staff still gave him a wide berth, but Dalton had never been nervous around the big dog. He'd told Callie that he'd grown up on a sheep ranch outside of Shoshone around Great Pyrenees dogs, which were similar to Anatolians but hairier.

"Here's your coffee, Callie," Dalton said. He handed her the cup before kneeling down to pet Ratchet. "Hey, big guy, you gotta go handle your business?" Dalton took Ratchet's leash from the desk. "That okay if I take him outside?"

"Thanks, Dalton. You're a godsend," Callie said before taking a small sip of the hot liquid. Sweet spices filled her mouth, and she sighed. "Man, that is good."

Dave, her producer, signaled her for the countdown, and she set her coffee on the desk. When he pointed at her, she flicked the mic back on and said, "We're back. October is only a week away, so don't forget to mark your calendars for the following events: on October 6, the Rock Canyon Harvest Festival will be held at the Silverton farm

with yummy food, games, and a haunted corn maze perfect for getting your chills and thrills. Then, on October
31, come out to the Rock Canyon Community Center for
Kat Country's Ghoulish Halloween Ball. Get yourselves
a babysitter, because everyone twenty-one and over can
enjoy dancing and drinks until two. Tickets are on sale
on our website and at the following retailers…"

After naming several local businesses, she continued.
"And now, our all-request hour. So get to your phones
and call 208-555-3KAT—unless you're driving or eating. No one wants to hear you talk around a mouthful of
bagel, and we all want you to make it to wherever you're
going safely."

Dave held up his finger, and she hit the button for line
one.

"First caller, what can I do you for?"

"Hi, I'd like to hear 'Teardrops on my Guitar' by Taylor Swift," a young female voice said over the line.

"Sure, honey. What's your name? And is there anyone
specific you want this going out to?"

"Um…do I have to say?" the girl asked nervously.

Callie smiled. Poor kid. "No, of course not. I'll get that
on the air for you right now."

"Thanks." The line went dead, and Callie flipped on
the track before taking the next call. By six twenty, both
lines were blinking, and she had half an hour of music
to play.

But Rhett had missed his call-in.

He'd been calling every morning at six thirteen and
hadn't missed a morning yet.

He's just a caller. Stop being a freak about it.

Besides, if he'd had romantic notions about her, he probably would have dropped a hint or two, especially since she'd started taking their calls off air when their conversations went on too long. And when she'd get angry waves from her producer and she'd have to go, he'd always just say, *"Have a nice day, Callie Jay."*

Unlike some of the other citizens of Rock Canyon, Idaho, he didn't call up to bitch and moan about politics or what was wrong with modern country music. In fact, just yesterday he'd said that he loved October because it was when all the fall drinks and colors started showing up. She was more of a spring person, but when Dalton had made a coffee run this morning, the pumpkin-spiced latte she'd ordered had been in Rhett's honor.

Callie glanced down at her cell phone and noticed the voicemail icon was on the top of her screen. She tapped it and held the phone to her ear. The robot voice said, "Hello. You have one new voicemail from…"

"It's Caroline Freaking Willis!"

Callie groaned as the robot continued. "At eleven twenty-five P.M."

"Oh, come on, Callie! I know you're avoiding me, and you won't get away with it! You go to Buck's and Hank's, so what's wrong with this?"

Callie shook her head. When Callie had met Caroline back in April, she'd sensed someone she could relate to. Someone who had her own demons and was fighting her own past—and she'd been right. Yet in all the time since, and as the two of them had grown closer, Caroline had never asked Callie about her past. She'd just taken her for who she was now.

Even though Callie loved Caroline for trying to bring her "out of the army tank you've climbed into"—Caroline's words—Callie had no desire to go to Caroline's sister's bachelorette party.

"You already agreed to DJ the damn wedding. Just because you have no desire to go out with a group of obnoxious women and watch some greasy dudes gyrate to 'It's Raining Men' does not make you weird. It just means you have taste."

Caroline had continued her rant, finally ending with, *"Fine, but I'm not through with you! If you think I'm going to this thing with just my sisters and their crazy friends, you're dreaming!"*

Callie deleted the voicemail. Dave held up his finger, and Callie picked up line one again. "You're on the Kat. What can I play for ya?"

"I was thinking a little Blake Shelton, actually," a deep voice said. The caller's smile was evident, even over the phone.

Rhett.

Turning off the "record" button, Callie tried to ignore the giddy butterflies fluttering through her stomach. "You're late."

"You noticed."

"Well, you've been almost OCD about the time you call, so it's a little hard not to notice."

"Well, as a matter of fact, I overslept this morning. Can I just say I'm actually flattered? Were you counting down the minutes?"

Callie's face burned, and even though he couldn't see her, she rubbed her cheeks with one hand. "Actually, it's just because you're the only person with any taste who calls in."

"Coming from you, I'll take that as a compliment."

"You should," she said, turning around in her chair so she couldn't see Dave and her tech, Sam, making kissy-faces at her. "Now, what Blake song do you want to hear?"

"Uh-oh, did I get you in trouble with the boss?"

"No, I just…there are just a lot of calls coming in, so I can't talk as long."

"I understand," he said, and there was a pause on the line before he cleared his throat. "Maybe we could talk more later? Off air?"

Callie's heart pounded. Was he asking for her number? Giving him her number made their interactions more than just a flirtation. What if he was dangerous? The scars on her body tingled with apprehension, a silent warning.

"I'm going to take it from your silence that I've freaked you out," he said, breaking into her panicked thoughts. "I'll let you get back to work."

He hung up before she could say anything. Without his trademark farewell.

Way to go, you paranoid freak.

Though really, Callie didn't think she was paranoid; she was cautious. Having your fiancé turn into a complete stranger—a violent stranger—six months before your wedding could do that to a person. Thinking of Tristan was painful, and she tried to push him from her mind. Tried to forget their past together. If she didn't, the nightmares might start up again—and the urge to drink herself into a stupor along with it.

Just then, Dalton came walking in with Ratchet. The minute he let him off leash, the large dog lumbered over and laid his head in Callie's lap, as if sensing her dark thoughts. Stroking his dense fur, she murmured softly to him until he sat and eventually flopped to the ground.

"Callie, you've got callers holding," Dave said over the intercom.

Pressing the button, she took the next call, but her thoughts were still on Rhett. Was she ready to let someone in and trust again?

She really wasn't sure.

EVERETT SILVERTON TOOK off the headset just after two and stretched his arms above his head, cracking his neck in the process. He had been sitting in the same position for five hours, counseling traumatized and frustrated veterans, and added to the two hours of farm work this morning, he was damn sore.

It was worth it, though, to have a safe place to come home to. Veterans coming back after long tours who realized that the world hadn't stopped while they were gone had it much worse. Despite the fact that he'd spent several months in a hospital overseas and had come home to a wife who couldn't handle his scars or his "issues"—as she'd kindly referred to his PTSD—he'd always had his father and brother. Some vets didn't have anyone—no stability, no job, and the adjustment often took its toll on their psyches. It was hard to come back from a world of violence—one where any minute a roadside bomb could go off or a sniper's bullet could take you out—unscathed.

Everett ran a hand over the scarred side of his face, every ridge and rough patch a badge of dishonor, of his failure to Robbie, his best friend. A constant reminder that Robbie's wife, Cara, and son, RJ, now had to live without him. In the end, the scars on Everett's body couldn't hold a candle to the abrasions on his soul.

Everett stood up and headed for the kitchen of his three-bedroom modular to grab a soda. His brother, Justin, had actually wanted to build a home for Everett on their land, but Everett hadn't needed a stick built. He was happy with his picked-from-the-lot manufactured home. It had cost him about fifty thousand for the house and all the amenities, but his place was serviceable and perfect for him.

"Hey, Rhett," Everett's dad called as he poked his head in through the open door.

Everett's gut clenched just hearing the nickname. Justin and his father were the only people who called him that, but now it was just a reminder of his crash-and-burn with Callie.

He'd started listening to the Kat when he moved home and had especially loved listening to Callie Jay in the mornings when she took over the show five years ago. She was funny, and the music she played wasn't just your run-of-the-mill modern country rock; she mixed in the old-school eighties and nineties. He had no idea what she looked like, since the station website only had a cartoon avatar for her instead of a photo, but he didn't care. Her voice, which was a low, husky rasp, was sexy as hell, and he found himself addicted to hearing her over the line.

Finally, a little over a year ago, he'd been unable to resist calling in to her all-request hour. And again the next day. And the next.

But despite how friendly their conversations had become, he'd had no intention of pushing for more. It was just fun. Besides, there was no guarantee that she'd be able to see past his scars. None of the other women he'd gone out with since his divorce had.

Which is why he'd been just as surprised as her when he'd subtly asked for her number this morning, but he hadn't wanted to say good-bye. If her reaction was any indication, though, he would not be calling the station again. She no doubt thought he was a creeper.

Realizing he'd left his dad hanging without answering, he called, "Yeah, what's up?"

"You mind going to the grocery store for me? I've got a meeting in Twin Falls in an hour and don't want to be late."

Fred Silverton was weathered and craggy, but his shoulders and arms told the story of a man who had worked hard his entire life. His alcoholism had spiraled out of control just after Everett's mom had died eighteen years ago, and it was only in the last six months—since he'd been diagnosed with pancreatitis—that he had begun seeking treatment. Things had been going well, so far, but while Everett believed their father was truly committed, Justin had his doubts—and it showed.

Justin had every right to his anger and resentment. Everett had spent two years picking up his dad at whatever bar he'd passed out at, but Justin had had it worse after Everett enlisted. But despite what Fred had put them through, they were still family, and family had each other's back.

"Sure, Dad, just give me your list." Everett abandoned his soda and stepped outside, only to be treated to a smack of cold air on his face. The wind blew crisp and hard this time of year, and he reached back inside to grab his jacket.

"Here," Fred said, handing Everett a scrap of paper.

"I'll head out now. I was going to go for a hike, but I can push that back until later."

"Well, I will probably go for coffee with my sponsor after the meeting and maybe have dinner with some of the guys after, so don't wait on me for supper."

Everett smiled and slapped his dad on the back. "Are we ever going to meet your sponsor? This woman who steals you away?"

Fred Silverton's leathery face flushed, and he grumbled, "It's not like that. She's too young for me."

His father was in his sixties, but Everett had a hard time believing a woman in her forties or fifties was too young for him. At least, that was how old he assumed his dad's sponsor was. It seemed crazy that someone any younger would be mature enough to be a good example for his father.

"Well, still, you should have her over to the house," Everett said. "Anyone who has your back and that you respect so well is welcome here anytime."

"Thank you, son." Fred cleared his throat. "I appreciate that."

Everett watched his father head to his truck. He definitely looked better, but he still seemed worn out. His pancreatitis flared up every once in a while; plus, he was just getting too old to work as hard as he used to. Which was where Everett and Justin came in.

Silverton Farms was running smoothly and successfully, but it had more to do with Justin's passion than Everett's. Everett had too much to do with his nonprofit, Stateside Support, than with the farm.

Right now, Everett's organization was active only in Idaho, but the hotline counseling was statewide, and he'd partnered with several other national organizations where he could direct vets for job and housing assistance. He spent anywhere from five to eight hours a day counseling over the phone, and although he avoided any kind of interviews, he'd hired a publicity crew just before Stateside Support had launched. They went on air and handled the TV appearances and radio interviews. He just wasn't big on parading around in front of strangers. Even though the people of Rock Canyon treated him with respect, he felt their pitying stares whenever he ran errands in town. If that was the way people who knew him reacted to his scarred face, how would an on-air interview go? And if they started asking questions about the fire...

Yeah, living the hermit life had its benefits.

He could have moved anywhere after he was honorably discharged and his marriage fell apart, but anywhere else, he didn't have his family. The awkward encounters here were worth dealing with, just to be close to his father and brother.

Pulling his keys out of his pocket, he climbed into his silver Chevy and brought the large diesel to life with a twist of the key. He usually let it warm up a bit, but he needed the drive to get out of his head and stop thinking about what an ass he'd made of himself that morning with Callie. He could blame his stupidity on being lonely, but it wouldn't be the whole truth. Every time he called in, his hands began sweating and his heart pounded.

It was a hell of a reaction to have to a woman he'd never actually met.

Maybe that's why he'd thought there was something more between them and that she might have felt the connection too. He'd even considered accepting the interview for Stateside that Eddie Kendall had scheduled with Callie's morning show, just so he could meet her.

But her silence had told him in no uncertain terms that was a bad idea.

Pulling the truck off the gravel road and onto the pavement leading into town, he shook his head. He'd been crazy to think she'd give out her number to some guy who called in to her station. What sane woman would? It was just that since he'd been back, dating had been tough—and not just because of his scars. Even months after he returned, he'd suffered from night terrors so severe that he'd wake up in a neighbor's yard, with no memory of how he'd gotten there. Even the backfire of a car could send him to his knees, screaming Robbie's name...

God, it was hard to think about the world without Robbie.

It was hard to relate to the cheery, small-town girls he'd taken out. He'd joined the marines at eighteen and done four tours in Afghanistan. He was twenty-seven when he was honorably discharged, months after he'd returned home to recover from his burns.

After everything he'd suffered and the five years of therapy he'd gone through just so he could function seminormally, the sheltered, small-town women he'd gone out with would never be able to comprehend the darkness that still hung heavily on his conscience. He was thirty-four now, and in the past eight years, he'd suffered more loss and pain than most people would in a lifetime. And although he'd met a few women he'd had things in common with, there just hadn't been that spark of interest. Which was why Callie Jay the DJ had taken him by surprise; the electricity between them sizzled, and they'd never even met.

Six minutes later, Everett parked his truck and headed into Hall's Market. On his way in, he passed a hay bale circle filled with pumpkins and thought about grabbing a few for Justin and Val's wedding. They were having a fall theme, and Val had mentioned something about pumpkin centerpieces on Pinterest. Maybe he should pick some up for them.

Pulling out his cell, Everett suddenly ran smack into someone coming out of the store and instinctively caught their arms.

Make that *her* arms.

Golden eyes stared up at him from a round, pale face, her mouth open in a surprised *O*. The way her wheat-colored hair flowed around her in a riot of curls made him think of a disheveled angel.

Then, the low rumbling of a dog's growl broke through the spell of his fascination, and Everett stepped back from the woman to find a giant tan dog watching him, its lips pulled back enough to flash its canines.

"It's okay," the woman said softly, touching the dog's head. The low growl stopped, but the dark eyes still followed Everett's every move.

"Sorry. I wasn't watching where I was going," he said.

"Neither was I," she said, holding up a torn newspaper that she must have been reading. "I guess this is why they say, 'Don't read and walk.'"

"I haven't heard that one before. Is there one for thinking and walking?"

"You know, I have heard thinking is hazardous to pedestrian traffic."

As he laughed, he watched her reaction to him—to his scars. Even now, eight years after a roadside bomb had taken out his Humvee, his best friend, and half the skin on his body, he waited for the inevitable awkwardness that followed an introduction. But as he studied her expression, he was surprised to find there was no pity, eye-shifting, or discomfort in her gaze.

Then again, she didn't seem to find the conversation half as amusing as he did. She hadn't cracked a smile once, despite her joke.

"I'm Everett Silverton," he said, holding out his hand.

She hesitated for a moment before taking it. "I know."

A zing of pleasure went through him. "How do you know?"

Her cheeks turned a dusty pink. "You're a local hero, and people talk."

"Ah," he said, a little disappointed when he caught her meaning. "So my scars gave me away, huh? I should start wearing a *Phantom of the Opera* mask; try to be a little more mysterious."

"No, you shouldn't," she said sharply.

"What?"

After a moment's hesitation, she said, "You shouldn't try to hide who you are. What you did...well, it was very brave. You should be proud of your scars. They're proof of your heart and your service."

The statement was so frank that Everett was a little taken aback. Even she seemed thrown by her words. Most people tiptoed around his burns, even his brother and father.

"Well, they definitely make a fascinating conversation piece," he said, trying to lighten the mood. "By the way, do you have a name, or should I just call you Whiskey?"

"Whiskey?" she echoed.

"Yeah." He tapped just below his eye. "Your eyes are the color of rich Scottish whiskey."

"Why Scottish?"

"I went there and took a tour of one of their distilleries. Nobody makes a clearer or better whiskey," he said, adding, "as the hangovers I suffered during that week will attest."

"I didn't know hangovers could be expert witnesses," she said.

"Are you forgetting Brad Paisley's 'Alcohol'?"

"Touché," she said, her lips twitching like she was fighting a smile.

"Your name is Touché?" he deadpanned. Her soft laugh was exhilarating.

"Callie. It's Callie Jacobsen. I'm actually the DJ for your brother's wedding." Callie tucked a stray curl behind her ear, just as the wind blew five more into her face.

What he wouldn't give to be able to reach out and push her hair back, the soft strands sliding through his fingers—

Everett's heart skipped a beat as her words sank in, and he realized she was *his* Callie. The Callie he'd been calling nearly every morning for over a year.

The one who pretty much thought he was a creep.

Justin had said he'd hired one of the Kat Country DJs, just not which one. What if he admitted who he was and she bailed on the wedding? Despite her friendly manner, there was nothing in her demeanor that said, *I am so attracted to you that I'll forgive the fact you freaked me out.*

Better to play it cool, at least for now.

"You host the morning show on the Kat?"

"Yeah, *Weekdays with Callie Jay*." Her tone was amused, even if her lips barely tilted up at the corners. Though she'd laughed, he wondered why she didn't smile. Instead, she just watched him with those amber eyes, as if she wasn't sure what to make of him.

"It's…it's a good show," Everett said, his voice sounding squeaky to his ears.

Get a grip, man. She doesn't know you're the crazy stalker.

"Thank you. Well, it was nice to meet you, but I'm actually late for something." Callie folded her ripped paper.

"Let me buy you a new *Rock Canyon Press*, as an apology for bumping into you," he said quickly. He wasn't ready for her to go yet.

"Really, it's not your fault—"

"It's fifty cents," he said, taking her paper and tossing it in a trashcan. "And it will make me feel better." He slid two quarters into the newspaper dispenser and waited for the click before opening it and grabbing another paper. "Here you go."

She took it slowly and seemed at a loss for something to say. "Thank you. It wasn't necessary."

"Happy to do it," he said honestly. The wind tossed her curls over her eyes once more, and Everett resisted another urge to brush them back, just so she would look at him again.

God, when was the last time he'd been so taken with a woman he'd only just met? At least, in person. If his desire to be near her was any indication, too long, apparently.

"Well, thank you again," she said and tucked the paper under her arm. "I guess I'll see you at the wedding?"

"Yeah, if not before." Everett wondered why she kept looking away from him. She had been so frank about his scars, yet she hardly met his gaze now.

Except for that first intense meeting of their eyes.

"Bye, then." She walked past him with her monster dog, those curls dancing around her shoulders like gold and moonlight ribbons.

"See ya." He was speaking more to himself, though, since she was already several yards away.

Now that he'd met Callie in person, there was no denying that the connection he'd felt had been real.

The question was, had she felt it too?

Chapter Two

"SO HOW ARE the wedding plans coming?" Callie asked Fred as they walked through Twin Falls's Old Town with Ratchet lumbering beside them. Since Fred had chosen her for his sponsor six months ago, they had taken to getting coffee after the meetings and talking about the stress of their lives. And although they tried to keep the specifics out, it had been inevitable that Fred would tell her his last name.

Silverton.

It had seemed like an incredibly small world when they'd realized they were from the same community, but it hadn't bothered either of them. There was an understanding that what they said during group and coffee stayed between them; neither wanted personal struggles broadcast back in Rock Canyon.

Callie had to admit, she enjoyed the older man's company. He reminded her a lot of her grandfather before he'd died, a roughneck cowboy who had given freely of his time and his bear hugs.

"Well, my son's bride has informed me that they're going to have a dry wedding." Fred's sun-weathered face broke into a smile. "Partly because of her pregnancy and to support my recovery, but also because my future daughter-in-law doesn't want a bunch of drunk assholes raising hell and causing chaos."

Callie smiled at Fred's description. Having met Valerie Willis, she imagined the words were spot on. She knew this wedding was very important to Fred, partially because he felt responsible for some of Justin and Val's past relationship troubles but ultimately because he just wanted his youngest son to be happy.

Of course, the fact that he was going to be a grandfather had Fred over the moon too.

"I can understand that," Callie said, taking a sip of her coffee. "I wouldn't want to be around a bunch of drunk people when I'm stone-cold sober."

Even when she went out with Gemma or Caroline, she usually was the only truly sober one. Caroline never got drunk—she had one or two drinks, maybe—but since bar consulting was her business, she tried to be never less than professional.

Still, watching everyone else relax and cut loose was sometimes hard on Callie. Especially following a letter from Tristan. She never opened them, but just seeing his name on the envelope sent her longing to dive head first into a bottle of Jack Daniel's.

She hadn't, though, not in over five years. Even though drinking may have made her problems go away for a while, they always came back with the hangover the next day. It was something her first sponsor had told her, and it had stuck with her over the years, especially when she was feeling weak.

Suddenly thinking of hangovers, Callie remembered Everett Silverton and his Scottish-whisky bender. He was not what she'd been expecting from the gossip she'd heard. She'd pictured a brooding, mountain of a man who could lift cars and stop trains with his finger. The exaggerated praise was proof enough of how much the people of Rock Canyon thought of him and his heroism.

But what had really surprised her was the fluttering she'd felt in her stomach when she'd looked up and met his gaze. His hands had burned a hole through her shirt sleeves, the heat of his touch sending goose bumps down her arms. She had barely noticed his scars, not with the way his light brown eyes had stared down at her, reminding her of her past obsession with a certain vampire hero from her favorite book series.

Of course, that had been before, when the thought of a dangerous vampire loving her forever had been romantic. But after the night of Tristan's attack, that fantasy—along with every other hope and dream she'd held onto—had been shattered.

"It's going to be beautiful though," Fred said, patting her hand and startling her.

"What?"

"The wedding," Fred said. "It's going to be beautiful."

"I bet."

Callie could imagine. Well, she could imagine what *her* dream wedding would have looked like. It had been documented in the wedding scrapbook she'd started after Tristan had first proposed—and tossed into the fireplace after she returned from the hospital. Even so, she still remembered the joy she'd felt as she'd filled it with pictures and clippings of everything she'd wanted to make her special day perfect. Callie had even signed up for an online service that had made them their own wedding web page, complete with registry links and engagement photos—photos her mother had paid to have done in Forest Hill, one of the most beautiful spots in the northern California foothills. The memory of standing atop the Forest Hill Bridge, holding nervously onto Tristan's arms, held a bittersweet place in her heart, one that belonged to another girl in another time.

"I've got you; I promise."

Tristan's deep voice echoed through her mind, a ghost from her past that she just couldn't shake.

Especially when he wouldn't let go.

Once he'd gotten out of the psychiatric hospital, Tristan had called her, over and over. She'd changed her number several times, but when he started following her—never too closely, or he'd have violated the restraining order she'd taken out on him—she'd realized he would never stop. Soon, Callie began looking for a new job, far away from her past.

After three months of living quietly in Rock Canyon, her lawyer had forwarded the first letter. Callie had never told her lawyer to stop, mainly because she was afraid of agitating Tristan. Instead, she just shoved them, unopened, into a drawer in her living room. One day, she hoped she'd have the courage to read what he had to say—but she knew she'd never be able to see him again. How could she face him after what he'd done to her, her mother, and their dog?

"Are you all right, Callie? You seem distracted." Fred broke into her memories.

"Yeah, sorry."

"Is something bothering you?"

Nothing I want to talk about.

"No, I was just thinking of stuff I have to get done."

"My older son, Everett—he does that to me. I'll be having a conversation with him, and all of a sudden it's like he's in another world."

At the mention of Everett's name, Callie's heart tripped up. "I was going to tell you, I met Everett today."

"Did you? How did he seem?"

Charming. She didn't dare say that aloud, though. Meeting Everett had been a surprise, and she'd barely caught herself before telling him how she knew his father. She never talked about her alcoholism and wasn't about to advertise it to a man she'd just met.

Especially considering how she'd been drawn to Everett and his smile. The scars on his face hadn't diminished his handsomeness; instead, they actually seemed to accentuate it. She'd avoided his light brown eyes because they were beautiful, like the crisp autumn leaves that fell from the trees in November. Her reaction to them had struck her dumb.

Well, for a minute or so, before his easygoing nature had helped let her guard down. He'd even made her laugh, which was something that rarely happened. Yet with the battle-scarred marine, her laughter felt effortless.

"He was nice. He bumped into me while I was reading my paper, and when it ripped, he bought me a new one."

"That sounds just like him. He's a good boy. Would give the shirt off his back to a stranger if he needed it." Fred paused, and Callie looked up in time to catch the flash of pain in his eyes. "I worry about him, though."

Every fiber of her being wanted to ask why, wanted to press for more, but she didn't want to seem like she was fishing for information.

"I just think he spends too much time alone," Fred continued. "When he first got home and was recuperating, I understood, but he's had time. He should be out, getting reacquainted with the world. And so should you, missy," Fred added, patting her hand.

"Oh, come on, I'm in touch with the world."

"Watching the news doesn't count."

"Does reading it?" she asked.

"No. I just mean, you should be out there, meeting a young man. A real man."

Callie's mouth twitched. "Oh yeah? And where do I find all these real men?"

"In the country, at church, on farms," Fred said, holding his fingers out as he named off places. "You would be surprised where the perfect man might show up."

His words caused a familiar ache to settle in her chest, but that wasn't his fault. Her thoughts drifted back to high school, when she thought she'd met the perfect blue-eyed boy in her sophomore English class. He'd come walking in, and the minute he'd caught her gaze, she'd known he was meant to be hers. Which was proof enough that there were too many outside factors for anyone to be *perfect* for another. There was no right *one*, no "forever and ever, amen," no matter what Randy Travis sang. There was *happy for now.* There was getting some good years together.

And then there were irreconcilable differences.

"Callie, I swear, girl, you're a million miles away and fading fast."

Fred's comment pulled her back again, and she shook her head. "Honestly, I think I just haven't had a good run in a while."

After she'd joined AA, she'd started running in the morning and at night. Anytime she started to feel helpless or out of control, she took her control back. She wasn't sure if it was the endorphins or the soreness afterward, but running always put things in perspective. She was alive. She had survived.

"Well, don't feel like you need to humor an old goat like me."

"Don't be silly. You know I enjoy your company."

"Same goes, but you should go home. Maybe take a nap or a jog, if that's what you like. Me? Well, I'd rather go home, sit down in my chair, and turn on some football."

Callie was thankful that Fred was so understanding. Sometimes, depending on what was weighing on her mind, she just needed to be alone. Actually, most of her free time was spent alone, watching TV with a bowl of buttered popcorn in her lap. Unless it was Karaoke Night at Hank's Bar. She hadn't accepted Gemma's invitation to go out until about two years ago, and even now, some nights it was hard as hell. But she pushed through her weaknesses because going out with her friends gave her a small semblance of normalcy, something she wanted desperately.

Still, she hadn't been to Hank's in the last few months, what with Gemma's being pregnant. Without Gemma as a buffer, going out with the rest of the group was awkward, especially with Gracie. Callie liked the opinionated blonde most of the time, but she was a little too wild for Callie on her own. Too many times, Gracie had mouthed off and caused a scene, and the last thing Callie wanted to be around was drama and violence.

She'd seen enough of that to last a lifetime.

AFTER HIS RUN-IN with Callie, Everett decided to head out for his usual hike. He still had several hours of daylight left and needed to burn some energy. When he worked hard during the day, he usually slept better. No night terrors. No lying awake, thinking of Robbie or Robbie's family. Sometimes he still used a sleep aid but not often. Not with his family history of addiction.

He stopped along the hiking trail and bent over to tie his shoelace. The late afternoon sky was just turning a peach color as the sun sank down. He loved coming here, not just for the peace and quiet but for the beauty that surrounded him. This time of year, the trails were becoming overgrown, but at least it was past tick season. He hated those blood-sucking bastards.

Once his shoe was tied, he dropped his pack onto the ground and pulled his water bottle out. He always came prepared for several hours: a couple of water bottles, protein bars, a windbreaker—and his Glock attached to his thigh, just in case. The chances of bumping into a large predator were slim, but it never hurt to be prepared.

Everett took a long drink from his bottle before shoving it back inside his pack and pulling it into place. He needed time to think, especially about his reaction to Callie.

When he'd married Alicia, all he had wanted was to settle down and start a family. Have a couple of kids who would jump into his arms when he came home and a loving wife to grow old with. It was what he had been working for.

Until a roadside bomb had blown those dreams to hell.

Everett couldn't blame his accident for his marriage going down the crapper. According to some of his friends' wives, Alicia had never been a one-marine woman anyway. When he'd come back hurt and with a long road to recovery, she'd bolted. Still, it had hurt like hell to wake up one morning and find that his wife had abandoned him. Granted, they had spent more time apart than together, but she could have at least had the decency to leave him a Dear John letter. Instead, she'd sent him a text: *At my mother's. I want a divorce.*

Since he'd come home, he'd been working on himself first, then on the farm, and then on Stateside. After a while, he'd started to think that maybe, if he met the right woman, he could have the family he'd always wanted. But he couldn't seem to find a woman who fit the bill.

Whiskey-hazel eyes flashed through his mind, and he shook his head. Callie was the first woman to spark anything inside him, but she hadn't exactly seemed enthralled with him when they'd bumped into each other. If she knew he was Rhett, his fiasco on the phone would make him persona non grata.

Maybe she's just shy and awkward in person. Maybe she has her own hang-ups, just like you.

Pounding feet alerted him to someone coming down the trail, and Everett looked up to find the woman of his thoughts jogging toward him. He could tell it was her by the blonde curls swaying as she moved and, of course, the giant dog loping beside her. As she drew closer, he noticed the loose T-shirt and sweats she wore, making her nearly shapeless. Her face was shiny with sweat, and her cheeks were flushed.

Just then her dog barked—actually, *barked* was too mild for the deep sonic boom that came out of the beast's muzzle.

Everett waved. "Hey, there."

"Hey," Callie said as she and the dog came to a stop. She removed her ear buds before asking, "What are you doing?"

"Hiking. I thought I was the only one who used this trail."

"No, I come down here often."

"Me too. I was trying to get down to the river, but I need to clear out the path." Everett took his pack off and began to reach in for an extra bottle of water. "Want a water?"

"Thanks, I'm covered." She held up the bottle already in her hand before popping it open to drink.

Everett's cock hardened without warning as he watched her place the mouth of the water bottle to her lips, the muscles of her throat working as she drank. Droplets of water rolled down her chin, and when she finished drinking, she held the bottle against her forehead and neck. Suddenly, he wanted to be the one trailing the bottle over her skin.

The erotic scene playing out in his head made his erection worse, and Everett shifted his pack in front of him. What the hell was wrong with him?

"So why did you want to go down to the river?" she asked.

"There's this place I like to go and relax. It's on a huge, flat rock overlooking the Snake River. It's just been one of those days, you know?"

"I'm having one of those days too," she said.

"I'm sorry. I hope my assault on your paper didn't affect it." He watched her lips twitch and hope flared inside him. That was pretty damn close to a smile.

"No, and thank you again for the replacement. Most people wouldn't have bothered."

"Maybe not, but it was my pleasure," he said.

"What's with the piece?" She waved her water bottle toward his thigh where his Glock was holstered.

"It's just in case I run into a bear or cougar. I don't need any more scars jacking up my pretty face."

"I see. I'm actually a little surprised to see you again today. We've lived in the same place for five years and never crossed paths before."

"Maybe it's fate."

She didn't look amused; she looked downright suspicious. "I don't believe in fate."

"Well, I don't have any other way to explain it. I've been using this trail since I was a kid, and aside from the good-weather months, I hardly bump into anyone out here."

He hadn't meant to come off as defensive, but he got the feeling she was accusing him of something, and he didn't like it.

"I'm sorry. I shouldn't have implied anything. I usually run earlier, but I had somewhere to be today, and…well, I'm sorry."

Everett let it go but couldn't ignore the questions that Callie's suspicion raised about her and her past.

"Well, we're going to keep going," Callie said, putting one of her ear buds back in.

"Be careful out here, especially at dusk."

"That's sweet, but I'll be fine."

Everett started to open his mouth to argue but changed his mind. "Have a nice day."

She paused, staring at him strangely before pushing in her other bud. "You too."

As he watched her run off, the dog loping beside her, Everett hoped fate would throw them together again soon. One thing was for sure: Callie Jacobsen was a mystery he wanted to solve.

Chapter Three

CALLIE WAS IN the dark, a blaring alarm screaming around her. The only thing louder than the noise was the sound of her heart pounding. She reached along the wall, trying to find the deactivate button, anything to quiet the sounds.

Blinding pain sliced through her back, and she fell to the floor. Writhing, she turned to look up at her assailant, knowing who it was before she even saw his face.

Tristan.

His face was twisted into a terrifying mask of hatred, and she tried to move, to pull herself across the floor and away from the glittering knife in his hand, but she was paralyzed.

The knife swung down toward her, and she screamed...

Callie woke up sobbing, the soft, wet brush of Ratchet's tongue on her face pulling her out of the nightmare. With shaking hands, she wrapped her arms around her dog and buried her nose in his fur. She breathed in the calming lavender-and-vanilla baby shampoo she used for his baths, and slowly, her trembling subsided. She flipped off the alarm clock on the nightstand when she realized it was still going, breathing a sigh of relief when all was quiet except for the sound of her heartbeat and Ratchet's panting.

God, it had been months since she'd dreamed about Tristan. Not since the last letter. It didn't make sense.

Climbing out of bed on unsteady limbs, she made her way to the bathroom and splashed water over her face. The cold was jarring but just what she needed to pull her completely out of her terror.

Ratchet sat next to her, leaning his body against her leg as if to reassure her. *I'm here. You have nothing to fear.* It was amazing how he could read exactly what she needed.

"You're such a good boy, Ratch."

His large tail thumped the tile floor as she undressed, avoiding her reflection in the mirror. She didn't need to see the scars to know they were there. All six raised lines—some jagged; others, clean white scars on her already pale skin. They were proof of her stupidity. She had put her faith in a man who had lied to her, and his betrayal had cost her everything.

Her mind drifted back to that night. She'd come home just after seven, since the radio station she'd been working at was just a few miles from her childhood home. Her mother had given the house to them as an engagement present and moved into the guest house. It had been so amazingly generous, Callie almost hadn't accepted, but her mother had squeezed her hands hard and said, *"No buts; it's yours."*

As she'd come through the door, she'd expected to smell dinner on the table and hear the sound of Tristan and her mother talking, or the click of Baby's nails on the tile floor just before she greeted Callie, barking happily.

But all she'd heard was the beeping of the house alarm. There'd been no barking, no laughter from the kitchen. Nothing.

And then she'd seen Baby on the floor of the darkened house.

"Baby!" she'd screamed.

She'd dropped to the floor, reaching out for her beloved pet but paused when her hands had met a warm, wet puddle. Thick liquid had covered her skin and even in the darkness, she'd known it was blood.

Callie had stood up, going for the light, but the incessant beeping wouldn't stop. She couldn't think with the noise. She'd reached up to turn off the alarm when the first slice of pain had exploded across her back.

Callie remembered falling to the ground, writhing and crying as a shadowy figure stood over her. "Please, there's money upstairs. Just don't—"

He'd leaned down over her, and she'd gotten a look at his face.

"Tristan?" But he'd looked nothing like the curly haired man who loved to make her laugh. His normally blue eyes were wide and black in the darkness, and his lips had twisted into a feral snarl.

"Who sent you?" he'd hissed, spittle dropping onto her cheek.

"Tris, it's me! It's Callie!" she'd yelled and put her hands up to push at his chest.

And then, as he'd pulled his arm back, she'd seen it: a knife, covered in something dark red and glistening. A knife from their set that sat in the corner of the kitchen—another engagement gift.

Suddenly, Tristan brought that knife down into her right shoulder. Callie had felt each snap of bone and muscle as he'd torn through them.

"Who sent you to kill me?" Tristan yanked the knife out of her shoulder, and she'd screamed in pain, the wet rush of her blood pouring out across her shirt.

Callie had sucked in air, sobbing hysterically as she'd tried to hold his arm back, that knife glinting at her threateningly. "Tristan, it's me! Your fiancée! It's Callie. Please, stop—"

"I'll make you talk, creature!"

She'd been no match for Tristan's strength, though, and the next sharp stab had struck her abdomen. She'd had no time to process how it was possible that the man she'd chosen to spend her life with was thrusting a knife into her, again and again. Callie had started to feel woozy, to watch the world fading away around her...

Before she'd blacked out, blue and red lights had flashed through the window, but she remembered nothing else.

Callie had woken up in the hospital days later, groggy from the painkillers they'd given her. The doctor had come by to see her, but she remembered only snippets of that conversation.

"Stabbed seven times…just missed the lung…had to repair your intestine…recovery will take time…you were very lucky…"

Lucky. She would never forget that. People told her that often, afterward. She was lucky to have survived. She'd hardly been able to understand what lucky meant until the police came in.

The officer had been so matter-of-fact, like a robot: Tristan had suffered a psychotic break and had been shot by police. He was recovering, but he'd been charged with second-degree murder, animal cruelty, and attempted murder.

"Murder? Who else did he…"

The looks on the officers' faces had been grim. "Your mother was found by the back door…"

She'd stopped listening after that. Her mother was dead. She had spent years trying to make up for her mistakes and in return, she'd been killed by her future son-in-law. A man she had loved and trusted.

A man *Callie* had loved and trusted.

Callie should have been more diligent. She should have made sure he was being treated, that he was safe to be around.

It was her fault—all of it.

When she'd gotten out of the hospital several weeks later, Tristan's parents had offered to let her stay with them while she'd recovered, but she'd refused. It wasn't their fault—she knew that—but she couldn't be surrounded by pictures of him, not when she couldn't get the image of his face, twisted with rage, out of her mind.

But she also couldn't go back to the house she and Tristan had shared. So she'd hired a cleaning crew and movers with the money from her mother's life insurance policy, and after burying her in the Carmichael cemetery, Callie had moved into a gated, one-bedroom apartment in El Dorado Hills. She'd changed her phone number and attended months of physical therapy for the damaged nerves in her shoulder. She tried to move on, tried to get better, but she couldn't sleep. If she slept, the nightmares would come, and she didn't want to see him there—or anywhere—ever again.

Even during Tristan's trial, she couldn't look at him. His lawyer had brought in character witnesses and mental health experts, all saying the same thing: Tristan was a good man, a wonderful son, but he had snapped because of untreated schizophrenia. He had no recollection of what he had done; therefore, how could he be responsible?

After a long recess—where the judge, the prosecutor, and Tristan's lawyer had spoken behind closed doors—they'd pled Tristan down to manslaughter. Guilty, but with a mentally ill addendum that allowed him treatment in a prison mental health facility and five years of psychological monitoring and probation. He was required to see a therapist once a week and have regular doctor's visits. It was a slap on the wrist, but the lawyer she'd hired to file a restraining order informed her that he could have been found not guilty; at least this way, he was paying for what he had done.

But being out of the hospital within two years didn't seem like punishment to Callie. Which had made his stalking worse. She'd switched jobs and was working at a tiny station in Placerville when one day, Tristan was waiting by her car.

"Callie, please talk to me. It wasn't me. I swear, I don't even remember it!"

The minute she'd seen him, she'd started screaming, blocking out his words, his voice. Her lawyer had gotten an updated restraining order, and he'd tried to enlist Tristan's parents' help.

"He's really better, Callie."

Callie had hung up on them and changed her number once more, but no matter what she did, she couldn't escape him. It was hopeless.

After that, everything in her life became tainted. Faster than she'd thought possible, Callie had fallen down a rabbit hole of pills and booze—anything to block out the pain, the nightmares, the fear. She'd hit rock bottom hard.

Her mother's face flashed through Callie's mind, and she jerked open the shower door in self-disgust. Even though they'd never had the healthiest relationship, it had gotten better once her mother had started working the program. Still, they weren't lying when they said alcoholism ran in families.

Like mother, like daughter. Only it had taken Callie just two years of heartbreak—not twelve, like her mother—to realize that drinking only exacerbated the problem. Callie had never dealt with stress and loss in the healthiest of ways. Most of the time, she'd run from her problems or just buried them in whatever she could get her hands on. In many ways, Tristan had been her salvation from an unhappy childhood.

Well, at least that's what she'd thought. In high school, she'd escape her mother's drunken rages and sneak off to his house where they'd get stoned and screw. Afterward, he'd just held her, telling her that she was always safe with him.

Unfortunately, he had been dead wrong without even realizing it.

Once Callie was all ready for work, she grabbed her cell phone off the charger, and skimmed through her messages: *Changed your mind yet?*

Callie shook her head at Caroline's persistence. Maybe it was about time to share the shadows of her past with Caroline, just so she would stop pestering her.

It could be fun, if you just let yourself go.

But she couldn't listen to that inner voice. If she let herself go, let down her barriers and boundaries for even one second, she could end up right back where she'd started—a foolish girl who had ignored all the danger signs.

Which was why her attraction to Everett Silverton was so unsettling. Seeing him yesterday on the trail had been a surprise, and her mind immediately had gone to the dark side, especially when she'd seen his gun. She'd been so caught up in the legend of a small-town hero that she'd started to soften, to enjoy his easy smiles and even his self-deprecating humor.

It was a dangerous thing to be lonely. It made you crave normalcy, someone to go out with and enjoy. Someone who might just chase the shadows and evil away.

Callie knew better, though. Especially with a guy who was already dealing with his own past. She'd heard too many news stories about good people who'd snapped. You never knew what someone else was capable of, no matter how long or how well you might think you knew him. She just had to keep reminding herself of that and to stay the hell away from Everett.

EVERETT POURED MORE coffee into his mug, trying to wake up, despite the fact that it was three in the afternoon. He had slept for maybe four hours the night before, and those hours had been restless—and intense. It was always like that when he dreamed of Robbie.

This dream had been different, though. In it, they had been sitting at his kitchen table, shooting the shit.

"So who's this girl you're obsessed with?"

He could have sworn it was really Robbie's voice. And as they'd gone back and forth, razzing one another, it actually had taken Everett longer than usual to realize he was in a dream. And like a hundred times before, he'd apologized to Robbie for not being able to save him.

"Bygones, man. I know you tried. Besides, no one else thought twice about saving his own ass before mine. Just you. Only why are you wasting your life bottled up like some fucking hermit? You got to live, so get your ass out there and do something."

But before Everett could respond, Robbie had burst into flames and disappeared. Which was fucked up, until Everett himself had started to catch fire and had woken up in a panic. Eight years had passed, but the excruciating pain of his flesh melting was something he'd never been able to leave behind.

He'd managed to get out of bed to shake the dream, but the lack of sleep was hitting him hard now. It wouldn't be a bad idea to take a little nap, especially with how bad the weather was outside. He'd been taking calls since seven and really had no reason to go out anyway.

His cell phone started blaring, and he slid his thumb across the screen to accept the call.

"Hello?"

"Hi, Everett, it's Gemma Bowers. I was just calling to let you know that your books came in. And I gotta tell you, you have the most eclectic taste of any man I've ever met."

"You tell me that every time I order." He'd been frequenting Chloe's Book Nook since getting back into town and loved ordering a variety of genres. He'd always enjoyed books, but it wasn't until he was deployed that he'd begun realizing their true value. He'd needed the distraction from the horrors he was witnessing, and now, books helped ease his loneliness.

Somewhat.

"Only because I admire the hell out of you for not just sticking to typical guy novels."

"Well, thanks. I'll come pick them up."

"Okay. See you soon."

So much for not going anywhere.

He wanted those books, though. He'd reread everything on his shelf and had been meaning to go to the library, but Mrs. Nelson, the librarian, loved to talk his ear off. Sometimes an hour would go by before he could get out of there. At least Gemma was friendly, without jawing away at him all afternoon.

Grabbing his keys and jacket, he pulled his hood up over his head. The rain pounded down on him as he ran from his front door to his truck. Everett shook like a dog as he climbed inside. He didn't mind the rain, especially a warm rain, but thunderstorms were another matter. The boom of a lightning strike could sound a little too much like an explosion, and he hadn't refilled his anxiety medication in a while, hadn't felt like he needed them. But last night's dream, plus his lack of sleep, had him on the jittery side.

Pulling out onto the main road, he headed toward the heart of town as the wipers whipped water off the windshield too slowly to give him a clear view for long. He was just coming around the bend when he saw a white Jeep pulled off the road and a woman in a bright red slicker bent down by the back tire. At least, he was pretty sure it was a woman.

He craned his neck as he passed, and in the front seat, he saw a large tan shape.

A dog.

"Well, shit." It was Callie. If it had been anyone else he'd have pulled off already, but he didn't want to give her the wrong impression.

Are you really going to be a chicken shit just because she hurt your pride?

Flipping his truck around, he pulled off onto the side of the road. His heart was pounding like a jack hammer as he jumped out of the truck and jogged up the road. Thunder growled above as he came up behind her.

"Looks like you could use a hand."

"SON OF A *bitch*!" Surprised, Callie spun around from her kneeling position so fast that she fell over, landing in the softening muck with a splat. She'd been too busy cursing the shredded tire and the pouring rain to hear Everett behind her until he spoke.

Callie shook her mud-covered hands and was sure she heard a snort of laughter from Everett over the pouring rain and Ratchet's muffled barking inside the Jeep.

"Hasn't anyone ever told you that sneaking up on someone is rude?" Callie glared up at Everett, who was holding his hands down to her. Even though he wasn't smiling, she'd have to be blind not to catch the amused gleam in his eyes.

Jackass.

Ignoring his offer of assistance, she climbed to her feet, but her bruised pride earned her even more mud as her jeans were soaked through. She tried to wipe off the muck, but it just smeared.

"They have, which is why I didn't sneak; I walked. I saw you huddled over and figured I could help."

"Thanks, but I've got this," she said.

Thunder erupted over their heads, and Callie felt like the sky was laughing at her too.

"You sure? You're shivering like crazy, and I can have this changed in under four minutes. I'll have you know I hold the Silverton family record for fastest tire change." Lightning lit up the sky, highlighting his cheeky grin. "And I've been told more than once that I'm good with my hands."

She didn't want to smile at his gentle teasing, but she was cold and miserable, and he was offering her a way out.

"I was just going to call triple-A for a tow—"

"It will be faster if I just change it; believe me. Here." Everett reached around her and opened the door to the Jeep. "Hop in, and I'll grab the spare from the back."

Callie's face burned with embarrassment. "It's not there."

"What?"

"I meant to buy another one, but these suckers aren't cheap and I just…I never got around to it." She leaned her head against the door, laughing humorlessly. "Pretty stupid, huh?"

"Well, yeah, but there's no use in me lecturing you when you already know."

Callie glanced at him sharply. "Thanks a lot, Dad."

"Come on; I'll take you to Jose's Tires, and we'll get you a new one."

"I told you; I can't afford it right now—"

"I'll take care of it. Don't worry."

"Um, no. I don't like being in anyone's debt." She squirmed under his thoughtful gaze and added, "Thank you, but I must decline."

"Well, *I* must insist. You can't just sit here on the side of the road until payday, and triple-A will ding you for using one of your get-out-of-trouble calls." Another crack of thunder shook the sky. "Look, I get it. You don't know me from Adam, but I can get you over to Jose's and get you a line of emergency credit. That way, you won't owe me anything, and I don't have to stand out in the rain. Sound fair?"

Her insides churned, and she cursed. If she'd just gotten a new spare when she'd bought her last set, she wouldn't be sitting in the rain at the mercy of a large former marine.

Who you can't seem to get out of your head.

And now she was about to get into a car with him and have to make small talk. What if he started flirting with ideas that she was interested in him as anything more than an acquaintance?

Why? Because you actually feel something for him, unlike every other guy since Tristan? You gotta start to move on sometime.

But moving on meant putting her trust in another man, and she wasn't sure she could ever make that mistake again.

"Okay," Everett said. "I really don't want to stand out in the rain while you debate whether or not I'm some dirt bag trying to scam you, so how about I run up to Jose's, get the tire, and come back?"

He was giving her an out and still offering to help her. If she was smart, she would take him up on the offer and climb up into the safety of her Jeep, away from him and his warm brown eyes.

He's Fred's son, and everyone says he's honorable. It's not like you're driving to Mexico. It's right up the road. He didn't even have to stop—most people wouldn't have.

"Wait," she said when he started to turn away. Grabbing Ratchet's leash and her purse from inside her car, she ignored the voices in her head. "We're coming."

Chapter Four

EVERETT KEPT GLANCING toward Callie out of the corner of his eye, but his view was blocked by her enormous dog sitting between them on the bucket seat.

"So where were you headed when your tire crapped out?"

"I was going to meet a friend for coffee."

Was that code for a date?

"Do you need to call him or her and let them know you'll be late?"

A few seconds passed before she spoke. Her tone definitely sounded amused. "Thanks, I'll let *her* know."

Everett started whistling, fighting a shit-eating grin.

Just because she doesn't have a date tonight doesn't mean she's not involved with someone.

The pessimistic voice dimmed his relief. Besides, with the way she'd fought his offer of help, he had no reason to believe he had a shot in hell with her.

But man, did he want one. Even soaking wet and covered in mud, she was a pretty sight.

Trying to catch a glimpse of her again, he met Ratchet's eyes. The dog stopped panting long enough to give him what could only be described as a look of warning: *Back off, asshole, or I'll rip out your throat.*

Everett unconsciously rubbed his neck.

He turned onto Main Street toward Jose's Tires and slowed down when he saw a Rock Canyon police cruiser coming from the opposite direction. Checking his speed, he realized he was going about ten over the limit.

Everett said a silent prayer. The last thing he wanted was to be pulled over with Callie in the car. Nothing killed a romance faster than a nosy member of RCPD asking questions and spreading the word.

The cruiser flashed its lights, a clear message to slow down, and Everett took his foot off the gas.

"Are we getting pulled over, Hamlin?"

Everett laughed. "Didn't peg you for a NASCAR fan."

"Well, there's a lot you don't know about me," she said. *But I'd like to.*

Everett glanced in the rearview mirror, relieved that the cop hadn't turned around. "So you're a radio deejay with an affinity for NASCAR and big dogs. What else should I know about you?"

"Why do you need to know anything?"

"Maybe I find you interesting." Okay, it was a bold move, but she'd asked. No, she'd basically dared him to make a move.

This time when he glanced her way, she was looking around Ratchet's head and caught his gaze. Those eyes of hers were like warm honey, and he imagined her lips were just as sweet.

He shifted in the seat, as just the thought of her lips stirred his interest. His jeans had *not* been made with comfortable erections in mind.

She sat back out of sight. "Trust me; I'm not."

He didn't believe her for one second, but he didn't argue.

Silence filled the cab until Ratchet sniffed at him, dragging his wet, drooling lips across the arm of Everett's jacket.

"I think your dog has an overactive salivary gland."

"He's just not a fan of car rides," she said.

"He's not going to puke on me, is he?"

"You know, I thought about teaching him to puke on command, but it wasn't in my dog training book."

He chuckled. "I'm glad, since, you know, I'm such a nice guy. Helping out a damsel in distress. I should definitely get more than a lap full of puke."

"You like to toot your own horn, don't you?"

Everett couldn't resist tapping the horn several times.

The husky sound of her laughter filled the truck, and satisfaction uncurled in his stomach. He wanted to hear more of it, wanted it louder and freer. There was still a hitch, as if she was scared to let herself go, and he wanted to get around that, to help her.

For some crazy, unknown reason, he felt like she needed him.

CALLIE STOOD NEXT to Everett, nibbling her lip thoughtfully, as he talked to Jose. In the last twenty minutes, she had laughed, teased, and smiled more than she had with any man in the last seven years, even her friend, Mike Stevens. But Mike didn't stir her the way Everett did.

"Jose Rameriz, this is Callie Jacobsen."

Everett's hand grazed her shoulder and despite the thick sweatshirt that separated his skin from hers, an electric shock raced down her arm. She looked up at him sharply, wondering if he'd caught her swift intake of breath, because his hand dropped back to his side suddenly. It was true she didn't like to be touched in most instances, but Everett's warm strength kept drawing her to him. She would have never gotten into his car otherwise.

"Hi, Callie." Jose held his hand out to her, his smile bright. He was a handsome man with light brown skin, almost the same color of a gingerbread cookie, and deep, soulful brown eyes. He was a good head shorter than Everett and less imposing too—despite his sleeve tattoos and the spider tat on his neck.

Or he's less imposing because he doesn't make your heart race.

Callie took his hand with a firm squeeze. "It's nice to meet you, Jose."

"Callie is a little strapped and was wondering about a payment plan for two tires. I can vouch for her."

It was on the tip of her tongue to tell Everett that she could speak for herself, but Jose's raised eyebrows and sly expression stopped her. Why did he look so amused? His gaze shifted between them, and her cheeks flamed as she realized that Jose probably thought they were sleeping together.

"Yeah, sure. We can work something out. What are the dimensions? I'll check out what we've got in stock." He held up a notepad and pen that he'd pulled from his pocket.

Everett rattled off her tire size, surprising her. How did he remember all that? She had issues remembering her social security number, which she'd been reciting since birth.

"Make and model? Year?" Jose asked.

"A two thousand four Jeep Wrangler."

"All right, just hang tight."

Jose headed into the back, leaving Everett and Callie alone.

"He thinks we're...involved," Callie hissed.

Everett glanced down at her, and she would have had to be blind to miss the unholy twinkle in his eyes. "So?"

"It's not true."

"Don't worry. Jose doesn't gossip."

Callie spluttered. "It's not about the gossip, it's that...I don't want or need a boyfriend."

"Okay."

His reasonable answer, followed by a nonchalant shrug, irked her for some reason. Had she read him wrong? Was he just this nice guy who helped out stranded women on a regular basis? Was she freaking out for no reason?

Neither of them said another word, and when Jose came back, she was thankful for the diversion.

"Okay, I got your tires, and here is the cost," Jose said, handing her a receipt. "Think you can pay them off by December first?"

Two months? That was very generous. "Yes, thank you."

"Awesome. I'll bring them up. I'm assuming you two can handle changing them?"

"Yeah, I've got it. Thanks, man," Everett said.

Everett and Jose did some kind of bro hug, and Jose disappeared once again.

"You two seem close," Callie said.

"Yeah, we grew up together. We both had it rough, although he had it worse than me."

Callie wanted to ask, but Jose and another man appeared pushing two tires up front before helping get them outside. The rain was still coming down, but the thunder was just a distant rumble.

When the tires were loaded, Everett and Callie jumped back into the truck. Ratchet met her with wet kisses, and she pushed him off with a laugh. When he finally settled down, he actually lay down, his slobbery mouth on her legs.

"Geez, I keep forgetting what a big son of a bitch he is. How much does he weigh?" Everett said as he pulled out of the parking lot.

Callie stroked Ratchet's head and velvety ears, and the warm calm only his love could bring spread through her. "He was a hundred sixty-four pounds at his last veterinary appointment."

Everett whistled. "What made you want such a big dog?"

Callie's hand stilled, settling on Ratchet's head. It wasn't really his size that had drawn her; it was something

she'd read online about Anatolians being loyal and protective, known for going up against animals three times
their size to keep their herds safe. Baby, her poor mutt,
despite knowing something was wrong with Tristan, had
been only forty pounds. No doubt, her size and age had
made it impossible to defend herself. She worried about
Ratchet, but he was strong.

And his strength had been what she needed.

"I actually just saw a picture of the breed in the paper
and fell in love. Besides, big dogs are more intimidating
than purse dogs."

"That's true, but whom do you want intimidate?"

You? She couldn't say that though, not out loud. Partly
because she couldn't bear to be rude to him after he'd
helped her out of a jam.

But also because she liked him. Probably more than
she should.

"I don't know. Purse snatchers? Burglars?"

"Ah, so he's like your buffer."

"Yes."

"It must be hard," Everett said. He reached out to
crank up the heater, and she watched his hands. They
were big hands with long fingers, and she suddenly wondered if they were rough or soft.

*Stop thinking about his hands, for fuck's sake! What
happened to keeping your distance and not getting
involved? Fantasizing about his hands is pretty damn
intimate.*

"What must be hard?"

"Feeling like you have to keep everyone at a distance."

His words stunned her. "I don't feel like that. I have friends."

"Sorry. I guess I misread the situation."

But Callie could tell that he didn't believe that, and his arrogance irritated her. "Look, you don't know me or what makes me tick, so stop assuming you do."

EVERETT DIDN'T SAY another word as he drove, taking a different route so he could pull up behind her Jeep. He'd obviously struck a nerve with her, and despite every gentlemanly fiber of his body telling him to apologize, he couldn't.

Because he knew he was right about Callie. Even if she wouldn't admit it.

Hell, he'd been there. When his wife left him, he'd been hurting from the loss of Robbie and then his friendship with Robbie's wife, Cara. He'd spent so much time alone that he started to think it was better that way. Even when he'd come home, he'd kept his brother and father at a distance, insisting he was fine. Therapy had helped him realize he needed to reconnect with the world so he could move on.

It was obvious from the way Callie behaved that she'd had a rough past. But instead of reaching out, she seemed to prefer being on her own.

The rain was barely drizzling when they arrived, and Everett opened the door to get out.

"I'm sorry I snapped at you." Her husky voice sounded strained, like the words had cost her.

Never one to hold a grudge, he smiled. "You were right. I was assuming, which makes me an ass."

Everett heard her soft laugh and closed the door behind him with a smile. He went to work on the tire, ignoring the sound of his truck door opening and closing and her sweet voice as she talked to her dog. The Jeep dipped and when she came around the front alone, he figured she'd put Ratchet inside already.

"I've almost got it."

"Thank you. This was really nice of you, especially when I haven't given you a reason to be."

Everett looked up at her, wiping the rain off his face so he could meet her gaze. "You seem to assume that just because people are kind to you, they want something. Sometimes people help because it's the right thing to do."

Her gaze shifted away, and he went back to tightening the nuts on the wheel. He'd said his piece, but knew he wasn't going to convince Callie with words that his intentions were honorable.

He had to prove it to her.

When he finished, he released the jack and gathered up all the tools, sliding them back in the spare tire kit. "I'll put this and the new tire in the back, and you'll be good to go. I'll haul this one off to the dump for you."

She knelt down next to him and took the kit from him, their fingers brushing. Despite the chill of their skin, heat sizzled between them, sending a shot of awareness down his throat. Her blonde curls were wet and falling out of her messy top knot, and drops of rain were clinging to her cheeks. Before he could stop himself, he traced the pad of his thumb across one, catching the cool droplet on his skin. Her amber eyes widened, and he dropped his hand, cursing his impulse.

"Sorry. You had something on your cheek."

Callie cleared her throat and stood up. "It's okay."

He climbed to his feet and couldn't help wondering if she'd felt something too. Was that why she kept pulling away?

But if she didn't want him, why was he pushing?

Because she doesn't treat you like a defective puppy she'd have to fix.

Grabbing her spare tire from the back of his truck, he slid it into the back of her Jeep. She stood back as he closed the door, and he could tell she was nervous—her hands kept twisting.

"Well, you're all set. You should get home and change out of those wet clothes. If you get sick, I'll have to listen to one of those ridiculous weekend deejays, and they play nothing but crap."

Everett started to head back to his truck, but she caught his hand. "Hey."

Just the touch of her hand sent his heart from a trot to a gallop. He loved the way her soft skin wrapped around his.

Facing her, he waited, afraid to move a muscle and scare her off.

But she moved so fast, he wasn't prepared when her lips brushed the scarred side of his face. He stiffened as the warmth seeped through his cheek, his stomach twisting up as a thousand thoughts and insecurities made him wince. Had the roughness repelled her? Why hadn't she picked the untouched side?

"Thank you. For being kind."

Callie dropped his hand and ran to her car, as if afraid he would come after her. As she started it and pulled forward, he was finally able to move again, backing up a ways to watch her disappear down the road.

Everett's hand came up to rest against his cheek, and he realized that he'd lied to Callie when he said he didn't want anything from her.

He wanted everything.

Pulling his phone from his pocket as he headed back to his truck, he called Eddie Kendall, one of his publicity managers.

"This is Eddie."

"Hey, Eddie, it's Everett."

"Hey, boss. You outside? It sounds like you're in a wind tunnel."

"I'm standing in a thunderstorm," he said, opening his truck door and climbing inside. "Better?"

"Yeah, I can hear ya. So what's up? Did you get the new program stats?"

"Yeah, and they looked great, but listen. I've been thinking about that interview you're doing Thursday on the Kat Country morning show. I don't have anything going on and can take it, if you want."

The line was dead quiet for a minute. "Um, okay. Sure, Everett, but…why? You never do interviews."

Everett rubbed his cheek where Callie's lips had been. "It's personal."

Chapter Five

TWO DAYS LATER, Everett walked into the Kat just before seven in the morning and smiled at the young man behind the desk.

"Everett Silverton. I'm here to talk about Stateside Support."

"Oh, yeah," the kid said, standing up with his hand out. "Pleasure to meet you, sir. I'm Dalton. Callie's in the booth waiting for you."

Everett shook Dalton's hand and liked his grip. "Good to meet you too." Something about the way the kid held himself made him add, "Have you served?"

"Not me, but my older brother and my father were both in the army. I would have joined, but my mom had a fit backward," Dalton said. His ears turned red as he added, "Something about her baby not being a military man."

"Something tells me you weren't disappointed, though," Everett said with a smile.

"To be honest, no. I believe in our military, but I'd rather not spend my life dodging bullets and bombs—" Dalton cut himself off suddenly, stammering, "I'm...I'm...sorry. I...I...didn't...didn't mean anything..."

"What? You don't want to look as pretty as me?" he asked. Dalton paled, and his skin took on a bluish sheen Everett didn't like. "Hey, I was just kidding. Lighten up, and don't worry about offending my delicate sensibilities. I've got a thick hide."

Everett was used to people saying the wrong thing around him and then making things worse by rambling.

"Thanks, sir," Dalton said, taking a deep breath. "I'll take you back."

Everett followed, his heart beating faster the closer he got to seeing Callie. He rarely did publicity for the organization, usually leaving it to Pam or Eddie, who handled their social media and fund-raisers, but the chance of sitting in a small room with just her had been too good to pass up.

Besides, if he was going to really go for it with Callie, he needed to be completely honest. Which meant telling her that he'd figured out who she was when they first met. And that he was Rhett.

Would she freak out? He hoped not. She had enough of an emotional force field around her without dropping this bomb on her. He was hoping that once she realized who he was and that he was harmless, maybe she'd take a chance on getting to know him better.

And hopefully not think you're a liar...

Dalton stopped outside a door with an ON AIR sign lit up above it. The minute the light went off, he knocked.

"Come on in," Callie called.

Dalton opened the door and waved Everett inside.

"Your interview is here," Dalton said, and Everett stepped into the room.

Callie's eyes widened, and she looked down at her desk. Everett didn't know if she was just surprised or horrified, but his heart sank.

Stupid idea, Silverton.

Callie seemed to recover, though, and said, "I thought I was interviewing Eddie Kendall."

"I offered to take the interview." Everett held his hand out as Ratchet came out from under the table to sniff it.

"I see." Callie reached up to adjust her headband. Everett had a feeling he made her nervous, or maybe she just didn't like surprises. Either way, she was fidgeting something fierce. "Well, have a seat, and we'll have a little warm-up chat before we go back on air."

Now, why does she have to make it sound like you're about to pull her teeth out?

He sat down in the chair across from her and picked up the headset on the table. "So, Callie, where are you from originally?"

One of her eyebrows lifted. "I thought I'd ask the questions."

Why was she being so cold? After the tire and the kiss on the cheek, he'd thought she might be pleased to see him.

"I thought we were gonna chat," he said. He grinned, hoping to ease the strange tension. "Doesn't that mean the conversation goes both ways?"

She didn't smile back, and for a second, he thought she was going to kick him out; she looked so disgruntled.

"I'm from California," she said grudgingly.

"Huh." He bit back a laugh just as she looked at him sharply. Man, she was on edge.

"What does 'huh' mean?"

"Nothing. I'm just surprised they play country music in California," Everett said. "I thought you all drove electric cars and listened to Depeche Mode."

"Ha-ha, you're a funny guy," she said, and he could have sworn he saw a small smile.

"How come you don't smile?" he asked abruptly.

She frowned at him. "I smile."

"No, I think the most I've seen is your mouth twitch a little like this." He demonstrated, stretching his lips a little, and she glared at him.

"Maybe I don't like you."

Everett stared at her for a moment, hostility surrounding her like a shield. What the hell had happened in the last few days to make her want to push him away? Just when he thought he was making headway with her, she threw up walls and emotional blockers like she was Fort Knox. She was defensive, rude, and if she'd been anyone else, he would have already walked out the door.

But he didn't believe that she really wanted him to leave or to stay away. He just had to figure out how to get her to let her guard down.

"Me? But you called me a hero. Everybody likes heroes."

She coughed into her hand, and he knew she was covering a laugh. Satisfaction curled through him and suddenly, he sat forward, whispering, "I think you like me a whole lot."

She stilled, her gaze wide and nearly panicked. "Why would you think that?"

"Because you wouldn't fight so hard to be cool if you didn't," he said, wanting to crow when she blushed hard. Throwing her off balance was more telling than anything. When she was caught off guard, she revealed everything.

Especially that she *did* like him. So why was she fighting it?

"Whatever. We're about to go on air."

"Wait," he said. She paused and gave him an impatient look. It almost made him lose his nerve, but he knew they would have no chance if she found out later.

"Look, I feel like I need to tell you that...well, that first day when we met outside Hall's Market, I didn't know how to tell you who I was. And especially not after we met on the trail—"

"What do you mean? Who are you?"

"Rhett. You can call me Rhett."

Callie paled. "What?"

"I'm the guy who's been calling the station at the same time every morning for a year. I didn't know how to just come out and say, 'Oh, by the way, I'm the dork who tried to pick you up over the phone.' I just figured I'd tell you when the time was right."

"Hey, Callie, we need to get this show on the road," Dave said over the intercom.

Everett held Callie's gaze, one that said she'd rather gut him and throw him in the Snake River. "Sure. Go ahead and count us down."

As numbers sounded in his headset, he tried to talk to her again. "Look, I have no idea what you must be thinking, but I wasn't trying to pull anything. I was going to tell you. I was just afraid to scare you off."

Callie raised her coffee cup to her lips and didn't say anything.

Trying to break the ice that had formed between them, he said, "Considering how good you look glaring at me, I bet you're even more beautiful when you really smile." Callie missed her mouth, and coffee spilled down the front of her shirt. Everett was up out of his chair and rushing to her side before he could think about it. "Are you okay? Did you burn yourself?"

He reached out toward her, and she grabbed his hands, holding him back. "I'm okay."

Her voice was shaky, but when he looked at her, their gazes crashed hard. Everett couldn't stop thinking of her warm hands in his, and slowly, he stroked his thumb across her skin. He watched as her lips parted lightly, and she took a soft breath…

"You all right, Callie?" a voice asked in the headphones.

Callie jerked her hands away and slid her chair back. "I'm fine."

Everett realized then that he was on his knees at her feet. He had been so caught up in her that he hadn't noticed Ratchet sitting next to him, his large jaw open and breathing right down his neck.

He froze.

"If I move, is he going to take me out?"

"It's okay, Ratchet. Come here," Callie said, reaching out for the dog, who lumbered a few inches forward to lay his head in her lap. Both of them watched Everett warily as he stood up and walked back over to his seat.

As he sat, Callie spoke into the mic, her voice strong and steady. "And we're back with the head of Stateside Support, a nonprofit organization helping our military personnel readjust to civilian living. They offer counseling, job placement, and a multitude of other services. Please join me in welcoming Everett Silverton."

The sound of applause went off in his ears, and he looked over at the little box where two men sat at a large soundboard.

Pay no attention to the men in the sound box.

Everett chuckled at his silent joke. Callie was watching him suspiciously, like maybe she thought he was laughing at her.

The applause finally died down, and Everett said, "Thanks, Callie, it's great to be here with you. I was just trying to get used to the headphones. This is my first radio interview."

"Really? Well, I hope you enjoy yourself."

"Oh, I'm sure I will."

She glared at him warningly, and he suppressed a smile. She really was pretty with her scrunched-up nose and squinty, angry eyes.

Of course, he was probably treading on thin ice, so he didn't say anything more.

"Good. Now, I know you were in the military, but can you tell us a little bit about your service? How old were you when you joined?"

Everett took a deep breath as memories flashed in his head. He'd spent years in therapy working through them, but they were still gut-wrenchingly painful.

Especially the ones with Robbie.

"I joined the United States Marine Corps when I was eighteen and was honorably discharged when I was twenty-six."

"And if you hadn't been injured, would you have remained a marine? It seems like a lot of unnecessary risk to reenlist after you've already served your minimum enlistment."

Everett felt a pinch of irritation at her casual tone, like he'd just torn a ligament or something. As if serving his country was just an obligation he'd been trying to fulfill and not something he'd planned to make a career doing.

"You mean *if* my Humvee hadn't been hit by a road-side bomb and *if* I hadn't received second-degree burns over thirty-nine percent of my body, would I have reenlisted? Then, yes. It was an honor to serve my country. As it was, I did four tours, and although I wasn't able to retire from the military like I'd planned, we have a saying in the Corps: 'Once a marine, always a marine.' "

Callie's face paled, and Everett cursed himself, realizing how much he'd revealed about his pain and bitterness over his scars—and his life. He'd planned for it to be a career, to retire at forty and come home to live out the rest of his life in peace, to be with his family and grow old with his wife. Instead, that plan had been cut short, and now he had nothing except for Stateside. He'd poured everything into it, and although he believed in the organization, it hadn't been his plan.

Surprisingly, her hand came across the table and covered his. "I am so sorry."

The moment was charged between them, and he was loath to break the connection, but he didn't want her pity. That was the last thing he wanted from her.

He pulled his hand away gently. "It's all right. My experience and the experiences of my friends gave me the idea for Stateside. When we came home, we all suffered, both physically and mentally, but it was hard to admit that we needed help."

Callie pulled her hand back, and he noticed the burning red of her cheeks. She probably thought he was rebuffing her, but he wasn't. He wanted to tell her, but the show was live and she was already moving on with the interview.

"There are other organizations out there similar to yours, aren't there? What makes Stateside different?"

The moment was over, and although it was a fair question, her condescending tone made it seem like a dig.

"Yes, there are a lot of very good organizations out there, and like them, we're here to talk, to listen, and to help, but mostly Stateside is for the people on the fence about needing assistance. Military personnel are proud and have been taking care of others for so long that it's often hard for them to admit they need help."

"How do you convince them if they're on the fence?"

And she comes out swinging.

"Wow, you're really going for the deep stuff, huh?"

She raised her eyebrows. "I am just curious about what sets you apart, Mr. Silverton."

"To answer your question, we're different because even though we're based in Idaho, we have resources nation-wide. We have open dialogue with our vets, and we stay with them from the moment they call our hotline to the moment they get back on their feet. Our counselors are available twenty-four hours a day, seven days a week. But more than anything, it's because most of us have been there. Because we are staffed by veterans, our counselors and job advocates can better understand the struggles our military men and women face coming home. That's what sets us apart."

Callie had recovered, but her expression was so mixed up, he wasn't sure what she was thinking. But apparently, it wasn't "I need to get the hell out of here," because she continued the interview.

"It sounds like you provide amazing services and dedication. What about military personnel with serious mental health issues, like PTSD?"

"Grief counseling is a major part of our organiza-tion. We are taught to tamp down our emotions so we can stay levelheaded in a hot zone, but many of us lose friends and even family during our service, yet we never really process the loss. We try to help people with this and especially with the guilt associated with making it home when others didn't."

"You sound like you've experienced this." Her voice was soft.

"Yeah, I came home in pain and with severe PTSD. I'd lost my best friend and more. I know what these guys are going through, and it's hard, but we're still here, and we have got to respect that."

Everett hadn't meant to choke on the last sentence, but talking about counseling reminded him of the years he'd sat in his therapist's office trying to open up about Robbie's death and how it felt to be a survivor. It had been a long and painful struggle.

Callie muted her mic, her expression blank, but he saw something lurking in her eyes. Something warm and caring, and he felt a flash of hope that he hadn't ruined everything. That they could talk after the interview, and everything would be back on track. "Do you want me to wrap it up?"

Running a hand over his face, he shook his head. Despite the ugly images and memories haunting him, being near Callie made him content—and excited for the first time in years. He had something to look forward to, something to chase the pain away. "I'm fine. Sorry."

She nodded and flipped her mic back on, all business now, but he knew better. She could be angry with him if she wanted, but she couldn't deny the connection between them.

"What about support for their families?"

Everett cleared his throat. "We offer marriage counseling, but there are other organizations that focus on the particular stresses military families endure."

"But don't you think you need to explain to the families the signs they need to look for, in case their loved ones' mental states take a dangerous turn?"

Everett paused, studying her face and the hollow look in her eyes. Had someone in her family experienced PTSD?

"PTSD is often triggered by something out of the veteran's control. We do educate family members about the signs that may mean their loved ones are struggling, but our main focus is to make the individual feel like he or she has somewhere to call and ask for help from people who know what the vet has been through."

Everett noticed the way Callie was squeezing the mic, like she was struggling internally, and he wanted to ask what ghosts haunted her. All his attempts to be funny and even his mild irritation with her coldness melted in the face of her obvious pain. He wanted to pull her into his arms, to comfort her and tell her he would keep her safe.

As if sensing his mistress's agitation, Ratchet climbed out from under the table and nudged Callie.

Callie shook her head and stroked the dog's head, as if she was coming out of a dream.

Back in peppy DJ mode, Callie concluded the interview. "Well, thank you so much for coming in and talking to us today, Everett."

"No problem, Callie, anytime," he said, holding her gaze.

She looked away and listed Stateside's number and website. Through it all, Everett could tell her hands were shaking and that she was distraught. Something had definitely happened to her. His thoughts kept straying to her concern for the military personnel's families. She'd seemed so worried that they weren't protected or informed enough. Was she worried about him and his own PTSD? His antagonizing her probably hadn't helped. He'd definitely fucked up.

And he realized that as attracted as he was to her, he first needed to gain her trust, to be her friend, if he ever wanted anything more with her. Which meant some serious groveling was in store.

Callie stood up with her headset still on. "And for all the men and women who protect our great nation, here's a little Craig Morgan."

Everett stood up too, removing his headset, but before he could say anything, Callie had hers off and was heading for the door, her dog close behind.

Maybe groveling was an understatement.

CALLIE STORMED OUT of the studio and caught the surprised looks on Dalton's, Dave's, and Henry's faces.

"What? I need some air."

Heading for the back door with Ratchet close on her heels, she pushed the door open and sucked in the cold air. Inside her head, a battle raged.

What is it about him that rubs you wrong?

After she'd impulsively kissed his cheek on Tuesday, she'd wanted to choke herself. For someone who swore she wanted nothing to do with him, she sure was wishy-washy about where she stood, and Callie hated herself for it. When he'd walked through the door today, she'd been so thrown that she'd lashed out and been a bitch. She'd had every intention of apologizing after the interview; then he'd dropped that Rhett bomb, and she'd nearly hurled.

How had she not recognized his voice? Not known who he was? All her fears that he was following her, that their bumping into each other had been more than a coincidence had been spot on. She suddenly wished that she'd taught Ratchet how to "sick balls."

Are you really freaking out about that, or is it because when he called you beautiful, you wanted to melt?

God, she was a glutton for punishment. When he'd been kneeling by her side, staring up at her with those concerned eyes, she'd stopped breathing, and her heart had crashed into her breast bone. Then he'd gone and stroked her hand with the pad of his thumb, and a jolt of red-hot awareness had shot all the way to her stomach as she imagined those big hands stroking everywhere.

She could forgive herself that momentary weakness, but the way he'd talked about his organization with so much passion had only stirred the pot, so to speak.

For the first time in what felt like forever, she wanted a man. Wanted him bad, in the worst way possible.

And he was the wrong man. If there was ever a man who was totally, crazily wrong for her, it was Everett Silverton.

Ratchet woofed softly and turned. Callie swung around to find Everett standing behind her, his hands in his jacket pockets.

"Are you okay?"

"I'm fine," she said, willing him to stay where he was and not come any closer.

"You just rushed out of there and I—"

"Why didn't you tell me who you were?"

"You mean, why didn't I tell you I was the idiot who had attempted to ask for your number on the air and only succeeded in epically freaking you out? Not exactly a conversation starter."

"You deliberately withheld information. Information that was important—"

"Why? So you could think up a reason for why I'm not right for you? Or why we can't be friends?"

"You're telling me that none of these 'accidental encounters' have been planned?" she asked.

"No, I'm not saying that." She sucked in a breath, ready to go off, but he continued. "I'm saying that after Tuesday, I felt something that I haven't felt in so long, I hardly recognized it. I'm saying that I wanted to see you again so badly, I called up one of Stateside's publicists and asked to take this interview myself so I could be near you. I don't do interviews, because I can't stand to have people pity me. I thought you were different, I wanted you to be different, and so, yes, I arranged to see you again today, but that's it. Every other meeting was just luck. Or fate or whatever you want to call it. It was the universe telling us that there is something here. Can you honestly tell me that you feel nothing?"

He didn't give her a chance to answer. "Look, I know I threw you by not telling you right away that I was Rhett, but honestly, I was embarrassed. I'd made an ass out of myself with a woman I had never met but thought was amazing. I'm sorry, and I hope you can see it for what it was. That it's not a deal-breaker. That I didn't set out to lie or deceive you. That I was just trying to save my pride, what little I have left."

Callie's throat knotted up. If she had been any other girl, none of this would have happened. She would have flirted back, and after that first meeting, she would have said yes to a date with Everett. Maybe they would have already slept together, had long phone conversations, and when he'd shown up today, maybe she would have teased and touched without any reservations.

But she was fucked up. Tristan had fucked her up and her life and her family, and she couldn't just forget that. It clouded every choice she made, and Everett had admitted to having PTSD. He'd said that sometimes there was no telling when an episode could happen. She just couldn't get involved with someone again who was unstable.

"But if you want me to leave you alone, I will," Everett continued. "If I see you around, I won't approach you, and I won't bother you again."

"I don't trust you."

Everett ran his hands over his head and blew out a deep breath, the air fogging in front of his face. "I get it, believe me. You've got baggage. I don't expect you to just take my word with no evidence to back it up, but can you honestly tell me that I've given you any reason *not* to?"

She couldn't, not besides the fact that he hadn't divulged he was Rhett, and even then, she hadn't been exactly open and friendly. He hadn't been wrong in thinking she'd have assumed the worst.

"I get that you're scared of taking a chance on me, but I think we could be friends."

"Friends?" Callie almost snorted. She doubted that Everett had only friendship on his mind.

As if reading her thoughts, he grinned. "Fine, I want more, but we gotta start somewhere."

Everett started to back away from her. "So if you want to get started sooner rather than later, I head into the South Hills almost every clear Saturday to go hiking. There's this great hiking trail that takes you to the top of the mountain. It's such an amazing view; it can almost make you feel like you're a step away from heaven."

She remained silent, waiting.

"Anyway, it's off Sweet Water Road, and it's called Moose Head Trail. In case you ever need to clear your head."

Callie cleared her throat. "Thanks."

"Any time." A wide smile stretched across his lips. "And just so you know, I'm usually there at eight in the morning, if you're ever nervous about walking alone."

Callie bit her lip in amusement. "I'll remember that."

"Good," he said, before heading back around the corner. "Have a nice day, Callie Jay."

Her stomach flipped over with delight, and she hated how mixed up she was.

Suddenly, "Wild Flower" blared from her pocket, and Callie pulled her phone out with a sigh.

"Hello, Caroline."

"I feel like you're avoiding me."

"No, I'm not avoiding you. I've just been tired."

"You are full of shit, and you know it! Now, Gabe is working late on a bike with Chase, so I'm coming to get you tonight."

"Seriously, I—"

"Unless you're going to say, 'Of course, Caroline, my loving friend,' I don't want to hear it. I'm coming by at seven, and you, Miss Thang, had better be rested and in a damn-good mood!"

The back door to the studio swung open, and Dave poked his head out. "You ready?"

"Yeah. Caroline, I gotta go," Callie said, heading toward Dave.

"Damn. Good. Mood!"

Callie hung up the phone with a groan.

Chapter Six

"You know this is kidnapping, right?" Callie said as she climbed into Caroline's Corolla.

"Please, you know you want to come play with me." Caroline tossed her long dark hair over her shoulder. Callie caught herself envying her friend's straight hair as she pushed her own unruly curls off her forehead.

"What I *want* to do is sit at home watching side-splitting comedies with a bowl of popcorn drowned in butter."

"Wah, wah," Caroline said.

"Seriously, where are you taking me? I thought you had given up the whole bar scene unless it has to do with business." Callie relaxed into the seat as Caroline pulled away from the curb.

"I did."

"So?"

"Don't you want to be surprised?" Caroline asked. "We are going to the Haunted Houses of Albion! It's opening weekend, and it's going to be *epic*!"

It took a split second for Callie to process that before panic lit her body on fire.

"Take me home," Callie said, her throat constricting. The last thing she wanted to do was go to a place that glorified crazy people and murder, even if it was supposed to be fun. She'd already lived through that once.

"What? Why?" Caroline asked. "Come on, it'll be great—"

But Callie wasn't going to give into Caroline, not about this. "If you want to do something else, fine, but if you want to go walk around with people dressed up as psycho clowns and mental patients, I'm going to pass."

Caroline didn't say anything for several moments; she just stared straight ahead.

Why had she snapped? She could have opened up a little and told Caroline why, instead of jumping down her throat. But she didn't want to tell anyone, didn't want to watch their looks of horror turn to pity.

She didn't deserve pity. Everything that had happened to her, she'd brought on herself by believing Tristan when he'd sworn he was fine. For months, he'd told her it was just exhaustion, that he was spread too thin, and she'd tried to make his life easier, enlisting her mother to help make dinners and making sure he got plenty of rest.

But that hadn't worked. Instead, she'd come home to a living nightmare, and there was no way in hell she was going to experience it again for entertainment.

Taking a deep breath, Callie broke the silence. "I'm sorry if I spoiled your night."

"Naw, don't worry about it. I'll just go with my sisters."

"Sorry, it's just..." Callie wasn't sure she wanted to get into her past with Caroline. She enjoyed their fun, uncomplicated friendship. Caroline knew about her drinking and that Ratchet was trained as a therapy dog, but Caroline had never pressed her about why she needed one, and she was grateful. She didn't talk to anyone about Tristan.

"Hey, really, it's fine. I have issues with bowling alleys, so we're even."

"Noted," Callie said, adding, "So what do you want to do instead?"

"We could go to a movie. Grab some dinner and some coffee?"

"Sure," Callie said, relaxing into the seat.

"How about the new one with Rachel McAdams?" Caroline asked.

Yeah, because watching a picture-perfect romance is exactly what you need when you're all tied up in knots about a guy.

"Or we could go see something funny that doesn't make me want to gouge my eyes out."

"Och, lassie, but ye've got nah romance in ya soul."

"Okay," Callie said. "That was the worst Irish accent I've ever heard."

"Mmmm, I thought I nailed it...and it was Scottish."

Callie burst into laughter. "Hashtag, fail."

"You are just on comedic fire tonight. Okay, so accents aren't my thing. You know what totally is, though? Bacon cheeseburgers from Jensen's."

"A bacon cheeseburger sounds great."

"Good. Now, Gracie said you two were planning Gemma's baby shower. Please tell me she's kidding about not finding out the sex?"

"I wish I could," Callie said. "It's driving Gracie nuts."

"I am so glad my sister found out they were having a boy. I hate shopping for unisex stuff."

"When are you having Valerie's shower?" Callie asked, a slight pain in her chest. Everyone around her seemed to be moving on and planning for the future.

You could have that, if you would only let go of the past.

"Not until January. I'm going to make her a baby book with pictures of her and Justin at certain ages, so they can compare and see who the little guy looks like."

"Wait—you're going to scrapbook?" Callie asked.

"No, I'm ordering it online. I'm not fucking Martha Stewart!"

Callie snorted. "We all know that."

"Oh, I have another favor to ask!"

"Um…no?"

"Shut up. Look, I was going to avoid it, since about sixty-six percent of Rock Canyon's citizens still hate my guts, but Val and Justin are putting together the Rock Canyon Harvest Festival out at the Silverton farm on Saturday, so I feel like I need to go support them. Wanna be my date?"

Callie made a face in the dark. She had avoided most of Rock Canyon's community functions, mainly because she just didn't like being in a crowd, but it had more to do with the location and who she'd be most likely to bump into.

You can't avoid Everett forever.

No, but she had managed to not bump into him once, prior to last week. As long as she avoided his home, and even his dad…

Oh, God, what if he told Fred he was interested in her? What would Fred say?

No, she was definitely avoiding the festival. Besides, the people of Rock Canyon were a touchy-feely bunch when they liked you. Even Mrs. Andrews had patted her arm once to tell her how much she enjoyed a segment she'd done. Callie had thought Gracie and Gemma, who were with her, were going to fall over in shock.

The thing was, she hated to be touched, but especially by people she didn't know.

Except when it comes to a certain former marine. Then you become a quivering puddle of goo.

She had been thinking about his offer of friendship all day and was half tempted to show up on Saturday with Caroline, just to shock and surprise *him* for a change. But then the little sane voice in her head piped up, screaming about what a bad idea that was, how she just needed to keep her distance, and that she had all the friends she needed.

"Ellie is going to be dressed up in the haunted corn maze. And you know they'll have elephant ears…what do you think?" Caroline asked.

Callie leaned her head back and sighed. "You know I hate crowds."

"I'll be your buffer, and you know how intimidating I can be."

Callie almost smiled. It was true; even though she was only five foot three, Caroline had an icy stare that froze most people in their tracks. Those closest to her knew it was all an act, but if anyone was going to chase people away, it would be her.

"Fine, but you'd better not ditch me, or you will face the wrath of Callie."

"I would never, especially since you so sweetly agreed to come to the bachelorette party," Caroline said slyly.

"I said no such thing!"

"Really, 'cause I could have sworn—"

"That you were delusional? Yeah, I pretty much knew that."

Caroline huffed. "Come on! You don't have to look; I can blindfold you. We're only going to the strip club for an hour or so after Becca comes over to Val's and shows us some *pleasure enhancements* from her shop."

Becca owned Sweet Tarts Boutique, a cute clothing shop with a black-curtained area filled with anything you could possibly think of to spice up a relationship. Most of the women in town loved it, even the ones who hated to admit it, but Callie had never found a reason to go in. Besides, she was more of a T-shirt and jeans kind of girl, and the clothes Becca sold were sleek and showed off a great deal of skin. Something she didn't do anyway, not when people might start asking about her scars.

"So basically, everyone is going to be drinking while they look at sex toys and then get all riled up watching greasy strippers...and then what? Are we heading to a bar too, just to strike a rowdy brawl from the bachelorette checklist?"

"No. By that point, I imagine everyone will be so horned up, they'll just want to go home and jump their honeys' bones," Caroline said, amused.

"Nice, do you have to be so crude?" Callie ground her teeth.

"I could have said bone, singular."

"Ugh," Callie said with a groan.

"Okay, you have been in a mood all week, and I want to know what I did. Normally, you just snort and call me a pervert when I joke about this stuff, so what gives?"

The truth sat on the edge of her tongue—that she was interested in a guy and was struggling with her feelings. But she didn't want to have any feelings for him, and if she told Caroline, they would start analyzing, and then it would be real. It was better to just ignore and avoid, and eventually, the feelings would go away. Like a bad cold, they just needed to work their way out of her system.

"I've just been tired this week. Lots of stuff on my mind. I might be coming down with something."

Caroline was silent, and Callie knew she didn't believe her, but in typical fashion, she didn't press. "Okay, well, I still think you should come to the bachelorette party and be my sober buddy. Of course, Val won't be drinking, but she doesn't need alcohol to get crazy."

"Somehow, the thought of a pregnant girl gone wild is even more disturbing than Becca bringing out the vibrators and strap-ons."

"Oh, I don't know," Caroline said, looking her way. "I think Becca's hot in a Kat Dennings, *Two Broke Girls* way. She's snarky, and she's got great boobs—"

"Wait, you've checked out her boobs?" Callie coughed with laughter.

"Hey, I can notice if a woman is pretty or not," Caroline said defensively. "Besides, I was just thinking, you know, that you might have noticed...too?"

Callie swung toward Caroline, her jaw dropping into her lap. "Are you asking if I'm gay?"

"In a back-ass-wards way, yeah."

Callie couldn't seem to shut her mouth; she was so damn surprised. Did *everyone* think she was gay? Not that there was anything wrong with it; she'd had plenty of gay friends growing up, and her cousin, Miranda, had been with her wife for years, but...

"I'm not a lesbian," Callie finally said.

"Okay, I just thought—"

"What? That because I wasn't jumping on some guy's jock every weekend, that I don't like men? I like men."

"I'm sorry, I just—"

"Does everyone think I'm gay?" Callie asked.

"No! Like I said, I was just asking because, like *you* said, I've never seen you up on someone's cock."

"What's wrong with being picky or discreet?" Callie said, her voice rising. "Just because I don't advertise my

conquests, doesn't mean I'm not getting any. I am con-
quering all kinds of ass."

"Fine, I'll just call you Callie, the ass conqueror," Caroline said as she parked in front of Jensen's.

"I'm sorry for being snotty. I just...it's hard for me to
open up about stuff," Callie said.

Caroline turned the car off and twisted in the seat to
face her. "And I get that, believe me. The past is a murky
pile of shit, but I figured after being friends for a while,
I'd eventually know *something* personal about you. Like
whether or not you were into dudes or had a boyfriend."

"Believe me, I like dudes. I'm just not...dating anyone," Callie said quickly, but something struck her about
how Caroline had said it. "Did someone ask if I was seeing anyone?"

"Well, actually, Jenny Andrews, who is living with
Ellie, mentioned that her friend was interning for you
and that he talks about you all the time," Caroline said
before opening the car door.

"Dalton?" Callie laughed.

"Yeah, I think that was his name. Anyway, she thought
he might have a crush on you, and I thought you might
want to know. In case he's cute."

"Are you kidding me? He's a kid! Barely legal!"

"That didn't stop Mrs. Robinson." Caroline winked in
the dome light.

"Gross, dude; you are a perve."

"There's my friend, Callie. I missed her."

Caroline climbed out of the car, and Callie followed suit.

"Look, I prefer men. I like them older, taller, and I like a nice set of broad shoulders."

And if he has light brown eyes and an easy smile, all the better.

"Oh, yum. Who would have thought we'd have the same type?" Caroline opened the door to the restaurant and held it for Callie.

Callie walked through, talking over her shoulder to Caroline. "Wrong. You like bad boys with motorcycles. I prefer nice guys who—"

Callie walked smack into someone. "Oh, I'm so sorry, I wasn't paying"—Callie looked up into Everett's light brown eyes and swallowed hard—"attention."

How had this happened? What were the odds?

"We have to stop meeting like this."

"Hey, Everett."

Everett looked beyond Callie to find Caroline holding the door open. He took a step back, pulling Callie along with him and almost plowed into his dad.

"Sorry, Dad."

"It's all right, son."

But Everett wasn't even looking at Fred, although he was suddenly glad he'd decided to go to dinner with him. With Justin and Valerie doing a bunch of wedding and baby stuff, he and his dad were left to their own devices most nights. He'd been ready to make a frozen pizza and read, but his dad had convinced him that Jensen's sounded better than anything in his fridge.

Who would have thought it would lead to bumping into Callie and having her just about fall into his arms?

"Hey, Caroline," Everett said before his gaze strayed back to Callie. Caroline had been to the farm many times because of Val, so he didn't need to introduce her, but he was excited for his dad to meet Callie. It was stupid and corny, but he wanted his dad to like her too.

"Callie, this is my father, Fred. Dad, this is Callie Jacobsen. She is the deejay Val and Justin hired."

Callie looked a bit like a deer in the headlights for a moment, but then she surprised the hell out of him by smiling brightly at his dad. Her lips wobbled a little, but she reached out her hand to Fred. "Hi, Fred. How are you?"

Fred pulled Callie in for a hug, further shocking Everett. "I'm good, Callie girl. Just had a big dinner and discussed the Harvest Festival next week. Everett isn't much for crowds but has agreed to help set up, since it's such a big job."

"That's wonderful. Caroline was just telling me about it in the car. I'll still see you Monday, though?"

"What?" Caroline's jaw dropped open.

Everett was right there with her. There was such an ease between his father and Callie; it was like they were old friends. And what was Monday?

"Of course, but why don't we get out of the doorway and sit down? We already ate, but I wouldn't mind some pie and coffee," Fred said, crooking his elbow for Callie.

Callie looked up at Everett, and her teeth were worrying her lip, as if she was waiting for him to protest.

He wanted to know how the hell they knew each other and why Fred hadn't mentioned it before. Why hadn't *she* mentioned it?

"How do you two know each other?"

Callie hesitated before straightening her shoulders and meeting his gaze. "I'm your father's AA sponsor."

Everett looked between them in disbelief. "That's a joke, right?"

"Why would I think that was funny?"

She was serious. When they'd met, and she'd said she'd heard about him—had she been talking about his dad? What had he said about him?

And after everything that had happened with his dad growing up—the drinking, the late-night pickups, the drunken fights and hungover *I'm sorrys*. How could he be drawn to a woman like her?

And how could she be his father's sponsor? What was she, thirty? How the hell did she have the experience to mentor a man twice her age?

The room started closing in on him, and he couldn't breathe. The three of them were staring at him now like he was crazy, like he was the one acting weird, but how was anything about this normal? Of all the fucked-up coincidences...

Then it struck him. She'd known. This whole time he'd been flirting with her, pouring his heart out and apologizing to her for keeping Rhett a secret, she'd been hanging onto this.

He had to get out of there. If he didn't, he was going to lose his shit. Everett wasn't much for shows of temper, but the rage, the disappointment, the hurt...it was just too intense. Too much.

"I...I can't deal with this."

Everett turned, furious with himself and Callie, and passed Caroline, who was still holding the door. It was bad enough worrying about his own lineage and addictive personality, but fall for a person who already had those problems? How fucked up would it be to get involved with Callie and try to build a life together, only to have it all fall apart later when she fell off the wagon?

He wasn't even thinking as he climbed into his truck. If his dad wanted to have pie and coffee with her, then she could drive him home.

AT HOME, TWO hours later, he still couldn't wrap his head around it. Lights passed by, and he looked out the window but couldn't see anything. He was tempted to walk over to his dad's place in the dark and have it out with him, but suddenly, the headlights were back. Only this time, they were pointed directly into his window.

Shit.

A soft knock on his door told him it wasn't his dad, and he took a deep breath before opening it.

Callie stood there, the porch light illuminating her nervous smile.

"Caroline dropped me and your dad off at my place, and I brought him home."

"Thanks," he said.

She was doing that hand-twisting thing again, and he waited for the apology he knew was coming.

"You know it was immature to just take off and leave him, right?"

"Excuse me?" He hadn't been expecting that.

"Just because you found out something you didn't like, you took off and left your dad stranded. It was thoughtless and rude, and you should be ashamed of yourself."

"What about you?"

"What about *me*?"

"You go off on me about not telling you I was Rhett. Meanwhile you're going to AA with my dad, having some kind of weird relationship with him, and you don't think that's something I should have known?"

"First of all, no, my being in AA is none of your business, and second, being your dad's sponsor is not weird."

Everett laughed; he couldn't help it. It was like he'd landed in some crazy land where rationality was a thing of the past. "The thing is, you knew who I was. If you two are so chummy, then you must know what he did to us. You must know about the late-night bar pickups and all the times I cleaned up his puke. You must know about that time I had to break up a bar fight he started when I was sixteen. Didn't he tell you about what he put us through?"

She stared up at him with sad eyes, and he hated it. "Yes, he told me."

"I *told* you I was interested in you. I made it fucking obvious! So when would it have been a good time for you to tell me you were a recovering alcoholic?"

"There is never a good time to tell anyone that, and honestly, I haven't been in the position to need to. I've only told Caroline and Gemma, and they're my friends. They understand and accept me. I haven't dated anyone since…well, since before I started AA."

"How long have you been in?"

"Since I was twenty-five, so five years."

It was too much, too intense.

"Look, I just stopped by to tell you that it was really crappy to do that to your dad. I'm sorry that you found out this way, but as far as your feeling entitled to my life story, you haven't earned it. I've known you for four days, and I think you're a nice guy, but I learned a long time ago that looks can be deceiving."

And with that bomb of information, she spun around and walked off his porch to her Jeep.

Chapter Seven

"IDJIT," FRED MUTTERED as he walked by Everett.

Everett sighed at the familiar word, which he'd heard all too often from his father this week. The morning after he'd found about Callie's past with AA, he'd gone about his business until his father had caught him in the barn and started in on him.

"I raised you better than to be a rude, self-righteous son of a bitch!"

Which had started a whole other blowout.

"You didn't raise me—Mom did. And when we lost her, we lost you too. Can you understand why I wouldn't want to go through that again?"

His father had spluttered, kicked over one of the old milk jugs, and stormed out of the barn. Since that morning six days ago, they'd barely said two words to each other.

"Are you ever going to tell me what the hell happened between you and Dad? He hasn't called either of us *idjit* since Valerie and I were having problems."

Everett looked up from the hay bale he was stacking to find his brother watching him with curiosity and concern. It was the day of the Rock Canyon Harvest Festival, and they'd been working all week to get things ready. The corn maze was set up and filling with costumed people, ready to jump out and say *boo*. Food vendors were putting up their tents, and Everett was trying to get the hayride ready.

"We're just having a difference of opinion," Everett said.

Justin took a pair of hay hooks and lifted another bale from the ground up to Everett in the bed of the truck. "But what about?"

Everett debated whether or not to tell Justin. Callie hadn't seemed ashamed of it, but it wasn't his secret to tell either.

"I found out something about a woman I was interested in, and it's made me rethink whether or not I want to get involved with her. Dad thinks I'm being an idjit."

"Well, tell me the big secret, and I'll tell you if I agree or not."

Everett glared at his smirking brother. "Why would I want your opinion?"

"Because I am in a loving, committed, mature relationship—"

"Justin Matthew Silverton, I am going to kick your *ass*!" Valerie hollered from outside the barn.

It was Everett's turn to smirk. "You were saying?"

Valerie came stomping into the barn seconds later, her simple black maternity dress covering up her small, rounded tummy. Everett thought his soon-to-be sister-in-law looked like a disgruntled kitten, what with her dark hair pulled back from her face in a ponytail, showing off bared teeth and slitted eyes.

She was holding something in her hand that looked a little tie-dyed. "You are never allowed to do laundry again! Look at what you did to my new top!"

"I'm sorry, sweetie. I was just trying to help. I could hear you throwing up, and I know how that wipes you out, so—"

Valerie burst into tears and sank onto a hay bale, burying her face in the ruined shirt. Justin looked up at Everett helplessly.

Everett shrugged. "Don't look at me. Women confuse me, even when they aren't hormonal."

"Shut up, Everett!" Val wailed.

Everett covered up a laugh with a cough as Justin went to sit next to his distraught fiancée, putting his arms around her. "I'm sorry, honey. He's a jackass. We'll get you a new top, okay?"

"I'm so sorry I yelled at you," Val said and wrapped her arms around Justin. She began kissing him everywhere she could reach, and before Everett could blink, they were caught up in a passionate embrace that made him both uncomfortable and envious.

"Why don't you two take that elsewhere? Some of us are trying to work."

Justin flipped him off, and Val pulled back, glaring as she stood up.

"Come on." Val tugged Justin to his feet and after whispering something in his ear, he was hauling her toward their house.

Everett hopped out of the truck and picked up the next hay bale, his mind drifting back to Callie. He hated to admit it, even to himself, but he missed her. It had been hard not to search for her in town, and he couldn't even count how many times he'd taken the long way home past the radio station, just hoping to catch a glimpse of her. For a man who was determined to forget her, he was doing a piss-poor job.

"Damn idjit!" his father yelled as he drove past on his quad.

Angrily, he tossed the bale into the back and vowed to ignore his father's obnoxiousness. Everett was doing what he knew was best for him.

At least, he thought so.

Considering how badly you wanted her to understand your mistake, aren't you being a little hypocritical? Don't get too judgmental. You're not exactly a saint.

Little niggles of doubt had been worming holes into his convictions for six days, and he'd been cursing fate for a week. Why would it have thrown her right in his path more than once and given them this magnetic connection if they weren't supposed to be together?

"WANT SOME CARAMEL corn?" Caroline asked as they walked past a row of food tents set up on the Silverton

BAD FOR ME 97

farm. Callie had tried to get out of going to the festival, but Caroline had begged her.

Her reluctance didn't have anything to do with the chance that she might bump into Everett. None at all.

"No, thanks. I'm not really in the mood for popcorn."

"Since when?"

Since she'd gone through two huge boxes of the buttery microwavable kind. She'd never eaten as much popcorn as she had since knocking on Everett's door.

When she'd gone to his front door, she'd been upset with him and had been ready to give him a piece of her mind, but then she'd seen the deep sorrow and disappointment beneath his anger, and she'd deflated.

He'd had a point. Standing in his shoes and remembering the twelve years her mom had spent in a wine-induced haze, she knew without a doubt that she didn't want someone like that for herself. Someone unreliable, who was ready to go off the deep end at any time...

He's got a bomb ticking inside him too.

It was better this way for both of them. She knew that deep down. But there was a part of her that wished things could be different. She had just started to come around to the idea of liking him, of wanting something more than a TV dinner and a slapstick comedy every night.

But that was over now.

"I'm just not in the mood," Callie said. "Besides, I was promised elephant ears."

"And you shall have them, as soon as you tell me what is going on with you and Everett Silverton. Have you at least talked to him?"

Callie, Caroline, and Fred had talked about everything under the sun that night after Everett left, but Fred hadn't asked her why his son was so angry with her. She'd hoped it was obvious, that she wouldn't have to talk about it. But Caroline had pestered her the next day like crazy, and she'd told her they'd bumped into each other a few times. That he'd come in for an interview at the station, but other than that, they were just friendly acquaintances.

"No, I told you a thousand times, there is nothing going on—"

"Hey, Callie!"

Callie turned to find Dalton and a group of teenagers walking toward them.

"Who is that?" Caroline asked.

"Dalton, the intern at my station."

"Ah, the one with the crush on you."

"He does not have a crush on me," Callie hissed under her breath.

Dalton broke away from his group of friends, swaggering toward her as only a young cowboy could.

"Um, do you not see the look in his eyes? It says, 'Oh please, older and more experienced hot woman, I need you to show me the ropes and teach me a few new tricks.'"

"Will you shut up?"

"Ride it, my pony."

"I am going to take out your windpipe."

Caroline laughed and backed away. "I'll go get us some food and drinks, but you still owe me. I don't care if I have to hold you down and waterboard you—you will talk!"

Callie made a face at Caroline's retreating back before turning back to Dalton. Still, Caroline wasn't wrong about the very-interested look he was giving her.

Damn it!

"Hey, I didn't know you were going to be here," Dalton said.

"Well, technically, I was blackmailed into coming, but either way, I'm only here for the food."

"Are you sure? If we hurry, you could take a hay ride with me."

Ruh-roh. Dalton was definitely looking at her with interest. How had she missed that?

"You know, I would, but my friend is fighting with her boyfriend and needs me tonight. Maybe another time?"

"Yeah, sure." He seemed so disappointed that she almost took it back, but what good would that do? She didn't want to lead him on, and even if she wasn't interested in someone else, there was no way she'd date an eighteen-year-old kid. "Well, I'll go catch up to my friends. See you around."

Dalton jogged off as she was saying bye, and she saw a pretty blonde watching him sadly. Yuck—young unrequited love, the stuff of sleepless nights and misery. Not that she'd experienced much of it in high school herself, of course. She'd started dating Tristan when they were sixteen, and though they'd argued, the fights had never lasted long. Callie was so glad she was over all that.

Aside from all the moping you've done in the last week, sure, you've really matured.

It was true she'd been more depressed this week than she had been in a long time. Of course, receiving another letter from Tristan the day before hadn't helped. Callie wondered why the frequency had picked up again. In the last two years, he'd only written a few times, but this was the second letter in a month.

She didn't want to know badly enough to read them, though. She wasn't ready.

All around her, families played games, and kids ran around, squealing happily. Life hadn't been that joyous since before her dad left when she was eleven. He'd been having an affair for years and finally decided he would rather marry his mistress than be with them. At first, she had gone to stay with him every other weekend, just like the courts said, but once their first child was born, she'd ended up spending most of the time there on her own anyway. They were so busy cooing over the new baby, but she couldn't even call him her little brother, not when she'd always felt like an outsider with them. After her father's new wife had gotten pregnant with their second, a girl, and they talked to her about sharing the room that was supposed to be hers with the baby, she had stopped going. At first, her father had called and sent cards twice a year, but after a while, he became just a memory.

He'd come to her mom's funeral, so she could at least give him that, but he hadn't been someone she could lean on for support. He was practically a stranger, and besides, with three other children, he didn't really have time to devote to a grown child he hadn't had a relationship with in ten years.

Callie started walking between the vendors' tents set up along the gravel driveway, but her dark thoughts blocked out the laughter and activity around her.

Sure, she had some extended family, but her mother had been the only person she'd been close to, and even so, their relationship had always been complicated.

Still, at least when her mom was alive, she'd had *someone.*

As she passed by the food and game booths, she noticed a large tree with a swing close to Everett's house. She was a little surprised she hadn't seen him yet, actually. Maybe he was in the haunted maze, dressed up as a goblin or ghoul and jumping out at people. She'd seen Justin dressed as a scarecrow and Val as a witch when Caroline and she had first pulled in.

Or maybe he's inside his house, avoiding the crowds— and you.

She headed toward the swing, surprised there wasn't a gaggle of children surrounding it. Of course, it *was* away from all the other activities, shrouded in darkness. If the moon and Everett's porch light hadn't hit it just right, she might not have seen it.

Once there, Callie sat down gingerly, testing the swing's weight-bearing capabilities. When she was comfortable that it would hold her, she pushed off. She'd grown up with an old plank swing her grandfather had built her in their backyard and had spent most of her childhood out there, thinking, or crying, or laughing—depending on the day…and on whether or not her mother had fallen off the wagon.

It was still crazy to her that after all the years she'd spent taking care of her mother—enduring her insults, drunken anger, and later, her whispered apologies—that

Callie would still end up going down the same path. Coping with her pain by getting drunk, often to the point of blacking out and not remembering the night before. Anything to mask her fear and self-loathing.

After two years of hangovers and nearly blowing her career, Callie had gone to Folsom with some friends, renting a hotel room so they wouldn't have to drive. Two Adios Motherfuckers later, she was toast. Usually, she could drink more, but upon finishing the second drink, she'd immediately started feeling woozy. Her *friends* had ditched her for a couple of guys they'd met, and after she'd finished puking in the bar bathroom, she'd stumbled back to the hotel. The last thing she remembered was getting into the elevator before everything went black.

When Callie woke up, her head had been underwater, and she'd come up gasping. Still out of it, it had taken her a minute to realize she was in her hotel room and that somehow she had ended up in the bathtub. The water was still running, and she was wearing nothing but a black camisole.

For days after, Callie had freaked out, wondering what had happened and how she'd ended up in the tub. But the real nightmare was that she could have died. Again. She could have drowned or slipped and cracked her head open. A million scenarios had played through her mind until she'd finally said, "That's it. I'm done."

The next day, she'd attended her first AA meeting and began turning her life around.

Kicking her heels back, Callie soared higher on the swing, breathing in the crisp, cool air as it stung her cheeks. She smiled with pure joy, flying higher and higher. Closing her eyes, she held on to the ropes and propelled herself toward the sky.

"I was right," a deep voice said from below, breaking through her bliss.

Her eyes flew open, and she dragged her feet against the ground, slowing down. Her gaze swung through the dim night to find Everett standing nearby.

"You are insanely beautiful when you smile."

Chapter Eight

EVERETT'S OBSERVATION WAS almost bitter. He'd been asking for a sign and here she was, smiling like a golden angel and just as innocent as she'd swung higher and higher.

"What are you doing here?"

The question came out harsher than he'd meant it, but he wanted her so bad that his hands were shaking. He'd had been sitting in his living room with the window open, the cool air and the sound of distant laughter blowing in as he'd read his worn copy of *The Power of One*. No romance tonight, not with the way he'd been feeling; he'd just wanted something familiar, comforting. Something he knew the ending to and wouldn't be surprised or disappointed by. Then he'd heard it—the familiar creak of the old tree swing. He'd put his book down and peeked through the blinds, expecting to find a couple of kids pushing each other.

Instead he'd seen a woman in the moonlight, pumping her legs until she was swinging high enough for her face to come out of the shadows.

Callie.

Heart hammering with excitement, Everett hadn't even thought about why he shouldn't get up or why he shouldn't walk out of his house. Though really, he should've just let her be and left things as they were.

As he'd drawn closer, he'd noticed her eyes were closed. Before he could call out to her, she'd smiled to herself and even released a husky, raw laugh.

A laugh that had gone from his heart to his groin in one straight shot.

Callie was bundled up in jeans and a puffy jacket, but her blonde curls had flown behind her in a mix of gold and crystal, flashing like streaks of lightning in the moonlight. His hands had itched to get tangled up in that mass of curls as he imagined pulling her against him, kissing those sweet lips until she relaxed, breathing in her sweet scent and holding her. Forgetting all about why she was bad for him and why things could never work between them.

But before he could think better of it, he'd opened his mouth and told her she was beautiful.

Only instead of jumping into his arms at his compliment, she was now staring at him like he was a Peeping Tom.

Callie hopped off the swing like it was on fire. "Sorry. I just needed a minute alone."

"You do that a lot," he said, taking a step toward her.

"What?"

"Want to be alone."

"So?" she said irritably. "What's wrong with wanting a little privacy?"

"Nothing. It's just...when you spend so much time on your own, you start to get lonely."

"Why do you care if I get lonely? You want nothing to do with me, right?"

He kept getting closer to her. "I did say that, didn't I?"

"Yeah, you did, and I'm sorry to have bothered you—"

"Do you know why I holed up in my house with a book I've read at least a dozen times instead of having fun with my family and the rest of my hometown?" He had her nearly backed up against the tree and wanted to press himself into her and feel her soft curves.

"Because hayrides and haunted mazes creep you out?" she asked quietly.

"Hmm, no, I actually like Halloween," Everett said.

He was a foot away now, close enough to touch her.

"Then what?"

Everett leaned over her, his arm against the tree. He ignored the bark biting into the flesh of his arm and the warmth of her body calling him closer and said, "Because I was afraid if I saw you, I'd forget everything I know and everything I've been telling myself about you."

"Like what?" Her small, pink tongue darted out to lick her lips, and his cock grew heavy with need.

"That you're bad for me. That if I get involved with you it will destroy me."

He saw something flash across her face before her expression shuttered. Hurt? Longing?

"Then leave me alone."

He should. He should turn around and head back into his house, locking the door on her and his desire.

"I can't. I can't stop. You get to me, and I'm not strong enough to walk away."

A soft cry escaped her just before his mouth came down, claiming hers.

God, she tasted like fresh honey. His tongue slipped inside to sweep along hers, delving into her warmth as his hand came up and tangled in her hair. He wanted closer, wanted to surround himself with her scent, her body, and push all of the doubt from his mind.

Everett came out of his fog of desire when Callie shoved at his chest, turning her head away from him. She was breathing hard, panting.

"I am not a plaything. You keep saying that I'm not what you're looking for, but the truth is, I wasn't looking for you either. You popped into my life and sought me out. Then you learned something you don't like about me, and suddenly I'm this toxic thing you have to resist?" She pushed him hard, and he backed off. Every word was true, and it made him feel like an asshole.

Because he was acting like one.

"I've got a newsflash for you. Being self-righteous and judgmental doesn't make you a good person. You don't know me or what I've gone through, and yes, I've made some bad choices, but they were *mine*. I've taken responsibility for my addiction and changed. And that's all anyone can do, but I don't need you telling me you want me or that you're better than me."

In the distance, someone began calling her name, and Callie turned without saying anything else.

He couldn't let her go, not with that statement hanging between them. In three strides he was behind her, his hand on her arm. Callie stopped but didn't turn. Everett moved closer until the top of her head sat just under his chin; then he gently pulled her unruly curls back over her shoulder. She was still as a statue, even when he leaned down to whisper against her ear.

"You're right about everything, and I'm sorry. I'm a self-righteous prick, but I don't think I'm better than you. You just scare the hell out of me." Everett was so tempted to kiss the pulse point below her ear. "I never wanted to make you feel less-than, Callie, and hurting you is the last thing I want to do."

Seconds ticked by, and she said nothing. He was still scared shitless, but he couldn't ignore this thing between them. Distance and avoidance hadn't made his desire for her go away, hadn't lessened his infatuation, and her passionate speech only made him want to keep pushing, peeling back her layers until he could see right into her soul.

And just when he was sure he'd blown it, she shocked the hell out of him.

"What's the first thing?"

CALLIE COULDN'T HEAR Caroline calling for her, not over the pounding of her heart and the blood thundering in her ears. The trail of Everett's fingers on her neck still burned pleasantly, and she had a sudden urge to lean back. To trust him. To believe him.

It was that insanity that had led her to ask him a loaded question.

He probably thought she was daring him to kiss her again, and maybe she was. Maybe she was tired of being scared, of jumping at shadows. It had been too long since she'd let a man touch her because she truly wanted him, rather than just to get her rocks off. She wanted him in a second-chance-at-happiness kind of way—one she never thought she'd want again.

But Everett's warm breath on her bare neck made her shiver, and anticipation raced through her.

"The first thing I want to do with you," he said, close enough that his lips grazed the skin just below her ear, "is take you hiking tomorrow."

Callie's eyes flew open in surprise, both at his words and the fact that she had closed them in the first place. "That's it?"

His deep, masculine chuckle caused an ache to pulsate between her legs and her nipples to tighten. "Oh, no, honey. That's just the start."

"Callie!" Caroline's shout broke through her desire, and Callie saw her over by the tents, coming toward them.

Callie couldn't look at Everett as he stepped away from her. Instead, she fidgeted with her hair and jacket as she started toward Caroline on wobbly legs.

"Have a good night, Callie Jay."

The nickname whispered so sweetly made her stomach flip, and she turned around to say good night, but he was already heading back toward the house.

"Hey! I got you an elephant ear and a mocha," Caroline said, coming up alongside her. "Was that Everett?"

Callie reached out for the coffee. "Yeah."

Suddenly, Caroline was almost nose-to-nose with her. "Oh my God."

"What?" Callie said, jerking back.

"You have the hots for Everett!"

"I do not," Callie said before taking a drink.

"Um, yeah, your eyes are totally dilated, and you're all flushed—"

"If I'm flushed, it's because it is freezing," Callie said. "Now give me the sugar you promised me."

"I don't think *I* have what you're craving." Caroline laughed as she knelt down to pull an elephant ear out of the bag.

"God, you are a pervy horndog," Callie said and took the pastry.

"Don't even try to lie. I know the signs of a woman in lust."

Callie walked back toward the tents. "I'm ignoring you."

"Oh, come on! Let's talk about boys."

Laughing, Callie shook her head, excitement rushing through her veins, something she had been missing. She'd been playing it safe, holed up and keeping the world at bay. Maybe she did need to get out and live again. Maybe go for a morning hike.

It sounded like a very good start.

Chapter Nine

"I'M SO GLAD you could make it."

At seven forty-five, Callie stood at the bottom of the trail that Everett had mentioned, Ratchet by her side. Most of the landscape was rock and sagebrush, except for the cluster of trees closer to the top of the mountain. Staring up at the steep climb, she wondered if maybe she'd bitten off more than she could chew.

"I'm not sure mountain climbing was what I had in mind," she said.

Everett stood next to her, his wide shoulders covered by a warm jacket. On his head he wore a black beanie with a little brim pulled down over his forehead. He looked like a model for L. L. Bean or Cabela's.

Except for the scars.

Ratchet kept inching closer to her leg, as if leaning on her would somehow show Everett who she really belonged to. Running her hand over the big dog's head, Callie said,

"I like to run, but my trails have little hills and bumps. That thing looks like you could base-jump off it."

"It's not as hard as it looks," Everett said before starting up the hill ahead of her.

Callie stared at his back dubiously but followed after him, asking herself for the hundredth time why she'd thought this was a good idea. Climbing a mountain with a man she hardly knew sounded like the start of a bad made-for-TV movie.

"The view from the top is amazing and totally worth the climb," Everett called back over his shoulder.

They had only been climbing for twenty minutes, and thanks to her afternoon runs, she was in pretty good shape. Still, the steep grade made her muscles protest slightly. "I hope so."

"Trust me."

Give me a reason to. She didn't say it, but the thought still lingered there. Trusting the wrong person had cost her everything she held dear.

"You're awfully quiet back there," Everett said.

Callie stopped and took a few deep breaths as she looked out across the valley. She'd been so lost in thought she hadn't even been aware that they'd made it a third of the way up the mountainside.

"Wow." Staring out across the green and yellow landscape, she felt truly lucky for the first time in years.

Everett came down a few steps to stand next to her, and she resisted the urge to shy away from him. Tristan would never completely leave her alone, not when he'd left his *mark* on her, but she had to remember that Everett wasn't Tristan. She couldn't constantly compare the two, or she was going to make herself crazy.

"We haven't even reached the top yet."

"Still, this is pretty impressive," she said, rolling her shoulders and tilting her head. She needed to shake off the past and just enjoy this. Live again. It was what she wanted, right?

"Come on. If you think this is impressive, the view up there will blow your mind," he said before picking up the pace again.

She followed behind, a little surprised that he hadn't mentioned anything about last night or even asked what had made her show up today. "So you do this every Saturday?"

"Just about. In the winter, the trail gets lost in the snow, and in the summer you have to watch for ticks, but right now, it's pretty much perfect."

Yuck, ticks? Suddenly, Callie needed to scratch everywhere, as if she could feel tiny legs making their way across her body. "I hate ticks."

Everett laughed. "Don't worry; it's too cold for them right now."

Callie stopped to scratch the side of her calf anyway.

"What? Did I give you the heebie-jeebies?"

Callie looked up to find that he'd turned around and was watching her with a grin. It amazed her how easily he seemed to smile, especially given all that had happened to him.

"How do you do it?" she asked, surprising herself.

"Do what?"

"Relax."

Everett seemed stumped for a moment but then said, "I guess I just finally decided not to let my hang-ups destroy me. If I sat around and dwelled on everything that's wrong with my life, I'd never find the beauty in just being alive."

Callie stood up, shaking her head. "You make it sound simple."

"Yeah, well, I don't mean to trivialize whatever you're trying to get past," he said, reaching out for her hand and lacing his gloved fingers with hers. The gesture was sweet and comforting, although she wasn't quite sure who was comforting whom. "I just mean that I came back a hot mess, and I'm still working through it, eight years later. But I also know that there's a reason I survived."

"What's the reason?" Callie was unable to look away from his intense gaze.

"Haven't figured it out yet."

WHEN CALLIE PULLED her hand from his, Everett let her. He'd told himself he needed to go slow, to not push her. Whatever it was that made her jumpy wouldn't be helped by his forcing his attentions on her. Still, he couldn't help it. She was like a wild rabbit—skittish as hell but so soft, you just had to touch her.

Taking up the rear, he decided to change the subject to something a little less personal. "For a woman who seems to prefer older country, you sure play a lot of Taylor Swift."

"She's a popular artist," Callie shot back without stopping.

"With whom? Twelve-year-old girls?"

"And I bet you just *love* Kenny Chesney's new song," she said.

"As a matter of fact—"

"Kenny Chesney lost his roots right around his third album."

"I was just going to say I'm not a fan of his new stuff," he said.

"Oh."

Everett liked that she was so passionate about the music she played. "So, who's your favorite band?"

"Diamond Rio. You?"

"I thought you said it was Little Texas."

Callie paused. "You're right. I did tell *Rhett* that."

"So, which is it?"

"I guess it depends on the day," she said.

"What made you fall in love with country music in the first place? Aren't you a California girl? Shouldn't you like rap and alternative?"

"I grew up in a small town in California, and my mother was originally from Tupelo, Mississippi. She raised me on the greats: Patsy Kline, George Jones, Johnny Cash, George Strait, and Garth Brooks. Plus, we have cowboys and FFA, just like you do."

Everett held up his hands. "Pardon my faux pas then."

"If I must."

She turned around and kept walking, missing his grin.

"So where's your mom now?"

They broke through a patch of trees, and she took so long answering that he almost repeated himself.

"She died."

"Shit, I'm sorry. What happened?"

Callie stopped again and leveled him with a hard look. "I don't want to talk about it, okay? Some things I like to keep private."

"What about the rest of your family? Friends from your childhood?"

"There's no one."

She was shutting him out again, and it hurt. Stepping up alongside her, he reached out to touch her face, running the back of his hand from her temple to her jawline. Her breath caught and her mouth trembled, as if she wanted to fight her attraction to him.

"I understand having demons, Callie. I think if you let me inside your walls, we could help each other."

Everett didn't wait for her but dropped his hand and kept climbing. If she wanted to let her fears control her, he wouldn't push. He could feel something pulsing between them, something warm and incredible, but if she didn't want to let him in enough to find out what it meant, that was on her.

The sound of feet and paws behind him let him know Callie and Ratchet were moving too, but it took a few seconds to realize the sounds were getting closer, not farther away. Smiling to himself, he continued on through the trees, hope flaring to life in his chest with every step.

When the grove of trees opened up, he stopped. "We made it."

He sensed her beside him and turned to watch her face light up as her amber eyes swept over the view. "Oh."

"Yeah, oh."

THE VIEW WAS spectacular, just like he'd said it would be. Green and gold squares showed where farm fields met, and there were patches of trees scattered about. To Callie's right, the Sawtooth Mountains rose up like slate-gray arrowheads, clouds drifting across their peaks. The sky was robin's-egg blue with puffs of white clouds drifting past, and to the south, she could see the dark gray of distant thunderheads making shadows across the land below.

"You were right," she said, with awe making her voice soft. "This was worth the climb."

Everett sat down and patted the spot beside him. "Have a seat. Take it in."

Despite everything she had said to him, he still wanted her around. "I'm sorry."

"For what?" he asked, staring out.

"Everything. Snapping at you, accusing you of stalking me, pushing you away—"

"Before you get too carried away, I think we've both apologized enough, don't you?" Everett took his hat off. "Besides, I get accused of stalking women at least three times a day, so it's really no big deal."

"Shut up," she said, laughing as she sat down next to him. The minute she did, Ratchet tried to crawl onto her lap. "No, you are too big to be a lap dog." Finally giving up the fight, she let him lay his front legs and chin across her.

"He's a good-looking dog," Everett said, holding out his hand. Ratchet lifted his nose to sniff the digits, and then lay back down again.

"Thanks," Callie said, rubbing her dog's soft ears. "He thinks he's a cat, though."

"How's that?"

"He rubs his head on me like he's scenting me," Callie said. Her lips twitched as she warmed to the subject. She loved talking about Ratchet's antics. "Especially when my hair is wet. If you think my hair is scary now, you should see it after he tackles me and gets it all tangled."

"I like your hair." Everett reached out to finger a curl that had escaped from her ponytail.

Callie's heart stuttered as their gazes clashed. "It's a mess. I can't even straighten it."

"So, don't." He tucked the curl behind her ear, his fingers lingering there, and whispered, "Curls are sexier anyway."

The pit of her stomach flipped over at his warm tone and words. "I'm not trying to be sexy."

"You don't have to try," he said, leaning toward her. "You just are."

Callie closed her eyes as Everett's lips brushed hers, softly searching, and she sighed. "Everett…"

"Mmmm?"

She forgot her protest as his tongue snaked out and ran along her bottom lip, making her shiver. Callie felt Ratchet move before Everett had a chance to deepen the kiss, and she opened her eyes to find him standing with his head between them, nose-to-nose with Everett.

"If I tell your dog I don't want a kiss, is he going to take the rest of my face off?"

"Ratchet, it's okay." She patted the dog's side and finally pulled him back by his collar. He moved reluctantly until she was able to cup his face in her hands and smush his cheeks.

"Are you jealous, or did you think he was hurting me?"

His large tongue snaked out toward her face, and she turned away with a laugh. She caught Everett watching her intensely, and a lump of unease rose in her throat at his unreadable expression.

"What?"

"I want to make you laugh like that."

"Like what?"

"Like you're free."

Everett stood up then and reached out for her hand. She took it and let him help her to her feet, grabbing his arm with her other hand when the world spun a little.

"Whoa, that was weird."

"Sometimes the altitude can make you lightheaded if you aren't used to it." His arm snaked around her waist, and she felt his lips brush the top of her head. "But you can lean on me for any reason."

The seriousness of the offer was only strengthened by the way she felt in his arms. Safe. Secure. Protected. And the urge to do exactly what he wanted—to let herself go and put herself in his care—scared the hell out of her.

She was so out of her element with Everett Silverton. He was too good to be true, which usually led to something bad.

They started back down the mountain silently, even as Everett hung onto her hand. Callie wished she knew what he was thinking, what he was feeling. For some reason, she felt like she needed to fill the silence.

"My mom was an alcoholic too."

Everett stopped and looked at her. "What?"

"My mom was an alcoholic. Wine was her drug." With a bitter laugh, she added, "To this day, I still can't stand the smell of it."

"But…why?"

Callie moved past him down the trail, but he kept pace with her, his hand still gripping hers. She could feel his questioning gaze on her as she stared at the ground. "I can't…it's hard to talk about, but I just wanted you to know that I understand what you went through with your dad. Sometimes we don't deal with pain or trauma well, and it's just easier the use a bottle to block it out. I've been on both sides of the coin, and I started working the program because I didn't want to live my life that way."

Everett squeezed her hand. "I was scared for a long time that I was going to end up like him, especially after I came home. I was dealing with so much shit, and I was so tempted to take a bottle and sink into oblivion."

"But you didn't."

"No."

Callie could feel the space between them growing. Did he think she was weak for giving in? Was this it? Had she shared too much?

When they reached the trailhead, Everett released her hand, and it felt like all the warmth in her body left with him.

Callie walked over to her Jeep and loaded Ratchet inside, while Everett stood off to the side, waiting. When she shut the door and turned, he looked as awkward as she felt.

"Thank you for showing me the trail. And I'm sorry—"

"I thought we weren't going to say sorry?"

Her heart squeezed. "You're right. I just…"

"What?"

"Nothing," she said. "I'll talk to you later, I guess."

It looked like he was going to say something more, but he stopped.

As he turned to walk away, panic overwhelmed her and before she knew what she was doing, she reached out and put her hand on his arm. "Everett."

When he faced her once more, she took a deep breath and stepped up to him. Climbing up onto her tiptoes, she kissed the corner of his mouth and wrapped her arms around his shoulders. If this was going to be the last time she saw him, she was going to kiss him. And let herself go.

With a groan, Everett wrapped his arms around her, lifting her against him. She stiffened as he set her on the hood of her Jeep, and his hand cupped her face.

"Trust me, Callie."

Then Everett's mouth covered hers gently, his warm lips coaxing hers open. Kissing was something she had purposefully ignored in the few sexual encounters she'd' experienced since Tristan. In fact, she hardly ever encouraged anything more than some light touching before the main event.

Sex was a way to chase off the demons. Once she'd given up alcohol, she'd had no outlet to calm the roller coaster of emotions that would sometimes overwhelm her. Fucking helped, and running did too. But it never gave her quite the same kind of calm she got from drinking or screwing a stranger's brains out.

Intimacy definitely wasn't what she was after with sex, especially when it meant explaining why she had seven-inch-long scars from her shoulder to her abdomen—the reason she never took her shirt off during sex. Men could think she was in a hurry or imagine she'd had a bad tummy tuck; she didn't care. Each of them was nothing but a dick to her.

But Everett's kiss reminded her exactly what she'd been missing.

Heat flowed back through her as she opened her mouth and let him in, her tongue touching his. Lights exploded behind her eyelids as he moved closer, his hands releasing her face to slide along her neck and shoulders. He tasted amazing, and when his body pressed flush against her, a low moan escaped her.

She remembered kissing as being fun and flirty, but this wasn't lighthearted. This was intense. Need raced through her body as she held on to the broad shoulders she'd been lusting after since the first time she'd bumped into him. She wanted to stay like this forever, lost in his amazing lips and his warm scent.

And then, just like that, he was gone.

Blinking slowly, she refocused on his face, smiling tenderly at her.

"Have a nice day."

Huh?

He reached up to pull her hands from his shoulders, bringing first one set of knuckles and then the other to his mouth, kissing them softly. When he released her hands, he didn't say anything else. Just turned his back on her and walked toward his truck.

And all Callie could do was stand there, trailing her fingers across her lips.

Chapter Ten

ON MONDAY AFTERNOON, Callie sat in the back of
Chloe's Book Nook, her friend Gemma Bower's book-
store. She had agreed to come by and have lunch with
them so they could plan Gemma's baby shower, but she'd
hardly touched her salad, too distracted by thoughts of
Everett. Absently, she fed Ratchet a bite, tuning out the
argument around her.

"Come on, Gemma. Who wants to go to a baby shower
during the holidays?" Gracie McAllister said, throwing
up her arms.

"Lots of people!" Gemma's pretty face was fixed in an
ugly scowl as she stared down her best friend. "If we wait
until after, I'll be eight months and *huge*. I'd like to be able
to walk around without waddling at my baby shower."

Callie sighed, staring off into space. She hadn't heard
anything from Everett since Saturday, but she hadn't
been able to get him or his kiss out of her mind. It was

crazy to think that with one short, slow kiss, he had literally made fireworks explode in her brain. Maybe that's why she couldn't concentrate.

"Come on, Callie, weigh in here." Gracie burst in on her thoughts.

"Gemma's right," Callie said, not caring either way.

"Damn it!"

"Yes!" Gemma jumped up and danced, despite her already protruding belly. Gemma and her husband, Travis, had found out in July that she was eight weeks' pregnant with twins, and since then, she seemed to be growing at super speed.

"Fine," Gracie said, grumbling. "We can do it the week before Thanksgiving or the week after, but if it's too close to Christmas, I'm afraid people will skimp out on prezzies."

"Travis and I were going to tell people not to bring gifts anyway."

Gracie's face suddenly began to turn an unhealthy purple.

Callie jumped in on this one. "Okay, now that's crazy."

"Dude, you are having *twins*! You are going to need double *everything*, and besides, shopping for a baby shower gift is the best!" Gracie made a face before adding, "Unless your best friend decides not to find out the sex of the babies just to piss you off."

"We want it to be a surprise." Gemma shot Callie a pleading look.

"I think it's sweet to do it this way," Callie said and winked at Gemma.

"Screw that! It means I'm stuck buying baby shit in yellow, green, brown, and orange," Gracie said. "Those are shit colors, literally. You want me to shop for things that are the color of shit."

"You can put a boy in pink," Callie offered, earning a look of disbelief from her friends.

"Uh, yeah, I have a feeling Travis would have something to say about that. And animal prints. He's put a strict ban on leopard, tiger, zebra, and cheetah."

Callie shook her head, a small smile playing across her lips. "So, I guess the babies' rooms won't look like the Jungle Room at the Fantasy Inn."

"Travis wants to wait to decorate until they are born."

"And you're okay with that?" Gracie asked doubtfully.

"Since I got to make all of the decisions with Charlie for the first nine years, I am taking the passenger seat on this pregnancy." Gemma rubbed her rounded stomach with a smile. "Besides, it's really cute to see how excited Travis is."

Callie could understand where Gemma was coming from. Due to a lot of miscommunication and distrust, Travis had taken off to become country music's hottest rock star while Gemma had stayed in Rock Canyon, raising the son he didn't know he had. When they'd run into each other years later, they had fallen back in love, but those years Travis had lost with their son still rubbed him raw.

"Just remember that these are your babies too, and your opinion counts." Gracie was always protective of Gemma's feelings, and Callie admired her loyalty. "Do not let him guilt you into doing something you don't want."

"Travis doesn't guilt me, ever," Gemma snapped.

"Fine, then don't guilt yourself," Gracie shot back.

"Enough," Callie said, shaking her head. Sometimes, Gemma and Gracie acted more like sisters than best friends with their bickering. "Why don't we have it the week before Thanksgiving? That gives us a little over four weeks to plan and get the invitations out. And since fall colors are 'shit colors'"—Callie gave Gracie a pointed look—"we'll need to get creative to make it cute. Maybe we can make a gift-card tree out of a dead tree branch and glue fake leaves and clothespins to it. Maybe put an owl on one of the branches?"

"Oh, owls are so cute!" Gemma said enthusiastically.

"An owl theme would be darling," Gracie agreed.

"Fabulous." Callie stood up and gathered the remains of her lunch.

"Where are you off to?" Gracie asked.

"I have a date."

"With who?" Gemma asked.

"A hot blond guy with big brown eyes who adores me."

Gracie's expression was skeptical. "Are you talking about your dog again?"

"Maybe." Callie picked up Ratchet's leash from the floor, ignoring their irritated looks.

"You are such a tease." Gemma rolled her eyes.

"I just like to see you guys get all excited when you think you're going to hear something juicy."

"Speaking of gossip, did you read Miss Know It All's blog this morning?" Gracie said.

Callie snorted. Gracie was obsessed with Miss Know It All, their own small-town gossip girl. MKIA had started off with a column in the local paper over a year ago and had since branched off into an online blog, with a tip line and everything. Many people thought Gracie herself was MKIA, but Callie didn't think Gracie would take shots at her friends the way MKIA had in the past. Gracie had faults, but stabbing people in the back wasn't one of them.

She did, however, love gossip of any kind.

"Hmm, looks like Kirsten Winters went home with…holy shit!"

Callie stopped at the door, unable to resist anything that surprised the hell out of Gracie. "What is it?"

"Listen to this," Gracie said and began reading aloud. "'There are a few things you can count on at the annual Rock Canyon Harvest Festival. For instance, Mrs. Andrews will be complaining about something.' True that."

Gemma shot Callie a grin. Mrs. Andrews was a very unpleasant woman and for some reason, a favorite target of Miss Know It All.

"'There will be at least one kid who pees on the hay-ride'"—Gracie wrinkled her nose as she continued—"'and a couple hookups, despite the family-friendly atmosphere. But it seems that one of the town's homegrown heroes may have found his Cinderella,'" Gracie said, her voice rising excitedly. "'Several people saw Everett Silverton, who is known for his bravery and reclusive nature, pushing a mysterious woman on the swing outside his home. One person even reported that there may have been a kiss or two exchanged—'"

"What?" Callie yelped, earning a hush from Gemma.

"'Though the woman could not be identified, she is described as average in height and weight, with curly blonde hair.'"

Suddenly, two pairs of curious eyes turned on Callie intently.

"What are you looking at me for?"

Gracie looked back at her phone and read, "'Some of the suspects include Jillian Davis, Amanda Meyers, and…Callie Jacobsen.'"

The eyes were back on her, this time with eyebrows raised.

"She just wrote that no one could identify her accurately. It could be anyone with blonde hair," Callie said, backing toward the door.

"Me thinks the lady doth protest too much," Gracie said.

"Hamlet has a point," Gemma added.

Callie glared at both of them. "He didn't push me on the swing."

"But there was kissing?" Gracie asked.

Callie looked at Gemma pleadingly, but Gemma grinned. "Oh, no, I am dying of curiosity."

"Traitor."

"Face it. There's no escape," Gracie said. "We know where you work and live, and if need be, we will call your satellite provider and deny you all your must-watch shows."

"There is nothing to tell. We just talked."

"Talked about what?" Gemma prodded.

"The festival, books…stuff."

Gracie and Gemma grinned at one another before Gracie said, "So you talked about *stuff*."

"Good stuff?"

"And that's my cue," Callie said, escaping out the back as Gracie yelled, "Resistance is futile!"

EVERETT HAD JUST finished up a call with a veteran when there was a knock on his door.

"Yeah, come in."

Justin stuck his head in, grinning from ear to ear. "Hey, bro."

Everett raised his eyebrow at his brother's sly tone. "Hey, *bro*."

Justin came in holding a copy of the town paper and straddled one of Everett's kitchen chairs. "Have you read the paper today?"

"I have not. Something interesting?"

"Now that you mention it, it seems you were the highlight of Miss Know It All's column." Justin held the paper out to Everett.

"What? What the hell are you talking about—" Everett stared hard at the blurry picture of him and Callie standing a few inches apart by the swing. You couldn't make out the faces, but Miss Know It All listed Callie as one of the suspects. "Shit."

Callie was going to hate this.

"So who is she?" Justin asked.

"None of your damn business." Everett got up to grab a beer from the fridge.

"Wow, we're touchy, aren't we? Get me one too, will ya?"

"You come over here to spread gossip, and now you want to drink my beer? You're lucky I don't shoot the messenger."

"I grabbed your mail on my way up, if that sways your decision on the beer and the shooting."

Everett opened the fridge and took out the beers. After he handed his brother one, he sifted through the envelopes until he came across one with a return-to-sender stamp.

Damn.

Picking up the offending letter, he tossed it in the trash.

"Cara still not taking your letters?" Justin asked somberly.

"Nope."

"I'm sorry, man."

So was he. Cara had been a good friend. Robbie, Cara, and he had all enlisted at the same time and had been thick as thieves. When Robbie and Cara had gotten married, Everett had been standing by as a witness, and when Cara had found out she was pregnant, she'd told Everett first because she'd been bursting with happiness.

But that was before the bomb—and the fire. It was before he'd come home without Robbie.

At first Cara had tried to pretend that she didn't blame him, but after Cara had given birth to RJ, and Everett had come by to see them at the hospital, she'd broken down, sobbing that her son would never know his father.

"I hate you, Everett, because every time I see you, I wish it had been you and not him. And then I hate myself."

Cara's sister had escorted him out, promising that Cara had just needed time. But after that, the cards he'd sent every year on RJ's birthday, with money for the kid's college fund, were sent back. Finally, he'd stopped sending money and just sent the card. As each day, month, and finally year went by, Everett grew less certain that Cara would ever forgive him. He'd been told more than once by his father and brother to give up, but he couldn't. Not until he had closure.

"Man, I don't know why you keep putting yourself through this," Justin said. "What happened to Robbie wasn't your fault. You busted your ass to save him and almost died because of it. She should have been thanking you, because some men would have just bailed—"

"I know how you feel, Justin."

"Okay." Justin played with his beer label. He looked like he wanted to say more about Cara, but Everett didn't want to hear it.

"Valerie dropped off the playlist for the wedding this morning."

"To Callie?" Everett tried to sound casual.

"Yes to Callie. She is our DJ."

"So what did you pick for your song?"

"I voted for 'Honky Tonk Badonkadonk,' but we went with 'At Last' by Etta James."

"Cool." But Everett was preoccupied with thoughts of Callie. He realized suddenly that he didn't have her number or any idea where she lived.

It made seeing her again a little hard to accomplish.

"So what do you have set up for my bachelor party?" Justin asked.

Everett pushed Callie from his mind briefly. He was actually excited for his brother's bachelor party, mainly because what Justin had asked for was so low key. "I rented Buck's out for the night and set up a poker tournament with your friends. Shit-ton of beer and poker. Real wild night."

"Did you know that Val's going to a strip show?"

"Now, that seems like a double standard," Everett said. "Didn't she say no strippers?"

"No, I said *I* didn't want strippers."

Everett smiled as he slapped his brother's shoulder. "You're a good man."

"Yes, I am." Justin held up his bottle to tap the neck against Everett's.

Everett took a long pull of his beer, trying to think of a casual way to ask Justin for Callie's number. He didn't want to make it obvious or have his brother start asking questions.

"You know, I'd like to add a song to the playlist, if you don't mind. Maybe I could get Callie's number?"

"Dude, if you want her number, just ask."

"I am asking," Everett snapped.

"What are you gonna do for me?"

"How about *not* sharing the time you wet yourself during your first-grade Christmas play when I deliver my best-man speech?" Everett kicked at the back of Justin's chair as he walked by and sent him careening to the floor.

"You fucker."

"Total accident, I swear. Now, about that number…"

Chapter Eleven

CALLIE COULDN'T GET Everett or his insanely awesome kiss out of her head—or the fact that it had been almost five days since she'd seen or heard from him.

How is he supposed to get a hold of you? It's not like you volunteered your phone number, and you're unlisted!

Callie cursed the little voice in her head and jerked her car door open. She was in a pissy mood. On top of the letter she'd received from Tristan last week, Valerie Willis had dropped off the playlist for their wedding, and their first dance song had nearly sent Callie into hysterics.

What were the odds that they'd choose the same song as she and Tristan?

When she started to download the songs into the playlist folder on her laptop, she hadn't wanted to listen to that song, even briefly. She hadn't listened to "I Love the Way You Love Me" by John Michael Montgomery since she'd started planning her wedding with Tristan.

They had been standing in the kitchen, making dinner, and she'd pulled out her iPod. Pressing the screen, she'd come up behind him and wrapped her arms around his waist.

"What do you think of this one?"

He'd grabbed her hands from around his waist and lifted them to his lips.

"I think this is perfect for us."

But as she'd dropped the file into the playlist, it had started playing. Even the first few bars had made the urge to drink strong enough that she'd considered heading out to Hank's. Instead, she'd called her sponsor, Tim.

It had helped, thankfully, but between that, work, and wondering where she stood with Everett, she'd been in a bad mood for days and distracted to boot. So distracted, that this morning, she'd left the freezer open. All of her frozen meals—which tasted like cardboard anyway, no matter what spices she added—were ruined. And then she'd been depressed because she'd become that single woman who relied on frozen dinners because she didn't want to go through the trouble of cooking for one.

"Stay, Ratchet." She slammed the door to her Jeep in the Hall's Market parking lot. On warm days, she left him at home, but it was barely forty degrees out. He could chill for ten minutes with the window cracked.

Once she'd grabbed a cart, she headed toward the frozen food, glancing down the aisles as she passed. And suddenly she saw Everett, holding a box of something in his big, masculine hands.

She paused, at war with herself. Should she head down and say hi, or pass him by? Was his silence a sign that he'd lost interest?

Or maybe he thinks you aren't interested and is giving you space?

Before she could even process her decision, she was rolling down the aisle, staring at his profile. From this side, she saw the unblemished part of his face as he grabbed a few more packages of…

Shells and cheese? Gross.

"Okay, I can't let you eat that," she said, stopping a few feet from him.

Everett turned toward her, and that easy smile stretched across his face. "Oh yeah? But it's so tasty."

"No, it's nasty. Your taste buds have just been too corrupted to realize it." Callie realized her heart was jumping like a jackrabbit as he put back the last box and took a few steps toward her.

"So where are you headed with that empty cart?"

"Frozen aisle." She resisted the urge to fiddle with her hair as he drew closer. She'd just tossed the unruly curls into a messy bun and that, combined with her oversized sweater, yoga pants, and Uggs, meant she probably looked like she'd just rolled out of bed.

Yeah, super-hot. Not.

"What are you buying in the frozen section?"

He leaned on her cart so he was only a few inches from her, his body radiating heat. God, she wanted to warm her hands on him, starting with those amazing shoulders—

Callie stumbled back at the sudden derailment of her thoughts and hit the shelves, knocking several cans to the ground.

"Oh my God." She knelt down to pick up the cans, all the while refusing to look at him.

From under her lashes, Callie saw him squat down, and his hand reached out for hers. "Hey, stop, jitterbug. They're just cans."

Looking up then, she met his gaze. "I don't know how to do this."

Everett seemed taken aback, but then his expression softened. "I know how you feel."

Callie laughed softly. "Yeah, right. You're way too charming *not* to be good at this."

"Only because I have to overcompensate for only having half a face," he said.

Callie pulled her hand back, suddenly furious. "Stop doing that."

"What?" he asked.

"Making a joke about your scars." She grabbed at the scattered cans.

"Why does it bother you?" The question hit her right where it hurt.

Because he doesn't need to be ashamed of his scars.

"I just think you're better than that."

"See, you can't say things like that to me and expect me to ask you out."

Her gaze flew up and she caught his smile. "I thought maybe you…you weren't…interested anymore."

"I am, believe me. I got your number from my brother two days ago, and I've just been staring at it," he said. "But I wasn't sure how you felt, so I just decided to let fate give me a sign."

"I told you I don't believe in fate."

"And yet, here we are." He stood up to put the last can on the shelf before turning back to face her. "How would you feel about getting some food at Jensen's with me?"

"What about your groceries?" Callie eyeballed the beer and chips in his cart dubiously.

"Most of this is for Justin's bachelor party tomorrow, but I can come back for it. Justin said you had the playlist. Are you all set for the wedding next weekend?"

At the mention of the playlist, her spirits dimmed momentarily. "Yeah, all good."

"Great. So should we go then?"

If you don't say yes, you might as well forget about him. No man is going to wait around forever, especially not a guy like him.

"Okay, but I have Ratchet in the car," she said.

"Do you want to take him home and then meet me?" he asked. Callie hesitated, and Everett spoke swiftly. "Or I can grab the food to go, and you can come over to my place. Ratchet is more than welcome to hang out with us."

"Okay," she said. "I'm going to head home first, but I'll see you in about twenty minutes or so?"

"Great. Good thing you know where I live. Makes things easier."

"Yep," she said. "See you soon."

Callie turned, the burn of his gaze on her back. She hurried out of the store to her car, jumping inside and pushing away Ratchet's kisses as she burst into excited giggles. Grabbing Ratchet's face between her two hands, she kissed his muzzle. "We have a date, buddy."

His jaws split open, and he panted happily as she turned on her Jeep. After she backed up and exited the parking lot, she checked her appearance in the mirror, grimacing. He'd asked her out, despite her looking like a monster. It was amazing she hadn't scared him away with her baggy, tired eyes and *Bride of Frankenstein* hairstyle.

Driving through the heart of Rock Canyon, she smiled. When was the last time she'd had dinner with a man? Too long, for sure.

Sixteen minutes later, she was staring at her closet in sheer frustration. Nothing in the blasted thing looked right, especially with her wild hair. She'd thought about jumping in the shower to get it wet, but then she'd have to dry it again and—

She was getting off track. Her hair was a lost cause. She needed clothes. She'd already settled on a pair of cotton boy shorts and a simple white bra, but what to put over it was proving to be a hellish decision.

Glancing down at Ratchet, she asked, "Casual is okay, right?"

The big dog just perked up his ears and tilted his head.

"Right." Reaching in for a simple button-down and a pair of nice jeans, she dressed quickly. She was just hopping into her black boots when her cell phone blared Lady Antebellum's "Lookin' for a Good Time."

"Yeah?" She tucked the phone between her shoulder and cheek as she struggled with the other boot.

"Hey, just letting you know I just got the food, and I'll be home in about ten minutes," Everett said.

Callie leaned back on the bed, yanking on her boot. "Okay."

"You all right?"

"Yeah—*huh*—why?"

"It sounds like you're struggling with something," he said.

Callie realized she'd forgotten to unzip the boots, which was why they weren't just slipping on. It had been so long since she'd tried them on, she'd forgotten. They were an impulse buy on a shopping trip with Gemma and Gracie a few months ago, when it was still too hot for boots, but they had called to her nevertheless.

"Callie?"

"Yeah, sorry, I'll be there."

Sitting up, she tapped the end button and fixed her boot situation. What the hell was wrong with her? So distracted she couldn't even put her shoes on.

Finally making her way out the door, she loaded Ratchet up in the back of the Jeep and headed down the road toward the Silverton farm, her hands sweating. What if Everett had asked her over with expectations? It had been a while, and he definitely wreaked havoc on her lust buttons, but he wasn't like the guys she used to get her rocks off. They were faceless, nameless men who she'd given her body to and nothing else.

Everett was different. She actually liked him. When she thought about him, she pictured more than just an hour or so of perfunctory fucking. She pictured getting caught up in him and getting to know everything he loved, the things he took pleasure in.

For the first time in seven years, she saw a future where she wasn't alone.

Being only two streets away, the drive took a few minutes. The long dirt road the Silverton farm was located on reminded her of an old country painting. Lines of trees flew past, opening up to flattened cornfields surrounding three houses within a few acres of each other and a big red barn. There were no remnants of the Harvest Festival besides a flatbed truck filled with hay bales.

After pulling up next to Everett's truck, Callie got out of the Jeep and stared up at the simple modular home that was so different from the two ranch houses nearby. She'd never seen Everett's home in the daylight, but the brown house with the wooden front porch suited him. It wasn't fancy, but it was homey and welcoming. Especially with the big oak in the front yard that held their swing.

Their swing? Now when had she started thinking of it that way?

After retrieving Ratchet, Callie headed up the short stoop to his front door. She had hardly knocked when Everett opened the door, but Callie forgot to lower her arm anyway. He was obviously in the middle of changing his shirt, his hard, washboard stomach exposed as he held the door open.

"Sorry, I was trying to clean up quickly." He yanked the gray cotton shirt all the way down over that delicious, golden skin, and Callie closed her mouth, swallowing, embarrassed that she had been mere seconds from drooling.

"It's okay."

"Food's in here." He stepped back to allow her inside, and she studied the interior of the modular. It was an open setup, but the worn, dark brown couches, solid oak kitchen table, and other masculine touches made it seem lived in. Under the smell of cheeseburgers coming from the fast-food bag and the cedar smoke in the fireplace, she could smell Everett's clean, subtle cologne, and she licked her lips.

"I like your place," she said.

"Thanks." He stooped, grabbed something off the ground, and threw it toward the trash. "Sorry for the mess, but it's usually just my brother and dad who come over."

"It's fine, believe me. You should see my place."

He gestured toward the table, and she sat down, her hand on the clip of Ratchet's collar. "Do you mind if I let Ratchet off leash? He's potty trained."

"Of course."

She unclipped Ratchet's leash to let him explore.

"Do you want a Coke?"

"A Coke would be great."

Everett got up, and she opened the lid of her lunch, eyeing the diner burger and fries hungrily.

"You look like you're starving." Everett held out the red can. "Do you want a cup with ice?"

"No, that's okay," she said, taking the can. "Actually, I don't even keep mine refrigerated."

Everett paused halfway into his chair. "You mean you like *warm* soda?"

"Yeah, why?" She knew what was coming and bit back a smile.

"That's fucking nasty."

Callie choked on the fry she'd just bitten into as she laughed. "You eat processed cheese. I wouldn't be casting any stones, if I were you."

"No, but seriously, how can you? That's like warm beer!"

"I've just always liked it that way," she said.

"Weird." Everett flipped open his container and sighed. "God, I love Jensen's. Not every diner knows how to make a bacon burger."

Callie took a bite of her own burger, the juicy meat and zing of mustard doing the rumba on her tongue. When she swallowed, she shrugged, just to be a pill. "You obviously haven't been to In-N-Out Burger."

"Actually, I have," Everett said, taking her by surprise, "and I still say Jensen's is better."

"That's ballsy." She munched on another French fry. "So, when did you have In-N-Out?"

"When I graduated from Camp Pendleton."

Callie had been to Camp Pendleton once for a cousin's Marine Corps graduation, and they'd spent the rest of the weekend at a San Diego hotel so her mom could get drunk at the hotel bar. She hadn't even gotten to see Legoland or Sea World before they'd headed home. "How did you like California?"

Everett shrugged. "It was different, and some parts were awesome. But there's no place like home."

Callie cringed inwardly. She'd thought the same thing, until her home had been turned into the place of nightmares.

For several minutes they ate in silence, though Callie stole glances at Everett. He still looked like a military man, with his hair buzzed close around his head, exposing the shell of his ear and the burns scars that were pale white. She could only imagine how painful they must have been, and she wanted to reach out and touch him. Still, she'd noticed Everett always watched for how people reacted to him; he did not like to be pitied.

But even the scars on his face that puckered into the collar of his T-shirt couldn't hide the beauty of his eyes and mouth or the hard muscles working beneath his shirt. He'd said that the scars covered nearly 40 percent of his body, but she hadn't seen any burns along his stomach. She imagined helping him take off his T-shirt once more and running her hands over his skin, tracing the ridges of muscles as she explored him and learned every scar, every birthmark, and mole until it was burned into her brain.

"Can I ask you about…about what happened?"

"With this?" He gestured to the scarred side of his face, and she nodded. "I was stationed in Afghanistan along with my best friend, Robbie. We were headed back to the base, and then…"

She reached out for his hand when his eyes closed in a grimace. "It's okay. I'm sorry I asked."

He opened his eyes and squeezed her palm. "Naw, it's fine. It's just…I only remember waking up to this high-pitched ringing in my ears, and it was hot. I could see my brothers scrambling out of the door and someone tried to help me. Over the ringing, I could hear Robbie yelling and screaming. I got to him as the fire started creeping over his legs and realized his arm was pinned, and I…this isn't exactly light dinner conversation, but I managed to get him loose and carry him out. Only the fire spread to me before I got us far enough away to drop and roll. Our unit tried to put out the fire on both of us, but not before it felt like the skin was just melting from my body."

"Oh my God." She couldn't stop the exclamation, her hand covering her mouth as she watched the pain fill his eyes. He had been through so much and come out of it stronger. She envied that.

"When they put out the flames on Robbie, they found a piece of shrapnel embedded in his back. It was so deep, it was hard to see, but it had severed the aorta. He'd bled out. They rushed me to the closest hospital, and I had to stay there for months as I healed. Afterward, I was honorably discharged and returned home. But when my wife found out all the medical care I'd need, she split."

Callie's insides burned as she thought about Everett's coming home in pain and having lost so much, only to be abandoned by the woman he loved. "What kind of person would leave her husband like that?"

"It was for the best, so don't lose any sleep over it. Turns out she was really just looking for a marine to marry." Everett finished off his beer. "She wanted the uniform and the status, and when I couldn't give her that anymore, she took off."

Callie had the urge to track down the former Mrs. Silverton and clobber her. "You deserved better."

"I survived." He closed his container. "You done?"

She realized she'd been so engrossed in his story, she had stopped eating. It was fine, though; she was full anyway. "Sure."

Everett stood up and cleaned off the table. When she stood up and tried to help, he said, "No, you're my guest."

"But you cooked! Well, sort of."

"House rules. Now get out of my kitchen," he said.

Callie walked over to a large bookshelf on his wall and stared at the packed shelves. She heard the water shut off behind her and called, "You do read a lot."

She heard his footsteps behind her but concentrated on the titles. Suddenly, a pink paperback caught her eye, and she pulled it off the shelf.

Raising her eyebrows, she turned to face him and smacked his chest with both the book and her hand, he was that close. "Did you like *The Duke and I*?" Looking up at him, her amusement dimmed at the intense gleam in his eyes.

"Do you always snoop around a man's bookshelf?" His obvious teasing relaxed her, and she turned around, putting the book back.

"I just had no idea you were into romance." The heat of his nearness warming her arm and shoulder, and she was tempted to lean back into his body and let him wrap that heat around her.

"I'll read just about anything, but this was actually sent to my unit while we were in Afghanistan. I read it about four times before I was sent home."

His breath rustled the hair on the back of her neck with every word, and she shivered.

"Are you cold?"

"No."

"You were shaking."

"I'm fine." She turned around to face him, her back to the wall of the bookshelf. "So, *The Duke and I* was so good that you read it four times?"

"It was fun, but more to the point, it had a happy ending," he said sadly. "Not all of us get one of those."

Callie's heart ached for him and the things he must have seen over there, but she was afraid to touch him. She had only ever loved one boy, and he'd known everything about her. He'd been her friend, her confidant, her lover. It had been sweet and simple, and she'd been so sure of everything until it had gone to hell.

What was happening with Everett was different because of who she was now. It was messy and scary and arousing and exciting, and all of it had her on edge, unsure of who she was supposed to be. She couldn't be the simple, fun-loving girl she'd been with Tristan; she'd seen and been through too much for that.

Should she flirt? Should she play the seductress or the tease? If she was just the woman she'd become—one who loved popcorn and PG movies—would that be enough for him?

Unable to face him with so much confusion and uncertainty rattling around in her head, she turned back to the bookshelf, skimming across the spines to distract herself from him.

"So you read romance, Tom Clancy—"

Suddenly, his hand reached past her and pulled another book off the shelf. "Even Shakespeare."

He held the worn copy of *Much Ado About Nothing* out, and she took it. "So I guess this means you're cultured and sophisticated."

"Or I just like to read."

God, she could almost feel his lips against the skin on the back of her neck; tingles were already electrifying her skin. "So you read anything?"

"Yep, anything. Even you."

This time she didn't have to imagine the sweet brush of his lips just below her hairline. They kissed a burning trail up the side of her neck to her ear, the warmth of his breath spreading everywhere.

"I think you want me, but you're afraid to admit it, even to yourself."

His mouth closed over the pulse below her ear, and the hard, fast suction made her back bow. She reached out to steady herself against the bookshelf, and he covered her hands with his, lacing their fingers. Then he pushed them up over her head, the motion bringing his front flush with her back.

"I think you avoid looking at me because you're afraid I'll see how your eyes liquefy when you're thinking about me touching you, kissing you. Rubbing my hands all over your body until you're wet and throbbing."

Her nipples tightened against the cotton of her bra, and she moaned as he nipped along her skin. She pushed back into him involuntarily and when he pushed against her, she could feel her panties grow damp. She squeezed her legs together, trying to control the throbbing need building with every word and teasing touch.

"Please." Her voice was harsh, and she sucked in a deep, shuddering breath when he released one of her hands.

"What do you want, Callie?" His fingers slid across her neck and over her collarbone.

"I thought you already knew."

Everett's hand stopped, hovering over her breast. "I want to hear you say it."

Callie whimpered as she tried to turn in his arms, but he pressed into her, pinning her with his body. Panic started to claw its way to the surface, and as if sensing her distress, he immediately let her go.

She turned around to face him, his hand still clasping hers against the bookshelf.

"I'm sorry. I got carried away."

But her fear was gone now that she was faced with the worry in those kind brown eyes, and she found her gaze drawn to his lips. Those full lips, which had been so gentle on hers just days before, were so close. She could lift up just a little and keep this thing going—

Callie realized the lips were moving. He had asked her something. "What?"

"I said, do you want to watch a movie?"

Callie looked away from Everett's gorgeous lips toward the brown sofa, the fire that crackled from the fireplace, and Ratchet watching them from a few feet away.

A movie meant sitting on the couch, closely, and possible cuddling.

God, was she sweating through her shirt? That was embarrassing. Did she smell? She was tempted to use his bathroom, just so she could check.

"Sure, that sounds great." She took a deep breath when he walked over to the TV, and she realized how close she'd come to letting him have his way with her against the bookshelf.

Just the fact that things had gone as far as they had showed her she was starting to trust him. Maybe there *was* hope for her again.

Everett squatted down in front of the DVD shelf, the fabric of his jeans pulling tight across his ass and thighs. What was it they said about asses so tight you could bounce quarters off them?

"Okay, I apologize for my movie collection, but I think the last new movie I bought was *Dumb and Dumber*."

"Are you kidding?" Callie leaned over to take off her boots. Might as well get comfortable.

"No, I mostly watch Netflix, if anything."

She set her boots by the door and came back to take a seat on the couch. "Well, we can browse on that," she said, though she was really enjoying the view of him bent over.

Everett stood up, and Callie decided he looked good in every position.

"So, what will it be?"

Chapter Twelve

"I CAN'T BELIEVE you chose this movie." Everett stretched his arm across the back of the couch. He was still fighting a raging hard-on, and the sweet scent of Callie was wreaking havoc on his control, but he needed to slow down with her. She was like a wild animal who'd been raised in captivity; she'd be relaxed and responsive one minute but jumpy if you moved too suddenly.

The fact that her dog hadn't growled at him once or even tried to get between them was progress. Instead, Ratchet was lying across half his shoe at that very moment, letting out rough snores.

"You suggested a Halloween-themed movie." Callie leaned forward to set the remote on the table. When she did, her shirt rode up in the back, and he could have sworn he saw some ink on her hip. "And since I'm not a fan of horror movies, it was either this or *Hocus Pocus*."

"Bette Midler? No thanks. Still, I didn't think you would pick *A Nightmare Before Christmas*." As she sat back against the couch and under his arm, he noticed the way her breasts strained against her button-down shirt, and suddenly, he wanted to touch her so bad he hurt. He wanted to unbutton that shirt and spread it open before using his hands and mouth on every inch of her skin. Damn, just the thought of getting to explore everything Callie Jacobsen had hiding under that conservative top was making him crazy.

"It's one of my favorites."

Her simple statement brought him out of his lecherous mind, and he smiled as she became totally transfixed by a children's movie, like it was the most amazing thing she'd ever seen.

The opening song came on, and Everett leaned toward her. "Are you humming?"

"No." But a small, betraying smile spread across her mouth.

Everett groaned and dropped his head in his hands.

"What? You don't like humming?" Her voice shook with laughter.

"It's only second to whistling."

She started whistling a jaunty tune, and he lifted his head, scowling at her. "That's your first warning."

Her lips were still pursed in that sweet little "o" when he heard the barest, high-pitched noise escape them.

"You asked for it." Before she could move, he attacked her ribs with the wiggling digits.

Callie squealed and pushed at his hands, trying to crawl away from his tickling fingers, but he didn't stop his torture, loving her uncontrollable giggles.

"Stop, please!"

He ceased, and was about to come up with something clever to say, but watching her amber eyes sparkle in the firelight, Everett lost his train of thought. The red flames cast a golden light across her cheeks and showed off the layers of blonde in her hair. She was beautiful and ethereal, and a wave of protectiveness came over him. He wanted to learn all of her doubts and fears and help her forget them. He wanted her to trust him and to know that he would never betray her, never hurt her.

Before he could second-guess himself, Everett ran his finger across her bottom lip, his thumb spreading up along the soft skin of her cheek.

"Callie," he whispered, leaning into her slowly.

Only her lips met his a lot sooner than he'd intended.

She'd met him halfway, her lips open wide under his. It was all he could do not to pull her hard against him and thrust his tongue inside, but he kept his lust in check, his hand sliding gently into her curls.

Her small moan against his mouth was followed by her hands gripping his shoulders as she scooted closer to him. His tongue slipped inside her mouth finally and tangled with hers, while his cock strained against the constraints of his cotton boxer briefs and jeans. He'd been telling himself that he had to have imagined how good she tasted, and he was right.

She tasted better.

Sweet with just a hint of tartness.

He sucked her tongue into his mouth before releasing it to run his lips down her chin. Finding the place just under her ear, he left a trail of kisses until he reached the pulse of her neck.

"God, Callie, I want you."

For a second, her body tensed, but when he flicked his tongue against her earlobe and sucked it into his mouth, teasing it between his teeth, she melted against him once more.

Everett started to ease her back onto the couch, and she let him, her neck tilting to the side, giving him better access. He felt her shiver as he nipped her skin and slid his hand up her body until he covered her breast with his hand. Massaging it through the shirt, he brought his mouth back to hers.

He felt her palms slip down his arms and sides until they began creeping under his T-shirt. Her fingers skimmed over his back, and he knew the minute they met his scars. She stilled, her touch so light it was barely there. He stopped moving, kissing her lightly as he waited for her reaction.

"Do they hurt?"

"No."

Without another word, her hands were back, firmer as they moved up to his shoulders, and he let out a shaky breath of relief as he kissed her again, harder, desperately. Most of the women he'd been with had avoided touching or talking about his scars, but Callie acted like they were nothing unusual. Her sweetness had him aching to be inside her. He wanted to show her that if she just trusted him, they could be amazing together. In and out of bed.

Moving to the buttons of her shirt, he took the top one between his thumb and forefinger, ready to flick it open and see her. He wanted to pull down her bra and suck her nipples into his mouth. Tongue them into hard peaks as he exposed her down to her belly button.

But one of her hands caught his as she broke the kiss. "Don't."

Her voice sounded almost panicked, and he laced his fingers with hers before taking a shaky breath. Sitting back up, he brought her with him. "Sorry. I got carried away."

"It's okay," she said before tucking a few loose strands back. "I…I liked it."

He nuzzled his nose against her ear. "I liked it too."

She let out a deep breath, like she'd been holding it, and he smiled, playing with her hands.

"I'm not in any rush," he said.

He didn't press her about why she'd stopped him. It was only their second date, after all. Using their linked hands, he simply pulled her against his side and wrapped his other arm around her shoulder. She fit perfectly.

Everett didn't say anything else. He just cuddled her and waited for her to realize he wasn't going to try anything else. He could tell the exact moment she decided to believe him and leaned into his warmth. Triumph coursed through him at the small gesture. He would win Callie over. He had been waiting years to meet her.

Everett had a feeling that for Callie, he might just wait forever.

THE END CREDITS rolled, and Callie blinked her heavy eyes. It was only nine, but she was usually lying in bed at this time. Turning her head, she caught her breath when she saw Everett's head tipped back against the couch, his mouth open slightly.

"Are you asleep?" she whispered.

When he didn't respond, she slipped out from under his arm and climbed to her feet. As she stood over him, she covered her mouth to smother her giggles.

Some hot date, huh? You put the guy to sleep.

Looking around the room, she spotted a quilt on the back of the rocking chair in the corner. She grabbed it, planning to cover him up and sneak out, but as she tucked the blanket around him, she found herself lingering.

If he hadn't been burned, he would have been almost too handsome. With a square jaw and Roman nose, he was exactly what a man should look like. Not pretty or metrosexual like most of the guys she'd grown up with in California.

Callie hesitated for a second before touching the scarred side of his face gently, sliding her fingers over the ridges of skin. She was drawn to Everett; there was no denying it. He was strong and steady, the kind of man who would put his life before someone he loved.

Like his best friend.

Callie wondered about the man whom Everett risked so much to save. He seemed so put together now, but with everything that happened to him, it was hard to imagine he wasn't a mess.

When he'd gone for her shirt earlier, she'd almost asked him to turn off the lights first. But she'd chickened out, afraid he might feel her scars and ask her about them. How could she explain about Tristan and her past after hearing his story? He'd been scarred saving someone, being selfless and a hero. She had ignored warning signs because she was afraid of what they meant. She had been selfish, living in her own little happy existence, when deep down, she'd questioned Tristan's excuses of exhaustion and stress. She'd been worried, afraid that his blackouts and strange behavior had meant more, but she'd buried her head in the sand, and it had cost lives, while Everett had saved them.

He was better than she'd ever be.

Then what are you even doing here, fondling his face like a creeper?

Because she wanted him. And though she might not deserve him, she didn't care. He was everything she wasn't, and he thought she was beautiful. He wanted her too.

Without thinking, she bent over him and kissed his open mouth.

Suddenly, rough hands gripped her arms hard, and she reared back with a startled scream.

"Callie, fuck!" Everett said, releasing her.

Callie scrambled to her feet, trying to get away from him, but her ankle turned funny when her foot caught on something. With a cry of pain, she fell to the floor, tears blinding her as the sharp hurt began to throb.

Ratchet let out a ferocious growl just before his tongue began showering her face, but she was in too much pain to push him away.

Then Everett was kneeling next to her, a dark shadow with the light of the fire behind him, and for a split second, she saw Tristan in his place.

"Oh, God, Callie. Are you okay? Fuck, I'm sorry." Everett's worried voice broke through her panic, and she closed her eyes, taking deep, shaky breaths.

You are safe.

Ratchet was still hovering over her, focused on Everett, and she reached up to pat him. "It's okay. I'm all right."

The growling stopped, and he backed up a step, letting Everett get closer.

Suddenly, Everett was carrying her against his chest as he stood up, his arms under her shoulders and knees.

"What are you doing?"

"I'm going to take a look at your ankle." He set her upright on the couch and went to turn on the lights. She winced as she tried to put weight on her foot, and the throbbing only intensified.

Everett knelt down by her feet. "Which one?"

"I'm fine," she said, her voice strained.

He reached for the injured foot and rolled up her jeans. "Is it this one?"

"Really, you don't have to—yow!" she yelled when he picked it up and pressed his fingers into the tender muscles.

"Damn, it's swelling," he said grimly. "We should take you to the hospital and get it X-rayed."

"I'm sure it's fine. I'll just ice it when I get home." The last thing she wanted to do was spend the night in a hospital, being pinched, poked, and prodded. Especially with Everett looking on, wondering why she was refusing the pain meds they'd offer her.

"Oh, you know, I used to be a major pill-popper and alcoholic. No big deal."

"Callie, you might have fractured something."

Ratchet kept trying to push between them, and Callie stroked his head, trying to calm him. "It's probably just a sprain, and all the doctor's going to tell me is to take it easy and keep my weight off it."

"If you won't go to a hospital, then you'll just have to stay here. You can't drive on it, and besides, leaving you alone when you can hardly walk isn't safe. If the swelling hasn't gone down by tomorrow, I'm taking you in, even if I have to throw you over my shoulder."

"If you hadn't freaked out when I was putting that blanket on you, I wouldn't have twisted it in the first place." Callie watched the guilty pain on his face and instantly wanted to take her words back.

"I think you were doing a lot more than tucking me in," he said softly.

She looked away from his penetrating eyes. "And that's why you grabbed me like I was attacking you?"

"No, I…" Everett cupped his head in his hand and took a deep breath before he spoke again. "I sometimes forget where I am, especially when I first wake up. All I knew subconsciously was that someone was hovering over me…and I reacted. But I would never hurt you, not in my right mind."

He was talking about his PTSD, but she was hung up on his words. *In his right mind.*

"Look, I appreciate the offer and everything, but I just want to go home. Sleep in my own bed, and besides, I have to feed Ratchet in the morning."

"I can drive you home before work—"

"I have to be there at four thirty in the morning!"

"I'll set the alarm for three. Is that enough time? And you can take care of him then. As for tonight, I'll take the couch, and you can take my bed." His persistence was wearing her down. She didn't want to keep arguing with him, and she was hurting.

Before she could argue more, he had scooped her up again and was walking to the back of the house. When he flipped on the light, she found herself in a simple bedroom with a bed and dresser; no photos or pictures on the wall.

"How long have you lived here?"

"I bought the house a little over five years ago." He lay her down on the bed before gently tucking a few pillows under her ankle.

"Your decorating style is almost too simplistic." Her tone was angry and insulting, and she hated that she felt helpless. She was so confused; it was one thing to hear that he had PTSD, but to experience it, even briefly, had been frightening. She wanted to be home, where she could overanalyze and convince herself that she was better off away from him, instead of lying in his bed, with him caring for her and looking like a lost puppy.

"I know. I've been meaning to hire a decorator. Know anyone good?" Everett gave her a wink before going to the closet. How dare he try to be charming when she was busy being angry with him?

And scared.

Initially, yes, she'd been spooked by his reaction, but he'd only grabbed her. If she'd been startled awake from a deep sleep, how would she have behaved? Probably have come up swinging, if she had to guess. Could she really blame him for scaring her? She could call Caroline to come get her if she needed, but despite her initial fear, she wanted to know more about his PTSD. Was it severe? Did he act so secure and adjusted to make up for his inability to control his fears when he was most vulnerable? Had he ever hurt anyone?

He pulled out a blanket and spread it over her. "I'm going to get you some Tylenol and an ice pack. I'll be right back."

He was being so careful, so gentle with her; it was as if she was made of porcelain. Callie wiped at her suddenly wet eyes as he left the room.

Everett came back with a glass of water and a blue ice pack. He set the water next to the bed and sat down. "Okay, I'm going to put this on your ankle, and I want you to take these." He held up a small packet of pills. "It's just Tylenol, but it should help a little."

"Thanks." She checked the package to make sure it was just Tylenol, and not Tylenol PM or anything with codeine. When she'd started the program, her sponsor had given her a list of safe pain relievers to use, and most of the over-the-counter ones were okay. Callie broke open the package and popped the white pills into her mouth before taking a swig of water to wash them down.

"So does that happen a lot?"

BAD FOR ME 163

"No, not anymore." He adjusted the cold pack on her ankle and covered her foot with the blanket.

"Have you ever hurt anyone?" *Please say no.* She didn't think she could get over it if he said yes.

"I clocked an orderly once who'd come to get me for surgery. I'd been deep in a night terror, and when he tried to wake me, I came out of it swinging. Of course, just the pain of moving had been intense enough to wake me up. I had nightmares almost every night, and sometimes I would freak out and have no idea where I was. I started seeing a shrink after my wife left, and she taught me some exercises to help bring me back to reality, so to speak," he said. "And gave me a prescription for anxiety pills. Which I hardly ever need anymore."

As if sensing her trepidation about his revelation, he added, "I am not that same guy anymore, Callie. I worked through it. I hope you'll believe me. I don't know what happened in your past, but I get the feeling someone hurt you. I won't."

"You scared the crap out of me." She couldn't believe she said the words out loud, but they were true. He had scared her, but it hadn't really hurt. And to be fair, he'd been badly burned and hopped up on pain meds when he'd hit the orderly. It was a long time ago.

His hand drifted up to rest on her shin, and his face was so twisted with regret that Callie just wanted to cover his hand with hers. "I really am sorry."

His pain hurt her, and her stomach tied in knots. He was this amazing man, and he wanted her. He had pushed aside her recovering alcoholism to be with her and give her a chance. Could she do the same? Put her worry on the back burner and have a little faith in him? A little trust?

Surprising herself, she said, "It's okay."

His face lit with relief, and he even gave her a small smile. "Some date, huh?"

"Definitely not what I was expecting."

A wet nose pushed into her hand, and she wondered how she hadn't noticed Ratchet following them into the room.

Probably because you've been focused on Everett.

"Well, if you need anything, I'll be in the living room."

"Okay. Thank you for taking care of me."

"You got hurt because of me. It's only right I make amends." He took her hand between his, and she knew he was going to apologize again. "I really am—"

"Sorry. I know," she said gently. "I forgive you. We all have our hang-ups, right?"

He bent over and kissed the palm of her hand, the press of his lips burning against her skin. "Just holler, and I'll come running."

"Good night," she said.

As he left the room, Everett paused in the doorway, a cheeky grin on his face. "You know, this was not the way I was hoping to get you into my bed. My way would have included wine and roses."

Before she could respond, he shut off the lights and disappeared down the hall.

Minus the wine, it would have been better than this.

Chapter Thirteen

CALLIE WOKE UP as pain exploded in her ankle.

"Argh!"

Ratchet's wet nose pressed against her arm in the dark, and she brushed him off impatiently as she tried to take deep breaths, willing the pain away. It was 2:30 A.M., but it felt like she'd been asleep for only an hour. Her eyes stung, even in the darkness of the room.

Swinging her legs off the bed, she bit her lip to keep from crying out as she hobbled toward the door where the light switch was. When her hand found it, the light blinded her.

God, she felt hung over, and she hadn't even been drinking.

Now *that* was some bullshit.

Blinking until her eyes adjusted, she limped back to make the bed. The ice pack Everett had put on her ankle had melted, and the pillow was now soaked with water.

Once she had straightened up the room, she grabbed the ice pack and opened the door. "Come on, Ratch."

He padded behind her as she walked slowly down the hallway, bracing her weight against the wall. She tried to be quiet, but Ratchet's heavy breathing was louder than an angry bull in a library.

Callie made it to the living room and looked over the back of the couch to find Everett stretched out, his bare feet hanging off the arm. He had a worn quilt pulled over most of him, but the light from the flickering TV revealed his jeans bunched up on the floor.

Just the thought of him in nothing but a pair of boxer briefs was drool-inspiring.

He looked so uncomfortable and exhausted that she felt too guilty to wake him. Moving toward the coffee table, she picked up his phone and swiped through to alarms, deleting the one at 3:00 A.M.

Besides, she'd been taking care of herself for a long time. She could handle a little sprain without putting him out even more than she already had.

It felt like forever, but she finally made it to the front door, only to remember she'd worn her calf-high boots. Using the flashlight app on her phone, she examined her ankle, which could officially be called a "cankle" at this point. There was no way she was going to squeeze that boot up over it.

Barefoot it was.

Gathering the boots up, she ushered Ratchet out the front door and wondered what Everett would think when he woke up to find her gone. She should at least leave a note, but her ankle was throbbing badly, and her other leg was getting tired. If she went in search of a pen, she would definitely wake him up, stumbling around. And he deserved some rest.

The minute her feet hit the ice-cold gravel, she made up her mind. She'd just send him a text when she got to work.

"DALTON, I SAID I'm fine!" Callie snapped when he tried to help her out of her DJ chair eight hours later. "Will you stop hovering?"

"You need to stay off it," he said.

"Thank you, Sergeant Obvious. I guess that would explain the funny hitch in my giddy-up."

"I can help you out to your car. You're just being stubborn."

Yeah, she was, but for good reason. She didn't like relying on anyone. And if she were to allow any man to put his hands on her and help her, it would have been the sexy, sleeping one she'd left this morning.

Callie had sent Everett a text around five, afraid if she sent it too early it would wake him. It had taken her three drafts before she'd finally sent *Thank you so much for taking care of me.* And all he'd sent back was, *You're welcome.*

It was so curt that the "maybe you shouldn't have snuck out without a word" conversation she'd had with herself now seemed to have some serious merit. He was obviously upset with her, but it had seemed cheesy as hell to send *You were just so adorable sleeping, I couldn't wake you.*

Dalton's hands grabbed her as she stumbled a bit, and she gave him an ugly look. "I made it to work today all by my lonesome, and I will make it home the same way." She shook his hand off as she made it to the studio door. Dave and Sam both stood off to the side, hands in the air like she was packing heat.

Dalton wasn't as bright.

"It won't hurt you to just lean on someone else for once." She ignored him as she led Ratchet to the front of the station. Honestly, Callie was already tired from hopping around on one foot all morning. She stopped in front of the door, breathing hard, and waved her hand. "Fine. Can you hold the door open for me?"

That adorable boyish smile appeared. "I'd be happy to."

Caroline's comment about Dalton's possibly having a crush on Callie popped into her mind, and Callie looked away from his barely legal cuteness. She did not need him getting the wrong idea.

Especially when she had some pretty major feelings going for Everett.

So what should she do? Should she call him and apologize? Show up on his step with a tube of cookie dough and offer to make him cookies?

No, that was something she'd have done as a teenager, not a grown-ass woman.

Outside, she walked the ten feet to her car and saw Everett's old beat-up truck parked next to her Jeep. He was sitting in the driver's seat, watching her. Callie stopped moving, but Dalton plowed into her back, catching her when she started to tip forward.

"Whoa, sorry. Why did you stop?"

Everett's door opened, and he stepped out.

"Oh," Dalton said.

Callie wasn't looking at Dalton, though. She was too busy watching Everett lumber toward them, his mouth twitching like he was fighting a smile.

Wait—if he was mad at her, why would he be trying not to smile?

"So she wouldn't let you help her either?"

"Nope," Dalton said, chuckling. "She's stubborn as a mule and twice as—"

"Hey, I am standing here, and try to remember, I'm your boss."

"I was gonna say twice as cute," Dalton said.

"Right."

Everett was standing in front of her now, looking down at her with those light brown eyes that made her knees weak. Of course, that made her tip a little, and Everett reached out to cup her elbow, warming her skin through her sweater.

"I'll take care of her; don't worry. I know how to handle her."

"Handle me?" She'd meant to come off sounding threatening, but her indignation sounded a little squeaky. Though that might have been because he'd stepped a little closer, and the strength of his body was giving her flashbacks to their hot-and-heavy make-out session last night.

"Yep, just like a wild filly," he deadpanned.

Ratchet had the nerve to nuzzle Everett's outstretched hand and then lean into him. *Traitor.*

"Well, I guess I'll take off then." Dalton looked like he wanted to do something more, but his gaze was latched onto Everett. "You'll make sure she gets home safely?"

"Yeah," Everett said.

Dalton said a soft good-bye and loped toward his truck.

"He likes you."

"No, he doesn't," Callie said. "Besides, he's just a kid."

Everett gazed down at her intently, and she squirmed under his scrutiny.

"What? He is."

"He looks grown up to me," Everett said.

"Are you jealous?"

"No, because I know he doesn't mean anything to you."

"Why? Because you can read me?" Callie asked.

"Yep. Can't you read me?"

She couldn't. His expression seemed mild, but his gaze was filled with heat. But was that anger or...

She blushed. Had he been thinking about last night too?

"I'm sorry."

"For what?"

"For taking off this morning without even a howdy-do."

"Oh, that," he said. "Yeah, I went back to check on you, and you were gone. I figured I'd scared you off."

"No!" she cried. "I mean, I just needed to get home. Really, you were super-sweet."

"Sweet?" He looked horrified. "Sweet is the kiss of death for a man."

"Not to me."

The hand on her elbow moved up to her chin, tilting her face up until their eyes met. "I am sorry, Callie."

He sounded so earnest, his eyes so pained, that she didn't want him hurting. Not for something that wasn't his fault.

How can you readily forgive Everett, who you hardly know, and not yourself?

Because Everett had sought help and was working on his PTSD. Tristan had ignored his symptoms, lied to her, and cost her everything because of it.

"You didn't really hurt me, just startled me," Callie said. She realized that his hand had slid up to cup her cheek, and she was actually leaning into his touch. When had that happened?

"I was just going to head home and watch some TV. Do you want to join me?"

Her invitation seemed to surprise him, but it surprised her too. She really liked him. Callie had a feeling that if she was ever going to trust any man again, it would be Everett.

"I can't," he groaned.

"Oh." Callie could feel her cheeks burning again. "It's Friday, right? The big bachelor party."

"Yeah, and I'm heading over to Buck's to help set up."

"Well, I hope you have a blast," Callie said. Her leg was aching anyway. "I should go, though. I need to ice this bad boy again."

Everett shook his head. "I bet it's been giving you hell and yet, you drove and walked on it all day."

"More like limped," she said. "Besides, I can drive with my left foot."

"And I'm guessing if I dumped you over my shoulder and drove you home, you'd throw a wall-eyed fit?"

"Probably."

Suddenly, Callie found herself upside down over his shoulder, looking into Ratchet's big brown eyes. "Some guard dog you are." Said dog didn't do anything more than wag his tail at her admonishment.

Everett started to carry her to his truck. "He understands that I'm just trying to help you."

"I need my car and like you said, I already drove myself this morning. I am fine!"

"I'll get some help and bring your car by this afternoon. I just need directions." He opened the truck door and set her on the front seat. Next to her was a colorful array of flowers in a bouquet, which he reached across her to pick up.

"You do realize that I have been taking care of myself for years, right?"

"Maybe it's about time you let someone else take the wheel." And with that piece of advice, he placed the flowers in her lap and shut the door on her surprise.

As Everett loaded Ratchet in the backseat of the truck, Callie fingered the soft petals, tears stinging her eyes. She couldn't remember the last time a man had given her flowers. She held the bouquet to her nose, breathing in the sweet mix of fragrances.

Everett climbed into the driver's seat, and she looked up from the flowers. His gaze was tender when he reached out to slide his hand behind her neck. As his rough thumb rubbed along her jawline, her eyes closed, waiting for him to close the distance and kiss her. When nothing happened, she opened her eyes to find him watching her, his lips twisted in amusement.

"I really want to kiss you, but I didn't think you would enjoy having an audience."

Noticing the tilt of his head, she glanced toward the front of the station. Just outside the entrance, she saw Dave on his cell phone, his mouth hanging open.

Covering her face with her hands, she sunk down into the seat. "Oh my God."

Everett took the hint and started the truck. He backed up slowly, patting her knee. "If you need me to have a talk with him, I will."

Callie peeked out from between her fingers and saw he was dead serious. "Yeah, no. You'd only fuel the flames of torment."

"You've got a bit of a dramatic side."

"No, I swear. Your phone calls in the morning were regular enough to incite Dave to break out into song."

"What song?"

Callie grimaced and broke into a sing-song voice. *"Callie and Rhett, kissing in a booth—"*

Everett burst out laughing. "In a booth? What did he rhyme it with?"

"I usually put him on mute when he started, but I'm sure whatever it was, he thought it was clever."

"Well, I'm sorry you work with a couple of idiots." He slid his hand across the seat and took hers. Their fingers tangled, and she let him hold her, loving his rough palm against her own. It was a lovely gesture, and no matter what he thought, Everett showing his sweet side wasn't turning her off to him.

Not at all.

EVERETT PULLED INTO Callie's driveway and was reticent to release her hand. It felt good to share something as simple as this, though Everett was still unsure about what Callie was really thinking or feeling. She was so guarded and independent, but then suddenly, he'd catch a glimpse of the vulnerable woman who seemed to want to trust him.

But there was more to her than just the sad shadows that lurked behind her whisky-hazel eyes. Callie was lonely. He could sense it because he was lonely too. He wanted someone to come home to, to share a life with, and to love again.

No, he didn't just want someone. He wanted *Callie.*

But last night, after he'd woken up and realized he'd grabbed Callie, he'd been sure she was going to run. It didn't take a rocket scientist to realize that someone had hurt her, and grabbing her arms in a vice grip because he was too fucked up to realize he'd been dreaming had probably sent her into a déjà vu tailspin.

But instead, she'd been understanding and kind. A complete 180 from his ex-wife.

"God, I can't sleep with all your moaning and screaming! Go sleep on the couch, for fuck's sake."

Then again, Alicia hadn't ever been the sensitive type. She'd grown up in a military home and had wanted to marry a military man. He'd met her when he was almost twenty-two and getting ready to deploy. After knowing each other for less than a week, he'd bought her a ring and promised her a wedding when he returned. But she'd convinced him she loved him, that she *knew* they were right for each other, and she didn't want to wait.

So one trip to Vegas later, he had a wife, and over the next four years, they spent a grand total of eight months together. When he'd come home for good, Everett figured that they would start creating the life he'd imagined, but after she walked out, he'd spent a lot of time in therapy, trying to figure out why.

It had come down to wearing blinders, especially when he was lonely and scared. Alicia had come into his life just before he went into a hot zone, unsure if he'd make it back. Having her waiting for him had given him something to come home to.

With Callie, it was different. He was lonely, sure, but he wanted to be with her because of how she made him feel, not because he was trying to fill a void. With Callie, there was fire and electricity. There was desperate need and wanting that created an ache inside him when he couldn't hear her voice or watch the sunshine dance across her hair.

It was official. He was a fucking goner.

"Well, thanks for driving me home," Callie said. A gleam of humor danced in her eyes. "Even though it was against my will."

Before she touched the door handle, he used their linked hands to tug her toward him and tangled his free hand in her hair.

"I owe you a kiss," he whispered, his lips a fraction away from hers.

"You make it sound like you don't want to kiss me." Callie's warm breath fanned across his lips.

"If you don't know how badly I want to kiss you, then I'm doing something wrong."

His mouth covered hers, and the air in his truck grew humid. Sweat trickled down the back of his shirt as she met each thrust of his tongue. Her hand still held his, but he could feel the fingers of her other hand inching up his thigh, and his cock grew in response, hardening against his jeans. With each scrape of her nails or slide of her thumb, his dick twitched and flexed.

Wanting to be closer, Everett released her briefly only to pull her toward him more tightly. Mindful of her ankle, he gently urged her leg over his lap so that she straddled him. Once Callie was seated on his lap, he groaned into her mouth.

He wanted to remove everything she had on, inch by inch. To press his mouth against her collarbone, to trail kisses downward until he took her breast into his mouth and sucked until she was writhing against him.

His hands had just slipped under her sweater and began to ease it up when she grabbed his wrists. "Not here."

It took all his self-restraint not to drop his head back and curse.

His cell vibrated against his leg, breaking the tension, and he tilted his hips to get it out. When she tried to climb off his lap, he put his hands on her thighs and shook his head. "Not yet."

Everett answered the phone when he saw Justin's picture. "I'm busy."

"Dude, you were supposed to be here ten minutes ago," Justin said.

"And I *will* be there, but I had something I needed to do."

"Well, hurry up."

Everett swiped the end button, grumbling.

"You did say you had to help out," Callie said.

Glancing up at her, with her hair falling wildly around her face, he grinned. "They can get started without me."

But before he could pick up where they left off, she stopped him. "Can we just slow down for a half a second?"

Damn it, he had been too eager again and freaked her out. "Yeah, sure."

"I just…I love kissing you, but…I don't take my shirt off. For anyone."

Everett wasn't sure what to say to that. "Okay."

"Okay? That's it? No questions?"

"Oh, I have plenty." He stroked her neck with his fingers, and she almost arched and purred like a cat. "But something tells me they would come out all wrong and leave me sounding like a pervert. And I'm enjoying this open dialogue too much to risk saying something that will offend you."

"Now I'm wondering what kind of questions you think would offend me."

"Tough." Everett brushed her mouth with his. "So how do you feel about hands under the shirt?" His other hand hovered at the bottom of her sweater, and he felt her shiver.

"I'm not sure."

"Then I'll just wait until you are."

Chapter Fourteen

"WHAT THE HELL am I doing here?"

Callie was sitting next to Caroline on Val's lumpy sofa, surrounded by a room full of women who had obviously started partying long before the party had officially begun a half hour earlier. Val had rented the house to her sister, Ellie, and Jenny Andrews, Mrs. Andrews's youngest daughter, and the sisters had decided to have the party there because it was closer to town than the Silverton farm.

Although Callie had a feeling that Jenny's mother would take issue with her eighteen-year-old throwing back shots and "whoo-hooing" like a sorority girl.

"You are keeping your very good friend from murdering her sisters." Caroline wrapped her arms around Callie's shoulders and squealed in her ear, "I am so glad you came!"

Callie wasn't quite as elated as Caroline, but if she'd stayed home by herself, she'd have gone bat-shit crazy.

Especially because she couldn't seem to get the taste of Everett off her lips or the heat of his fingers brushing her skin out of her mind.

The warmth of the room and the twenty bodies in it was making Callie sweat, and she wiped a few beads from her forehead, even as she swore it had nothing to do with her thoughts of Everett.

Suddenly, Ellie came into the room yelling, "What's up, bitches? Who wants beads?" Dangling from her hands were dozens of multicolored necklaces.

"I thought this was a bachelorette party, not Mardi Gras."

"Yeah, well, you know Ellie. The wilder the better." Caroline held out her hand for a necklace as Ellie passed.

Callie shook her head at the beads and would have said more, but just then the bride-to-be plopped next to her on the couch.

"How's it going?" Val was decked out in a white veil covered with neon-colored condoms. Apparently, it was some kind of weird tradition among the women of Rock Canyon; at least three other women said they'd worn the same tacky veil to their bachelorette parties. They claimed it was good luck, but Callie thought all of it was silly.

"Great." Callie wasn't sure what else to say but was saved when another woman screamed from the doorway.

"Look who's here!"

Becca came into the room in a dress the color of blood, her black-and-red hair swept back into high pig-tails. She wore black-and-white striped tights, visible over the tops of her calf-high boots. Callie thought Becca looked awesome.

And Caroline did have a point; she did look a lot like Kat Dennings, right down to the great boobs.

Self-consciously pulling at the front of her sweater, Callie watched as women began to file into the room. They moved the couches and chairs around into a half circle, and people started sharing laps when they ran out of other places to sit. When everyone was quiet, Becca stepped in front.

"Good evening, ladies." She held the handle of a black bag on wheels and bent down to open it. "Are we ready to get naughty?"

The room cheered, including Val, who'd officially blown out Callie's eardrum.

Becca spread a tablecloth across the nearby coffee table, and Callie leaned forward, trying to figure out what the design was...just before she burst out laughing. Tiny hearts and penises decorated it. Callie wondered where the hell Becca had bought fabric like that; she must have ordered it online.

"First, I'm going to talk about intimate accessories. These are your flavored lubes"—several colored tubes were set across the cloth—"then your massage oils"—metal containers and a pink spikey glove were added—"and finally your *tools*."

When Becca finished laying out the items, she described each and its purpose. Callie had assumed she'd be bored, but she found herself tuning into everything Becca said—and picturing Everett more than once.

"The lube comes in strawberry, raspberry, and watermelon and is perfect for body-tasting. And it's safe for all those *intimate* areas." Becca winked.

Callie imagined having Everett on his back, naked and hard. She'd pour a little lube into her hand, warming it between her palms before she lovingly stroked him from base to tip, her hands sliding over him easily until she leaned over, adding her mouth to the mix—

Caroline pinched her side. "Callie will do it!"

"Do what?" Callie said.

"I need a volunteer to try this next item." Becca came over and pulled Callie to her feet before handing her a bottle and a bag of cotton swabs. "You just take this bottle of Fired Up and squirt two pumps onto a Q-Tip. Don't use any more than that, or you might become uncomfortable."

There were a few giggles around the room, and Callie had a bad feeling about where she was supposed to put it. "Um…uncomfortable where?"

More snickers sounded. "You just dab it on your clit, and then come back and tell us how it feels."

Callie flushed and handed the stuff back to her. "You can pick someone else."

"It's not bad; I promise." Becca held the bottle out for her again, but Callie shook her head. Taking pity on Callie, Becca patted her arm. "Okay."

Caroline groaned as Callie sat back down, and Becca picked Ellie in her stead. "Just leave them in the bathroom in case anyone else wants to try it throughout the night."

Ellie did a little shimmy all the way down the hall, and the room burst into hysterical laughter.

"Why didn't you do it? That stuff is awesome. It makes you all…" Caroline gave her an eye-rolling, mouth-open expression and started moaning.

"Okay, Sally, can it."

"While we wait for Ellie to come back, let's talk about masturbation," Becca continued. "I, for one, am happy to live in a time when a woman can take control of her sexuality and her own orgasms. For some people in long-term relationships, this is a good thing. A lot can play into how often we have sex, and men can face a lack of interest too. We all remember the old headache commercial, but the truth is, it's not just women who can lose their sex drives. Sometimes, you have to shake things up in the bedroom to rekindle passion.

"Take this little baby." Becca held up a black battery pack and cord leading to a spiky blue circle of silicone. "This is the Builder Duo Three Thousand. Now, the Builder doubles as a vibrating cock ring for couples, or"—she popped off the ring to show a silver egg-shaped vibrator—"a do-it-yourself battery-operated buddy. You can also buy different sleeves, like the Gripper"—Becca slipped what looked like an octopus arm over the vibrator, complete with little suction cups—"the Lizard, the Porpoise, and the Porcupine."

"Wow, who knew spikes were sexy?" Caroline asked.

"Feel it. It's supple, and mixed with the vibration, it's amazing." Becca brought it over and turned it on for Caroline to touch, a sheepish grin on her face. "I love mine."

Callie eyed the spiky sleeve and didn't think it looked sexy at all. Or comfortable.

Just then Ellie came back from the bathroom, and the room broke into cheers.

"How does it feel?"

"It's like...cold? And then hot, with some tingling." Ellie did another little wiggle that had the room in hysterics.

"Just give it ten minutes, and it'll have you really squirming. Perfect if your partner wants to play with you or if you want to play with him. Just give his tip a little dab"—Becca winked at the room, proving she was truly comfortable with any subject—"and stroke away."

They moved on, and Becca passed around each item she demonstrated. There were glass dildos with tattoos, and vibrators with piercings. Callie was mortified, especially when a rubbery sex aid called "Coco" started making the rounds.

"She's the perfect companion for a blow job, ensuring that your hand won't tire and your gag reflex won't ruin the fun."

Okay, there's never a good enough reason to say "gag reflex."

Handing the wiggly, pink thing—"Coco"—off to Caroline, Callie got up to use the bathroom.

Luckily, half the room was already hammered and had forgotten about Callie's failed demonstration—thank God. The last thing she wanted was to listen to cat calls and teasing, no matter if they thought it was all in good fun. Being sober in a room of giggling, sex-crazed women had to be one of the dimensions of hell that Buffy never mentioned.

Callie locked the bathroom door and went to the sink to splash some water on her face. As she dried it with one of the towels, the little bottle of Fired Up caught her eye.

No one has to know you tried it.

Curiosity was a dangerous thing, especially when Callie remembered how Ellie had been squirming in her chair. Picking up the bottle, Callie read the ingredients. It was made with basic stuff, including peppermint.

How bad could it be?

AT BUCK'S, HALF a dozen poker tables were set up for Justin and his friends. Each table held about four men, and they rotated two players out every three games.

Everett sat at a table playing with Justin, Eric Henderson, and Jared Brown. Eric ran Buck's Shot Bar for his dad, and Jared had been Justin's best friend since elementary school. It had actually surprised Everett that Justin had picked him to be best man instead of Jared, but Jared didn't seem to mind.

Despite the fact that Everett was currently on a winning streak, he'd have rather been with Callie, even if they weren't doing anything at all. He'd been trying to figure out what she was hiding and why she didn't like taking her shirt off. She seemed fit and felt good, from what he could tell. He had his own body issues, especially after the fire, but what were Callie's? He thought she was beautiful.

"It's your call, Rhett." Justin tossed back another swig of his beer casually, but after years of playing games with him, Everett knew his brother's tell. Anytime he bluffed, he was doing something with his mouth: drinking, chewing gum, or biting his lip.

Everett glanced down at his cards and smirked. "Call."

"Son of a bitch," Jared said, folding.

"He could be bluffing," Eric said.

Everett showed his cards—a full house. Justin cursed and dropped his hand on the table. "I'd call you a damn cheat, but I know how good you are."

Everett chuckled as he swept the chips toward him. They had been playing poker since they were kids, but back then, it had been for Halloween candy and jelly beans. Their mom's four brothers, all younger than her, had come for Christmas one year and had gotten a kick out of teaching their nephews to play.

"I think that's my last hand anyway." Everett dumped the chips into his bucket as he stood up. Each man had shown up with a hundred-dollar buy-in to help pay for everything. After that, it was on them how much they played.

The men around the table groaned.

"Come on, man, it's only nine thirty," Jared said. "Besides, I want a chance to win my money back."

"You've had two and a half hours to win it back. Face it, buddy, my brother whooped all our asses."

"I'll see you all later." Everett made his way over to the table where Sam Weathers was playing cashier. Taking his cash, a little over four hundred for the last couple of hours, Everett headed out to his truck.

After climbing inside and warming it up, Everett grabbed his phone from the floorboards. It had been dying earlier, so he'd left it in the truck to charge. There was a missed call from an out-of-area number and a text message.

It was from Callie.

Why do some women find sweaty, half-naked men gyrating all over them appealing?

What the fuck? Where the hell was she? Everett's fingers flew as he typed. *No idea. I don't swing that way.* Then, after debating how she might take it, he added, *I thought you were staying in.*

The minute he sent it, he dropped his forehead to his steering wheel and groaned. Did that text make him sound like a jealous, controlling asshole? Well, at least one of those descriptions was right. His phone beeped.

I needed to get out of my head. So I let Caroline drag me to Valerie's bachelorette party.

Was that a good thing or a bad thing? Had she been thinking of him and wanting to put the brakes on whatever they had going, or...

Maybe she hadn't been able to stop thinking about him.

Trying to seem casual, he typed, *Did it work?*

Beep. He read her message and his heart skidded to a halt.

No. I can't stop thinking about you. ;-)

His heartbeat came back like a freight train, the exhilaration of her words bringing him up off the steering wheel to drum a beat on the dashboard.

When he finished celebrating, he replied, *I'd say I was sorry, but I'm not. I can't stop thinking of you either. ;-)*

CALLIE LIMPED INTO her house with a black bag sporting the Sweet Tarts Boutique logo in one hand and her phone in the other. She was actually glad she'd gone to the party, even if the strippers had killed every tingly feeling the Fired Up gel had created. After everything with Tristan, she'd never had her own bachelorette party, but she imagined it would have been a lot like Valerie's. Except for the strippers. They were just so slimy and fake.

Unlike Everett's texts.

She still couldn't believe she'd been brave enough to text him the truth, that she couldn't stop thinking of him. When he'd taken so long to reply, she'd assumed she'd freaked him out.

But she hadn't. Instead, she'd ended up sitting in the back of the all-male revue, glued to her phone as she'd gone back and forth with Everett for the last hour. It had started with her making fun of the girls waving their dollar bills and his telling her how glad he was that Justin had opted for a guy's night of poker and beer, and grown into questions about their likes and dislikes. All the way home, they'd traded texts, much to Caroline's irritation, since Callie wouldn't tell her who she was talking to, but Callie wasn't ready to talk about Everett. Not yet.

The last text she'd sent had been to ask what he was going to spend all of his poker winnings on. Just as she knelt down to greet Ratchet, her phone beeped.

"What do you think he said, Ratch?" She turned her face in time to avoid a lick on the mouth and stood up.

As she flicked her thumb over the screen, she read, *Our first date, for one thing.*

If she was a romantic, she'd have sighed. *I thought we were already on date number three. Hiking up a mountain, remember? And food and a movie usually constitute a date.*

She made it to her bedroom with minimal hobbling since the Tylenol she'd taken in the car had started to kick in. Callie set the Sweet Tarts bag on her nightstand as she changed into her pajamas, loving that it was finally cool enough to wear her soft flannel ones with sock monkeys all over them.

Her phone went off again, and she climbed into bed before reading it.

That was hanging out, not a date. Dates require leaving the house.

Flipping off the bedside light, she smiled. *Duly noted.*

Settling back against the pillows, she listened to Ratchet's panting and thought about how surprised Becca had been when she'd placed her order. Luckily, everything she had wanted, Becca had brought with her—and she'd promised discretion.

When Caroline had asked on the way home what Callie had bought, she'd told her bath salts, which was so far from the truth she'd had to smother a laugh.

Now, sitting next to the bed was a bottle of Fired Up gel and Tasty Lube in strawberry. She'd bought the stuff because, eventually, Everett and she were going to end up in bed together. And when it happened, she wanted to be prepared.

Her cell started blaring Cole Swindell, the ringtone she'd picked for Everett that afternoon. "Hi," she said, holding the phone up to her ear.

"Hey, you home?"

His deep voice rose gooseflesh on her body. "I just got home a little while ago."

"What are you doing?"

"I am lying in bed, listening to Ratchet breathe."

"Sounds like fun times."

Her stomach fluttered nervously. "Just how everyone should spend a Friday night."

"So besides the strippers, what else did you girls get into?"

"Oh yeah. We went to a biker bar and got tattoos—"

"Speaking of tattoos, what's the one on your hip?"

Callie's breath caught. "When did you see that?"

"You shirt rode up on the couch last night."

Callie rubbed her hip. Originally, it had been a heart with Tristan's and her initials woven together inside, but she'd had it covered years ago with her mother's name and the date she'd died. The black, broken heart had destroyed any evidence of his name, but she'd never talked about its meaning with anyone anyway.

"It's a tattoo for my mom."

"I'm sorry."

"It's okay, really. It's been a long time."

"Yeah, but losing a parent never gets easier. I lost my mom when I was a teenager, and it still eats at me."

"How did she die?"

"Car accident. She rolled off an embankment during a snowstorm, and no one found her until the next day. They said she died on impact, but the thought's always there, wondering if someone had found her just a little earlier…"

Maybe she'd be alive now. She knew exactly what he was saying. She'd had the same *what-if* thoughts too. "I understand how you feel. My mom was…attacked, and I always wonder if I had come home just a few minutes sooner, maybe she'd be okay."

"I've learned that you'll drive yourself crazy looking back and wondering what you could have done better. You're better off learning from it and moving on."

The conversation was quickly spiraling, and she didn't want to give him a chance to ask about her mother's attack or her own past. God, why had she opened up the can of worms by asking about his mother's accident?

Because it's natural to ask your partner about his past.

"So after the tattoo parlor, we were going to run off to Vegas and elope with a couple of Duck Dynasty wannabes, but then we found out they had bad credit."

Everett laughed and the tightness in her chest eased. "Well, that's too bad. Sorry your plans fell through and you got stuck with me."

"I wouldn't call it stuck…"

"Brat."

"No, actually, I started the evening off surrounded by drunk, screaming women and dildos."

"Come again?"

"They arranged for Becca from Sweet Tarts to come in and do a sex toy demonstration. If you liked the stuff, you could buy it."

Everett's laughter exploded over the line. "Get anything good?"

He was messing with her and she knew it, but she blushed anyway. Wanting to throw him off, she lowered her voice in what she hoped was a sexy purr. "Wouldn't you like to know."

"I would, actually," he said, purring right back, the sound sending bolts of desire between her legs.

"Well, too bad."

He chuckled, and she smiled in response. "Now I'm imagining all kinds of gadgets and gizmos—"

"I didn't buy any toys," she said swiftly.

"Oh really?"

"Yeah, they were too much. One of them was even pierced, and I just can't imagine why anyone would want that."

"I guess because some women are into pierced tongues and…other things," he said.

An image of a Prince Albert piercing burned into her brain. "Ugh, and now I'm picturing it."

"Sorry."

"Wait, were you trying to save my delicate sensibilities?"

"Trying."

"Well, you didn't quite succeed, but that was very chivalrous of you."

"I'm chivalrous all the time," he said, sounding affronted.

"Of course you are." Callie smirked.

"Why do I get the feeling you're mocking me?"

"Not mocking. Placating."

"My mistake."

A few moments went by before she said, "Flavored lube."

"What?"

"I bought flavored lube." Callie thought she heard him suck in his breath. "And this gel called Fired Up."

"What does it do?"

"It…it…you put it on…" She couldn't seem to form a coherent sentence and finally blurted, "It makes your clit tingle."

Silence stretched on the other end, and she wondered if the phone had given her false confidence to say stupid things.

But then he asked softly, "Have you tried it yet?"

It was her turn to hold her breath. "Earlier at the party, but it's stopped working by now."

Callie could almost hear the wheels in his head turning before he asked, "Wanna try it again?"

Chapter Fifteen

EVERETT WAITED, HALF expecting Callie to hang up on him. From the moment she'd mentioned being in bed, his mind had been racing with thoughts of her in slinky nighties or nothing at all. And then she'd turned flirty and sassy, so unlike the shy yet friendly woman he'd come to know.

Had he pushed too hard? Is that why the phone had dropped into dead silence?

And then she said, "Hang on."

"Okay, what would you like me to hang on to?"

"Smart ass. I'm going to try it again."

Holy fucking shit balls.

His cock was raging under his quilt, and he slipped his hand beneath.

It was quiet for a few seconds, and his heart hammered so loudly in his ears, he almost missed it when she spoke. "I'm taking off the plastic."

"That's hot," he said, laughing.

"I know."

Part of him was sure she was just messing with him, but what if she wasn't? His tongue moistened his dry lips as he waited for more.

"I'm pulling down my pajama pants. And now I'm taking some of the gel and rubbing it on me."

Her breathing hitched as she spoke, and Everett closed his eyes, focusing on the soft sound of her voice. The little puffs were driving him crazy, and he had to know what was happening.

"How does it feel?"

"It's cold right now, but it'll warm up in a minute." Her tone was husky, warm, and he wanted to hear more. She had taken them down this road. If he played along, would it scare her off? It wasn't the first time he'd had phone sex, but somehow with Callie, it felt new.

Taking a leap of faith, he said, "Why don't you try rubbing it into your clit?"

The line was dead quiet, and he was sure she had hung up.

"Okay."

He released the breath he hadn't even known he'd been holding. "Tell me everything."

"Like how I'm sliding my hand into my pajama pants?"

He pushed his hand under his boxers and waited for more.

"Or that my fingers are inside my panties and pushing between my legs?"

"Christ." Everett was hard as a rock and shocked as hell. He was sure she'd have told him to fuck off, but considering how nervous she was when they were together, he imagined this was good for her. Sex on the phone gave her a chance to experiment, to test the waters and yet remain in control.

Taking his cock in his hand, he started stroking his length, imagining her blonde curls spread over her white, lacy pillow. Her eyes closed and her lips wet and parted.

"I'm rubbing my clit in short, fast circles, and it feels so good."

"Fuck, Callie, do you know how much I wish I was there right now?"

"Oh yeah?" Her voice was siren sweet and just as enthralling. "What would you do if you came in and found me like this, playing with myself?"

She was practically inviting him to play, and he was more than happy to jump in and share his fantasies. "I'd cover your hand with mine and lacing our fingers together."

"Hmm, that seems counterproductive."

Everett smiled at her teasing. "I wasn't finished."

"Oh, well then, please continue."

"I'd move our fingers in a small circle over your clit until you were moaning, and then I'd take over, using just my thumb as I slipped one finger inside you, then two."

"Now that my hand is free, I'd slip it under the back of your shirt and down your boxers to grab your ass." Her words made him close his eyes, and he could almost feel her touch. "I'd push at the top of them until they were around your ankles."

"How do you know I'm wearing boxers?"

"Because it's my fantasy."

"You've been fantasizing about me?" God, he hoped so, because he'd been doing nothing but all week.

"Oh, yes, just about every night...and during most of the bachelorette party."

Holy hell, she'd been thinking about him while looking at sex toys? His strokes became faster.

"Well, in *my* fantasy, your clothes disappear completely and there's nothing left between us. As I work your clit, I'd curve my fingers inside you until I found your sweet spot. The whole time I'd be watching you, your eyes half closed and your lips soft and open. I'd bend over and kiss you, flicking my tongue inside your mouth while my hand kept going."

Her breathing had become rapid puffs that he relished, but before he could continue, she spoke first. "I'd kiss you back, opening my mouth wide, even as my hand slid between us to find your dick. I'd cup your balls, rolling them gently in my hands until I heard you groan. Only then would I slide my hand around your shaft."

He was hanging on her every word, stroking himself as he imagined her with him, doing everything she said.

"I'd break our kiss," she continued, "so I could slide down your body and take you into my mouth, my tongue circling the head of your cock until you were begging me to take you all the way."

Everett pictured Callie with her lips wrapped around him, curls falling around her face, a golden curtain for naughty peek-a-boo. He could feel the pressure inside building as he increased the speed of his stroking.

"Are you tingly yet?" he asked hoarsely.

"OH, YES," SHE whispered back, eyes closed as she touched herself. The low drumbeat between her legs built in tempo as she taunted and teased Everett and herself. She'd never had phone sex before, but it wasn't as awkward as she'd always thought it would be. Listening to Everett's husky words and the hitch in his breath was erotic and sexy and turned her on like crazy.

"Imagine I'm laying you down on my bed, and I slip my hand up your skirt."

"I thought I was naked."

"Well, now you're in a skirt."

Callie laughed a little, taken out of the moment. "I don't wear skirts."

"It's my turn; you hush," he said sternly.

"Yes, sir." She smiled.

"As I was saying, my fingers sneak underneath to touch you again. You're so wet, I want to be inside you now, but I just put my mouth on you instead, sucking and licking you until I can feel you arching to meet my mouth. I'll flick my tongue over your clit, taking it between my teeth lightly. I can feel your legs trembling as I love you, fingers and mouth everywhere."

Callie pressed hard into her clit, rubbing faster as the pressure built, his words crashing into her. A soft moan escaped her lips as the first wave of orgasm washed over her.

"Oh, God, Callie," he said, his voice strained.

A few seconds later, she heard his low groan and rapid breathing. "Come for me, Rhett. Please."

He chuckled in her ear, and it was like a caress across her skin. "I already did."

She stretched and groaned. "I've never done that before."

"What, phone sex?" he asked.

"Yeah. Hang on, okay?"

"Sure."

She got up and walked into her bathroom to wash her hands. When she flipped on the lights, she squinted at herself in the mirror. Her cheeks were flushed, and her hair looked like it had been messed by actual hands.

Callie wondered if Everett looked just as rumpled.

She climbed back into bed and grabbed the phone. "Still there?"

"Yep," he said. "But I think you wore me out."

"Oh, I did, did I?" she said, playing with her hair.

"I wish you were here with me, so I could hold you."

Her chest tightened. Part of her wondered how she would be able to look him in the eye when she saw him again. She wanted him, so badly, and had thought of little else, but was she ready to have him over, in her bed? To be intimate with a man, and not just fuck and leave, would be a big step. Tristan was the last man she'd shared anything more with, and she definitely didn't want to think about *him* right now.

But Everett had been so understanding, so amazing, that part of her wanted to throw caution to the wind and say, "Come over."

"Really? Now?" he asked.

Holy shit, did you just say that out loud?

"Oh, I…"

He didn't say anything, as if waiting for her to be clear.

Why had she said that aloud? Panic started to claw up her throat as she tried to speak, prepared to tell him that she wasn't ready.

"It's up to you." Everett was clearly letting her off the hook. "I'm okay with lying here, just talking. But if you want me to come over, I promise I won't touch you unless you want me to."

Trust. He was asking her to trust him with her safety, in her sanctuary. She hadn't slept next to a man in seven years, but the thought of having Everett's arms around her was a temptation she couldn't resist.

"Come over," she repeated.

"On my way."

Callie stared at the clock while she waited for the sound of Everett's truck and was amazed when it only took him about six minutes to pull up outside. Climbing out of bed, she headed down to the front door, ignoring the twinges of pain in her ankle. She opened the door before he even reached the top step of her porch.

His lips quirked in an amused pout. "Were you listening for me?"

"Yes, what took you so long?" she said.

"Had to grab my toothbrush." He held up a backpack.

"That looks like a lot more than a toothbrush." She stepped back against the door to let him inside.

As he passed by, he stopped and leaned over her. "I packed a change of clothes for tomorrow."

"Tomorrow?" she repeated, unable to look away from his face in the moonlight.

"Yeah, our date is at six A.M." His mouth was only an inch away and driving her crazy. "So we'd better get some sleep, because I don't want you whining that you're tired."

"I get up at three thirty every morning." Why was he just hovering like that? Why wouldn't he just kiss her?

He seemed to be waiting for something and suddenly, his words came crashing back. *I won't touch you unless you want me to.*

Reaching up behind his neck, she looped her arms around his shoulders, bringing his mouth down to hers. She traced his lips with her tongue until they opened and she pushed her way inside. He finally circled her waist with his arms, pulling her tight against his hard body as he met each thrust of her tongue. Callie ignored everything around them, lost in the warmth of Everett.

Suddenly, something flew into the side of her head and she jerked away from Everett as she felt movement in her hair. Screaming, Callie slapped at whatever it was, while Everett flipped on the light.

"What the hell? Callie, hang on. Let me look."

Callie tried to hold still even as she felt whatever it was struggling in the strands of her hair. And it was big.

"Is it a bat? What—"

Everett pulled her snarled curls apart, and something fell out into his hand, twitching. It looked like a moth, but it was twice as big as any moth she'd ever seen.

"Holy shit, *that* was in my hair? Is it mutated or something? Moths aren't that big normally."

Callie realized that Everett's shoulders were shaking. In fact, his whole body was rumbling with silent, suppressed laughter, and she scowled at him. "Why are you laughing? I was just attacked by a gargantuan insect, and my hair actually snared it!"

Everett was wheezing as he walked out onto the porch and set the moth on the railing. She was tempted to slam the door on him and his mirth, but then she thought about the way she must've looked, screaming as she danced around, bad ankle and all, flapping her hands at her head.

Her lips twitched, but just a little.

"Okay, ha-ha, it was funny." She shut the door behind him as he came back inside.

"I'm sorry," he said, sucking in air.

"No, you're not."

"I am. I shouldn't have laughed while you were being attacked by a big-ass moth."

She knew he was messing with her, and she sniffed derisively. "No, you shouldn't have. It wasn't very chivalrous of you."

"Pardon me, my lady," he said, bending over to pick her up in his arms. "Very unknight-like."

"Unknight-like?"

"Hey, I've read a medieval romance or two. And Sean Connery is a bad ass."

Callie burst out laughing as Everett carried her against his chest, past Ratchet, who sat at the edge of the hallway watching them.

"Come on, Ratchet," Everett called over his shoulder. Callie leaned around him to find her dog following behind them.

"He used to growl and warn people off if they even looked at me funny, but you pick me up and he just looks bored."

"That's because he knows you're safe with me," Everett said. He poked his head through the door of her bedroom. "Wow, this is not what I was imagining."

Callie glanced around the room defensively. "What were you expecting?"

"I don't know. Simple lines, nothing girly."

Callie blushed. A down comforter with blue and purple flowers lay rumpled on her bed. A bulbous lamp the same shade of purple sat on her nightstand, which was part of her mother's oak bedroom set. On the walls were different country music star art canvases that she'd special ordered and gotten signed over the years, and in the corner was a guitar signed by every member of Diamond Rio.

"This looks like the room of a fifteen-year-old girl." Everett set her on the bed, still looking around the room in amusement.

"Hey." Callie was insulted. "It does not."

"Yeah, I'm pretty sure my high school girlfriend had that same George Strait poster," Everett said, pointing.

"First of all, that is a canvas, not a poster. Therefore, it is art."

"Um…"

"And second of all, every *piece of art* on this wall is pretty to look at." Callie pointed to Luke Bryan, Chuck Wicks, and Billy Currington, all live at their concerts. Concerts she'd seen from the front row and backstage.

"So this is what girls feel like when they walk into a teenage boy's room and see a centerfold on the wall." Everett played somber, but she saw a mocking twinkle in his eye.

"You…they aren't even close to being naked." Callie reached back for a pillow.

"I don't know…Billy's shirt is riding a little—hey!" he said when she hit him in the face with the pillow.

She swung again, giggling when he tried to block her aim. Callie squealed as he took the pillow from her and tried to scramble back across the bed but gasped when she put pressure on her ankle.

Everett sat on the bed and picked up her ankle, clucking his tongue. "See what happens when you're ornery?"

"You're the ornery one. I was just defending the integrity of Billy Currington's abs."

"I think he's safe from my scrutiny, at least for now."

Without warning, Everett unzipped his sweatshirt and peeled it off, revealing a plain gray T-shirt that hugged his shoulders and upper back, showing off mouthwatering muscles.

But when he started pulling his T-shirt up over his head, Callie panicked. "What are you doing?"

Everett pulled the shirt all the way off, and Callie sucked in her breath. Yes, the muscles were definitely impressive, but it was the red, puckered flesh along his side that made her want to wrap her arms around him. It was one thing to touch the scars, but to actually see them...well, all she wanted to do was kiss her way along the scars and tell him they were beautiful. That *he* was beautiful.

"I figured you were going to see them eventually." His tone was flat, emotionless. Callie hated that he thought his scars might be a deal-breaker, that she might find him less desirable because of them. Which would never happen; she thought his scars were beautiful.

Isn't that the same way you feel?

But she had good reason. Anyone who thought Everett was anything less than a sexy hero was a fucking idiot.

Everett was holding himself ridged, as if waiting for her to say something. At that moment, Callie realized that Everett didn't just want her; he needed her.

Was she the only one who saw his scars for what they were? A mark of his selfless, heroic nature?

She had been so engrossed with her own hang-ups, she'd ignored the fact that Everett had experienced hell too. And even though he seemed like he had it all together, he was human. He was lonely.

"Come here, please," she said.

Everett kicked off his shoes and lay on his back next to her. Without waiting for an invitation, Callie curled up against his side tentatively and slid her palm across his chest until her fingertips rested on the edge of his scarred tissue. Callie could feel how tense he was and knew he was holding his breath. "Relax. It feels like I'm lying on a statue."

Everett released a deep breath, and she took a risk, tracing the raised and puckered flesh with her fingers. She flattened her palm against his side, waiting for him to tense up again, but he didn't. So she stroked his skin, her cheek resting against his warm chest, and sighed.

"What was that sound for?" he asked.

"You feel good," she said. "Solid and strong."

And he makes you feel safe.

She felt his lips against her forehead. "What can I say? I work out."

"And eat your Wheaties, obviously." She ran her hand across his abs and laughed when he flexed under her touch.

"Don't forget, drink my milk and *eats me spinach*."

If anyone had told her a week ago that she would be lying in her bed with a hot, half-naked Everett Silverton, she would have thought they were cracked out. But now, with her head on his chest and his gentle fingers stroking her back, nothing felt more right.

"Thank you for coming over," she said drowsily.

"Any time you need me, I'll be there. Okay?"

"Okay."

Chapter Sixteen

EVERETT SNUCK OUT of bed while Callie continued to sleep, smiling as he listened to her and her dog snore softly in unison. He'd said he was going to wake her early, but when the time came, he hadn't had the heart to disturb her.

Instead, he drove into town to the Local Bean Coffee Shop and grabbed a *Rock Canyon Press* on the way in. As he stood in line, waiting to order, he came across a teaser on the front page:

Who was the hottie that hero Everett Silverton was seen shopping with? Turn to page seven to find out!

Everett ripped the paper open and saw an article, along with a picture of him and Callie, bent over, picking up canned goods in Hall's. He wracked his brain, trying to remember if someone had been watching them, but he couldn't remember anything besides Callie's face.

Speculation has been running rampant about who Everett has been seen courting on numerous occasions this past

*week. Several sources are convinced our cool-as-hell radio
DJ Callie Jay has stolen this war hero's heart. The two were
seen bonding over spilled cans on aisle eight just two days
ago, and an eye-witness spotted them making out in Everett's truck outside of Callie's work the next morning. And in
case you need any more proof that these two are shacking
up, this author has since learned that Callie left her Jeep at
work to ride off into the sunset with her Prince Charming!*

*What do you think, dear readers? Could there be
another Rock Canyon wedding in our future? Stay tuned
for more in the "Caverett" chronicles.*

Had she really Brangelina'd their names?

"Next," Gracie McAllister called.

He looked up and realized she was talking to him.

"Sorry—can I get two pumpkin lattes and"—he
craned his neck to look in her pastry case—"two vanilla
spice muffins?"

Gracie smiled and leaned across the counter. "If
you're buying for Callie, she prefers the cheese Danish.
Just saying."

Dammit! Everett knew it was a trap, but he still wanted
to get what Callie would like. "I'll take one of those instead."

Gracie crowed, drawing the attention of the whole
shop.

"Knock it off." Everett handed her a twenty-dollar bill,
praying she would stop laughing like a loon.

"Oh, I can't wait to tell Gemma. She is going to die."

Scowling, Everett took his change and went to wait for
his order. He ignored some of the stares, though whether
they were because of his scars or the article, he didn't care.

When he'd first come home, he'd been so angry about everything that he'd lashed out at a few people who had blatantly stared at his scars. He'd finally been able to replace the anger that came from their obvious rudeness with humor, which he'd found could be just as effective at making people look away.

Last night, when he'd taken off his shirt, he'd been expecting Callie to pity him, despite her previous kind words about his scars. In the past, he'd tried not to draw attention to his burned skin when he was seeing a woman, just shut off the light and get to business, but with Callie, he wanted more than fumbling in the dark and a quick release.

So he'd shown her everything and she'd made him feel normal, like she didn't even see the scars, only it had been better than that; she'd seen them, and they didn't faze her.

"Here you go, Everett," Gracie called.

She held out a drink carrier and baggy to him, and when Everett reached out to take it, Gracie added quietly, "Tell Callie I said hi."

Everett gave Gracie a warning look, but her grin never wavered. "I will."

Everett pushed out of the crowded coffee shop and went to his truck, wondering why Callie and he were drawing so much interest. Was it because they were both private people?

He drove back to Callie's house, thinking how little he knew about her. Everything he did know was superficial, except for her mom being dead and her history with alcohol, but even that she'd even been vague about. She knew about his past, about his best friend and his scars; he didn't even know her parents' names.

Give her time. You've only known her two weeks.

He knew that, but for him, it felt like longer. Like he'd been waiting for her forever. It reminded him of the things his mother used to say about love and soul mates. She'd been a firm believer in fate, that one day, when the person who was meant for you in every way was near, it would hit you like a lightning bolt. Everett had always been happy thinking he'd eventually find someone to love and share a life with, but after meeting Callie, he understood exactly what his mother meant; Callie was meant for him.

He just needed to be patient, to let her learn to trust him. He knew she was starting to. And once she let go, she'd realize that he was meant for her too.

Everett pulled into Callie's driveway and gathered up their breakfast. When he came through the door, Ratchet was waiting for him, his large tail thumping against the ground.

"Sorry, buddy, this isn't for you."

Everett ignored the dog's snort and headed down the hall to find Callie still in bed, spread out on her back, the covers twisted around her legs. Her hair half-hid her face, except for her mouth, which hung open.

Everett set the bag and drink carrier on the nightstand next to her black Sweet Tarts bag and lay down next to her. He gazed down at her face, before sweeping over the slope of her neck and chest. One of the buttons of her pajama top had come open, spreading the neck open.

And that's when he saw it: a white puckered scar, about half an inch long.

Could it be from surgery? Had Callie been hurt in an accident?

Or had she been there when her mother was attacked?

As if sensing his eyes on her, Callie twisted toward him, her eyes opening slowly. "Are you watching me sleep, creeper?"

Everett laughed. "Actually, I ran out to get caffeine and breakfast. I was just about to wake you up."

"What'd you bring me?" she mumbled, squinting at him.

"Pumpkin latte and cheese Danish." He pulled the drink out of the carrier and held it out to her.

Callie's eyes popped open. "How did you know I liked cheese Danishes?"

"Gracie told me." Everett took the page from newspaper containing Miss Know It All's column from his sweatshirt pocket. "We made the paper, and she guessed that I was buying you breakfast."

Callie groaned and took the paper from him, ignoring the drink as she sat up and rubbed her eyes. "I'm surprised Gemma and Gracie haven't called me on three-way yet to find out what's going on."

"I think they're giving us some privacy," he said.

"Yeah, right. Gracie is going to badger me until I give them every detail. She's like a very tenacious Chihuahua."

"I thought you two were friends."

"We are, but she can be a lot to take in sometimes."

"Yeah, tact isn't exactly on the top of her vocabulary list," Everett said.

"Oh, God, what else did she do?" Callie flopped back onto the bed with a groan.

"Nothing, really." Everett threaded one of Callie's blonde ringlets around his finger. "She was semidiscreet."

"I take it back; she is my mortal enemy. Initiate *Mortal Kombat* fighting stance." She punched the air above her in some kind of crazy fighting style.

Everett held out her drink to her again, chuckling. "Has anyone ever told you that you're adorable when you imitate nineties video games?"

"No, but thank you." Callie sat up and accepted the drink. After taking a sip, she made an "mmm" sound that went straight to his groin. "You were right about these pumpkin lattes."

"You'll find I am right quite a bit." Everett grinned when she made a face.

"Spoken like a true man."

"I'm sorry. Did I come off as an alien previously? I'd hate to give the wrong impression." Mock sincerity oozed from his tone.

"Ha-ha, funny man. I just meant that despite the several times you've gone all he-man on me, you aren't a douche bag."

"Hey, now, why is it when women tell men they are always right, it's acceptable, but when a man says it, he's a douche?" Everett shook his head, frowning sadly. "I smell sexism at its worst."

"Oh, please, men were never oppressed and denied basic rights like voting," Callie said, amending, "Well, not white men, at least."

"Okay, this conversation is spiraling, so I'm just going to drink my latte and stare at the prettiest girl in the room," Everett said.

"Smart man."

"Man, I had no idea how mean you were."

"It's only because you're holding my food hostage." She reached past him for the bag, but he held it away from her.

"Hey, there is a toll." Everett tapped his lips with his other hand to emphasize. "Sugar for sugar."

"And I had no idea what a lame pickup artist *you* were," Callie said, leaning forward, her lips pursed.

Taking her drink from her hand, he ignored her protests as he set it next to his. "I may be a pickup artist, but considering I'm in your bed, I'd say I'm anything but lame."

Callie rolled her eyes and grabbed the bag away from him. "Whatever."

"You only say 'whatever' when you don't have a comeback."

Callie said nothing, just shooting him a glare. He gave her an answering grin as he bit into his food, licking the crumbs from his lips.

"So where's this first date going to take place?" Callie asked.

"I thought we'd go for another hike and have a picnic. It's almost ten, so if we hurry and get ready, it will be time for lunch."

"Did you forget about my ankle? I'm not exactly able to climb mountains at this point," she said.

"Have no fear, Whisky. I have a plan."

"THIS IS YOUR plan?"

Callie had gotten ready in record time for their picnic, and while he'd showered at her place, she'd added an ankle wrap to help give her extra support. But an hour and a half after she'd agreed to this harebrained first date, she found herself staring down at Everett, who was squatted down before her, motioning for her to climb onto his back.

"Yep, hop on."

"You cannot carry me wherever we're going," Callie protested.

"Sure I can; it's not far."

Callie shook her head. "You have lost your damn mind!"

She unclipped Ratchet's leash. She usually let him walk off-leash when there was no one else around, and this trail by the river was definitely remote.

"Woman, get your cute little ass on my back and stop your caterwauling." Everett had an evil gleam in his eye that made her wary. Not that she was actually scared of him, but he did have a mischievous side that usually didn't bode well for her.

"If you don't cooperate, I'll just have to use my signature move and haul you off like a caveman."

Callie pulled the backpack with their lunch onto her back and climbed up. Once she was situated on his back, she reached up and yanked on his ear lightly.

"Ow!"

"That will teach you to threaten me," she said, wrapping her arms around his shoulders.

Everett's hands supported her thighs as he lifted her higher on his back. "You ready?"

"As I'll ever be."

Then Callie hung on tight as he started moving. They hiked through the underbrush, and Callie resisted asking Everett if he was tired every five seconds. He'd been the one insisting he could carry her, calling her "woman."

He deserved to suffer.

Callie kept pushing low-hanging branches out of their way and had ducked her head several times already. "Are you trying to take my head off?"

"Nope, I like your head right where it is."

Ten minutes later, they broke through the trees, and Callie let out a soft, "Oh."

"See? You always doubt me."

Everett came to a stop, and Callie slid off his back, hobbling a little until she caught her balance again. She stared out over the rush of rapids in the river and a small waterfall just below. This must have been the place Everett had been talking about the first time they'd met. It was about twenty-five feet above the Snake River and gave her a beautiful view of the canyon, the river, and the trees along the edge.

Everett took the pack from her and pulled out the large flannel blanket she'd said they could use. As he spread it across the flat rock they were standing on, Callie watched him with mixed emotions rushing through her. In just the short time she'd known him, he'd shown her that there were still things worth taking a risk for, whether it was a view or the chance to be close to another person.

It was amazing how comfortable she felt with Everett, almost as if she could see right into his soul. It was ridiculous, of course, but his mix of teasing and gentleness had a way of pulling her out of her shell, of making her feel safe and warm and able to be herself. The girl she used to be before—only better. More aware and not as naïve, but still able to find joy in a little banter and horseplay.

Everett brought out the best in her, traits she'd thought were lost and buried.

"Thank you."

Callie sat down next to him on the blanket and he gave her a puzzled look. "For what?"

"For surprising and delighting me." Callie reached out to cradle the back of his neck and bring him closer to her. Everett didn't resist, and when their lips met, Callie jerked as a shock of electricity shot through her body.

His mouth opened wide, his tongue tracing her lips before thrusting inside. She scooted closer, her arms going around his neck, and pressed her chest to his. Her nipples hardened, and she sighed into his mouth.

Callie found herself being lowered gently onto her back as Everett covered her body, one of his hands gripping her waist. She wanted him to move his hand up and touch her breasts, to relieve the hard nubs, and she arched against him, hoping he would get the message. When his hand finally skimmed up her side, she wanted to cry out, "Hallelujah."

Everett's large palm covered her breast and squeezed gently, kneading her flesh through her long-sleeved cotton shirt. Whimpering against his mouth, she slid her hands down his back, settling on the waistband of his jeans. She needed to be closer to him, to feel him pressed against her, and she hooked her legs around his hips, raising her pelvis to his.

Everett's hand left her breast and traveled down her body, until it reached the top of her jeans. She felt him working the button open and heard the *rrrrft* of the zipper before his warm fingers slid inside.

He broke the kiss, pressing his lips against her cheek, working his way down her neck. Everett didn't try to move her shirt up, just kissing her through it until he reached the tips of her breasts. When his mouth closed over her nipple, tonguing her through her shirt and thin cotton bra, she cried out, gripping the back of his head. Everett sucked and pulled on her flesh, while his hands worked to push her jeans down her hips. She lowered her legs to help him.

The fact that they were out in the open for anyone to see was the last thing on her mind.

All she cared about were Everett's hands on her body.

With her jeans around her knees, it left her open and vulnerable, something she would have hated with anyone else but Everett. But over the last few weeks, he'd changed something inside her, brought a warmth back into her life that she hadn't been prepared for. But it left her sure that Everett was a good man. He proved it with every gesture, in his laughter and eyes, in the way he held her hand and didn't press her for more than she could give.

She knew, deep down, that she needed him, just as she'd needed Ratchet to get her through recovery. But she didn't just need Everett; she wanted him, every part of him.

She trusted him, trusted that he cared about her and would never hurt her, would never betray her trust.

And she wanted to honor that in every way she could.

His mouth lowered, kissing each of her ribs over her shirt, even as he slipped one finger between her legs, circling her clit lightly. Her back bowed at the first shock, trembling with pent-up desire. When that finger pushed into her already wet center, she lifted her hips, biting her lip when the pressure on her ankle sent a zing of pain up her leg.

"Shh, don't move." His mouth was against her belly, and the heat of his breath felt amazing against the cool autumn air. "I'll take care of everything."

Before she could protest, he'd picked up her bound legs and pulled them over his head. Despite his instructions to hold still, she squirmed when he buried his mouth between her legs, pushing his tongue inside her.

God, she'd forgotten how amazing oral sex could be. As he pressed his tongue against her clit, licking the little nub until it almost hurt, her cries rose. His fingers spread her, giving him better access. He took her clit into his mouth and sucked her, just as his finger curled up within, rubbing that sweet spot just inside.

And suddenly she was weightless, lifting off the ground as an orgasm rushed over her. Callie buried her hands in her hair and stared up into the bright blue sky, sure any minute now she was going to float away.

After she came back to herself, she realized Everett was sliding her pants back into place instead of off. She watched him, his face pinched in concentration.

"What about you?"

He finished buttoning her pants and leaned over her, smiling. "Me? I'm hungry. How about you?"

BACK IN THE dirt parking lot a few hours later, Everett helped Callie into his truck, stealing a kiss just before he closed the door. The day had gone better than he'd imagined.

Okay, so maybe not better than he'd *imagined*, if the raging hard-on he'd been sporting most of the day was any indication, but it had still been great. After their picnic, they'd cuddled on the blanket, staring out over the water. All in all, they'd stayed out there longer than he'd expected, but Everett wouldn't have changed a moment of it.

"Come on, Ratchet." Everett loaded the big dog into the back of the truck. Ratchet had shown up the moment the picnic basket was opened, soaking wet and dripping river water on them as he shook off. They'd used the blanket to mop themselves off, and it had given Everett an excuse to pull Callie back against him and wrap her up in his arms again.

Everett jumped into the front seat and reached across for Callie's hand. "Did you have fun?"

Her amber eyes burned brightly at him, and the soft smile on her face stole his breath. "It was a perfect day. Thank you."

Everett kissed her fingers. "See? This is why you should always trust me."

"So I'm learning." Her words hung between them, heavy with meaning. He didn't need her to say what she was thinking out loud; he could hear the gears in her mind turning.

Don't disappoint me.

It was the last thing he wanted to do.

Chapter Seventeen

A WEEK LATER, Callie got out of her Jeep, cursing as she pushed the skirt of her new black dress down. She'd needed to be at Justin and Val's wedding early to make sure the equipment worked fine, but thanks to her friends' meddling, she was nearly twenty minutes later than she should have been.

Damn Gracie and Gemma. If she had just worn the simple black suit like she'd planned, she wouldn't be messing with the hem of her dress, afraid she was going to flash everyone her *good girl*.

At least they had been able to work a miracle on her curls. With several bottles of hair-care products, Gracie had managed to first straighten and then arrange Callie's hair in loose waves over her shoulders. Gemma had helped her perfect the smoky-eyed look she'd kept messing up because her hands were shaking so badly.

"Why are you so nervous?" Gemma had asked.

The truth was that Callie would be seeing Everett for the first time around other people and had no idea what to expect. Would he ask her to dance? Kiss her in public or hold her hand? Or would he be too busy with best-man duties?

Not that she wouldn't be busy herself, but not so busy she'd be able to ignore Everett.

Callie walked into the old Silverton barn where they were having the wedding and reception and stopped in the doorway. Empty stalls along the edges of the huge barn framed wooden benches and the long white strip of cloth being used as an aisle. People were milling around, adding last-minute touches here and there, but Callie didn't see Everett.

Disappointment coursed through her. Despite her protests that she didn't care about dresses and smooth hair, she'd actually been excited for Everett's face when he saw her.

Oh, well, he'd see her soon enough.

Callie saw Justin helping another guest move one of the benches, cursing when he knocked off some kind of decoration on the end. The benches had no backs, but someone had nailed cornucopia horns filled with beautiful arrays of flowers to each end. Callie almost giggled when Justin picked up the decoration he'd dropped and all the flowers fell out. His face flushed an unhealthy shade of purple until Ellie Willis ran over, gathered up the flowers, and patted his arm. If Callie knew Ellie, she was probably telling him to calm the fuck down, and by the way Justin laughed, it had worked.

Farther down the aisle sat a simple white arch, covered with flowers of orange and deep purple and woven through with green vines. Callie looked up toward the hayloft to admire the twinkling white lights and crepe-paper decorations, which prettied up the old barn-wood ceiling and walls. Pictures of Justin and Valerie were hanging around the room in white frames, including one of Justin kneeling in front of Valerie, kissing her stomach.

Just then she spotted Dalton inside one of the empty stalls, working on some wires for the speakers. She headed over to him slowly, walking carefully in the heels Gracie had picked for her, to avoid tweaking her ankle again just when it was starting to feel better.

"How's it going?"

"Almost ready; I just have to—" Dalton looked up at her and stopped talking, his eyes bugging out of his head.

"What?" Callie self-consciously tugged her dress up and then down.

"You…you look…holy shit."

Callie laughed. "Thanks, I think."

She walked around him and pulled her laptop out of the messenger bag she was carrying. Once she was finished hooking up all the wires and cords, she looked up and realized Dalton was still staring at her. "Dalton! Why are you staring at me like that?"

"I'm sorry, it's just…you don't look like you. I mean, you're always pretty, but tonight you're…"

"Beautiful," a deep voice said.

Callie turned and found Everett standing a few feet away, dressed in a black tux that looked tailor-made for him.

"Wow," she said.

"I was thinking the same thing." He began walking toward her with purpose, and her stomach dropped out, anticipation sending tremors through her body as she waited for him to take her in his arms and kiss her in front of God and everyone.

"Everett! I need your help over here!" Justin yelled from across the barn, and Everett stopped, much to Callie's disappointment.

"I'll be back." He gave her a last, heated once-over before loping away.

Dalton made some kind of choking noise, and Callie turned to him, irritated that Everett hadn't even taken the time to kiss her. "What?"

"Nothing." Dalton flipped out a pocket knife to work on some wires.

"Come on, out with it, kid," Callie said playfully.

"I'm not a kid." Dalton jerked to his feet suddenly. "And if you'd dressed up like that for me, I would have taken the time to kiss you."

Callie's mouth dropped open as Dalton walked away. Everett had been right about Dalton's little crush. And she had hurt his feelings.

A few minutes later, people started filing into the barn and were shown which side to sit on. When Dalton came back to finish the setup, neither of them said anything. Callie clicked on the folder labeled "Pre-Ceremony

Music" and the instrumental music for "I Cross My Heart" by George Strait flowed out of the speakers.

Callie searched for Everett and found him helping a stooped older woman to her seat. He looked up, as if sensing she was watching him, and his eyes lit her on fire. The woman said something to him, drawing his attention away once more, and Callie checked the time, her hands shaking.

Her reaction to Everett was sometimes terrifying and more intense than anything she'd ever experienced.

Even with Tristan.

With one minute to the start of the ceremony, Callie got on the mic. "Good evening, ladies and gentleman. We're about ready to start the bridal procession, so if you could please take your seats, we can get this show on the road."

Everett and Justin took their places under the arbor, along with another man in a tux who must have been Justin's best friend, Jared. Watching Everett's expression as he touched Justin's shoulder—the sheer happiness lighting his smile—brought tears to her eyes. He dropped his hand from Justin's shoulder and took a formal position, his gaze straying her way, with that joy still in his smile. Suddenly, she wondered how he'd look at his own wedding. Would he wait for his bride patiently, or would he come down the steps to meet her?

If I was his bride, I wouldn't be walking down the aisle. I'd be running straight into his arms.

The thought was like a punch in the gut. But even though her head told her it was crazy to think like that so soon, she couldn't stop imagining what it would be like to share forever with Everett. To marry him and share a life. To bear his children and experience all the joys she'd once dreamed about before...

Callie wiped at her cheeks and looked down at her laptop. She was making an idiot of herself, blubbering before the bride even walked down the aisle.

Callie clicked on the wedding processional folder and increased the volume just as Val's youngest sister, Ellie, came sashaying down the aisle, her long dark hair spilling down her back in rich curls. The deep forest-green bridesmaid gown was simple chiffon and accented her curvy figure beautifully.

Moments later, Caroline came through the door in a similarly styled gown but in plum purple. Unlike her younger sister's loose hairstyle, Caroline's dark locks were piled up on top of her head, with curls escaping the topknot becomingly. Caroline looked over at Callie and winked.

Once Caroline took her place, Callie switched to the bridal march and everyone stood as Val—a vision in a white empire-waisted bridal gown that hid her baby bump beautifully—came through the door on her father's arm. Her dark hair was slicked back from her face, hidden by a long veil. She was smiling widely as she looked down the aisle at her husband-to-be.

Callie was a little surprised that Edward Willis had shown up today, although Caroline had mentioned that he was trying to make things right with his three daughters. Some of the things she'd heard about him, though, would've been hard for her to forgive, but at least he was making an effort. That counted for something.

The ceremony was relatively short, barely fifteen minutes. When the preacher said, "You may kiss the bride," Callie turned up Faith Hill's "This Kiss," and the whole room cheered.

After Justin and Val walked down the aisle as husband and wife, Callie took the mic. "All right, folks, while the bridal party and immediate family take pictures, I'm going to play some of the bride and groom's favorite songs. Don't mind the people moving the furniture around. They're just setting up for the reception. So mingle, grab a glass of punch, and just have a good time."

Sitting down finally, Callie rested her aching ankle while she watched people meander around.

"Well, look at you, Callie," Mike Stevens said. She glanced up into his warm brown eyes that crinkled at the edges when he smiled. "You are the prettiest girl here."

Callie knew Mike was trying out a new image, that of a "smooth-talking pimp daddy"—his words, not hers—and had even ordered a custom motorcycle from Caroline's boyfriend, Gabe, but Mike just couldn't shake his good-guy roots. No matter how smooth or bad he tried to be.

"Please. How many times have you said that already?"

Mike gave her a sheepish smile. "Fine, but you do look beautiful."

"There he is, the real Michael. We were all wondering what happened to him," Callie said.

"Ha-ha, come on. I haven't been that bad."

"Bad, no. Bordering on a split personality disorder, you betcha."

"Well, being the good guy hasn't done anything for me so far," Mike grumbled.

Just then Callie saw Everett come back inside with Jared. "That's just because you haven't met the right girl, the woman who will appreciate all your charms. Even the nerdy ones."

"Okay, what's up with you? You're practically glowing with happiness."

Everett was heading toward them now, and Callie blushed as he looked between her and Mike.

"I see," Mike said.

Callie knew he'd seen Everett coming toward them and snapped, "You see nothing. And so help me, if you embarrass me, I will tell Gracie. You know how much she loves to hatch revenge plots."

"How did I never see the underlying evilness in you?"

"Hey, Mike," Everett said, coming around the DJ booth. "Can you give us a minute?"

"Sure thing." Mike shot Callie a wink as he backed away.

Before she could say anything, even a hello, Everett had her in his arms. As his mouth covered hers, kissing her thoroughly, she had no choice but to hang on tight. When he pulled away, they were both breathing hard.

"Sorry, but you look so fucking beautiful, and I've been dying to kiss you all night."

"Really, you'll get no complaints from me."

Everett smiled, running his hand along her cheek. "I was supposed to come in and tell you they're right behind me."

"Okay, I'll get the music ready." She started to disengage from his embrace, but he held fast.

"Not just yet."

Callie was smiling when he kissed her again, but she quickly opened her mouth, getting caught up in the stroke of his tongue, his lips, his rock-hard body pressed against her in a tux that made him look like James Bond.

Would anyone miss them if she pulled him back behind the barn?

"Hey, son."

Callie and Everett broke the kiss at Fred's greeting and turned.

"I'm glad to see the two of you on such good terms."

"Maybe now you can stop calling me idjit?" Everett kept his arm around Callie's waist, and she leaned into him.

"The wedding turned out beautifully." Callie reached out to squeeze Fred's hand.

"Here come the bride and groom," someone yelled, and Callie cursed at the interruption.

"I guess that means I have to get back to my best-man duties." Everett gave her one last kiss on the cheek. "I'll come find you when the dancing starts. I don't care if you're in charge of the music; you are taking a break."

Everett sauntered off, but Callie held on to Fred's hand, wanting to be sure he wasn't upset about them.

"I care about him, Fred."

"I know, sweetheart." He squeezed her hand in return, with a smile. "I'd be proud to have my son with a woman like you."

Callie's eyes stung, and she sniffled, trying to hold back tears at his sweet words. "I see where Everett gets his kind heart."

"Oh, I can't take all the credit. My wife was a saint."

"I'm pretty sure Everett has a bit of the devil in him, if his sense of humor is any indication."

"Ah, well, *that* he definitely got from me."

Callie laughed and released his hand before setting the dinner music to play. Tracy Byrd's voice rang out over the speakers as Justin and Valerie came back inside, with the rest of the bridal party behind them. When everyone took their seats for dinner, Callie sought out Everett again, and he blew her a kiss from across the room.

Things seemed to be going so wonderfully, and for the first time in seven years, she was happy.

"So HOW'S IT going with Callie?" Justin asked once they'd finished dinner and were getting ready for the toast.

As he'd been doing all night, Everett glanced Callie's way and found her leaning across the DJ booth, smiling at one of the Thompson brothers. Everett wasn't jealous, though. Callie had been looking his way just as often, and her soft, tender gazes told him he had nothing to worry about.

He had been floored when he'd seen her in that little black dress, her hair glossy and longer than he'd expected. But when he'd kissed her, she'd still tasted like his Callie Jay, like sunshine and whisky. And he couldn't get enough.

"She's amazing, man," Everett said.

Justin slapped his back. "That's great. I'm happy for you. I like to see you in a good place. You ready for your best-man speech?"

"As I'll ever be." Everett grimaced but grabbed his glass of sparkling apple cider before heading out in front of the bridal table.

Tapping his fork against the side of the glass, he waited until the room quieted down. Staring out at the sea of faces, Everett tried to pick out a few friendly ones. Eric Henderson and Gabe Moriarty were standing over by the drink station, watching him. Because it was a dry wedding, half barrels of ice with sodas and water had been set out with the sparkling apple cider for the toasts, but he'd heard a couple of the guys grumble about no booze.

To tell the truth, he wouldn't have minded a little liquid courage himself.

"In case you don't know who I am, my name is Everett, and I'm Justin's older brother. What can I say about my brother?" Everett gave Justin an evil grin, and his brother made a pounding motion with one hand into the other. "Well, what can't I say? As a kid, he was a pain in the ass, always getting in the way."

The crowd chuckled.

"But then he grew up and became a man. He started to build a life for himself, and when Justin first brought Valerie home, I knew that she would someday be my sister-in-law. She fit in too well with our family to ever be anything but."

A collective "aw" emerged from the room.

"But more than that, she loves my brother, even after she learned about his lack of culinary skills." More laughs. "And that was all I needed to know. There's no doubt my brother is a lucky man, but I think Val's lucky too. Because my brother looks at her like she's the center of his universe. To find the kind of love they share is rare."

Looking across the room at Callie, their gazes locked and held. "I just hope someday to be as lucky as my brother."

Her eyes were so wide, they seemed to swallow her entire face.

Addressing the whole room again, Everett held up his glass. "Everyone, raise your glasses and enjoy the sparkling apple cider as we toast my brother and sister-in-law, Justin and Valerie Silverton."

The room cheered as Everett took a drink from his glass. While Justin and Val went off to cut their cake, Everett made his way over to the DJ stand.

"Did you know that being the best man is highly overrated?" he asked Callie.

"You don't say."

"Oh, yeah. The only thing I want to do right now is pick you up and carry you out of here."

"I just might let you do that in a few minutes." She fiddled with the laptop for a minute or two before calling Dalton over.

"What's up?"

Everett's eyebrows raised at the kid's cold tone. Had Everett's relationship with Callie put a bee in Dalton's bonnet?

Either Callie was ignoring it, or she hadn't picked up on his attitude. "I'm going to announce the first dance and then take a break. Can you press play on this folder, and after the song ends, say, 'At this time, Justin and Valerie would like to invite all of their friends and family to join them on the dance floor'?"

"Yeah, I think a *kid* can handle that."

Callie's lips thinned, and Everett wondered if she'd told Dalton he was too young for her. Was that what all the hostility was about?

"Thank you."

Everett stood back as Callie announced the first dance and noticed that she seemed stressed as she did so. Her voice shook toward the end, and when she came out of the stall and took his hand, he could feel her tremble.

"Hey, are you okay?"

"Yeah, I just need some air."

Everett let her drag him outside and through the dark until they were around the back of the barn.

"Have I told you again how gorgeous—*oof*!" Everett wasn't prepared for Callie to push him back against the barn and plaster herself against him.

"Kiss me."

He straightened up a little and pulled her into his body, taking her mouth gently. He could hear muffled music inside and pulled back a little. "Hey, don't you want to see Justin and Val dance?"

She shook her head and tried to pull him back down to her.

"Why not?"

"I hate this song, okay?" Her words were sharp and oozed enough irritation that Everett pulled back to see a wildness in her expression he didn't like.

"Callie, what is going on?"

"Nothing." She slid her hands down his shoulders, leaving a trail of heat as they traveled over his stomach to the bulge in his pants. He groaned when she cupped him through his slacks, caressing his balls and cock.

Raw need surged through him as he grabbed the back of her neck and brought her mouth back to his, devouring her lips. Still, he knew something wasn't right; her motions and kisses were too desperate, too angry. Was she thinking about her mom? Whoever had hurt her in the past?

He turned Callie until he had her pressed back against the old barn and his hand inching up her thigh. Even if she was kissing him to chase the ghosts away, she was still kissing *him*. And he couldn't resist the sweet call of her need.

He took her ass in both his hands and lifted her up, rubbing his cock against her until she was writhing. She moved her hips against him, thrusting against her center until she was moaning into his mouth and clawing at his shoulders. Everett felt her reach between them and jerk on his belt. She had almost gotten it undone when he pulled his mouth from hers, breathing harshly.

"Callie, baby, what are you doing?"

"What do you think I'm doing? I want you inside me."

Everett groaned and lay his forehead against hers.

She stilled and her voice sounded small. "I thought...don't you want me?"

He let her slide down his body, pulling her skirt back into place before he cupped her face. "Of course I do. I want you so bad I'm hurting with it."

"Then why—"

"Because I don't want our first time to be against the side of a barn during my brother's wedding reception. I don't know what kind of war you're fighting, but I want the first time with you to be in a bed, where I can take my time making love to you."

"I got it." She sounded choked up and pushed at his arms and chest. "Get off me."

He backed up and let her go, but he tried to stop her when she started back toward the barn.

"Callie, I wasn't trying to be mean—"

"Just forget it, Everett. Leave me alone."

Everett let her go, watching her shadow disappear around the corner as his stomach knotted up.

You did the right thing. She'll see that.

Chapter Eighteen

BY A QUARTER to ten, the wedding was winding down, and Callie couldn't wait to get the hell out of there. She'd seen Everett a few times throughout the night, but he hadn't looked at her once. Not that she could blame him. She'd left him standing alone after jumping him like a nymphomaniac.

She'd just wanted a distraction, something to take her mind off the pain and sorrow that came rushing back at the first few bars of "Amazed." There was a reason that song got no play during her radio show, but it had been unavoidable tonight. She couldn't very well tell Justin and Val, *"Oh, gee, I'm sorry, but that was our song, my ex-fiancé and I, and things did not end well, so I won't be playing that."*

When Everett had come over to her after the toast, it had been the perfect opportunity to escape. But he hadn't taken what she'd offered, and she felt so stupid now, she couldn't even look at him.

Callie flipped on Shania Twain's "I Feel Like a Woman" and tried to catch Dalton's eye as Valerie threw the bouquet. When he finally looked away from Jenny Andrews, she waved him over.

He crossed the room slowly, grating on her last nerve with every lumbering step. "Yeah?"

Callie's patience was at an end. "Okay, look, I know you're pissed at me for calling you a kid, and I'm sorry, but if you can't be professional and do your job without sulking, then why don't you just leave?"

Dalton's eyes bugged out of his head at her words, and she stomped away to grab a soda from one of the barrels. She knew that under normal circumstances, she would have never snapped at him like that, but she was still reeling from Everett's rejection.

This was one of those nights she craved a beer and quiet. Anything to blot out the humiliation of throwing herself at a man she was seeing, only to have him reject her because he wanted their first time to be special. If she was another girl, she might have thought it was sweet. But all it did was make her feel like a sex-crazed idiot.

Why did he have to make such a big deal about sex? She'd instigated it. She'd been ready and raring to go, so what was his problem?

Popping the top of a soda, she took a few deep drinks.

"I don't suppose you're ready for that dance now."

Everett's deep voice was rough and so close she could almost feel him against her back. "I'm not really in the mood for dancing."

The first few bars to Diamond Rio's "Love a Little Stronger" poured out of the speakers, and she turned to find Everett holding his hand out to her.

"It's too fast."

He grabbed her hand and pulled her with him. "We'll two-step."

"I don't know how."

"Don't worry. I'm a good teacher."

Callie let him lead her out onto the floor, and when he put his arm around her waist, bringing her into his hard body, her nipples tightened involuntarily. He'd lost his jacket, and as his feet shuffled across the floor, she found herself laughing as she tried to keep up.

"I think you overestimated your talent."

"Naw, it just takes practice. In a few songs, you'll be leading me."

An awkward silence stretched between them as they danced. Callie turned her face away, trying to think of something to say, some way to explain her actions and why she'd just needed him to "go with it," but nothing sounded appropriate.

"Callie." His mouth was pressed against her ear, a low whisper as he spoke. "I feel like we've got something amazing. Something that's going to last. I look at you, and I see my future." Her throat tightened with emotion as he continued. "But it's almost like we take two steps forward and four back, every time. You let me in a little, and then you push me away. I just need you to know that I'll wait. I'll be here for whatever you need, whenever. Just don't shut me out, baby. Please."

She couldn't hold back her tears much longer. "Excuse me." Callie pulled away from Everett and hurried toward the doors of the barn, half expecting him to follow her. She passed through them and ignored the cold as she slipped between the cars until she reached her Jeep, but she was boxed in.

"Son of a bitch!"

She glanced back and saw Everett come through the barn doors, looking around. She ducked down by a car door and waited, watching him through the window as tears trailed down her cheeks, leaving her face chilled. Everett walked across his lawn to his front door. He turned one last time, his porch light highlighting the broadness of his shoulders, before he disappeared inside.

What was wrong with her? She was an emotional mess: a raging bag of lust one second and a petulant, crying child the next. She hated that he said all the right things and was so reasonable and put together when she just wanted him to lose control with her. To stop fighting his impulses and trying to uncover her secrets, layer by layer. Why couldn't he leave her past in the past, and when it did crop up, just help her forget it?

Her feet were killing her, and the heels weren't exactly steady on the uneven gravel, so she kicked them off and picked them up, wincing as the hard rocks bit into her feet. Still, it was better than turning her ankle again.

Callie walked back to the barn, her vision blurred with tears. She kept wiping them away as they spilled over, but more appeared in their place. Leaning her forehead against the barn wall, she sobbed, her whole body wracked in misery.

How was she going to explain why she'd needed to walk away from him if she could hardly understand it herself? What if he realized she was too messed up and decided she wasn't worth it anymore?

Maybe she should see a shrink. This moment alone made it crystal clear she couldn't make heads or tails of her own mind.

She ignored the people exiting the barn until Caroline's concerned voice spoke up behind her. "Callie? What happened?" Caroline's hand rested on her shoulder, but Callie waved her off.

"I'm fine, I just need a minute."

"You are not," Caroline said firmly. "You're crying like your prom date ditched you for your best friend."

"No, I just…" Callie turned and realized Caroline wasn't alone. Gabe was standing behind her in the light coming from the open barn, his smile a flash of white on his dark face.

"Hey, Callie," Gabe said.

"Hey."

"I'll drive you home," Caroline said to Callie before she glanced at Gabe lovingly. "I'll see you tomorrow?"

"Of course." He came forward to give Caroline the kind of kiss that created steam. When they pulled away, Gabe said to Callie, "Feel better, okay?"

"Thanks." Callie waited until he was gone before she spoke again. "You didn't have to stay."

"Yes, I did." Caroline put her arm around Callie's waist. "If *The Big Bang Theory* has taught me nothing else, it's that you always offer your friend a shoulder to cry on and a hot beverage when she's upset."

"I still have to help Dalton clean up the equipment."

"You stay here, and I'll let Dalton know he can handle it on his own—no buts. You need to go home, put a warm wash cloth on your face so your eyes don't puff up, and then tell me everything so I know who I have to kill."

"No one did anything to me, Caroline. This was all my fault."

"See, all I'm hearing is that someone made you cry, and considering you never cry, I'd say that's a big fucking deal. And I will decide whose fault is whose."

Callie gave up and leaned against the side of the barn as she waited, watching the light in Everett's window as if it were an oasis in the desert—sweet salvation—and yet, it seemed to slip through her fingers.

"THAT IS SOME hard-core drama right there. This is the kind of drama that reality shows go for before epically failing."

It was past midnight, and Caroline had driven Callie back to her place, where Caroline had still insisted on staying over. Callie was grateful for the company, especially since she was afraid if she was left alone with her thoughts, she might drive herself insane analyzing Everett, their relationship, and her own personal shade of crazy.

"But I don't want this drama." Callie tucked her legs under her. "I don't want *any* drama.

"Ha, with a man in your life? Good luck with that. Gabe makes me so nuts, sometimes I want to whack him over the head with his baking sheet."

"His baking sheet?" Callie asked.

"Please, you think I could make a crème brûlée without burning the shit out of it? The man should be on *Master Chef*, although I don't think he'd just sit back and take being screamed at."

"No, I think if someone screamed in Gabe's face, he would break their jaw," Callie said, laughing.

"True that."

"Did you seriously just say 'true that'?"

"What? I think I owned it," Caroline said.

"Um, no, it disowned you. Big time."

"Well, at least it got you smiling again."

The reminder stole the smile from her face. "What am I going to do?"

"Why don't you start by telling me what happened. Maybe I can help. As someone who knows how to keep secrets and has a totally dark and twisted past, I am an expert on how to be an idiot in this respect."

"Gee, thanks."

"What? If there's one thing I've learned from Gabe and my sisters, it's that the truth only hurts for a while. Lies can fester and poison a relationship."

"So basically, you're calling my entire life a large, oozing sore?"

"Yep, so pop it open, get all the gunk out, and everything will be okay." Caroline tossed a fluffy white kernel of popcorn in the air and caught it in her mouth.

"And you couldn't have come up with a less disgusting analogy?"

"Nope. I enjoy disgusting you."

Callie wiped buttery hands on her pajama pants and took a deep breath.

Caroline grabbed her hands and squeezed. "Callie, we have been friends for a while, and I have shared so much with you because I know you understand. You should know this is a judgment-free zone. No matter what you say, I will be right here."

Callie let Caroline hold her hands, the wheels of her mind turning as she considered what Caroline was saying. She'd shared her alcoholism, which had been a big step in itself, and Caroline was right—she'd never been anything but supportive.

But talking about Tristan? She could feel her breathing shorten and her heart beat skip as anxiety began racing through her veins.

Start off with how you're feeling and go from there.

"It's like one minute, I'm amazed at how happy Everett makes me, and I want to share everything with him. My past, my pain, my struggles…I want to share what makes me tick."

"Oookay," Caroline said, dragging out the word. "That doesn't sound bad; that sounds healthy."

"Except when I try, it's like I clam up."

"But why? What are you so afraid of?"

"How is he going to feel when I start dumping my dark-and-twisty past all over him?" Callie asked, a lump of emotion in her throat. "With you, we're friends. We're not looking into the possibility that we could build a life together, a life that could snap in half if I go off the rails. After what his dad put him through, I'm still surprised he took a chance on me."

"Okay, hold up. You went on a major bender, true, but then you cleaned up, got your shit together, and have been sober as a judge ever since. Do you have plans to go totally off the deep end?"

"No, but how many recovering alcoholics do you know who plan to start drinking again?" Callie asked.

"Okay, point taken, *but* you are fully committed to not letting that happen, so if you ask me, that's not something you need to be stressing about." Caroline grabbed a handful of popcorn and tossed some back, chewing as she continued. "And as for the past, why don't you start by sharing *something* with him, give him a little taste that says you're trying to move on and you want to move on with him? And if he doesn't take the gesture as the freaking diamond it is, then to hell with him."

"I'd hardly call my past a diamond." *Maybe a lump of coal.* "The thing is, he is this amazingly tender guy who's been through his own hell, and yet, he still sees joy and beauty in life." Dashing at her wet cheeks, Callie laughed at herself. "I swear, I have cried and felt more since meeting Everett than I have in years."

"And this is a good thing? Crying? Drama?" Caroline's tone said she was crazy if she said yes.

"No! I mean…being with him is like waking from a nightmare." It sounded cheesy even to her ears and when she caught Caroline's wide smile, she wished she'd kept her mouth shut.

"You love him."

Callie choked on her popcorn. "What?"

Caroline sat back against the couch, shaking her head. "Oh, believe me, I fought it too, but you are so over the moon for that man, you are practically dancing on a layer of clouds."

"I am not. I like him. I respect and admire him, but it's too soon to drop the L-bomb."

"Deny it all you want, but so far tonight, I've called him a dirty dog, an asshole, and a prick. But every time I try to trash-talk Everett, you defend him." Caroline looked like she was adding the final piece to a puzzle in her mind, and Callie would have denied it, but it was true.

"To be fair, I've only defended him because he hasn't done anything wrong. I'm the one acting crazy."

"If you don't act crazy, then how is he going to know you really care?" Caroline flipped her hair and did a Valley Girl impression. "You would be like, 'Pshaw, I can do better,' if he meant nothing to you."

"How would you know?" Callie asked, rubbing at her tear-filled eyes. "You've never seen me broken up over a guy before. Maybe that's just my defense mechanism—to pretend like I don't care."

"Aw, we are so alike. I knew there was a reason we were friends." Caroline set her bowl of popcorn down. "Is this where I hug you and say, 'There, there'?"

"I think so," Callie said, sniffling again.

Caroline scooted across the couch and put her arms around Callie's shoulders. "There, there."

"Thank you." Callie lay her head against her friend's and closed her eyes as the seconds ticked by.

"Can I stop now?" Caroline asked.

"God, yes."

Both of them laughed as they pulled away, but Callie was the first to sober. "So how do I fix this?"

"It sounds to me like you both want the same things, but you're being a chickenshit about it. So you have two choices: suck it up and let him in, or move on. My sister Ellie is always saying the best way to get over a guy is to get under a new one."

But it wasn't about sex, it was about the way Everett made her feel—like she'd been brought out of the darkness and back into the sunlight. How could she give that up when she hadn't even known she was missing it?

Chapter Nineteen

"COME ON, CALLIE, work with us. We only have three weeks until the shower."

Callie looked up from her phone, which hadn't so much as beeped in twelve hours. "What?"

"You know, staring at a phone does not make it ring any sooner," Gemma said. She had no idea how much her words hurt.

After Caroline left that morning, Callie had lay in bed with Ratchet, watching reruns of *How I Met Your Mother* until Gracie had called to remind her that they were meeting today to finalize the invitations for Gemma's baby shower. Callie had tried to tell them she didn't feel well enough to go out, but they had just moved the planning to her house.

"I think I like this one better." Gracie pointed to an invitation with a large brown owl and a border of fall leaves. "We can print the words inside the leaves, and it would be super-cute."

"I like it," Gemma said.

"Yeah, it's great." Callie got up to make some more coffee. She heard Gracie whisper something to Gemma but couldn't make out the words. It didn't matter, though. As much as she cared about them, she didn't want to get stuck talking about her personal problems. Gemma knew a little about her addiction, but Callie had never breathed a word to Gracie, just in case she decided to open her big mouth.

Now, it almost didn't matter. Caroline knew; Everett knew. Most likely Everett had told his brother, who had probably told Valerie. Eventually, the whole town would find out that Callie was a recovering alcoholic, and what if they grew curious? She was actually surprised no one had ever thought to Google her. It was one of the reasons she had kept such a low profile; if she didn't draw attention, people wouldn't become curious about her and stumble upon the incident with Tristan.

After filling up the water basin of her Keurig, she replaced the lid and pressed the on button. While she waited for the water to warm up, she stared out the window at the gray sky. The wind rattled her windows, and her walls groaned with the force of it. Storms rolled through pretty steadily in Rock Canyon, especially from August to November.

Callie saw a flash of white coming up the road, and she stopped breathing. As the beat-up truck pulled in next to her Jeep, Callie ran a hand over her messy braid, wondering if she had time to run back to the bathroom and clean up a little.

"Did I hear a car?" Gracie called from the living room.

"Yeah, I think they made a wrong turn." Callie walked toward the door, grabbing her coat off the hook. "I'm just going to see what's going on. I'll be right back."

"Be careful. You don't want to end up like those people in that movie *Wrong Turn*," Gracie called.

Callie opened the door and found Everett halfway up the stairs.

"Hi." She shrugged into her jacket and wrapped her arms around herself.

"Hey." He stopped at the edge of the porch. "Do you have company?"

"Yeah, Gemma and Gracie. I'm helping them plan Gemma's baby shower."

"That's...fun." He shoved his hands into his pockets as the silence stretched between them.

"I'm sorry I ran out on you last night."

"I can't expect you to bare your soul to me after only a few weeks. But I need you to believe me when I tell you—I wanted you so bad last night, it killed me to let you walk away."

"I know. But it was stupid to put you in that position. I don't know what I was thinking."

"I think you've been hurt. And I would do anything to know the *what* and *who* of that, but I can be patient. Just...please, Callie, don't walk away from me. Don't shut me out again, okay? Because I just want to be close to you."

Suddenly, his arms were there, pulling her against his chest. Callie breathed Everett in, wrapping her own arms around him, and all the stress she'd been carrying since the night before melted.

"I'm sorry," she said, closing her eyes.

"Me too." He kissed the top of her head, his breath ruffling the strands.

"Aw!"

Callie and Everett pulled apart just enough to find Gracie and Gemma watching them from the doorway, identical grins of mischief on their faces.

Callie glared at her friends but introduced them anyway. "Everett, these are my friends, Gemma Bowers and Gracie McAllister."

"I think you were freshmen at Rock Canyon High when I was a senior." Everett broke away from her to shake their hands.

"Oh, so you were in the same grade as Eric Henderson," Gracie said.

"Yeah, Eric's a good guy," he said. Gracie snorted as Gemma and Callie grinned. "Am I missing something?"

"No, it's just…you called Eric Henderson a good guy, and I vomited a little in my mouth." Gracie covered her mouth and pretended to gag again. "See? It happened again."

"You don't like Eric, huh?"

"Actually, she likes him a lot but won't admit it," Gemma said, earning a glare from her bestie.

"I like Eric like cats like water," Gracie said.

"So, a lot?" Gemma said.

As the two began bickering, Callie took Everett's hand. "Wanna come in for some coffee and look at a lot of owls?"

"Owls?" Everett repeated.

"Yeah." Callie raised her voice into a high squeak as they walked around Gemma and Gracie. "'Cause they are so cute!"

"I heard that!" Gemma and Gracie said in unison.

EVERETT COULD HEAR Gracie and Gemma teasing Callie about him as they said their good-byes, and he smiled when he could almost hear the blush in her responses. Last night, he'd spent a lot of time analyzing Callie's reaction to Justin and Val's first dance song. Part of him had thought about holding out and waiting for her to come to him, but he had never been a wait-and-see kind of guy. Not with the way he felt about Callie.

The door shut loudly, and Callie came into the living room, looking worn out. "Finally."

Everett felt the same way, though he was eager to hold her again. Holding out his arms, he pulled her down until she was cuddled against him.

"They are nice, but man, they fight like Justin and me."

"I know! Maybe it's part of growing up together, but ugh, it can make me crazy sometimes." She grabbed the television remote off the coffee table. "What do you want to watch?"

"You." He trailed his lips against the side of her neck to emphasize his desires, and she giggled. When he'd shown up on her porch, he'd been worried she would send him packing, but instead, she'd seemed genuinely happy to see him. And when he'd pulled her into his arms, she'd held onto him just as tight.

For the first time since they'd started this, he knew for sure she felt it too—their connection. The raw need that had him craving her whenever she was near. But along with that need came worries, and although he kept trying to bury them, some of her reactions to situations worried him. Whatever had happened to her in the past, she wasn't dealing with it. Not with the way she withdrew and held herself back from the world. Every bone in his body wanted to bring it up, to talk about it and help her, but he was afraid if he mentioned it now, she'd pull back even further.

Patience, Silverton.

"You don't want to watch me. I'm boring."

"Not to me," he said, nipping her skin, delighted when he felt her shiver.

While she clicked into the streaming video service, Everett concentrated on touching and tasting her, his hand slowly caressing her hip beneath the black yoga pants she was wearing.

"So, romantic comedy or slapstick?"

He pretended to consider her question seriously. "Slapstick."

"And here I thought you were going to say rom-com."

"What man worth his salt says yes to a rom-com?"

Callie leaned back and tilted her mouth up to kiss him. "A man who enjoys reading romance novels, perhaps?"

"What are you talking about? I don't read romance novels."

EVERETT WAS TEN minutes late picking up Justin and Val to take them to the airport, but it had been worth it to finish watching *Uncle Buck* with Callie. He had never seen the old John Candy comedy, but after seeing Callie belly laugh for an hour and a half, it was his new favorite movie.

"I can't believe you were late. This is my honeymoon, man." Justin's grumbling was slowly chipping away at his good mood.

"We'll make it up on the drive and besides, it takes twenty minutes to get through security at the Boise Airport and you allotted"—Everett looked at his clock on the dashboard—"an hour and a half."

"Fine. I'm done arguing."

"Thank God for that." Everett looked in the rearview mirror at his sister-in-law, who'd fallen asleep. Her head was tilted to the side, and her mouth hung open as she snored softly. They'd barely been on the road forty-five minutes, but she'd been out within twenty. "Is Valerie okay? I've never seen anyone fall asleep that fast."

"Yeah, the fried chicken or something gave her heartburn, so she was up half the night. Had to drive to Twin Falls to get her some antacid, so sorry if I'm being a dick."

"No, you were right. I should have been on time." Everett signaled and merged into the left-hand lane to pass a semi. "It's just that things with Callie and me are complicated, and I just had to see her."

"Well, she seems nice, from what little time I've spent with her. And Dad seems to like her. I saw them talking a couple times last night."

Everett debated telling Justin about Callie and Fred's association and decided it was better he hear it from him than find out later. "Callie and Dad are in AA together, actually. Callie is the mystery sponsor Dad is always sneaking off to have coffee with."

Everett saw Justin turn to look at him out of the corner of his eye and waited for the disbelief, the anger...

The laughter?

Justin was bent over laughing. "Oh my God, I thought you were serious for a minute. Dating Dad's sponsor. Very funny."

"I'm serious."

"No, you're not, because if you were seriously dating an alcoholic after what we've been through with Dad, I'd have you committed."

Everett took in his brother's attempt at humor, knowing that just below the surface he was simmering. His brother was even-tempered, just like Everett, but when he was stressed or worried about someone he loved, he could blow a gasket quick.

Several minutes ticked by before Everett tried again. "She went through a bad time, but she's been sober five years—"

"What? Did she start drinking in infancy?"

Everett took a deep breath, remembering his own reaction to Callie's addiction. Listening to Justin's sarcasm gave him a better perspective on what a judgmental, self-righteous asshole he'd been. "Don't be a douche."

"No, I'm serious. I want to know what it takes to be a sponsor. I mean, I figure you've had to get into some *shit* to be able to counsel others—"

"Just drop it. I shouldn't have told you."

"*You shouldn't have told me?*" Justin's voice rose. "I'm your fucking brother, for Christ's sake! I'm the guy who was there for you when that bitch of an ex-wife left you high and dry. I'm your family. I just don't want you putting your faith in someone who's only going to let you down."

"What's going on?" Valerie mumbled from the backseat.

"Nothing, honey. Rhett's just being a dumb-ass."

"Hmm."

Everett gripped the wheel so hard his knuckles practically glowed white in the darkness.

"Look, all I'm saying is that with everything you've been through, don't you want someone more…stable?"

"Callie *is* stable. She's got her addiction under control, and she makes me happy. You don't have to like it, but if you really want to be on my side, you'll give her the benefit of the doubt."

Justin sat up against the door, his face set in a hard, unreadable mask. "I think you're settling because you don't feel like you deserve any better, but—"

"If I were you, I'd shut my fucking mouth—unless you want to walk to Boise."

Justin did what Everett suggested, and neither said a word for the last hour of the car ride. When Everett pulled up to the departure drop-off, Valerie woke up with a yawn.

"So, what did you guys talk about?"

Chapter Twenty

"I JUST THINK you should call your brother," Fred said to Everett on Halloween morning, five days after Everett dropped Val and Justin at the airport. Everett was gathering hay bales for the Rock Canyon High School Carnival and had someone coming by at noon to pick them up. He'd had to defer all of his Stateside calls until then, which meant he'd be working later than usual. Callie had been okay with it, though, since they were just planning to hang out at her place and watch movies anyway.

Everett still hadn't reached out to Justin, even though they'd called home several times to tell Fred how much fun they were having. They'd even sent Everett a couple of beach shots.

But he was still boiling from Justin's assumption—actually from telling him that Callie wasn't worth anything, and he was just settling for her. Fucker. He should have made Justin walk.

"There will be plenty of time to kick his ass when he gets back." Everett hooked one of the hay bales and carried it closer to the barn door.

Justin and Val had barely disappeared into the airport before Everett had called his dad to vent his frustrations. But while he'd been looking for vindication, his dad had tried playing devil's advocate.

"Justin is protective of you, and he had it rough too. Try to cut him some slack."

Everett had hung up on Fred and turned up the music, switching to an old Toby Keith CD. A little "The Angry American" made him feel a hell of a lot better.

Only his brother's condescending tone still stuck in his craw five days later.

Fred stuck a piece of hay between his teeth and talked around it like a cartoon farmer. "I'm not saying your brother doesn't get too big for his britches. Hell, there are still times I'd like to turn him over my knee and give his rear a good smack, but he is who he is, and we just got to accept him, faults and all."

"And I do, but that doesn't mean I'm just going to take him sticking his nose in my business and shooting his mouth off about things he doesn't understand."

"Fine, I'll let you two work it out then." Fred sat back in his chair and folded his hands across his chest. "How is Callie, huh? You know, it would be nice to have her over for dinner after they get back. Maybe give your brother a chance to eat his words."

"Excuse me if I'm not eager to subject her to Justin's judgmental ass just yet."

"Just think about it. No matter what your brother has to say, I love that little girl and wouldn't mind if you two made a real go of it."

Everett tried not to be jealous of his dad, knowing it wasn't a romantic love, but Fred could understand Callie in a way Everett couldn't. It was hard to swallow. "If Callie wants to, then fine."

"Good. What are you kids up to tonight, anyway?" Fred asked.

"Well, Callie just wants to stay in. Watch a couple movies and eat some salty snacks," Everett said, shrugging. "She isn't big on Halloween. Not sure why."

"Have you asked her?" Fred said.

"No. I'm giving her a chance to trust me. I just want to focus on getting her to believe me when I say that I accept her past, no matter what other skeletons might be hiding."

"But that isn't true, is it? Everett, since you were a kid, you were never one for mysteries. You've wanted to know every detail, every surprise waiting for you, and you've wanted things at face value. How do you know she won't tell you everything if you just sit her down and ask her?"

Because she's been holding back from me since I met her.

His phone rang in his back pocket, and he pulled it out to see Callie's smiling face flashing on the screen. He answered it immediately.

"Were your ears burning?" Everett asked.

"Huh? No, I was just calling to tell you that I can't hang out tonight."

"What's up?" Everett said, disappointed.

"Harold from the station was supposed to DJ the Ghoulish Halloween Ball tonight, but he's got the flu, and no one else can cover."

"Well, that sucks. What about after?"

"The party doesn't end until two, so unless you want to have another slumber party—"

"Are you kidding?" He lowered his voice so his dad couldn't hear. "There is nothing better than holding you all night and waking up next to you in the morning."

"Oh yeah, with my crazy Medusa hair and dragon breath, I'm super-sexy."

"You are." Everett leaned against a stack of hay as he added, "And tonight I'll show you exactly how sexy I think you are in a million, tiny little ways."

"Are you trying to talk dirty to me in the middle of the day?" He could hear her soft laughter, and it warmed him to the core. It was amazing that just four weeks ago she had barely smiled in his presence.

"Now don't be silly. You've heard me talk dirty. I start talking about sliding my hands—"

His father cleared his throat behind him.

"What was that?" Callie asked.

"My dad. Who doesn't know when to make himself scarce."

"Oh my God, were you saying that stuff in front of Fred?"

"He couldn't hear me." Everett pointed toward the door, hoping his father would take the hint, but he just stayed put and muttered something Everett couldn't hear.

"I'm going to die of embarrassment," Callie moaned into the phone. "I have to go."

After she hung up, Everett turned back to his father, scowling. "Don't you have an elsewhere to be?"

"And miss out on the chance to torture my eldest son? Nope, I'm free as a bird."

CALLIE HAD TAGGED along with Gemma and Gracie, who'd wanted to go to Twin Falls to pick up a few things for the baby shower. Even though it was still two weeks away, Gemma didn't want to forget a thing, and Callie just wanted to kill some time.

She was definitely not looking forward to the Halloween ball, which was why she never volunteered to host it. She preferred to spend Halloween locked inside her house with Ratchet and her Buffy box set, but there'd been no one else to handle it.

But the worst part was not being with Everett—although his suggestion of a slumber party did thrill her to her toes. They still hadn't had sex, not because she didn't want to, but after her botched seduction, she'd decided to let him take the lead. And though they'd made out and gotten into some heavy petting, he'd been handling her with kid gloves since.

Which was frustrating as hell, especially when all she could think about was having her way with his sexy ass.

Gracie pulled into the Magic Valley Mall parking lot, which was the biggest shopping mall around, unless they wanted to drive to Boise, which none of them did.

"That is so awesome that you are going to DJ the ball tonight," Gracie gushed as they climbed out of her car.

"Oh, yeah, woo." Callie waved her finger in a whoop-tie-doo circle.

"Who the hell are you? How does anyone hate Halloween? Halloween is an excuse for a plain-Jane to dress up like Cinderella or a sexy pirate and to score some midnight booty." Gracie closed one eye and made her hand like a hook. "Argh."

Gemma laughed loudly, while Callie rolled her eyes, fighting a smile. "I'm not interested in anyone's booty."

"Not even Everett's?" Gemma asked, giving Callie a sly look.

Callie flushed.

Gracie whooped as Callie held the door to the mall open for them. "Oh, she's interested! Is Everett going with you tonight?"

"No, he's coming over after, I think." They walked through the food court, and Callie's stomach rumbled. She'd forgotten to grab lunch today, but nothing really sounded good.

Except for maybe Everett, naked, with a side of piping-hot sex?

"Callie, have you learned nothing from me? Nothing good happens after eleven at night," Gracie said. She slowed as they passed by the Buckle and picked up a pair of beautiful cowboy boots on display outside. "Please be on sale. Please be on sale."

Gracie turned the boots over, and from the way her face fell, Callie assumed they were definitely not on sale.

"Actually, I would like to argue the point that *most* good things happen after eleven," Gemma said, grinning.

Exactly. Callie was hoping that tonight was the night. Everett would come over. It would be late, and as they snuggled up in her bed, one thing would lead to another...and *boom*, they'd be knocking boots. So to speak.

Gemma took the boots from Gracie's hands and set them back on the rack. "You cannot afford three-hundred-dollar boots."

"How did you know they were three hundred?" Callie asked.

"Because every pair of boots she buys from there are *at least* that, and it's why she's constantly behind on her credit card."

"Not true. I always pay cash for my clothes and put business expenses on credit cards."

"Regardless, we are here for baby shower supplies, not boots," Callie said.

"And back to what I was saying," Gracie said. "If you just let Everett come over, and he doesn't have to put in the effort, all you'll ever be is a booty call."

"It's not a booty call if we aren't having sex." Callie ignored their surprised stares as she looked in another store's windows.

"With the way that man looks at you?" Gemma asked.

"Do we need to have *the talk*?" Gracie lowered her voice, adding, "Or a sex-ervention?"

"Geez, Gracie, you're like a thirteen-year-old trapped in the body of a grown woman," Callie muttered.

"I know; it keeps me young." Gracie slowed down as they passed by Hot Topic. "What are you wearing to the ball?"

"Jeans and a sweater." Callie refused to look at whatever had caught Gracie's eye, sure it was something she'd never wear. She hadn't been in Hot Topic since she was thirteen and spent a summer writing bad poetry and dying her hair ink-black.

"Nope, that won't do. I can see I'm going to have to help you. It seems to be my calling, showing the fashionably challenged and repressed how to make the most of the goods God gave them." Gracie flounced into the store ahead of them, like a queen expecting her handmaidens to follow.

Callie looked at Gemma. "Can't you control her crazy?

"Believe me, I have tried."

"Come along, wenches!" Gracie said before disappearing inside.

Callie and Gemma sighed simultaneously.

"Should I start running now, or…"

"It wouldn't do any good; she'd only catch you." And with that warning, Gemma headed in after Gracie.

Callie weighed her options and finally walked through the large entryway. "There's nothing to fear but fear itself."

Unless you went shopping with a bubbly blonde on a mission.

"COME OUT, CALLIE, or I'm going to drag you out."

Callie tried to ignore Gracie, who stood on the other side of the curtained dressing room. She still had no idea how she'd ended up inside the square cubby of no escape, staring at herself in the floor-length mirror. The black pleather Batgirl costume was tight and short, definitely two things that made her uncomfortable. Besides, the low-cut bodice showed two scars, along with a generous amount of cleavage.

Someone started grabbing at the curtain, and Callie heard Gracie mutter something about looking for herself.

"Hang on, you lunatic!"

"Well, I wish you'd just come out and show us! I'm sure you look hot."

"Do they have anything with more coverage up top?" Callie asked.

"Hang on," Gemma said.

Callie hoped that meant Gemma was going back to look.

"Why do you want to cover the girls up?" Gracie asked.

Callie looked down at her usually unimpressive breasts, which currently looked like a couple of water balloons about to shoot across the room. Even if the scars weren't an issue, when a costume posed a potential wardrobe malfunction, she wasn't interested. "Because I look like my chest is going to explode."

"Here—let me see, and I'll tell you if it's too much." Gracie's hand came around the black curtain, and Callie swiftly whacked it away.

"No."

"Ow! Dude, you did not have to hit me."

"Well, stop trying to come in here, and I won't have to whackadoodle you," Callie said, shimmying out of the clingy costume. "Didn't your mom ever teach you boundaries?"

"She tried."

"And failed, obviously." Callie stood for a moment, studying her body in just a plain white bra and bikini briefs. Her fingers traced the six scars she could see, the first across her right shoulder. The second and third had been just under her collarbone and below her breasts. Three raised white lines marred the skin of her abdomen, and the last was on her back. It was strange to see them healed, especially since she could still remember lying on the floor and feeling the wet warmth of her blood pouring out of her before she'd drifted into nothingness.

Callie jumped when Gracie spoke again.

"Hey, what the hell does whackadoodle mean, anyway?"

She didn't want to look at herself or remember that night. Covering her body, she looked away from the mirror and gathered up her T-shirt, covering her chest with it. "It's something my mom used to say when I was being a pill. Basically, cruisin' for a bruisin' but funnier."

"I think I got something," Gemma said. She thrust the item through the curtain. It appeared to be a black robe in a plastic bag, but as Callie turned the package over, she got a look at the picture and description. It was nun's habit—with half the habit missing. It would definitely cover her chest, but by the looks of the skirt, it stopped about midthigh and if she even thought about bending over, she'd be flashing her butt cheeks.

Holy slutty habit, Batman.

"How is something like this not illegal?" Callie ignored their laughter and pushed the costume back out through the curtain. "If I'm going to dress in a naughty costume, I don't think a nun is the right choice. Besides, it's just tacky."

"But you said you wanted something that covered more up top," Gemma argued.

"How about something that doesn't scream 'hooker wear'?" Callie muttered.

"Hey, maybe I'll see if Caroline wants to come out with me," Gracie said.

Callie stared into the mirror, her expression puzzled, while Gemma said exactly what she herself had been thinking. "Where the hell did that come from?"

"Since Callie will be deejaying, and you're…well…too round to party, I need a new wing woman. Someone who doesn't mind getting her sexy on."

"I'm pretty sure Gabe would have a problem with her getting her sexy on," Callie called out.

"Damn it, I am too young to be the last single person in my social group."

"Mike's single," Gemma said.

"Yes, but I am not going to date Mike. It would be incestuous at this point."

"Okay, I'm going to look for something else for Callie while you ponder your spinsterhood," Gemma said.

"Hey, I am single by choice!" Gracie was quiet on the other side for a minute before speaking to Callie. "Maybe I should be the nun. It's not like I'm getting any anyway."

"You can have it." Callie could just picture Gracie in the skimpy costume, having no problem rocking something like that and looking good doing it. But if a blasphemous black habit with a strip of white was all Callie had to choose from, she'd just wear a pair of cat ears with her jeans and T-shirt.

Callie stuffed the costume around the curtain for Gracie to take. "You could totally pull this off."

"I know," Gracie said. "But if I wore something like this, the dickhead would show up and find some way to make me feel like an idiot."

"Are you talking about Eric? I thought Eric liked you." Actually, Callie wasn't quite sure what their deal was, but she thought it was attraction.

"Liked? Eric likes to pick at me. He doesn't like me." Gracie's tone was irritable as she added, "Can we just not talk about him, for once?"

Whoa, talk about touchy subject.

"Sure, of course. And hey, look, I don't need a costume—"

"Wait, I've got it!" Gemma squealed and a few seconds later stuffed something through the curtain.

Callie forgot what she was going to say and looked over the costume. For the first time that day, she didn't make a joke.

It was perfect.

What would Everett say when he saw her in it?

"HEY, MAN, THANKS for coming."

Everett walked into the crowded community center with Eric Henderson and looked around at the strobe lights and purple bulbs casting an eerie glow in the darkened room. After Callie had called to cancel their date, Everett decided to surprise her at the ball, but he hadn't wanted to show up alone. Eric had agreed to come, and sporting a Jason hockey mask, a leather trench coat, and ripped-up clothes, he was terrifying. Everett searched for the DJ booth in the dark, his face feeling stiff under all the zombie makeup.

Eric rubbed his hands together. "No problem. Women running around in sexy costumes? Who would miss this?"

Finally, Everett spotted Callie standing with a woman who was wearing black cat ears, a mask, and little else.

"Come on." Everett started toward the booth, which was under a huge inflatable cemetery sign and surrounded by several tombstones. As music blasted through the room, he looked over the dancing couples, spotting at least four Little Red Riding Hoods, and one person dressed as a urinal. Classy.

Eric followed behind him before tapping his shoulder and pointing to line of girls in short, tight costumes, dancing up close and personal with one another, but Everett looked away. He wasn't interested in anyone but Callie.

Once they reached the booth, the masked cat turned toward them, her blonde hair curling around the cat ears, but Everett barely glanced at her. Instead, his gaze devoured Callie, whose dark blonde hair fell down her back in waves, shining in the strobe lights. She wore a simple sleeveless knit top, her arms bare and beckoning to him to stroke her soft skin.

"What's up, kitty cat?" Eric yelled to the other woman, tipping his mask back.

The kitty cat wrinkled her pert nose under her mask, and Everett realized it was Gracie McAllister.

"Hey, Buffy, can I borrow your stake?" Gracie held her hand out to Callie, staring Eric down through her mask. "I need to stab something undead."

Everett understood then and chuckled when he saw Callie wave the wooden stake in the air. A few days ago, when he'd been inspecting her DVD collection, he'd been surprised to find a mint-condition box set of the *Buffy the Vampire Slayer* series. The rest of the shelf had been filled with comedies and kids movies, but for that one set.

"What's this?" he'd asked.

"It's Buffy. You've never seen Buffy?"

"I'm sure I've seen an episode or two, but I thought you didn't like violent movies."

"I don't like serial killer, slasher films, but Buffy is different. It's funny, quirky, and no matter what obstacles she faces, she always wins. She's not perfect; she makes mistakes, but she always saves the day."

That conversation had said so much about her, it had stuck with him.

"Gracie Lou, you know stabbing me is that last thing you want to do." Eric was loudly laying on the charm, but by the look on Gracie's face, she wasn't buying his baloney.

Gracie huffed loud enough to be heard over the blasting music and waved at Callie. "I'll see you later."

She started to walk away but during the lull between songs, Eric yelled after her, "Why do you fight the inevitable? You know you want to have adorable kittens with me, pussy cat!" Gracie stuck her middle finger in the air, and Eric laughed, looking at Everett. "That woman is secretly in love with me."

"Must be some secret." Everett focus shifted back to Callie, who kept glancing between them curiously. "I'll see you later, Eric. Okay?"

"Yeah, sure, ditch your wingman." Eric held his hand over his heart. "That hurts, man."

"You don't know what hurt is...yet," Everett said with mock ferocity.

"Yeah, yeah, I get it. It's cool; I've got my own game to run," Eric said.

"Pretty sure the game isn't interested," Everett said.

"The fat lady hasn't sung yet, my friend."

Everett caught Callie looking his way again, but she still hadn't smiled or waved. It was dark in the place, other than the strobe lights. Could she not tell it was him?

He headed around the side of the DJ booth, and she held up her hand as if to stop him.

"Hey, you can't be back here...Everett?"

So she hadn't recognized him. "What do you think?"

She made a face, sticking her tongue out and wrinkling her nose. "I think you look disgusting. What is that all over your face?"

"Make up, a few fake scabs and blood...even some imitation pus." He wrapped his arms around her waist and pursed his lips, the stuff on his face shifting and crackling. "How about a kiss?"

"Ew, no!" She laughed, struggling. She reached out to grab her stake and held it under his chin. "Back off you, undead fiend. There will be no kisses for you until you're human once more."

"A rubber stake?" he said, amused. "I don't think you're going to do much with that, Whisky."

Everett leaned down toward her mouth, but she held him off. "Not with all that gunk on you."

"Aw, you're breaking my poor, undead heart."

Shaking her head, she stood up on her tiptoes and gave him a small, closed-mouth kiss. "How's that?"

"Eh."

"I'm working and do not have time to make out with my zombie boyfriend, no matter how sexy he is. For a dead guy."

"Boyfriend, huh?" He couldn't tell for sure in the dark, but he had a feeling she was blushing hard.

"I just…I mean…"

He lifted his hand and ran his thumb across her bottom lip, excitement shooting through him. Boyfriend. He liked the sound of that.

"I like that, although I'm pretty sure the other undead fiends are going to shun my ass for dating a slayer." Dipping his head, he put his lips right next to her ear, mindful enough to not drip any ooze on her. "I'm willing to risk it, though, to be with the sexiest woman in the world."

She gripped his shoulders and pulled back to stare up at him, a sweetly mischievous smile on those full lips. "I'm still not going to make out with you like that."

"Whoa, who said anything about making out? What, am I just a piece of rotting meat to you?"

"You're never going to stop with the zombie jokes, are you?"

"What's the matter with a little corpse humor?"

"Despite your rather revolting costume and terrible sense of humor"—one of her hands strayed downward to cup his ass—"I still find you unbelievable sexy."

"Oh, yeah? So, I'm bringing sexy back…from the dead?"

"Okay, I'm done!" Callie released him and turned back toward her laptop. Everett's gaze trailed down and in the flickering lights, he noticed the tight leather pants she was wearing, which hugged every curve from her waist to her calves.

Damn.

Just having her in his arms was turning him on, and he didn't want to let her go. He'd been holding back all week, but it was like he was suddenly possessed by a tiny demon that was making him painfully horny but too scared to act on it. Not that he was really scared of her, but after making such a big deal about their first time being special, it now seemed hypocritical to seduce her during *The Wizard of Oz* or after a marathon of her favorite *How I Met Your Mother* episodes.

Maybe tonight, if he set the mood right, things would be perfect.

As soon as he washed the shit off his face.

"So how's about you and I sneak off and find a little crypt for two?"

"I can't leave until one thirty, more like two, after the equipment is all packed up."

"Well, then, what if I just kept you company?" He played with the edge of her pants as his lips found her neck, nipping and kissing a trail down to the collar of her shirt. She tilted her head, and he reached up to move her hair out of the way, sucking on her skin. He pressed his hard cock against her, wondering if she knew what she was doing to him.

"Um, Rhett?" she said, stiffening.

"Yeah?"

"I think some of your ooze got on my neck."

Pulling back, he squinted. "Oh yeah, it did."

"Can you get it off, please?" she said.

Laughing, he wiped the goop of her neck. "How about we pick this up later?"

"After you wash your face."

"Deal."

Chapter Twenty-One

CALLIE'S HEART BEGAN thudding when she spotted Everett heading back from the bathroom. With all of that disgusting makeup gone, she definitely wouldn't mind if he started nibbling on her neck again—and maybe something more.

She hadn't recognized him at first, not with the layer of inch-thick makeup and baggy, ripped clothes. She'd been trying to keep her distance from all the masked people and made-up monsters dancing around the room, so when he'd first come around the side of the DJ booth, she'd nearly dropped him with a self-defense move.

But then the light had caught his eyes. Even with green and red gunk on his face, she'd recognize that sweet smile anywhere.

It was no mystery to her why he was here. He'd said he would love to come over after the ball for a sleepover, and she'd seen the way he'd checked out her tight pants.

Gracie and Gemma had both given her costume their wholehearted approval, and Callie had known it was right the second she'd put it on. It was comfortable and sexy without being obvious.

And with the way Everett's hands kept finding her hips and spreading across the soft pleather of her pants, she had a feeling he thought so too.

He pressed himself against her back and moved with her to the music, rolling her with his hands so her ass grazed the front of his jeans with every dip and sway. Keeping one hand on her laptop, she reached up to curl her other behind his neck, turning her head so she was looking up at him over her shoulder. Everett dipped his head and kissed her, releasing butterflies from her stomach into her chest. His tongue played with hers, and her nipples hardened into tiny nubs.

"Ahem."

The low cough made her break the kiss, but she didn't pull away from his hands when she faced Mrs. Andrews's disapproving sneer.

"You should really be doing your job instead of making a spectacle." She stuck a song request into the jar on the edge of the booth and flounced away. Everett took Callie's lobe between his teeth, biting down gently. "I do believe we've been properly chastised."

"I know. I can't wait to tell Caroline and Gracie that I've been officially initiated into the club."

"What club?" He pressed his mouth to her neck and sucked, sending a tickling quiver down her spine.

"The 'Mrs. Andrews Thinks We're Hussies club."

His surprised laugh sent a puff of warm air along her skin. "And why did you want to be a part of this club?"

Callie spun around in his arms and couldn't fight her sassy smile. "Are you kidding? Only the cool kids get scolded by Mrs. Andrews."

Everett shook his head before he kissed her again, and she held onto his biceps, loving the way they tightened under her palms.

"How much longer until we can go home?"

A thrill raced through her body as his raspy question. "About three hours."

He groaned loudly, clearly frustrated, before pulling back and giving her a wicked grin. "I guess that means we've got three hours of foreplay."

Lord, have mercy.

THREE HOURS AND eight seconds later, Callie shoved her fake stake into the back of her pants and walked toward Everett, who was leaning against his truck, arms folded. He hadn't been able to keep his hands and eyes off her legs and ass, which was fine with her, except that when he'd said they were going to have three hours of foreplay, he hadn't been kidding.

In fact, he'd kissed and touched and rubbed her so much, every nerve ending in her body was on fire, primed and ready to jump his bones.

"Do you have some kind of pleather fetish?"

He opened his arms to her without answering, and she walked into them gladly. As he closed his arms around her, she leaned against his hard body and hummed with pleasure.

She could stay in his embrace forever.

"Actually, I think I just have a thing for you in those pants."

His mouth settled over hers, his tongue tracing the outline of her lips, leaving a trail of tingles. Wrapping her arms around his neck, she stood up on her toes and rubbed her rock-hard nipples against him in response. Her breasts had been aching for him, and when Everett's big hands moved down from her waist to cup her ass, she moaned in protest. She wanted relief, and the feel of his hard cock against her stomach was the last straw.

"God, Callie, I want you so bad."

His tone was as pained and frustrated as she felt, and she shook with raw need, desire pulsing in her blood as she dug her fingers into his shoulders. "I want you too, Rhett."

A deep growl rumbled from him as one of his hands came up to hold the back of her head. Callie was caught unprepared for the rough passion that poured from Everett as he devoured her mouth. Her body caught fire, the cool air of the October night forgotten as she held on. Still, she couldn't get close enough to relieve the throbbing between her legs, and she made a soft whimper of frustration.

"Ow, baby!" someone yelled as he drove by, honking the horn.

Callie pulled away from Everett. "We should go."

"Yours or mine?" he asked.

"Mine's closer," she said.

Everett released her so quickly, she almost stumbled. Catching her elbows in his hands, he grinned sheepishly. "Sorry, I just—"

"Me too."

They climbed into their cars, and Callie led the way to her house. Without his hands and mouth to distract her, she began playing through different scenarios in her head. She had never been completely naked with anyone since Tristan, and if she bared everything to Everett, he was going to have questions. Was she ready to answer everything?

When they rolled up her driveway eleven minutes later, Callie didn't even have time to get out of her Jeep before Everett was there. Hands cupping her cheeks, he kissed her, his tongue darting between her lips, and she grabbed hold of him. Instead of crawling on top of her, he pulled her out, carrying her toward the house.

He broke their kiss and tried to open the door one-handed, but seeing his struggle, she reached down and did it for him. Spilling into the house and spooking Ratchet, Everett stumbled with her in his arms, and they bumped against a wall.

"Ow, geez, walk much?" she asked.

"Your damn dog was in the way!"

Her feet slid to the ground but Callie pulled his mouth back to hers, nipping at his lips and thrusting her tongue inside. She heard the door slam, and then they were fumbling down the hallway, hands everywhere on each other's bodies.

Everett's shirt went over his head, breaking their kiss, and Callie's gaze feasted on his hard, defined muscles. The scars that tattooed the side of his body only enhanced his masculine beauty, and a possessive joy washed through her as she realized this man was *hers*. She had come through hell, and he was her reward, her light at the end of the tunnel.

And damn, she could watch him strip forever.

Pushing open the door to her bedroom, she sat down on her bed and tossed her shoes across the room. Her eyes ate him up as his hands reached for the snap of his jeans.

Ratchet started to come into the room too, but Everett took him by the collar and pushed him out gently, shutting the door behind him. "Sorry, Ratch, but we don't need an audience."

Callie's giggles died as his hands returned to his jeans, the zipper shattering the quiet of the room with a loud *rrrrft.*

For weeks they had touched and kissed, but as Everett pushed his jeans to his ankles and stepped out of them, Callie realized that there was no way she would be able to turn back from this. Not that she wanted to, but this was the first step toward letting her walls down.

She wasn't sure exactly when she'd fallen completely in love with him. Maybe it was when he'd shown up the day after her freak-out and opened his arms to her so easily. Or perhaps it was that first day when he'd replaced her newspaper, just to be a nice guy. But maybe it was that very first *Have a nice day, Callie Jay* that had done the trick. Whatever the trigger had been, it didn't matter.

She was in deep, and she was perfectly happy right where she was.

His hard cock stretched the cotton of his boxer briefs, and she held her hand out toward him. When he moved closer, she grabbed the top of his briefs and pushed them down, her hands skimming up his hips, one palm touching nothing but smooth skin while the other met the bumps and ridges of his scars. She kissed and then licked the skin above where his cock bobbed, his salty, musky scent driving her wild.

Everett's fingers tangled in her hair as she pushed his underwear all the way to the floor. Callie cupped the sack of his balls, rolling them in her hands as she kissed his tip, licking away the drop of moisture gathered there.

"Fuck." Everett groaned as she sucked him into her mouth, her tongue laving at him. It was everything she'd imagined that night on the phone with him. Suddenly, Callie wanted to make him happy, to make him crazy with need.

She wanted him to need her the way she needed him.

Everett's hips jerked, sending his cock deeper into her mouth, and she ran her tongue under the head as she pulled back, circling the tip. "Stop, Callie, please," Everett panted.

She paused, and he released her hair, pressing her back on the bed. "My turn."

He knelt between her legs, his fingers curving under the waistband of her pants and underwear before pulling them both down and out of the way. Everett pressed his mouth against her pelvis just as his finger slipped inside and arched up. She rose off the bed with a cry when he pressed and swirled in a fast circle inside her. Electric shocks of pleasure shot out from her wet center and down the muscles of her legs, leaving her quivering.

As her hands touched the back of his head, his lips moved down, his tongue pushing between her legs. He licked her clit in short, frenzied motions, the combination of his fingers and tongue bringing on the rush of orgasm before she was prepared.

Unable to hold back any long, she screamed with release.

After a second or two, Everett lifted her back onto the bed before following her down.

"Wait."

She got up and went over to the window. With the room encased in moonlight, she could still see him clearly, and although she wanted nothing between them, she knew she wasn't ready to have him looking at her. At her scars.

After closing the curtains and plunging them into darkness, she crawled back onto the bed. Then Callie took a deep breath and, before she could talk herself out of it, pulled her shirt up and over her head.

Condom. She felt across for her nightstand drawer. Once she found the knob, she fished around inside, and finally took out a square foil package.

"Whatever you're thinking, no, I don't usually bring guys back here." Without waiting for him to deny it, she pushed him onto his back and climbed over him. "That doesn't mean a girl shouldn't be prepared."

"I had one in my wallet."

Holding the condom between her lips, she took his hands and placed them over her breasts. He squeezed her lightly, and she moaned, arching to press them into his hands. The rough skin of his palms wreaked havoc on her sensitive nipples, and it was glorious.

Ripping open the condom with her teeth, she slipped it over his hard-on. When he was completely sheathed, she lifted up to position his cock at her entrance.

"I'm glad you have an extra condom. I'm sure we'll need it."

Everett laughed until she pressed her hips down and closed her eyes as he slipped inside, stretching her muscles. His hands cradled her breasts, smoothing his thumbs over her nipples and sending frissons of heat down her spine.

When he was fully inside her, a slow smile spread across her lips. Callie was in bed with a man she loved, *completely naked*. No barriers. No walls.

"Are you ready for me?"

EVERETT COULDN'T SEE Callie moving above him, but he could feel every part of her. From the warm, wet delight of her channel to the hand on his chest and the other resting behind her on his thigh, he was caught up in the rhythm of her body dancing with his.

Her hips rolled and lifted over him, twisting in a seductive circle that brought him deep inside her. His hands rested on her hips, pressing her down as he thrust up beneath her.

When she'd closed the drapes, he'd had no idea she was going to take off her shirt, but once she'd placed his hands over her bare breasts he'd known it was a gesture of trust. She'd told him herself—she never took her shirt off during sex, yet she'd done just that with him. It didn't matter that she wasn't yet ready for him to see her; he'd felt her.

And she was amazing—soft, warm, and his.

But there was no way he could last forever, not with the way those little sounds of hers were driving him wild. She'd asked if he was ready for her, and he'd thought he was but that had been the shy and sweet Callie.

The woman above him was a siren, and he was completely under her spell.

As her breathing because rushed and uneven, he felt her muscles squeezing his cock, telling him she was getting close. God, he wished he could *see* her fully naked and riding him, her breast glowing in the moonlight, but he knew it was just a matter of time.

Her hips jerked, and she cried out, but he kept her moving, his hands rocking her hips in a steady, brisk pace, helping her ride out the orgasm until she fell forward onto his chest and sighed. "Mmmm."

Still hard inside her and throbbing for release, Everett pressed his mouth into her hair. "Callie?"

"Yeah?"

"You better not fall asleep."

"But I'm so"—he rolled them over until she was on her back and staring up at him with a mischievous smile—"tired."

Pushing himself up, he pulled out of her until just the tip remained inside and thrust hard, satisfied when she arched up with a wild cry. Everett kept moving in and out, slowly at first until she was gripping his arms. Sweat trickled down his back as his speed kicked up.

"Still tired?"

A soft moan escaped her when he thrust again, but then her breathless voice whispered, "Bored too."

"Ornery."

Coming down on his elbows, he kissed her, tongue slipping inside with every shallow movement as he took in her growing, high-pitched cries until he felt his body tumble over the edge. Tearing his mouth away, Everett came with a shout. His hips jerked several times as he rode the wave of pleasure, his heart pumping so hard he was sure it would burst.

Still pressing his chest against hers, Everett reached out and skimmed along her forehead, brushing her hair back in the dark. He bent down and kissed her, the scent of her subtle perfume and taste of her mouth drawing him deeper. Callie was the one thing he craved, and he wanted to lay it all out for her. Everything he was, everything that made him, he wanted to share with her.

But despite their bare skin, the darkness surrounding them felt like another barrier between them. He had sworn he'd be patient and was sure she would finally share herself with him when she was ready, but what if she didn't?

He could wait for her because despite all the push and pull, the ups and downs, he had fallen in love with her.

The only problem was, he wasn't sure if he could put his whole heart on the line...if she was only offering half of hers.

BASKING IN THE afterglow of their lovemaking, Callie waited for Everett to come back from the bathroom. She'd been so caught up in him, in the fun, the passion, and the joy of just being with him.

There was that word again—joy. It summed up everything Everett was. He was her joy.

The bathroom door opened, shining a bright light over the room, and she pulled the blanket up to cover herself. The light flipped off and she could hear Everett coming toward her.

Ratchet scratched at the bedroom door, whimpering.

"Sorry, buddy, but tonight she's mine."

The bed dipped under Everett's weight, and when he curled up behind her, his hands stroked over her arms, her sides, and her stomach.

She stiffened briefly as his hand stilled over one of the scars, but he moved it, resting it instead on the curve of her hip. Relaxing back against him, Callie snuggled in and reached for his hand, entwining their fingers with a smile.

"I think that was my best Halloween ever." Everett pressed his lips against the back of her head and the warm puff of his breath ruffled her curls softly.

"Mine too."

The room filled with a comfortable silence, but Callie couldn't rest, knowing she should say something more.

She should open up to him, let him know that she cared and that she did trust him.

"Everett?"

"Yeah."

She swallowed hard, her stomach flipping over as she took a chance. "I love you."

His arms tightened around her, and she waited with bated breath.

"I'm glad."

Laughing, she smacked his arm. "And you call *me* ornery."

His chest shook against her back but when his mirth dissolved, he turned her in his arms until they were face-to-face, although she couldn't really see him. But she felt his lips seek hers, sweetly coaxing hers as he breathed out.

"I love you too."

Chapter Twenty-Two

"I'M ALMOST READY," Callie called from the bathroom.

It had taken most of the morning, but Everett had finally convinced Callie to come to his place for dinner. Justin and Val had gotten home the day before, and his dad had called to say that Justin would be on his best behavior. They were going to watch the game, and Val's sisters were coming over to look at honeymoon photos. Callie had said she didn't want to intrude, but with so many people joining them, that argument fell by the wayside.

"Take your time." He grabbed a soda from the fridge and popped the top.

Everett took a drink and went back into the living room. Everything in Callie's house was older, as if she'd scoured antique stores to find just the right pieces. Everett was afraid to set his drink down on the side table because the fancy, intricate design of the wood looked vintage, and he didn't want to cause water damage. "Hey, where are your coasters?"

"What?"

"Never mind." He started opening drawers on the little table. When one opened wide, Everett stopped and stared. There were dozens of letters inside, all unopened. Everett took one of them and read the return address name on the front.

Who was Tristan Anderson?

Just then Everett heard the hair dryer shut off, and he put the letter back inside the drawer.

Callie came out of the bathroom a moment later, fluffing her hair out of her face. She was wearing a pair of jeans, with a flowing peasant blouse in rich crimson.

"What do you think?" She smoothed her hands over the shirt and jeans, looking nervous and adorable.

Everett got up with his Coke and set it on the bar. "I think you look beautiful."

Callie blushed. "Thank you."

He slid his hands over her hips and up her back, under the shirt.

"Ah, cold hands!" Callie grabbed behind her at his wrists.

"Sorry, I couldn't find any coasters."

He pulled his hands out of her shirt and kissed her, lazily playing with her lips and tongue until she melted against him, her mouth opening under his.

"What if we went back to the bedroom? I can do that thing you like…"

"But we'll be late," she murmured.

"No one will miss us."

He tried to pull her back down the hallway, but Callie laughed and wiggled away from him. "Yes, they will, and I'm not going to lie to Fred."

"Who said I was going to lie? We'll be there...eventually." Everett started to chase after her, but Ratchet stepped in front of him, leaning his weight on Everett's legs.

"See? Even Ratchet thinks it's a bad idea," she said.

"Ratchet doesn't think anything except 'where's my food, where's my master, and where do I do my business?'"

"Don't listen to him, boy." Callie knelt down to kiss the dog's muzzle, and Everett made a face.

"And I was going to kiss you again too." Everett smirked when she glared at him.

"I kissed his fur." She shrugged into her black peacoat and wrapped a paisley scarf around her neck. Everett loved her in jeans and a T-shirt, but the feminine details she'd added today, all for dinner with his family, filled him with pride that she loved him. That she was his.

And he loved moments like this, where they could tease and play. It almost made the lingering doubts worth it.

Almost.

"Still, I don't want to pick dog hair out of my teeth." Everett grabbed his coat off the back of the couch and came up alongside her as she opened the door.

"That's fine," she said. "You don't ever have to kiss me again."

"Whoa, now. Let's not be hasty."

Everett followed her outside and waited behind her as she locked the door. When she was done, she tossed her hair and sniffed. "If you want my kisses, Rhett, you're going to have to accept the good with the dog hair."

She walked past him with her little nose in the air, like she'd just put him in his place. Everett chuckled as he took two long strides and spun her around. Wrapping his arms around her, he kissed her again, murmuring against her mouth, "I'd do anything for your kisses."

"Mmm, I'll remember that." She nipped at his lips as she held onto his shoulders.

"What about *my* kisses?"

"Eh, they're okay," she said.

"Just okay?" Cupping her face in his hands, he took her mouth with scorching heat, swiping his tongue inside. "How was that?" he asked when he pulled back, breathing hard.

Despite the flush of her cheeks and her hazy eyes, she feigned boredom. "A little better."

"I'm going to have to just keep kissing you, I guess."

"I think you should."

FRED OPENED THE door with a wide smile, and Callie fought the nervous flutters she had about meeting Everett's family as a couple.

She knew Everett well enough to realize that bringing her to his home for Sunday dinner was a sign he was serious about her, if his heartfelt *I love you* hadn't been enough. Still, she'd been lucky enough to wake up before he'd been fully aware and was able to get dressed without him seeing everything. Despite her lingering hang-ups, it was weird how far they'd come in such a short time. Four weeks ago, they had only ever spoken on her radio show, and now she was about to sit down and get to know his family.

Everett had warned her the day after Justin left that he knew about her alcoholism, and she was actually relieved that the initial shock—and probably anger—had happened without her there.

Still, despite Fred's open acceptance of her, she was a little worried about Justin. She hardly knew him, beyond what Fred had told her about Justin's having taken care of him most nights when he was too drunk, but she knew Justin definitely still held a grudge. She couldn't imagine that he had been thrilled to learn about *her* past.

She just hoped he'd at least try to understand, for Everett's sake. Everett loved his brother, and despite their occasional disagreements, she could see that. And she wouldn't be the problem that drove a wedge between them.

"Callie." Fred stepped out onto the porch and pulled her into his arms. "I am so glad you could make it."

"Thank you for having me," she said.

Fred kept his arm around her and led her inside. "Come on in; everyone is waiting."

"How are the Broncos doing?" Everett asked behind them.

"They're up by seven."

They walked into the living room. Justin was sitting on the couch, watching the TV. He hardly looked up when they entered.

"Excuse Justin. He's tired after his honeymoon." Fred squeezed Callie's shoulders and her heart sank as she realized she'd been naïve. There was no way Justin was going to accept her or give her a chance. He was too jaded from his experience.

"The girls are in the kitchen, looking at honeymoon photos," Fred said.

Callie took the hint and gave the men a chance to talk. She smiled at Caroline and her sisters as she walked into the kitchen. "Hey."

"Hey." Caroline hopped up and gave her a hug. "So, you and Everett worked everything out?"

"Yeah, we did."

Callie noticed that Valerie kept glancing at her thoughtfully, as if she had something to say and was formulating a way to put it.

Ellie popped a potato chip into her mouth and smirked. "Congrats. He is smoking hot, even with the…well, you know."

Callie tossed Ellie a dirty look, and Caroline laughed. "You better watch what you say about Callie's man. Roar."

"I didn't mean anything by it," Ellie said.

"It's fine," Callie said.

"Everett's a good guy," Valerie said suddenly.

Every set of eyes, including Callie's, looked at Valerie in confusion.

"Yeah, he is," Callie said.

"No, he is the most selfless man I know, and he deserves someone who appreciates him."

"I know," Callie said. She was getting a little irritated with her stating the obvious.

Valerie stood up and leaned on the table. "Look, I like you, and you and my sister are friends. But if you hurt him, I will make your life a living hell."

"Val!" Caroline glared at her sister. "Back the fuck off."

"I thought you should know now, just in case you wanted to bail. Everett has been through enough without getting involved with someone who might fall off the wagon and decide her next drink is more important than a good man."

Callie didn't respond because everything she was thinking made her want to scream at a pregnant woman. This was exactly why she didn't talk about her past, because people looked at her like she was a loose cannon, like any moment she was going to fall off the wagon and become this hideous monster.

Taking a deep, calming breath, she said, "I don't have any intention of hurting Everett or anyone else. And to be quite honest, I've been sober for five years and was only off the rails for half that. I'd say, just going by the odds, I'll be okay. What I don't appreciate is someone threatening me because of my past instead of judging me on my present. I think that's a little ignorant, don't you?"

Val's face flushed crimson, but before she could move, Ellie was jumping between them and pulling her sister toward the back door. "Let's get some air, Val."

Callie watched them leave, regret churning in the pit of her stomach. Why couldn't she have just shut up instead of mouthing off?

You didn't deserve her threats or her attitude, and someone needed to call her out on it.

"Whoa," Caroline said next to her. "I can't believe you just called my sister ignorant."

"Sorry," Callie muttered.

"No, she was out of line." Caroline nudged Callie with her shoulder. "But take a little advice from me: if you ever go on a family vacation together, sleep with one eye open."

WHILE THE GIRLS finished making dinner, Fred, Justin, and Everett sat in uncomfortable silence, watching football.

The only problem was, Everett couldn't concentrate on the game with Justin radiating anger and those letters weighing on his mind.

Why did they bother him so much? Was it because they reminded him of the cards he'd send Cara, which always came back unopened? It did hurt that she'd never even bothered to read any of them, but he couldn't project that onto Callie. Whatever had happened between her and this Tristan, it was her business.

But who was he? He had to have been someone close to her to write so much.

Well, he couldn't do anything about the letters now, but he could deal with his brother's pouting. Everett, sick of the tension, finally tried to make amends. "Look, Justin—"

"Do you mind? I'm watching the game, man."

Everett sighed and grabbed the satellite remote, pausing it.

"What the fuck?" Justin snapped, reaching for the remote.

"I am trying to apologize to you!"

They grabbled and struggled on the couch, until Justin threw his hands in the air.

"Fine, you're sorry. I forgive you. Happy?"

"Yeah. I'm fucking ecstatic."

"Good."

Their father looked between them, his lips twitching. "God, I love these family gatherings."

"Dinner's on the table," Ellie called from the kitchen and the three men stood up.

Everett walked into the dining room and caught Callie's grim expression.

You okay? he mouthed.

She gave him the "okay" sign with one hand, but her strained smile said differently. Everett frowned, examining each woman's face until he saw Val glaring darkly at Callie.

Suddenly, Everett wanted to hit his brother. Whatever he'd told Val about Callie had obviously caused some tension, and who knew what else.

He pulled out a chair for Callie and when she sat down, he leaned over to whisper in her ear. "I am so sorry."

She didn't respond, and he took the seat next to her, glaring across the table at Justin.

"What's your problem?"

"You've got a big fucking mouth," Everett growled.

"Both of you, knock it off. We have guests," Fred said. While his father said grace, Everett reached under the table to take Callie's cold hand, threading his fingers with hers, but she still wouldn't look at him.

"Amen," everyone said after Fred ended his prayer. As the food was being passed around, Justin got up and started grabbing drinks for everyone.

"Callie, do you want some wine? Oh, never mind—I *forgot*."

"That's it," Everett roared, letting go of Callie's hand as he shot to his feet. "Get your ass outside, you little shit. I'm going to—"

"Stop!" Callie screamed.

The whole room went silent as she stood up, pushing her chair in clumsily. "This was obviously a mistake, so I'll go." Everett watched her dash tears from her cheeks, even as she spoke to his father with a brave smile on her lips. "Fred, thank you so much for inviting me. Maybe we can meet for coffee soon."

Caroline tried to reach out and stop her, but Callie avoided her hands.

"I'll come with you," Everett said.

"No, really, I'm fine. I just need to be alone."

"You are the woman I love, and you were just insulted in my family home. I'm coming with you."

She didn't argue again so he took her hand, turning to face his brother and sister-in-law one last time. "I don't care what your problem is. Callie makes me happy. She is a *recovering* alcoholic, and I trust her. I know you think you're looking out for me, but I don't need you," he said bluntly. "And you either need to apologize to her and get on board with our relationship, or you both can go fuck yourselves."

Everett pulled Callie out the door behind him just in time to hear his father start in on Justin, bellowing at the top of his lungs about how they treat guests in his house. Everett didn't try to speak to her; he just helped her into the truck and shut the door with a heavy sigh. So much for thinking his brother would support him. He tried to put himself in Justin's shoes, but he just couldn't. No matter what reservations he might have, he had no right to attack Callie.

Everett's fists clenched and flexed. He was tempted to go back in there and—

Callie was knocking on the windshield, as if sensing he was about to head back inside and deck his brother. She shook her head at him, pleading with him with those light hazel eyes, and he sighed again. As he climbed into the truck, he reached across and took her hand.

"I am so sorry for the way they treated you," he said.

"They're just protecting you," Callie said.

"What they don't get is that I don't need their protection. I trust you."

The letters flashed through his brain, but he pushed them back. They could hold on for one more day.

Chapter Twenty-Three

EVERETT SAT IN Callie's living room, staring at the coffee table and the letters it hid for what must've been the hundredth time in the last few days. He'd hardly been home since Sunday and when he was, he passed his brother as if they were strangers. But neither of them was ready to break, no matter how many times their dad laid into them about being brothers and to stop being idjits. Everett wasn't going to make the first move. Either Justin apologized, or he didn't, but Everett wasn't going to take the first step.

And even though his brother had been weighing heavily on his mind, Callie's secret stash of letters was eating at him.

He heard the water turn off in the kitchen. Callie hummed her way back into the living room but stopped just as she came up behind him.

As if he hadn't heard her.

"I'm not going to forbid your humming in your own house."

"Just in yours?"

"If you'll remember, I said whistling."

Callie laughed as she sat down beside him. "Wanna watch something?"

Everett glanced over at the coffee table again and decided it was time. "Actually, Callie, I want to talk about something."

"Uh-oh, this sounds serious."

"Here's the thing…"

"WE'VE BEEN DATING for almost five weeks."

Callie cocked her head to the side, unsure where he was going with this. "Okay."

"And I feel like we can talk about stuff now. You trust me right?"

Callie hated loaded questions, and unease settled in her belly. "What's this about, Everett?"

Everett sat forward with his head in his hands, and Callie's heart stopped.

Oh, Jesus, what?

"A few days ago, I was looking for coasters, and I opened that drawer over there. I found a dozen or more letters from some man named Tristan—"

"You looked at my letters?" She practically screeched the words at him. "Did you read them?"

"No, of course not, but I am curious. You have dozens of unopened letters, and it's been driving me crazy not knowing—"

"It's not your business."

He seemed to consider that, but instead of letting it go, he pushed back. "Callie, I've told you about my past, but getting to know you is like pulling teeth. Just give me something."

"I *have* given you something." She stood up and began pacing the room, wrapping her arms around her body like a shield. "I've given you my body, my heart, and my trust—"

"If you really trusted me, you would tell me why you have a dozen unopened letters rotting in a drawer." Callie gasped, but he just kept going. "You would tell about what happened to your mom, or anything before the past five years. Trust is about sharing your hopes, your fears, your past. But you only give me scraps of truth. I need more."

"And I need time." God, why did he keep pushing for more than she was ready to give? She had just started to think they were happy, that they could actually make this work, and now here he was, making demands and dropping bombs on her. "You can't just snoop around and expect me to pour out my life story. You act like five weeks is such a long time, like there's some magic timeline that tells me when I can share things that maybe I'd rather keep buried." She was breathing hard, trying to calm down, but she was too far gone. "Did you ever think about that? That I'm happy for the first time in what feels like forever, and maybe I don't want to taint that by dredging up the past?"

"Callie, whether or not you want to talk about it, you held on to those letters. You're the one not letting go and not dealing with whatever happened to you." His tone was slow, calm, coaxing, like he was talking to a child throwing a tantrum, and it infuriated her.

"Get out of my house." Her tone was filled with cold fury, and she didn't care. She just wanted to be alone. "You have no right to tell me how to live and deal with my pain. You're not perfect either, Everett."

"I never said I was, but I know what you're doing isn't healthy." He tried to reach for her, but she jerked away. The pain and hurt in his eyes gave her pause, until he started preaching to her about what she needed. Again. "You need to deal with this, or it's going to catch up to you one day and destroy you. And I love you too much to see that happen."

He loved her? If he loved her, he would accept her. He would let her come to him in her own time, instead of making her feel wrong or broken for wanting to stay in their happy little bubble.

Only he'd popped that bubble.

"You can't fix me. I don't try to fix you. Why can't you just let things be?"

The laugh he released was bitter and harsh. "Because I finally realized that you may love me, but you're not with me, not wholly. I can give you time, but I can't just sit around waiting for you to let me in. The minute I first heard your voice over the radio, I knew you were special and that you should be mine."

Everett walked over to her and cupped her face. She hated the sadness in his eyes, eyes that usually sparkled and shone.

"But if you can't give me all of you, then I can't do this."

He dropped his hand and turned away, heading toward the door. Callie's throat constricted as she realized this was it. She could either divulge everything she'd buried, everything that had contributed to her fucked-up state of mind.

Or she could let him walk away.

"They're just letters!" she yelled at his retreating back. "Everett!"

He stopped without turning around.

"Please, don't do this." She was trembling with desperation and searching for something, anything, that would get through to him. She just needed more time.

"I love you."

Everett came back toward her, and she almost sank to her knees with relief. As he kissed her roughly, she tried to pull him closer, to deepen the kiss, but he pulled away too soon.

Instead, he just stared down at her with sorrow lingering in his eyes. "I love you too."

And then he was gone.

Sliding to the ground, Callie gathered her knees to her chest and sobbed. Ratchet came out of the bedroom and sat beside her, whimpering. Wrapping her arms around his neck, Callie wailed into his dense fur. Everett had thrown down an ultimatum she didn't know if she could handle and walked out the door.

Taking her joy with him.

CALLIE GRABBED ANOTHER package of instant noodles, not caring that though it was only seventeen cents, that it was packed with preservatives. She needed salt and comfort food.

Pushing her grocery cart past the wine aisle, she kept her head straight, refusing to look. She was just miserable enough to consider giving into oblivion. Fuck the hangover *and* her sobriety chip.

After unloading her cart onto the belt, she zoned out during the cashier's inane attempt at conversation and handed her card over. It was like she was in a dream. The rest of the world blurred around the edges, dulled by her misery.

Taking her card back from the cashier's outstretched hand, she walked out of the store. After loading up her groceries, she drove home, her brain bogged down with a million creative ways to see Everett. But the simplest way to prove her love was also the hardest.

Just thinking about Tristan brought to the surface a colorful array of negative emotions: hate, self-loathing, rage, fear. She'd been a blank mask for so long that when her old self began to emerge with Gemma, Caroline, and later Everett, she'd wanted to keep the rest of it at bay. If she talked about it, if she told him everything, it would be like reliving the nightmare all over again. She just wanted to move on and leave it where it was—in the past.

If that's true, and you're fine, then why did you keep the letters?

Callie's pity party continued well into the evening, after she'd devoured two packs of instant noodles and felt like her entire stomach was going to come back up.

Sitting on the couch with a Sprite, her gaze kept shifting to the drawer of letters.

Ratchet was sitting on her foot, leaning against her leg. Scratching her dog's big floppy ear, she asked, "What would you do, huh?"

The dog moved away from her and wandered into the bedroom. Leaning back against the couch, Callie closed her eyes, willing her mind to be quiet.

A moment later, Ratchet was back, burying his head in her lap. She opened her eyes. In his mouth was the shirt from Everett's zombie costume, covered in slime and fake blood. It was disgusting and now soaked with dog slobber.

Still, holding up the dry side to her face, she could smell Everett on the cotton, and her eyes prickled. "Damn it, Ratchet."

The dog's tail thumped against the floor as she got up and opened the drawer, pulling every letter out and sorting them by date. She'd received the first letter a little over six months after Tristan had been sentenced, when he was sitting in a state mental hospital.

As she took the first letter and opened the seal, she realized her hands were trembling. She never understood why Tristan had begun writing her after everything that had happened, but the answer to why was right here in her hand.

But knowing what he was thinking…

What if he remembered everything and described it? Told her he was sorry? Or worse, what if it led to more unanswered questions? Like, why he'd been too afraid to ask for help. Had his fear been worth betting their lives that he wasn't sick?

Leaning forward with her elbows on her knees to steady them, she pulled out the one-page letter and read:

Calliope,

Somehow I imagined using your full name under different circumstances, like in our wedding vows. But calling you Callie feels like a privilege I've lost.

I can't imagine what you must think of me, although I've tried. I imagine you hating me, wishing I were dead, that you'd never met me. I don't blame you for any of it, and there is nothing I can say that will make it better. I know that.

I love you, Callie. I will always love you, even if you never forgive me. From the first time you looked at me as you twirled your hair around your finger, you were the girl that I saw myself spending the rest of my life with.

I was stupid and reckless. I thought I would get better, that I was just stressed. I swear, Callie, I would never have hurt you or your mom or put you at risk. I made a mistake. Please, forgive me. I will do anything.

Tristan

Callie's eyes burned and her jaw hurt from being clenched so hard. He *loved* her? How dare he say that after everything he'd done?

His words echoed what Everett had said—that he'd known the minute that they were meant to be. Only with

Everett, she knew he would have put her safety first. He would have sought treatment and help.

The next letter said exactly the same thing, except this time, he added in some details about his life in the institution, how much the medication was helping, and how much he missed her. She crushed that one into a ball and threw it across the room. On and on they went. Through fifteen months. Always telling her he loved her, that he was sorry, and that he was getting better.

After his release, the letters described some of the times he'd stalked her:

I know you don't want to see me, but I need to see you. I need to know you're okay. That you're happy. I hate to see you destroying yourself the way your mom did. I saw you take shot after shot until you could barely stand, and I hate it. I know I did this, but I just wish I could remember.

Her skin crawled at the thought of him watching her get drunk. What if he'd approached her when she was shit-faced?

The next set of letters congratulated her on joining AA and getting her one-month chip. After that, they changed, focusing less on her and more on how he was trying to live his life. How he was trying to make up for what he'd done.

I volunteered at the local soup kitchen on Thanksgiving.

I spent Christmas Eve at the hospital, delivering Santa's gifts to the pediatric ward.

I ran a 5K marathon to raise money for cystic fibrosis.

It didn't matter how many good deeds he thought he was accomplishing. Did he really think that would just wipe the slate clean?

Finally, she was on the last letter, the one from just a few weeks ago.

Tearing it open, she sucked in her breath.

Calliope,

I don't know if you are even reading these letters, but if you are, I hope you respond. I am living in Idaho now, but before you get the wrong idea, I didn't do it because of you. I moved here for a job opportunity and am living in Boise with my fiancée, Madeline.

I have loved you since I was fifteen years old, and I always will. But I waited seven years for a letter, a phone call, anything to tell me that you'd forgiven me and that you could move past it and give me another chance. When I met Maddy earlier this year, I never imagined that I would find love again, but I have.

I had to move on and live my life. I deserve to be happy and so do you.

I hope to hear from you,
Tristan

White-hot rage pulsated through Callie's body, building up inside until she was screaming out loud. Screaming until her lungs hurt. Screaming until she was hoarse.

He deserved happiness? He didn't deserve anything! Why should he get a nice, cushy new life and love when he hadn't even gone to prison for what he'd done to her mother? To Baby? To her!

Rubbing the scars beneath her shirt, she picked up her cell. Callie was afraid to call, afraid of what she might say, so she typed in the phone number he'd listed in the letter and texted him.

Tristan. It's Callie. Do you still want to meet somewhere in Boise?

She got up from the couch and paced, back and forth across her living room until her phone beeped.

Callie. Yes, are you available tomorrow? Noon at the Cheesecake Factory?

She had to be at the station then but didn't want to wait, didn't want to play the back-and-forth. She could call in sick to work for one day.

That's fine.

Beep.

I'm so glad you texted. Here's the address.

Callie stared at the text, at his excitement. Like they were just old friends meeting up to talk about old times.

Rationality went out the window as she reared back and threw her phone against the wall.

THAT AFTERNOON, EVERETT was sitting on his couch, cursing his impulsiveness and impatience when someone knocked on the door. He ignored the sound, willing whoever it was to take the fucking hint that he wanted to be alone.

No such luck.

Everett's door opened behind him, and he didn't bother turning around. He knew from the heavy footsteps that it was Justin. "What do you want?"

Everett heard his fridge open and the *pfft* of a beer being opened.

"Hey, those beers aren't for little pricks," Everett said.

"Come on, dude, I'm sorry." Justin sat down on the couch next to him. "I just don't want you to make a mistake. You've been through the ringer, and I just think you should find someone who isn't loaded down by baggage."

"You don't get it." Everett took a long draw of his drink and put his second glass of Jack on the coffee table.

"Then explain it, Everett, because I don't understand why you would fall for someone like that after everything Dad put us through."

"Because I love her, that's why. Because when I met her, there was this instant connection, this pull that told me *this* was it. She gets me, man. Why can't you understand that?" Everett laughed bitterly, rubbing his hands over his face. "When I came back here, you and Dad kept telling me that I was a hero. That I was something special because of all I've been through, but that didn't make me feel better, Justin. It made me feel weak. Like I was a freak everyone was staring at. I was angry all the time, and then I was making stupid jokes just to break the ice. And women? Forget about the women; they were clueless.

"But Callie doesn't even see my scars. She sees me. And she makes me feel like a man, the man I used to be. Don't you want that for me? Don't you want me to have what you have?"

"Of course, Rhett," Justin said, his expression pained.

"Then apologize to Callie. Give her a real chance and get to know her. Val, too. Did you know her mom was an alcoholic, as bad or worse than Dad? I flew off the handle when I first found out about her alcoholism, but she put me in my place really quick and in the same breath, told me she understood where I was coming from. She is an enigma, man."

"What if she still thinks I'm a dick?"

"Then we can look forward to more awkward family dinners, I guess. That is, if it all works out."

"Is that why you're nursing a bottle of whiskey? Did you two have a fight? About us?"

Everett poured another and shook his head. "I told her I needed to know more about her, and I think I pushed her too hard."

Justin patted Everett's back. "She'll come around. I saw the way she looked at you. She loves you too."

Chapter Twenty-Four

THE NEXT MORNING, someone started banging on Everett's door just as he finished with a caller and his pounding head protested the racket. It had been hard enough to get his ass out of bed this morning and take calls.

Taking off his headset, he got up to answer it, grumbling. Did they have to bang so hard?

The knocking continued, growing more insistent, and he knew it wasn't his dad or brother. They would have already walked into the house and started bitching at him about not answering the door.

Everett opened the door to find Callie standing on his doorstep.

"Hi," she said.

His heart squeezed, and he rubbed his eyes, hoping they weren't too bloodshot. "Hi."

"I know that we're in a weird place right now, but you also said that no matter what, you'd be there for me. Did you mean it?"

The question was said quickly, and she was carrying herself stiffly. Did she think he was going to tell her to take a hike?

"Umm," he said, leaning against the door frame. "Yeah, of course."

Her shoulders sagged, and he noticed that her eyes looked bruised. As if she'd spent all night crying and had hardly slept.

"Okay, I need you to drive me to Boise."

"Now?" he asked.

"Yes, right now."

"For what? You could have called and given me a heads-up at least," he said.

"Except that I smashed my phone last night, so I couldn't. I know that this is rude, out of the blue, and violates about a thousand social codes, but can you please, *please* drive me?" She paused, staring up at him with those warm whiskey-hazel eyes and added, "I need you to be there for me today."

"Are you going to tell me what this is about, or are you just going to leave me hanging like every other time?"

Callie covered her face with her hands and groaned. "Are you seriously trying to blackmail me right now?"

"Hey, if I'm going to play Jeeves, driving four hours round trip, I at least deserve to know what we're doing."

He could tell by the set of her jaw that she wanted to tell him to go to hell but didn't. Instead, she let out a heavy sigh. "I'll tell you," she said.

"Let me just grab my coat," he said, walking back into the house.

THEY WERE JUST passing Glen's Ferry when the question Callie had been dreading came up again.

"So why did I have to drop everything to take you to Boise?"

This was it. Time to disclose the horrors of her past.

"We're going to see Tristan Anderson, the man who wrote me those letters."

Everett said nothing as seconds ticked by, and then he asked, "Are you going to tell me who he is to you?"

Her stomach roiled, and she took a deep breath, trying to calm her nerves. The last thing she wanted to do was puke in Everett's car.

"When I was fifteen, I started dating this boy, Tristan. We dated all through the rest of high school and college. After we graduated, he asked me to marry him, and I said yes."

Everett's hands tightened on the wheel; she could tell by the sudden whiteness of his knuckles. Was he jealous? It would have been sweet at any other moment. But now a lump formed in her throat as she got going, even though the words poured out of her like a volcano.

"I was so happy; nothing could spoil it for me. Tristan had experienced mood swings and sometimes he'd have blackouts, but they were so few and far between, I didn't really piece anything together, you know? But when we moved into my childhood home, they became more frequent.

"As you know, my mom was a recovering alcoholic, and she had made a lot of mistakes. But she loved me and adored him, so she gave us her house to live in and moved out to the guest house. We still had meals together, but it was nice to have our own place when most married people were stuck in one-bedroom apartments.

"I thought that finally things were getting better. No more drunken rages from my mom, and we were finally able to have a relationship again. The stars had aligned, life was good, and I thought we were going to live happily ever after." She couldn't tear her gaze away from Everett's face, at the harsh grimace twisting his lips. Obviously, her talking about loving another man was tearing him up, and she wanted to reach across, to explain that it was different from what they had. The love she and Everett had was stronger because of who they were now. Then, she'd been a young girl with high expectations and ideals. Now, she knew what was real.

She could still remember those first few months. The laughter in the kitchen as they'd cooked their meals together. Popping fresh popcorn with real butter to have a movie night of whatever was new. Going to bed early, just so Tristan and she could make love, and falling asleep wrapped up together. It was like reliving someone else's memories.

"I started to notice that on top of the moodiness and blackouts, Tristan would sometimes talk to himself. No, it was more like he was talking to someone I couldn't see. Or someone was talking to him; I'm not really sure. He even told me someone was following him, but I never saw anyone. It just didn't seem right, and eventually I asked him to go see a doctor. He told me he had, but it turned out he was lying to me and to himself. His parents didn't even know he was having delusions until…"

Callie rubbed at a scar as it tingled and saw Everett glance toward her out of the corner of her eye. Without a word, he reached for her hand and held it, squeezing it in his long fingers and palm. The gesture was so Everett, lending his strength when she needed it, that she took a breath and continued.

"I came home from work one night, and the house was too quiet. That was my first sign that something was really wrong. It was dark, but I saw my dog, Baby, on the floor. She was lying in a dark puddle, and when I knelt down to help her, I realized my hands were soaked in her blood."

"Callie…"

Tears fell over her cheeks as she continued. "I didn't even see him. I was too busy trying to shut off the alarm. There was just a flash of pain in my back, and then I was on the ground with Tristan hovering over me with a knife, screaming nonsense. I kept trying to reason with him, but he was having a psychotic break. I couldn't do anything but lie there as he plunged that knife inside my body, over and over. I remember thinking, just before I passed out, that it wouldn't take long to die."

"My God, Callie." Everett pulled the truck off the freeway at the next exit and parked on the side of the road.

Without even being asked, he unbuckled himself and slid across the seat, taking her into his arms, kissing and stroking her hair.

"When I came to in the hospital, I found out that he had killed our dog and my mother."

"Jesus, Callie, you were lucky."

"Yeah, that's what the doctors said too. Do you see now why I didn't want to tell you? I ignored all the signs that something was wrong. I deserved—"

He squeezed her so hard she cried out. "Don't you dare say you deserved this. You did nothing wrong. Do you understand?" He loosened his grip and rubbed her back. "I'm sorry. But you cannot think like that. Tristan was responsible for what happened. You told him you thought something was wrong. You are blameless."

He buried his lips in her hair, and she melted into his embrace, closing her eyes and absorbing his strength, his faith.

"What happened after? Did they arrest him?"

She laughed bitterly. "Yes, but he had a really good lawyer who brought in all kinds of experts to testify on his behalf, and Tristan had plenty of friends swear that he was a good guy who was just sick. Which I suppose is true, but…it just didn't seem like enough, what he got.

"The judge agreed that the crime was horrific, but he didn't want to add to the tragedy by ignoring the truth." Callie snorted. "It was all bullshit. He was basically telling me that he felt sorry for Tristan and because of that, he allowed him to plead down to manslaughter. He was in a psychiatric hospital for less than two years, being treated for schizophrenia. Once they got him on the medication, they released him on medically monitored probation."

"I'm sorry, baby."

She sagged into him, drained. She'd told him, shared every detail of her past. She was on her way to meet the man who had haunted her nightmares, but Everett would be there.

She'd thought she would feel relieved or at least that Everett would look at her differently once she'd shared her past with him. Instead, he was watching her with that same, tender look he'd given her time and time again. And all she could think about was that now, she was about to face her worst nightmare—the man who had nearly killed her and had haunted her since. The man whose actions had nearly caused her to destroy herself.

"What made you decide to meet him?" Everett asked, as if reading her doubt.

"After you left yesterday, I sat down and read his letters. They started off as apologies and declarations of love." She snorted. "Can you believe that? Just because he can't remember, I'm supposed to forgive him?"

"No, of course not. What he did was unforgivable…but…"

But? What but?

"Maybe seeing him will help you move on."

Moving on. Everyone was moving on. She wanted to move on. So why did it feel like Everett was suggesting she let bygones be bygones?

"The last letter said he's getting married. Why does he get to move on with his life?" Everett didn't say anything, and Callie sighed. "Maybe this is a mistake."

"If you really feel like that, I'll turn this truck around and we'll go home. You'll never have to see him again."

Callie stared out the windshield at the rolling hills and flat farmland stretching for miles in front of her. She did want to move on. She wanted her life back. This was the first step, and she had to take it. It had been a long time coming.

"Let's go to Boise."

AT TWO MINUTES to noon, Callie walked through the Cheesecake Factory doors, Everett right behind her. Her legs felt rubbery as she crossed the tile floors toward the hostess stand, pausing when Everett touched her hand.

"I'll just be right over there, okay?" He pointed to a cushioned couch under the large window, and she nodded.

"I'll be fine." She could feel her smile shake a little, but A for effort, right?

"You will be."

She continued on, wiping her clammy hands on her sweater and jeans.

"Hi, I'm meeting someone. Tristan Anderson, party of two?"

"Yes, he's already seated. Let me take you."

Callie couldn't seem to slow her rapid breathing as she trailed behind the hostess, her gaze searching for his familiar face. The hostess stopped next to a booth, blocking the occupant.

"Here you go."

Callie walked around her and got her first look at Tristan since the day he'd been sentenced. His once-thick blond hair had thinned some, and he was stockier, like he'd been hitting the weights at the gym. Or eating too many burgers. But his eyes and his smile were the same—though they didn't make her weak with happiness or fear anymore.

Those emotions had been replaced by rage and frustration.

"Callie," he said, starting to stand.

"Don't."

Her simple command was quiet but said with an edge of steel that seemed to surprise him. Did he really think that she was going to hug him? Just act like they were old friends, happy to see each other?

Not fucking likely.

The hostess looked between them, clearly uncomfortable, and finally laid her menu down across from Tristan. "Your server will be right with you."

"Thank you."

Callie sat across from him, pressing herself back against the seat and keeping her legs away from the middle. She didn't bother picking up her menu, since her stomach was roiling so much she doubted she could hold anything down.

Tristan was watching her with eagerness as he picked up his own menu. "I'm so glad you made it. I figured the Cheesecake Factory would be easy to find, and it used to be your favorite restaurant—"

"Not anymore." She said it sharply. She hated the way he was looking at her, like he was just glad she was there, and it didn't matter what she said. "A lot of things have changed, haven't they?"

She hated that he looked so healthy and happy. Her mother was rotting in the ground, and he acted like he didn't have a care in the world.

"Yeah, they have." He paused, searching her face with a doe-eyed gaze. "You're still beautiful, though."

A memory flashed through her mind: Tristan standing behind her in the mirror as they got ready for a party. He'd come up behind her and kissed her bare shoulder. *You are so beautiful.*

Callie closed her eyes, choking back on bile at the next image: him leaning over her, his knife dripping red with blood.

Her blood.

"Please don't say that. Don't pretend that this is normal, just two old friends meeting for lunch to catch up."

"I'm sorry. I thought that when you said you wanted to meet, you were ready to forgive me." His hand started to creep across the table, like he was reaching for her, and she stared at it warily, as if it was a spider ready to strike.

He stopped moving when he caught her look and sighed. "I have been dreaming of little else for seven years. I guess it was just wishful thinking."

"You've been dreaming of my forgiveness?" She actually laughed aloud at the ridiculousness of it. "Do you know what my dreams are made of, Tris?"

His expression turned bleak, and his face paled. Satisfaction rolled through her; she'd finally managed to wipe that stupid expression from his face.

"I've dreamed of blood, pain, and tears. I've dreamed of begging for my life and the overwhelming fear when my attacker doesn't listen. There've been no puppy dogs and kittens for me."

"Then why did you come?" His face was expressionless now, a void, and it threw her for a moment.

"I...I came because I couldn't understand. What kind of man lies to someone he says he loves and then tortures her by sending her letter after letter, reminding her of his betrayal?"

"Callie, I wasn't in my right mind; you know that."

"You weren't in your right mind because you refused to see a doctor. You lied to me so I'd stop badgering, and I believed you because I trusted you. Do you have any idea what it's like to know that because you trusted the wrong person, someone you loved died? You killed my mother, Tristan. Right mind or not, how could you ever imagine I would still love you after that?"

His face actually seemed to crumple, and tears filled his blue eyes. "Because I don't remember, Callie, not really. I remember our love. I remember the fun we had."

Callie's skin was burning, her blood boiling through her veins. She could feel her face flush as she hissed, "And the letters? The letters you sent, one after another, telling me you loved me, begging my forgiveness, documenting your penances. I got a fucking restraining order. What made you think that writing me all that crap was a good idea? How did that benefit me? To be reminded constantly that you got off with a slap on the wrist while I was so terrified, I couldn't sleep."

"Callie, it wasn't me. I don't remember anything— nothing. It's like I blacked out and when I came to, I was in the hospital, and they had to tell me what happened."

"That's convenient for you. You're lucky. Because I can *never* forget that night. I look at you, and I remember slicing pain. Begging you for my life. My blood spilling out. And waking up in the hospital, with a doctor standing over me, telling me how *lucky* I was to have survived when my mother didn't." Then she thought of something. "Does your new fiancée know what you did? That you could snap any minute?"

"Yes, she knows everything. But I've been on a highly effective antipsychotic for years with no problems."

Callie didn't care if he'd had a lobotomy and was a drooling idiot. Any woman who would willing marry a man who had murdered someone, even if he now was on meds, was a few French fries short of a Happy Meal.

"Good for you." Sarcasm oozed from every word, each chosen to inflict pain. "Wanna know how I've spent the years since you murdered my mother and mutilated me?" Tristan winced, but Callie was too far gone. She wanted to hurt him. "For two years, I couldn't close my eyes without seeing you hovering over me with that knife. I took anti- anxiety pills. Oxy. And when those didn't work, I chased them with a bottle of whatever I could get my hands on. I self-medicated myself right down the tube. But you knew that, right? You were following me. Bemoaning and chastising me for destroying myself.

"I never meant—"

She banged her fist on the table. "You stop talking. It's my turn to tell you how I've spent my time all these years. After all, we can share our growth, right? 'Cause we've shared so much?"

Tristan looked ready to bolt, but she wasn't done with him yet. Not by a long shot.

"Then one day I decided I wasn't going to hurt myself anymore. You had already hurt me enough. But I couldn't get rid of the guilt I felt, and it's haunted me since. I don't trust people or let them in easily. So when I met this amazing guy, I kept pushing him away. I did everything I could to destroy what we had because I am still petrified of making a mistake. Of picking another *you*."

A pained grimace twisted his face, but she went in for the kill. "And this guy is the whole package. But what I especially respect is that when he had a problem, he sought help and dealt with it. Unlike you."

"I'm...I'm glad you're happy."

"Do I seem happy? No, I've tried. I want to be, but I don't know if I will ever truly be happy. You killed a part of my soul, Tristan. The part that believed in love and trust and that things work out for the best.

"I came because your letter said you deserved to be happy. Who the fuck said you deserve happiness? You didn't suffer. You weren't punished for your crimes. They *fixed you* and then turned you back out to live your life."

"I was punished, Callie. I learned from my mistake, and I know I can never make it right. But I've been trying. I lost the woman I loved, the woman I was going to spend my life with. My parents can still barely look at me; I never see or hear from them."

"At least they're alive." Her voice sounded cold, lifeless, even to her ears. And suddenly she felt like all the steam and anger was draining out of her, leaving her hollow.

"You're right. But I can see why you think I didn't suffer. I swear, Callie, I have spent *years* suffering, trying to make up for my mistake."

Another spark flared to life as she sneered. "A mistake is when you forget to pay for milk, not brutally stabbing two people and killing a dog."

He sighed. Tristan actually fucking sighed.

"You know what? This was a mistake," she said, climbing out of the booth.

"Callie, please don't go," he said, reaching for her.

"Don't touch me," she cried.

Several people looked their way, and Callie shook her head. "I have spent years bottling up how I feel about you, making myself feel guilty. I know you were sick and that you didn't know what you were doing. I know that deep down. What I can't forgive is that you lied because you were afraid. You didn't tell me how you were feeling; you just shut me out, and I let you. I can't forgive that your actions led to that night. You were selfish, and I looked the other way.

"And the letters you sent were even more selfish because they were a reminder, every day, every month, every year.

You meant them as a way to see if I had any feelings left for you, and I can tell you, at no point in the last seven years have I felt anything more for you than fear and loathing."

Then she ran, rushing past the wait staff and the reception area. Past Everett, calling her name, until she reached the parking lot, where she bent over and retched. Callie saw Everett's boots through her legs as he came up behind her and began rubbing her back.

"Callie…" he said.

"I just want to go. Please," she said.

"Sure."

She stood back up, and the world was spinning. She leaned against Everett, and he wrapped his arm around her waist. When they reached the truck, he handed her a bottle of water, and she took a large gulp and then used it to rinse her mouth.

Everett backed up the truck, and they were on their way back to the highway. Callie gripped her hands in her lap, trying to stop their tremors.

Why didn't she feel better? If anything, she felt worse. She had unleashed the fury on the man who had ruined her life, but instead of feeling calm and filled with all kinds of perspective, she just wanted to hit something. She wanted to scream and rage and fuck.

Everett didn't try to tell her he was proud, which she appreciated. She didn't think she could take a pep talk, especially when she didn't feel like she'd accomplished anything.

Instead, Callie stared out at the land, bare and flat, with heavy gray clouds hanging over, casting shadows along the yellow dirt. Even the land felt angry. Maybe that was just her projecting.

"Did he apologize?"

"Of course he did," Callie said hollowly.

"What did you say?"

"That he hadn't been punished or suffered enough to warrant my forgiveness." Everett remained silent, and she turned toward him. "What?"

"Nothing."

"I tell you that I don't forgive the man who murdered my mother, and you don't have anything to say."

"It's not my place—"

"Just fucking say it!" she yelled.

Everett's face flushed. "Fine. You told me he had a psychotic break and didn't know what he was doing. If that's the case, it's tragic and horrible, but it was also an accident."

Callie burst into hysterical laughter. "My mother's murder has been called many things, but never an accident."

"I'm just saying, I've known a lot of good men who— because of an undiagnosed medical condition—have done horrible things."

Callie clenched her fists, wishing she could take a swing at him. "What happened to this being his fault, not mine?"

"It *is* on him. He should have followed through with treatment, but…"

"But what?"

He looked over at her, regret heavy in his eyes, like he knew what he was about to say was going to piss her off. "No man wants to admit he's weak, especially when it's to someone he loves."

The air in the cab was suffocating her, and she needed to get out. "Pull over."

"What?"

"Pull the fuck over!" she screamed.

Everett took the next off-ramp and pulled onto a dirt road.

"Callie—"

She climbed out of his truck, slammed the door, and started running. She didn't want to be around him and listen to his sympathy. His understanding. Fuck understanding; how the hell could he rationalize what Tristan had done?

Inside her, turmoil and frustration raged. It wasn't the first time she'd felt so out of control, so angry that she wanted to lash out. It was part of why she'd continued to drink, the total oblivion that came from letting go and getting sucked into a dreamlike state. Being drunk had calmed her. She'd only been able to find one other thing to do that since.

Sex.

Callie heard Everett jogging behind her, and she picked up the pace, ignoring her still-tender ankle. Suddenly, he grabbed her arm and spun her to face him.

"Callie, stop."

She swung her arm at him, but he caught her wrist, so she swung with the other hand, but he caught that one too. Sobbing, she struggled, trying to hit him, but Everett just pulled her into his body, holding her tight. She hated him. Hated that he'd made her think he understood.

"I've got you. I've got you." He just kept repeating it, tightening his hold each time she moved.

But Callie didn't want love and understanding. She was fucked up beyond repair and nothing could fix her. She'd thought that she could have it all—Everett and a new life—but just seeing Tristan reminded her that she would always bear the scars. She would always be the lucky girl who survived—only to have pissed her life down the toilet.

Why did she continue to suffer while he got to find peace?

The comfort and safety that usually came over her with Everett wasn't happening. Instead her body pulsed from the back of her neck to between her legs, and she just wished he would grab her, bend her over, or lift her up—she didn't care. She just wanted to feel the calm.

But with Everett, sex was about love and so much more than filling a need.

Only she was beyond rationale or caring. She couldn't get Tristan's puppy-dog look out of her head, as if *she* had victimized *him*. Callie suddenly couldn't breathe and pulled her head back, gasping for air.

"God, Callie, I'm sorry. What can I do?"

What could he do? She got her hand loose and grabbed the back of his head, digging her fingers into his neck until he bent his head to hers. And then she kissed him, showing him what he could do to help with every harsh, angry move she made. She kissed him with teeth and tongue, everything inside screaming that she needed more. Needed this.

Everett lifted her into his arms and carried her back toward the truck at a jog. When the first raindrop hit her cheek she didn't care, didn't think. All she wanted was to feel Everett, hot and hard, inside her, fucking the anger and frustration away.

When he set her down to open the truck, she grabbed the front of his jeans, jerking the buttons and zipper open in a fever of need. Before she could blink they were both stripped from the waist down, and he had her pressed against the side of the truck.

Everett kissed her as his hand delved between her legs, his finger slipping between her wet folds, but she pushed his hand away. She needed to forget and just feel something beyond the rage that had her burning up inside.

"Fuck me, Rhett. Now."

Without an argument or excuse, he pinned her hands above her head, his eyes blazing down into hers, and her heart skidded to a halt. She'd just told him she didn't want his touch, rejected his sweetness.

And then his mouth slammed down on hers, giving her what she'd been begging for. Hard, hot fucking. This time, he wasn't telling her no. He was giving her what she needed.

She took what he gave and demanded more.

He lifted her up higher, cool metal at her back and solid muscle at her front. She heard him rustling through his clothes, and then he brought up a condom, tearing it open with his teeth. There was no twinkle, no laughter in his eyes now. Just a white-hot passion.

In one moment of clarity, she admitted—if only to herself—that she was using him to fix something broken in herself. She'd said she loved him, yet she was trying to chase away her pain with him as if he was any other of her nameless lovers.

She almost opened her mouth to stop him, to apologize and bear the turmoil on her own...

But he had already positioned himself at her entrance, and then he was thrusting into her, working himself into her tightness, and she was caught up in the sensation. He was big, and she hadn't been fully ready, but she didn't complain, her body adjusting to him as he slid home once more, and she forgot everything else but the raw need to drive every emotion away.

When his hands gripped her hips, and he took her mouth in a hard kiss, she moaned hoarsely into his mouth. This wasn't the sweet, tender lovemaking that Everett preferred, or the teasing passion he usually evoked in her. He pounded her against the side of his truck, shallow, fast strokes that hit her high up and built a pressure inside like nothing she'd felt before. A type of intense pleasure and pain that shot right into the core of her. She couldn't think about the cost, just that the storm would be over soon.

As his teeth bit down on her bottom lip and his cock jerked inside her, she shattered, screaming with pleasure and pain until she was limp as a rag doll, pulling away from his mouth to gasp for air. She wrapped her arms around Everett's shoulders, burying her face in his neck as she shook with the aftershocks. The sex had been raw and dark and hot.

And draining. She had spent every ounce of emotion, and now she was hollow, quiet. It was better than a shot of Jack, and she sank into him.

Everett slowly pulled out and lowered her to the ground as she winced at the soreness.

"Damn it, Callie."

He didn't say more, but she could tell he was angry now. Just as she was calm and serene, he was jerking on his clothes and cursing.

And then she remembered the look in his eyes, that bleakness. That void. She had used Everett to make herself feel better, and he'd let her.

Even though it had hurt him.

Maybe when she'd told Tristan she deserved to be punished, she'd been right.

She picked up her pants and dressed quietly, regret twisting her guts up inside. She'd taken out the worst parts of herself on Everett, and he'd done what she asked because he wanted to help, to make her feel better. She picked up her shoes and went around the side of the truck.

And as she climbed inside, she was sure that Tristan had killed a small part of her soul all those years ago.

But if she wasn't careful, she could do the same thing to Everett.

Chapter Twenty-Five

EVERETT PULLED INTO Callie's driveway an hour and a half later, biting the inside of his cheek to keep from yelling. He should have just kept driving instead of pulling off the road to try and comfort her. Whatever had happened during the conversation with Tristan had caused Callie to lash out violently. He'd been afraid she'd hurt herself or do something stupid.

"Fuck me."

And he had. He'd given her exactly what she'd asked for, only when it was over, he'd felt empty. And he'd hated himself for it.

Putting the truck in park, he sat staring ahead, waiting for her to say something.

"Thanks for taking me and I'm…I'm sorry."

Gripping the steering wheel, he wanted to ask what she was sorry about, but he held it in.

"I guess…"

"I can't do this, Callie." The words cost him, but he couldn't fix her. He couldn't make her love herself. Couldn't make her forgive herself so she could move on and be happy.

All he could do was give her the freedom to do it herself.

"What?"

"I thought that if I could just teach you to trust me, this could work, but I feel like every time I uncover something from your past, another shadow pops up, and I'm just playing whack-a-mole. You keep punishing yourself for something that happened to you, and today you used me to do it. And I let you, because I love you. If you were dealing with it and getting through it, then I could wait, but you aren't dealing. You're not moving on, and I can't have a future with someone who won't let go of her past."

Callie didn't say anything for a minute, and then finally: "Okay."

"Okay?" he said.

"You're right. Maybe I'm not ready for this. Maybe I still need time to deal."

The wobble in her voice told him she wasn't as calm as she wanted him to think.

"I love you, Callie. You know it, and I know it, but I won't wait forever. You need to decide what you want."

Before she left, he needed to give her one last kiss that wasn't angry or hurt or raw.

He wanted it to be about love. And hope.

Everett stroked her cheek until she raised those beautiful eyes to his, and then he kissed her, softly, sweetly, like it was the first time.

And possibly the last.

He pulled back, tracing his thumb across her skin before his hand fell away.

"If you can't forgive yourself, Callie, then you can't move on. And I deserve someone who loves me enough to let go."

CALLIE CALLED INTO work for the week, too lost to function. She was completely fucked up, a mess of epic proportions. It seemed impossible that in such a short amount of time she could have gone from a hermit, who was just a little gun-shy, to this lunatic head-case who hurt the people she loved.

By Thursday, even lying on the couch watching *How I Met Your Mother* didn't make her feel better.

Ratchet's head came up off the floor, and he let out a soft woof, but she didn't move. Her front door slammed open, and she heard several voices calling her name, but she just kept watching Ted try to fall in love with the Slutty Pumpkin.

Stop forcing it, Ted. It's over.

"Okay, this is sad," Caroline said above her.

Gemma squatted down next to her. "Callie, are you okay?"

"Peachy, except your big head is blocking the TV."

Gracie snorted. "You do have a round head."

"Shut up." Gemma stood. "We have to get her out of here. At least get her showered."

"She does smell pretty ripe," Gracie said.

"*She* is right here and smells just fine."

"If you think the smell of funk and Funyuns is fine…" Caroline grabbed the snack bag out of her hand.

"How did you know I was home? I could have been on vacation in the Bahamas."

Gracie answered that one. "The stalker boy at your station said you called in sick, but when he came by to check, your car was in the drive, you weren't answering the door, and it smelled like a dead body."

"You are full of shit!"

"Only about the dead-body smell, but he did knock for a while. He was worried, so he talked to Jenny Andrews, who talked to Ellie, who told Caroline, who called us."

"Seriously, wallowing in here is not going to bring Everett back," Gemma said.

"Who says I want him?" Callie said sourly.

"Um, the wallowing, moping, and all-out pitifulness."

Callie lifted her head to look up at Caroline. "You suck."

"No, this is what the rest of the world—who isn't throwing a pity party—calls a caring friendship. Now, get your ass up, shower, brush your teeth, and shave your legs. Not in that order." Gracie ripped off her blanket.

"And when you get out, we'll have coffee and a cheese Danish waiting for you," Gemma said.

"And then you'll explain what the hell happened and what the plan is for fixing it," Gracie chimed in.

"Oh, by the way, you made Miss Know It All's column again. Congrats," Caroline said, dropping the paper on her face.

"I hate you."

BAD FOR ME 335

The three women dispersed into different rooms—Caroline into the kitchen, probably to keep the coffee warm—and a few seconds later, Callie heard the shower turn on.

"I'm not an infant; I can shower on my own."

"Not according to the body odor permeating your house and burning my nostrils!" Gracie yelled cheerfully.

"Fucking smart-ass." Callie held the paper out as she climbed to a sitting position, scanning the page.

Is Caverett dunzo already? Sources say that the sparklingly happy couple are on the outs, and I am completely devastated, dear readers.

Sparklingly happy couple? Callie snorted.

I think the thing I liked best about these two was that separately they were quiet and withdrawn, each with an air of sadness that made you want to stop and hug them. But together, there was a spark. A connection that made them seem like two halves of the same whole. Call me a crazy romantic, but when these two were first linked, it was like a light bulb went off in my head, and I thought, "Oh yeah, that is brilliant."

So, if you're reading this, Callie and Everett, just remember: love can build a bridge, but someone's gotta take the first step.

If only it were that simple.

"Okay, the shower is going, clean clothes are on the bed…Callie! Get up and let's go! We don't have any time to waste!"

"Okay, here's my two cents," Caroline said, taking a sip of her coffee.

"Oh, please, regale us with your wisdom." Callie earned a glare for that. She had to admit, she felt better after the shower, but the hour-long story had been emotionally exhausting. She'd told them everything—from the night Tristan attacked her to the fight with Everett. A few details had been omitted; she loved these women, but they didn't need to know everything.

"You spent seven years beating yourself up about what happened to your mom," Caroline began, "and as long as you didn't open those letters, you could pretend that Tristan was suffering and punishing himself the same way you were. But when you actually read the letters and realized he was just a self-absorbed little douche anyway, all that anger and self-loathing came bubbling to the surface, and you exploded with it.

"The thing is, a guy like Tristan is never going to understand your side. He thinks that because he doesn't really remember, it doesn't count, but it does—big time. You just need to get right with the fact that he will most likely never take responsibility, and you need to forgive yourself. Because the way you feel isn't really about him; it's about you. You wanted him punished and that didn't work out, but if you dwell on him and his life, you're never going to have your own."

"And it sounds like Everett just wants you to be real with him," Gracie said.

"So if you go to him and hold nothing back, just lay it all out on the line, he'll forgive you," Gemma said.

"I don't know how."

"Think about it, Callie. If Everett wants you to forgive and love yourself, what is going to help you get there?" Caroline asked.

"When I was deciding whether or not I wanted Travis and if I could trust him," Gemma said, "I had to look at things from another perspective. I'd always thought that he didn't love me enough to stay, but when I watched our wedding tape, I realized I hadn't trusted his love because I didn't think I was worthy of him. The fault was with how I viewed myself, not with him."

Callie thought about Gemma's words. Everett had said more than once that he loved her sweetness, that she was funny and accepting. But deep down, she didn't see that in herself. She was constantly judging others, even her friends. Her eyes strayed to Gracie, whom she'd always held at a distance, calling her a drama queen in her head, but the truth was, when she'd needed help, Gracie had come through.

"And during my little…arrangement with Gabe, getting close to him scared the hell out of me. Being vulnerable is just not my thing, especially when it's with a man. Us Willis girls put the *d* in 'daddy issues.'"

"I hear ya," Gemma said.

"My point is, we all have reasons to hate ourselves. You just have to take it one day at a time."

Callie played with the lid of her cup, thinking about that. She'd learned the same thing in AA, although if she was honest, she hadn't worked the program like she should've. She'd never discovered spirituality or meditation, and although she had plenty of faults, she'd never made amends.

But none of the wrongs she'd committed lately stemmed from her alcoholism. The alcoholism was a symptom of her anger, self-loathing, and fear.

She could rework the program to help her move on. If she just took that first step, she could take the next.

My name is Calliope Jane Jacobsen, and I couldn't deal with the aftermath of my fiancé's attack. It nearly took my life, and it did take my mother's. Instead of seeking counseling, I drowned my guilt, pain, and fear in booze and pills. When I stopped using those, I started using people to make myself feel better, but the only person who can make me happy is me.

Callie rubbed the scar along the right side of her collarbone and knew what she had to do.

Chapter Twenty-Six

One Month Later

CALLIE WAS COMING back from Twin Falls, and she made a face at the snow flurries coming down. It was December 20 and after her counseling appointment that morning, she'd driven all over town, Christmas shopping. Luckily, Gracie's boots had been on sale for two hundred dollars, and she'd split them four ways with Caroline, Gemma, and Mike. She'd found a gorgeous messenger bag for Gemma, and for Caroline, she'd picked up a couple of cookbooks and some jars of brownie mix. Plus, she planned to tape a Bath and Body Works gift card inside one of the cookbooks. The men in her life had been a little harder, but she'd managed to get Mike, Fred, and the guys from the station done. Dalton was getting a new western shirt and a pair of rodeo headphones she'd found online.

She's been busy the last month; that was for sure. After starting her Twelve Steps over again, she'd pulled Dalton aside and apologized for the way she treated him at Justin and Val's wedding. Bless his heart; he had been more than happy to forgive and forget. And she was especially happy that he was over his crush on her. He'd even started dating this pretty little dark-haired girl from one of his classes. Callie was a little surprised he hadn't ended up with Jenny Andrews, who clearly adored him, but time would tell.

The last person on her list was Everett, even though she hadn't seen or heard from him since that day in her driveway. Caroline never resisted a chance to tell her that she'd seen him and that he looked good, and Gemma was constantly telling her about all the book orders he'd placed, hinting that he probably wasn't seeing anyone. But Gracie wasn't as subtle.

"I asked him straight up if he was dating, and he told me to mind my own damn business."

Callie tried not to think about it—not until she was ready. She was almost there; she just had a few more steps. Her counselor was happy with her progress, although her counselor had talked Callie out of attempting to make amends with Tristan. On that one, Callie was in complete agreement with Caroline; what she needed to fix had little to do with Tristan, and although she did owe him an apology, she wasn't sure if reaching out to him was a good idea. Despite how much he'd hurt her, he deserved to start over.

Callie pulled into Jose's Tires to get out of the snowstorm. She'd paid him off the month before, but he had told her that anytime she needed tires to come and see him, and he'd give her a discount. It was very sweet, and she would probably take him up on it in the next few months for her remaining two tires. In the meantime, she'd picked up a little thank-you gift for him.

Callie pushed open the door and shook the snow off, smiling brightly.

And then she froze.

At the counter, Justin and Valerie Silverton were talking to Jose.

"Callie, I'll be right with you, sweetie."

Callie blushed, avoiding the couple's gazes. Every time she'd seen them around town since that night at Fred's, she'd headed the other way. She had no desire to hear their opinions about her or why she'd bailed on Everett.

"I can come back."

As she turned to leave, Valerie called out. "Callie, wait."

She paused as Valerie came over, rubbing her hands over her large protruding belly.

"I know it's long overdue, but I wanted to apologize for my attitude toward you at dinner. We shouldn't have judged you without getting all the facts."

Callie hadn't been expecting that, especially considering the way Everett and she had been avoiding each other. "Well, thank you."

They stood awkwardly for a minute or two while Justin finished up with Jose. When he finally joined his wife, he cleared his throat before he spoke. "I know Val apologized, but I wanted to tell you that I was wrong about you. And we'd like to make it up to you, if you don't have any dinner plans next weekend."

"Um, can I get back to you? I'm just not sure."

"Of course." He seemed to be struggling for something else to say and finally just blurted, "He misses you."

A lump of emotion got stuck in her throat. "Tell him hello for me."

"You should really tell him yourself."

"Maybe I will."

"If you don't come by, Merry Christmas," Valerie said.

"Merry Christmas to you too."

They walked past her outside, and Jose said loudly, "Awkward…"

"Shut up, or I'm giving you a lump of coal."

EVERETT WATCHED THE snow fall from his window, the porch light highlighting the flakes of glittering white in the darkness.

It was almost midnight. He'd gone by his dad's house a few hours ago with the intention of carrying more wood inside for him, but he hadn't been there, which worried Everett. It was the anniversary of his mother's death, and his dad had been in a foul mood all day. When he'd said he was going to a meeting this afternoon, Everett couldn't keep his thoughts from straying to Callie, and he wondered if they still met for coffee. His dad didn't talk about it if they did. But tonight, Everett was afraid he'd bypassed the meeting and headed straight to a bar.

Everett tried his cell again, and after five rings, his dad picked up. "Hecklo?" It sounded like he'd hocked a loogie into the phone, his speech was so slurred.

"Dad, where are you?"

"Who is this?" There was a muffled fumbling; then, "Everett, my boy. Come join your old man for a little drink."

Irritation coursed through him. "How 'bout I just come get you, and you can have a nightcap?"

"Fine, fine. I'm at Buck's. Your friend Eric keeps telling me I can't have any more anyway."

The line went dead, and Everett cursed, shoving his arms into his coat sleeves. There went eight months of his father's sobriety down the toilet.

Everett resisted the urge to call Callie and tell her what was going on. No matter what had happened between the two of them, he knew she wouldn't give up on Fred, but he could handle his dad's drunken scenes.

Lord knew he'd been dealing with them for years.

Everett headed out and climbed into his truck. The cold air made it hard to start, and it gurgled and clucked at him as he set his phone in the nearby cup holder. Blowing into his ice-cold hands, he finally turned the key in the ignition and pumped the gas. "Come on, asshole, start."

The engine roared to life, and Everett said a silent prayer of thanks.

As he putted up the driveway slowly, he cursed his dad for being weak. The storm was bad—a complete whiteout—and he could barely see five feet in front of him. It would serve his dad right if he just called the Rock Canyon Police Department to pick up Fred and put him in the drunk tank for the night.

As he turned onto Old Mill Road and passed the turn-off that led to Callie's, his throat clenched painfully. God, he missed her. Everett was sure that things were over, but it didn't stop him from wishing that she'd just show up on his doorstep and pour her heart out.

Up ahead, out of the white, a dark shape suddenly raced in front of his truck. Everett clipped whatever it was with the right side of his bumper, sending his truck skidding on the wet snow. He saw the flash of headlights out of the corner of his eye and realized he was drifting into the other lane.

It was either hit the oncoming truck or swerve and roll off the road.

As he turned the wheel hard, his truck slid away from the headlights and felt almost airborne for a second. Suddenly, it jerked to a stop, and his head smacked against the steering wheel. The last thing he saw before he passed out was Callie's smiling face.

Chapter Twenty-Seven

"HAVE I TOLD you how much I love you?"

Callie shook her head and glared at the happy drunk in her front seat. "Don't think you can sweet talk me, Fred. I'm disappointed in you."

Fred frowned at her, the pout looking out of place on his craggy face. "But it was just a wee bit—"

"You be quiet until I get you home, but tomorrow, you're going to get an earful from me."

"I miss my wife," Fred slurred sadly.

Callie's heart constricted. She'd had no idea it was the anniversary of Fred's wife's death until he'd called an hour ago, telling her he needed a ride home.

Why he hadn't called Everett or Justin, she could only imagine, but they would have probably told him to go to hell. Either way, this was exactly how she wanted to spend her night…driving in a snowstorm and very likely carrying a drunk, babbling man into his house.

Just outside of the Silverton farm, Callie saw sparks on the side of the road and slowed down. Ratchet whimpered in the back, and she shushed him as she turned the Jeep to shine her headlights on the scene.

"What is it?" Fred mumbled.

Callie squinted through the snow and could make out a truck—a truck had hit a power pole and was stuck nose first in the embankment, with sparks flying over the top of it. "I'm going to pull to the side of the road and make sure the driver's okay."

"I'll go." Fred tried to open his door, and Callie grabbed his shoulder, pushing him back into the seat.

"Just wait. I'm going to park and be right back."

Callie flipped the Jeep around and pulled off to the side before grabbing her gloves and a flashlight from the middle console. Checking her mirror for oncoming headlights, she stepped out and flipped on the flashlight, shivering against the icy wind. As she neared the wreck, she noticed it was an extended cab and wondered if more than one person was hurt. Crawling down the embankment, she reached the driver's-side door and grabbed the handle.

And suddenly, a sickening fear overtook her.

She knew this truck.

Everett.

"Everett!" She pulled on the handle again, but it didn't budge.

She scrambled back up the hill, looking in the back of his truck for something hard, in case she needed to break a window. Grabbing a snow shovel, she tried the passenger-side door, but it was locked. Ducking her head, she swung the shovel as hard as she could and cracked the window, but it didn't break. Screaming in panicked frustration, she swung again, and the window shattered.

Throwing the shovel to the ground, she peered inside.

It was empty.

Spinning around, she looked off in the distance, but there was nothing but blackness and snow. Not even footprints, although with the snow falling so fast and hard, she supposed they could have been covered up.

Maybe he got a ride home.

Then Callie looked down at the shovel and back up to the broken window and started laughing hysterically.

Everett was going to be pissed.

Callie threw the snow shovel back into the bed of the truck and unlocked the door through the window. Sticking her jacket into the door, she managed to cover the broken window, hoping it would keep most of the snow out of the cab. She was pretty sure she had another sweatshirt in the car, and besides, she was going to take Fred right home anyway.

Once she made her way back to the Jeep, she opened the door with a laugh. "Fred, you are never going to believe what I...Fred?"

Fred was hunched over, and Ratchet was nudging him, whimpering. Callie climbed in and put her fingers to his neck. There was a pulse. Had he just passed out? She shone the light on his face and saw his chin was covered with blood.

There was blood everywhere, all over the front of him.

Yanking her gloves off, she grabbed her cell and dialed 911.

Be okay. Be okay.

And while she waited for the operator to speak, Everett's smiling face flashed through her mind.

Please be okay.

"It's NOT UNCOMMON for patients with advanced cases of pancreatitis to vomit blood, especially if they have a drink," the doctor said.

"But is he going to be okay?" Callie asked. She was standing in the hallway of St. Luke's Hospital in Twin Falls. She'd called Everett's phone a dozen times, but the minute that it went to voicemail, she hung up. She'd called Justin, who said he'd stop by Everett's place and then come to the hospital.

"We're running a few more tests, but he should be able to go home in a few hours."

Relief swept through Callie, and she reached out to take the doctor's hand. "Thank you so much."

"If you ask me, he really shouldn't be drinking at all. If there is any way to get him into a program, I'd do it."

"Callie!" She turned to see Justin rushing toward her and cried out when he wrapped her up in a huge bear hug.

"Thank you so much for picking him up and being there."

Callie hugged him back, smiling. "Of course." Her smile dissolved, though, as she looked around his shoulder. "Is Everett with you?"

"No, he wasn't home."

"Um, Justin, this is Dr. Wilson. He says Fred is going to be okay and can probably go home in a few hours."

As Justin turned his attention to the doctor, Callie pulled out her phone again. Hitting Everett's picture, she let it ring through to his voicemail. At least if he was hurt and someone was taking care of him, they might try to find his family. Maybe they'd hear her voicemail and call her back.

"Hey, it's Everett. Leave your message at the beep...and Whiskey?"—Callie's breath and heart stopped—*"I'm still waiting."*

Tears choked her as his voicemail beeped, and she tried to speak, but it came out kind of garbled. "Rhett, it's me. I broke the window of your truck because I thought you were inside, and I'm sorry, but I love you. Please...just please call me. Your dad is sick, and I am so worried about you."

"CAN I GIVE you a lift home?" Larry, the guy Everett had almost crashed into, asked.

They were standing next to his truck in the heavy snowfall, watching the tow truck driver, Carlos, connect a long, thick cable to his truck bumper. Everett was sporting a nasty headache from hitting his head, but overall, he was okay. Thank God, Larry had come back to help after Everett's car had hit that pole, or he might have frozen to death trying to find the nearest house.

It was terrifyingly ironic that on the anniversary of his mother's death, he had nearly died the same way.

"Thanks, a ride home would be great," Everett said, already feeling guilty for putting the guy out. Larry had driven him up to Jose's an hour ago, where Everett had managed to rouse someone to come back with them and tow his truck back to the garage. On the way back, Larry had swung him by Buck's, but Eric said Callie had already picked up his dad.

At least he knew his dad was safe.

Now, with snow covering his head and shoulders, he stared at the gaping hole that used to be his window. Some idiot had probably thought he'd left some valuables inside and stopped to take a look.

But what kind of idiot would be out in this, besides him?

Everett had searched his truck when they first arrived but hadn't found his phone and couldn't call Justin for a ride. The asshole who'd broken in had probably taken it.

The icy wind swirled the snow around them, sending chills up Everett's spine as Carlos started pulling his truck out of the ditch. The high-pitched whine as the cables cranked the heavy load made him grit his teeth.

Then, out of the corner of his eye, he thought he saw something big and black flopping against a fence just beyond the lights of Larry's SUV.

What the hell was that?

Everett started toward the shape, but Larry's voice stopped him.

"What are you doing?"

"Going to see what that is," Everett said, pointing.

Everett didn't hear anything else Larry said as he climbed down, his boots and legs sinking into the snow. When he was just a foot away, he reached out and grabbed the cloth.

No, not cloth. It was a wool coat. Dragging it off the fence, he tucked it under his arm and climbed back up onto the road.

"So what was it?" Larry asked.

"Looks like a woman's coat."

Larry looked at him like he was crazy, which was probably true. As Carlos finished up and handed him the paper to sign, he shifted the jacket up over his shoulders and could have sworn he smelled the sweet scent of Callie on the wind.

CALLIE CURSED THE large snowflakes covering the windshield. They were falling faster than her wipers could clear them, but she only had half a mile more to go. She had taken Highway 84 back home since the plows were out and working on the main roads first.

She still hadn't been able to get ahold of Everett, but Justin had agreed to stay with Fred so she could see if he was home yet. Valerie had been watching for him, but with the whiteout so thick, she couldn't see very well across the farm.

As she pulled up in front of his house, she threw the Jeep into park and climbed out. She could just barely see Everett's porch light through the blizzard and ran up the steps to begin pounding on the door. When he didn't answer right away, she tried the knob, but it was locked.

"Everett!" she yelled at the top of her lungs, banging on the door with all her strength.

Please be here. Please be okay.

Suddenly, a light came on inside, and she thought she heard someone running. The front door swung open to reveal Everett in a pair of sweats and a T-shirt, looking rumpled and so beautiful that she didn't hesitate to throw herself at him, causing him to stumble back into the house.

"Callie! Jesus Christ, you're freezing." He wrapped an arm around her and shut the door behind her.

Callie was so relieved to see him that she didn't care that she was probably strangling him. "Oh my God, I thought you were dead! I went to pick up your dad and I saw your truck, and I thought you were trapped, so I broke the window to get you out—"

Everett took her shoulders. "Wait—*you* broke my window?"

"Yes, but I put the jacket up so your truck wouldn't get ruined, but then your dad was vomiting blood—"

"What?" Everett's eyes bugged out of his head, and he started to head for the door, but she grabbed his arm.

"But he's okay; it was just his pancreatitis flaring up." Unable to control herself, she started giggling as she said, "The doctor said he should really stop drinking. What an idiot, right?"

When she finally sobered, she continued. "Then I couldn't get hold of you, and I tried to call, and I heard your voicemail—"

Everett actually flushed. "I dropped my phone during the accident, but I couldn't find it when we went back to tow the truck."

"So your brother's staying with your dad until he can be discharged, and I raced here to find you because Val couldn't see your house through the storm." She didn't think she'd ever spoken so fast in her life.

"It sounds like you had quite the night." His voice began shaking with laughter, and just that short burst showered her with warmth.

"The point I was trying to make is that I love you. I love you so much that if I lost you, it would kill all the beauty left in this world. Because you were the one who showed me that the world could be beautiful again. That love could be amazing and real.

"I've been working on myself, actually. I restarted the Twelve-Step program and have been trying to make amends with people that I've hurt." Her throat squeezed so tight, she could hardly get the words out. "Like you. I know all you ever wanted was to love me and be there for me. I know I shut you out and hurt you, but I've been trying to learn healthy ways to communicate. I'm seeing a counselor twice a week, and she's really helped me learn how to forgive myself. What happened wasn't my fault, but blaming myself gave me a sense of control in situations where I had no control whatsoever. It's a work in progress, and I'm learning to love myself...but I'm ready.

"Fate brought you to me," she said, sobbing now, "and I won't give you up without a fight."

Everett stared down at her thoughtfully, and just when she was sure he was going to tell her it was too late, he smiled. "But you don't believe in fate."

"But you do," she said, hope warming her like sunshine. "And I believe in you."

Before she could say anything else, he lifted her against him and wrapped her legs around his waist, taking her mouth with his.

Callie held on to the back of his head, opening her mouth wide. The kiss was messy, their noses bumping and teeth clacking, but neither of them could stop devouring the other.

"Fuck, Callie," he said against her mouth, his voice raw. Everett started carrying her down the hallway.

Heart pounding, she stopped him in the doorway. "Wait."

"Callie," he started, but she covered his mouth with her hand.

"Trust me." With her other hand, she patted the wall until she found the light switch. As she flipped it up and light flooded the room, she said, "You may continue."

His lips twitched as she pulled her hand away from his mouth. "I may, huh?"

"Will you shut up and kiss me?"

He did, his arms sliding up her back to tangle in her wet hair, and she moaned as he took her bottom lip into his mouth, sucking it sharply. When they reached the edge of the bed, she unhooked her legs and slid down his body. Her hands grabbed the bottom of his T-shirt and jerked it up, breaking away from him as he helped her drag it over his head.

She pushed him back, and he sat on the bed, watching her with eyes that were dark as burnt sequoia. Before she lost her nerve, she unbuttoned her coat and discarded her sweatshirt and bra, standing topless in her sweatpants.

No T-shirt. No bra. Just her skin and scars.

"Callie," he said, reaching for her.

She evaded his hands to push her sweats around her ankles, stepping out of them slowly in just her underwear. She was freezing without the warmth of his body, but she wanted him to look, to see why she had been so scared to let him touch her.

Closing her eyes, she waited for him to say something, anything.

She jumped when his finger trailed gently across her stomach.

"Look at me."

His command shook her to her core, but she did as he asked. Everett slid his finger over each white scar, watching her face as he did so.

"I love you," Everett said.

Her throat tightened with sobs as he wrapped his arms around her waist and brought her to him, kissing the scar in the middle of her chest, the one that had missed her lung by a millimeter.

"I'm sorry it took me so long to be ready," Callie said.

"You're here now." His lips lingered over the skin above her belly button before he brought his mouth back up to hers.

Callie lowered her forehead to his, releasing a shaky breath. "I wish I could take it all back."

"I don't." She pulled away from him, even as he continued. "If he hadn't attacked you, you never would have come to Rock Canyon. We never would have met. I hate that you went through hell for years and that you suffered. But without your past, you and I wouldn't have a future."

Her stomach fluttered at his words.

Everett's lips trailed across her chest again, the rough hair on his chin rubbing against her nipple, bringing it to a hard point. "When I think about a life with you, Callie, I see a house overlooking the canyon, with a clear view of the mountains. I imagine us curling up on the couch on weekends, watching stupid comedies and TV shows with two bowls of popcorn. Unless I can somehow bring you around to add just a little salt—"

"No way in hell."

"It doesn't matter, because when we start making out during the movie, you're going to be able to taste my salty popcorn."

"Gross."

His tongue reached out and flicked her nipple, sending a tingle of goose bumps across her skin.

"Are you cold?" The heat of his breath rushed over her wet flesh.

"A little," she whispered.

He stood up and pulled down the blankets covering the bed. "Come on." She crawled in, and he followed, spooning her and pulling the blanket over them.

"Jesus, your legs and feet are like icicles." Everett tangled his limbs with hers anyway, and she used his bicep as a pillow.

"That's why I'm glad I have you to keep me warm."

Everett leaned down to kiss her cheek, so sweetly it brought tears to her eyes.

"Thanks for not making me wait forever."

"I didn't want to waste another moment," she said, brushing her fingers across his cheek. "Life can change in an instant."

"You're right." His hand slid up her body to cup her breast as he trailed kisses along her jaw. "To making every moment count."

Sinking into the warmth of his mouth on her skin, she whispered, "Here's to forever."

Epilogue

One Year and Five Months Later

CALLIE HELD ON to Everett's hand as they walked onto the CSI campus and headed toward the Expo Center, a large heated indoor arena they used for the National Championship Rodeo team and community events.

When the local AA leader had approached her about talking to at-risk teens and college students as part of an initiative by a nonprofit called Healthy Solutions, she'd been unsure. The thought of traveling from school to school had made her anxious, so he'd organized a large fund-raising event for the area high schools instead. Teenagers and young adults from the Twin Falls area had been invited to come out, bid in a silent auction, and listen to several guest speakers who had abused alcohol and drugs as a way to cope with their traumatic pasts.

BAD FOR ME 359

Callie was the first speaker, and besides her initial apprehension, she was ready. At least, she hoped so. The last thing she wanted to do was disappoint the people closest to her. Especially the man by her side.

Everett squeezed her hand reassuringly, as if he could read her thoughts. "It's going to be fine."

"I know."

It was strange that Callie had been in AA for seven years now, but tonight would be the first time she'd spoken about what had brought her there. For years she had talked about her drinking, about feeling out of control, but she'd never shared what Tristan had done. And how she had dealt with the consequences of his actions.

As they went through the stage door, Callie was afraid she was going to throw up. It was one thing to stand up in a crowd of other addicts or even go on the local television morning show, but standing in front of five hundred teenagers and young adults was making beads of sweat roll down her back.

When she'd first started therapy over a year ago, all she'd wanted was to find a healthy way to deal with her unresolved anger and guilt.

But what had started out as a journey of self-awareness had become so much more as she began researching the correlation between addiction among young people and those who had suffered a trauma. From what she'd read, all of the statistics were betting against her and the kids she was trying to help. Still, she knew she wanted to make a difference, even if she helped just one person.

She just wanted them to know that they were not alone.

When they arrived backstage, the organizer of the event spotted them and waved Callie over.

"I have to go," Callie said.

"I'll be right up front." Everett gave her a deep, searching kiss before releasing her hand and heading for the exit.

She was all alone.

As CALLIE WALKED to the microphone, her heeled boots clicked across the stage and echoed throughout the auditorium. The sign above her head read, *Healthy Solutions to Trauma*.

Adjusting the mic, she cleared her throat. "Good evening. My name is Callie, and I was asked by the lovely people of Healthy Solutions to talk to you about my experience. Of course, I'm sure some of you are thinking you can handle your own problems, and you don't need help. I thought the same thing.

"I was just fifteen when I met a boy I thought I'd love forever. For seven years, we grew closer and finally, after we graduated from college, he asked me to marry him. I, of course, said yes.

"I didn't know that a few months later, the man I thought I'd spend my life with would get sick. That one night he'd suffer a psychotic break and murder my mother. And our dog. And finally, when I came through the door, he would stab me eight times in my chest and abdomen."

The lighting changed, but Callie didn't need to look behind her. The entire room gasped as they saw pictures of her wounds. She had given the organization the photos and permission to use them.

"The doctors told me how lucky I was too many times to count. I never felt lucky, though. I felt scared. And foolish. And guilty. But above all, I felt angry. At myself and at him.

"I didn't know what to do with my feelings. Without any family or support system, I was lost and struggling. I couldn't sleep without pain pills, and when those ran out, I added alcohol to the mix. Anything to help me forget.

"But the next day, everything would come back to me, and on top of that, I'd have a hangover. You ever heard of 'the hair of the dog that bit you'? Well, that was me. Soon my drinking wasn't just limited to nights, and I came close to flushing my career down the toilet.

"Once I hit rock bottom, there was no place to go but up. Only even though I got sober and started over, I still hadn't dealt with the pain of my past."

Callie searched the crowd for Everett, finding him in the front, next to his family and her friends.

"It wasn't until I met someone else, years later, that I took a hard look at the choices I'd made. At the way I dealt with stress, and I decided I wanted to change. To be happy. I went to therapy, and I started talking to the people I love. Opening up about what I was feeling and thinking. And I know I'm making this sound simple, but it's not. It's reprogramming your whole response to stress, and it is a long, uphill battle.

"I am still working through the process, but it is working. It's day-by-day, step-by-step. I'm not here to patronize you. I just want you to know that if you want something more than fear, hurt, guilt, anger, and help-lessness, then take the first step. Ask someone for help. Thank you."

The room broke into thunderous applause, the loudest cheers coming from the front row where Everett, Fred, Justin, Val, Gemma, Travis, Gracie, Mike, Caroline, and so many more stood. Callie's eyes filled with tears, cloud-ing her vision. It had taken her nine years, but she had finally found what she was looking for.

The ability to accept the things she could not change and forgive herself.

"HAVE I TOLD you how much I love you?" Callie asked.

Everett pushed her higher on the old plank swing, smiling. "Several times."

"Well, I just thought you'd want to know."

He did, every day. Since the night she'd shown up, baring everything to him, he'd never gotten tired of her love. And he couldn't be prouder of who she was. She had done exactly what she promised, working on herself even as she opened up to him, a little more every day.

"You were amazing tonight," he said.

Callie dragged her feet across the dirt, coming to a stop. Everett grabbed the ropes on either side and came around to look down into her beautiful face. The moon-light caught her pale blonde strands amid the gold and brown, and he still thought she looked like an angel.

"Only because I had you. When I think about all those kids who have no one, I just don't know how my story will really help them, you know?"

Everett knelt down next to her and took her hands in his. "You told the truth. You opened yourself up to a room full of strangers to help people going through what you dealt with alone." He leaned up and kissed her gently. "If you made even one of them think, then you accomplished everything you set out to do. You are a hero, Callie." Then, reaching into his pocket, he pulled out a black velvet box.

"Oh my God," Callie whispered.

Everett looked her in the eyes as he opened the case, displaying the simple white gold band. "I never thought I'd meet anyone who made me feel alive again. Not until I heard your voice on the radio, and I couldn't get you out of my head. And having you with me has made me happier than I ever thought possible.

"But I want more, still. I know I'm always asking you to give me everything you got, and this probably won't be the last time, but I'm hoping the woman you are, the one who has brought every part of me pure joy, will give me just a little bit more. I want you, Callie. I want every part of you, even the dark parts you don't like anyone else to see."

He pulled the ring out of the box and, with shaking hands, held it out. "What do you say, Whisky? Can you love me forever, dark and gnarly parts and all?"

Everett suddenly found his arms full of sobbing woman, and he fell to the ground with her on top of him.

"Yes!" she said, rearing up and over him, her hair falling all around their faces.

Her mouth covered his in a searing kiss, and he wrapped his arms around her, getting lost in the taste of her for a moment.

When he finally broke the kiss, he slipped the ring onto her left finger between them. Once the band was in place, he rolled until she was on her back, staring up at him.

"I have a confession to make," he said.

"Okay?"

"When I told you I wouldn't wait forever for you…"

"Yeah?"

"I lied." Everett waited until that smile softened her lips before he continued, "I would have waited, no matter how long it took."

Callie's hand cupped his cheek, her eyes sparkling with tears. "I'll never make you wait again."

Acknowledgments

THERE IS NO way I could get any writing done without my wonderful husband running interference with our children, so thank you, Brian, for your continued support.

To my awesome editor, Chelsey Emmelhainz, who continues to help shape my writing, my characters, and their actions. Thanks, love!

To my epic agent, Sarah Younger, for helping me deal with the tough stuff and for having my back! You rock!

For my family and friends, thank you for being there, encouraging and supporting me as I take this crazy adventure!

For my kids, for sometimes understanding that Mommy has to work and for bringing me joy.

To all of my wonderful author friends who help me through the self-doubt and stress, love you all!

For my Rockers; I love your guts.

And to every reader who has picked up one of my books and thought, "Eh, I'll give it a try," thank you for taking a chance on me! You are all amazeballs!

The love doesn't end here!

Keep reading for a sneak peek at Codi Gary's next
Rock Canyon romance

RULES TO BE BROKEN

Coming August 2015 from Avon Impulse.

An Excerpt from

RULES TO BE BROKEN

---

*Mike Stevens has been the good guy all his life—and
though he's never had a problem getting women,
he's ready for something more. So when he hatches a plan
to change his image from nice to naughty, that last
person he expects help from is his nemesis, Zoe Carver.
Zoe doesn't like or trust Mike but as his transformation
takes shape, she starts to doubt her first impression.
There are some great guys out there, but if she's grooming
this one for someone else, is she making the biggest
mistake of her life?*

ZOE WAS AT Mike's door forty-five minutes early, with
several shopping bags and an eager smile on her face. She
knew he would probably hate the leather chaps and at
least one of the shirts, but she'd wanted a variety so he
would have some choices.

Though really, there was no wrong choice.

She knocked hard and heard something crash inside. Mike answered the door a few seconds later, rubbing his hair with a towel. His scowling face was covered in shaving cream, but her attention was immediately drawn down to his bare, sculpted chest—and the fact that lower, he was wearing only boxer shorts. None of those stuffy collared shirts he wore at work had prepared her for those pecks or the ridges of his abs.

Holy hell, those are some nice abs.

Some male models had to rely on airbrushing to get muscles like that.

Mike's skin shone like he was still damp from a shower and when her gaze finally met his, he wasn't glaring anymore.

No, his expression was intense. Hungry.

She almost gulped, but that might've given him the impression that he affected her. He didn't, of course; she was just observing him. Closely.

"You're early." His voice was deeper and surly, but his obvious irritation didn't bother Zoe. He tossed aside the towel.

"Yes." But the shiver that shot through her lower belly did.

Still, she shouldn't be getting turned on by Mike, no matter how nice his body was or how rumbly his voice seemed. She had Tom, and he was exactly what she wanted: no surprises, an open book.

But even on his best day, Tom doesn't give you quivery, naughty feelings, now does he?

Mike reached out and took the bags from her hands, startling her out of her thoughts. When his cool fingers brushed hers, the simple touch burned her skin. His hair glistened with moisture, and the spicy, clean scent of his soap was delicious, intoxicating. Zoe almost leaned into him, but he was already pulling back, carrying the bags inside.

Ever the gentleman.

The thought sobered her somewhat as she followed him inside. Mike was a good guy, or so he said. Raised right, loved his mama, held doors open for ladies...

And yet the expression in his eyes when he looked her way wasn't good at all.

It was bad in the melt-her-panties-and-made-her-want-to-find-out-what-was-under-those-shorts kind of way.

"You look really good," he said.

She smoothed her hands over the black skinny jeans that disappeared into knee-high lace-up boots. She'd wanted to be comfortable yet sexy when they walked into the bar together, so she'd left her long hair down around her shoulders. She wore a purple sleeveless top with a low-cut neckline and her leather jacket.

She hated how pleased she was by the compliment.

"Thank you." Desperate to change the subject, she stepped up to him and ran her finger through his shaving cream. "Why is your face covered in shaving cream?"

"Because I wanted to dress up like Santa Claus. Why do you think?"

She knew she was playing a dangerous game, but she couldn't fight the overwhelming desire to tease him. Taunt him. Stepping into his body, she watched his eyes stray down to her lips and a zing of pleasure made her mouth tingle.

"If you're trying to shave off this prickly, dark hair"—she scraped off more, the fluffy wetness and scratchy hair beneath delicious against her finger—"don't. Bad boys nearly always sport a little scruff."

God, she wished she could touch him. She'd love to rub the palm of her hand across his cheek. Maybe slide her fingers up to grip his short hair and pull his mouth down to hers.

"Zoe." A dark threat lingered in his curt use of her name, and she bit her lip to keep from sighing.

"What?" she said when she finally trusted herself to speak.

"Whatever game you're playing right now, don't."

"Don't what?" She wiped the shaving cream on her finger off on his shoulder dismissively, watching his face for the irritation. Mike radiated anticipation instead.

Mike reached out and grabbed the towel he'd thrown off the couch, wiping the shaving cream off his face. "Don't think I won't give you exactly what you're asking for."

"And what's that?" Why did she sound so warm and inviting? It sounds like she was practically begging him to—

Suddenly, he grabbed her hand and pulled her along with him as he sat down in a kitchen chair, making her heart thunder in her chest. Before she could protest, he yanked her face down across his lap, and his arm held her in place as a hard smack came down on her ass.

"Ow, what the—fuck!"

Another whack.

"You son of a bitch, I will have your balls—"

Whack.

"Stop it!"

He released her, and she scrambled to her feet. As he stood up, she cranked back her arm and would've let it fly, but he caught it before she could, his chocolate-brown eyes boring into hers.

"Now go sit down and think about what you did."

Zoe caught the twitch at the corner of his mouth, as if he was trying not to laugh, and she might have been amused too, if her ass wasn't stinging.

And if a small part of her wasn't whispering that he'd surprised her.

But you hate surprises, don't you?

"You'll pay for that."

"Probably," he said, releasing her hand. "But it was worth it."

And as he strode past her toward the bathroom, she rubbed her posterior. It didn't hurt any longer, but she'd never been spanked in her life. She might have thought of it once or twice, but she had never imagined a sexy-as-hell, slightly nerdy *nice guy* would be the one dishing it out.

Great. Now she thought he was sexy.

About the Author

An obsessive bookworm, **CODI GARY** likes to write sexy small-town contemporary romances with humor, grand gestures, and blush-worthy moments. When she's not writing, she can be found reading her favorite authors, squealing over her must-watch shows, and playing with her children. She lives in Idaho with her family.

Discover great authors, exclusive offers, and more at hc.com.

Give in to your impulses . . .
Read on for a sneak peek at four brand-new
e-book original tales of romance
from HarperCollins.
Available now wherever e-books are sold.

CHANGING EVERYTHING
A Forgiving Lies Novella
By Molly McAdams

CHASE ME
A Broke and Beautiful Novel
By Tessa Bailey

YOURS TO HOLD
Ribbon Ridge Book Two
By Darcy Burke

THE ELUSIVE LORD EVERHART
The Rakes of Fallow Hall Series
By Vivienne Lorret

An Excerpt from

CHANGING EVERYTHING
A Forgiving Lies Novella
by Molly McAdams

Paisley Morro has been in love with Eli Jenkins
since they were thirteen years old. But after
twelve years of being only his best friend and
wingman, the heartache that comes from
watching him with countless other women
becomes too much, and Paisley decides it's
time to lay all her feelings on the table.

Paisley

I fidgeted with my coffee cup as I tried to find the courage to say what I'd held back for so long. Twelve years. Twelve years of waiting, hoping, and aching were about to come to an end. With a deep breath in, I looked up into the blue eyes of my best friend, Eli, and tensed my body as I began.

"This guy I met, Brett, he's—well, he's different. Like, he's a game changer for me. I look at him, and I have no doubt of that. I have no doubt that I *could* spend the rest of my life with him." I laughed uneasily and shrugged. "And I know that sounds crazy after only a few weeks, but, honestly, I knew it the first day I met him. I don't know how to explain it. It wasn't like the world stopped turning or anything, there was just a feeling I had." Swallowing past the tightness in my throat, I glanced away for a moment as I strained to hold on to the courage I'd been building up all week. "But there's this other guy, and I swear this guy owns my soul."

Eli crossed his arms and his eyebrows rose, but I didn't allow myself to decipher what his expression could mean at that moment. If I tried to understand him—like I always did—then I would quickly talk myself out of saying the words I'd been thinking for far too long.

"Eli," I whispered so low the word was almost lost in the chatter from the other people in the coffee shop. "I have been in love with you since I was thirteen years old," I confessed, and held my breath as I waited for any kind of response from him.

Nothing about him changed for a few seconds until suddenly his face lost all emotion. But it was there in his eyes, like it always was: denial, confusion, shock.

I wanted to run, but I forced myself to blurt out the rest. "I've kept quiet for twelve years, and I would've continued to if I hadn't met Brett. These last few weeks have been casual, but I know he wants it to be more. But if there is a chance of an us, then there would be absolutely no thoughts of anything else with him."

Eli just continued to stare at me like I'd blown his mind, and my body began shaking as I silently begged him to say something—anything.

After twelve years of being his best friend, of being used by him as a shield from other women, of being tortured by his pretending touches and kisses . . . I was slowly giving up on us. I couldn't handle the heartache anymore. I couldn't stand being unknowingly rejected again and again. I couldn't continue being his favorite person in the world for an entirely different reason than he was mine. I couldn't keep waiting around for Eli Jenkins.

This was it for me.

"Eli, I need to know." I exhaled softly and tried to steady my shaking as I asked, "Is there *any* possibility of there being an us?"

An Excerpt from

CHASE ME
A Broke and Beautiful Novel
by Tessa Bailey

Bestselling author Tessa Bailey launches the
Broke and Beautiful trilogy, a fun and sexy
New Adult series set in New York City!

Roxy Cumberland's footsteps echoed off the smooth, cream-colored walls of the hallway, high heels clicking along the polished marble. When she caught her reflection in the pristine window overlooking Stanton Street, she winced. This pink bunny costume wasn't doing shit for her skin tone. A withering sigh escaped her as she tugged the plastic mask back into place.

Singing telegrams still existed. Who knew? She'd actually laughed upon seeing the tiny advertisement in the *Village Voice*'s Help Wanted section, but curiosity had led her to dial the number. So here she was, one day later, preparing to sing in front of a perfect stranger for a cut of sixty bucks.

Sixty bucks might not sound like much, but when your roommate has just booted you onto your ass for failure to come through on rent—again—leaving you no place to live, and your checking account is gasping for oxygen, pink bunnies do what pink bunnies must. At least her round, fluffy tail would cushion her fall when her ass hit the sidewalk.

See? She'd already found a silver lining.

Through the eyeholes of the bunny mask, Roxy glanced down at the piece of paper in her hand. Apartment 4D. Based on the song she'd memorized on the way here and the swank interior of the building, she knew the type who would answer the door. Some too-rich, middle-aged douchebag who was so bored with his life that he needed to be entertained with novelties like singing bunny rabbits.

Roxy's gaze tracked down lower on the note in her hand, and she felt an uncomfortable kick of unease in her belly. She'd met her new boss at a tiny office in Alphabet City, surprised to find a dude only slightly older than herself running the operation. Always suspicious, she'd asked him how he kept the place afloat. There couldn't be *that* high a demand for singing telegrams, right? He'd laughed, explaining that singing bunnies only accounted for a tenth of their income. The rest came in the form of *strip-o-grams*. She'd done her best to appear flattered when he'd told her she'd be perfect for it.

She ran a thumb over the rates young-dude-boss had jotted down on the slip of paper. Two hundred dollars for each ten-minute performance. God, the *security* she would feel with that kind of money. And yet, something told her that once she took that step, once she started taking off her clothes, she would never stop. It would become a necessity instead of a temporary patch-up of her shitstorm cloud.

Think about it later. When you're not dressed like the fucking Trix Rabbit. Roxy took a deep, fortifying breath. She wrapped her steady fingers around the brass door knocker and rapped it against the wood twice. A frown marred her forehead when she heard a miserable groan come from inside the apartment. It sounded like a *young* groan. Maybe the douchebag had a son? Oh, *cool*. She definitely wanted to do this in front of someone in her age group. Perfect.

Her sarcastic thought bubble burst over her head when

the door swung open, revealing a guy. A hot-as-hell guy. A naked-except-for-unbuttoned-jeans guy. Being the shameless hussy she was, her gaze immediately dipped to his happy trail, although, on this guy, it really should have been called a rapture path. It started just beneath his belly button, which sat at the bottom of beautifully defined ab muscles. But they weren't the kind of abs honed from hours in the gym. No, they were natural, I-do-sit-ups-when-I-damn-well-feel-like-it abs. Approachable abs. The kind you could either lick or snuggle up against, depending on your mood.

Roxy lassoed her rapidly dwindling focus and yanked it higher until she met his eyes. Big mistake. The abs were child's play compared to the face. Stubbled jaw. Bed head. Big, Hershey-colored eyes outlined by dark, black lashes. His fists were planted on either side of the door frame, giving her a front-row seat to watch his chest and arms flex. A lesser woman would have applauded. As it was, Roxy was painfully aware of her bunny-costumed status, and even *that* came in second place to the fact that Approachable Abs was so stinking rich that he could afford to be nursing a hangover at eleven in the morning. On a Thursday.

He dragged a hand through his unkempt black hair. "Am I still drunk, or are you dressed like a rabbit?"

An Excerpt from

YOURS TO HOLD
Ribbon Ridge Book Two
by Darcy Burke

In the second installment of Darcy Burke's
contemporary small-town saga, the black
sheep of the Archer family is finally home,
and he's not looking for love . . . but he's about
to find it in the last place he ever expected.

Kyle Archer pulled into the large dirt lot that served as the parking area of The Alex. He still smiled when he thought of Sara coming up with the idea to name their brother's dying wish after him. It only made sense.

The hundred-plus-years-old monastery rose in front of him, its spire stretching two hundred feet into the vivid blue summer sky. The sounds of construction came from the west end of the property, down a dirt lane to what had once been a small house occupied by the head monk or whoever had been in charge at the monastery before it had been abandoned twenty-odd years ago. It was phase one of the project Alex had conceived—renovating the property into a premier hotel and event space under the Archer name, which included nine brewpubs throughout the northern valley and into Portland.

Alex had purchased the property using the trust fund left to each of them by their grandfather, then set up a trust for each sibling to inherit an equal share of the project. He'd planned for everyone to participate in the renovation, assigning key roles to all his siblings. And he'd made his attorney, Aubrey Tallinger, the trustee.

She'd endured copious amounts of anger and blame immediately following Alex's suicide because to all of them it had seemed unlikely that she'd established the trust without knowing what Alex had planned. But she insisted she hadn't known, that Alex had told her he was simply preparing in the event that he died young, something he'd convinced her was likely with his chronic lung disease.

However, things hadn't quite worked out the way Alex had envisioned. Not everyone had been eager to return to Ribbon Ridge, least of all Kyle. He shook the discomfort away. He'd fucked up. A lot. And he was trying to fix it. He owed it to Alex.

While Alex had been tethered at home with his oxygen tank and debilitating illness, the rest of them had gone off and pursued their dreams. Well, all but Hayden. As the youngest, he'd sort of gotten stuck staying in Ribbon Ridge and working for the family company. His participation in the project should've been a given, but then his dream had finally knocked down his door, and he was currently in France for a year-long internship at a winery.

Kyle stepped out of Hayden's black Honda Pilot. He'd completely taken over his brother's life while Hayden was off making wine—his car, his job, his house. Too bad Kyle couldn't also borrow the respect and appreciation Hayden received.

He slammed the car door. It wasn't going to be that easy, and he didn't deserve it to be. He should have been driving his own goddamned car, but he'd had to sell it before leaving Florida so the same shit that had driven him from Ribbon Ridge wouldn't also drive him from Miami.

But hadn't it? *No.* Things hadn't gotten as bad as they had four years ago. No one had bailed his ass out this time. He'd learned. He wasn't the same man.

An Excerpt from

THE ELUSIVE LORD EVERHART
The Rakes of Fallow Hall Series
by Vivienne Lorret

Vivienne Lorret, the *USA Today* bestselling
author of *Winning Miss Wakefield*, returns
with a new series featuring the three roguish
bachelors of Fallow Hall. Gabriel Ludlow,
Viscount Everhart, was a fool to deny the depth
of his feelings for Calliope Croft, but the threat
that kept him from her five years ago remains.
Now he must choose between two paths: break
her heart all over again or finally succumb to
loving her . . . at the risk of losing everything.

"Surely you've heard of the Chinese medicinal *massage*," Gabriel said, attempting to reassure her. Yet the low hoarseness of his voice likely sounded hungry instead. Slowly, he slid his thumbs along the outer edges of the vertebrae at the base of her neck.

"I don't believe I have," she said, relaxing marginally, her voice thin and wispy like the fine downy hairs above her nape teasing the tops of his thumbs.

"Taoist priests have used this method for centuries." His own voice came out low and insubstantial, as if he were breathing his final breath. As it was, his heart had all but given up trying to lure the blood away from his pulsing erection. *This was a terrible idea.*

He was immensely glad he'd thought of it.

His fingertips skirted the edge of her clavicle. Hands curled over her slender shoulders, he rolled his thumbs over her again.

Calliope emitted the faintest *oh*. It was barely a breath, but the sound deafened him with a rush of tumid desire. As if she sensed the change in him, she tensed again. "Are you trying to seduce me, Everhart?"

"If you have to ask," he said, attempting to add levity

with a chuckle, "then the answer is most likely *no*." Yet even he knew differently. The *most likely* was said only as a way of not lying to himself. He wanted to seduce her, slowly and for hours on end.

For five years he'd wanted to feel her flesh beneath his hands. For a moment this evening, he'd even thought this one touch would be enough to sate him. He hated being wrong.

Those pearl buttons called to him. He feathered strokes outward along the upper edges of her shoulder blades, earning another breathy sound. Only this time, she did not tense beneath the heat of his hands.

"I've read—*heard* stories," she corrected, "where the young woman is not certain of seduction until it is too late."

Gabriel caught her quick slip and was not surprised. Her penchant for reading was another aspect of her character that drew him to her. Earlier today, in fact, he'd spotted her disappearing through the library doors.

Unable to control the impulse, he'd found a servant's door off a narrow hall and surreptitiously watched her from behind a screen in the corner. Browsing the shelves, she'd searched through dozens of books. Yet her method fascinated him. She only viewed the last pages of each book. When she found one she liked, she clutched it to her breast and released a sigh filled with the type of longing he knew too well. He had little doubt that she sought the certainty of a happy ending. All in all, it had taken her over an hour to find three books that met her standards. Yet, instead of being bored, he'd been enthralled by every minute.

And now, here they were . . .

Under the spell of his massage, her head fell forward as

she arched ever-so-slightly into his hands. Rampant desire coursed through him. Even so, he was in no hurry to end this delicious torment.

"I cannot imagine that a woman would not suspect an attempt at seduction in some manner." He leaned forward to inhale the fragrance of her hair, the barest scents of rosewater and mint rising up to greet him. "Aren't all young ladies brought up with the voice of reason clamoring about in their heads?"

His gaze followed the motions of his fingers, gliding over her silken warmth, pressing against the supple flesh that pinkened under his tender ministrations. He'd always wondered . . . and now he knew she felt as soft, if not softer, than any one of his dreams.

"Curiosity has a voice as well," she said, her voice faint with pleasure. "And are we not all creatures put upon this earth to learn, just as you have learned this *exquisite* medicine?"

And sometimes curiosity could not be tamed.

It was no use. Did he truly imagine he could resist her? "Well said, Miss Croft."

Unable to hold back a moment longer, Gabriel gave in to temptation, lowered his head, and pressed his lips to her nape.